Praise for the Misty Point Series

"A charming holiday tale of fresh starts, friendship, and love with a heroine even Scrooge couldn't resist."

—Sheila Roberts, *New York Times* bestselling author, on *The Winter Wedding Plan*

"This second book in the Misty Point series continues to develop the relationship between sisters Kate and Charlotte Daniels—and their cousin Bree—with grace and sincerity. Charlotte proves a compelling heroine, a single mom determined to rise above her past mistakes and finally make her family proud."

—RT Book Reviews, four stars, on *The Winter Wedding Plan*

Praise for *Mistletoe on Main Street*

"The passion and tension between Luke and Grace are equal parts tender and intense, and their journey back toward each other is a sweet and nostalgic one. With a down-home feel throughout, this story is sure to warm any reader's heart. A delightful read."

—RT Book Reviews, four stars

"Sweet, tender, and burgeoning with Christmas spirit and New England appeal, this engaging reunion tale sees one couple blissfully together, artfully setting the stage for the next book in the series."

—*Library Journal*

Praise for *A Match Made on Main Street*

"In the latest in her Briar Creek series, Miles brings us a book filled with crisp storytelling, amusing banter, and charming, endearing characters. The love between Mark and Anna is genuinely deep, and the tension between them is fiery. Miles's modern romance will lure readers in and keep them turning the pages."

—RT Book Reviews, four stars

Praise for *Hope Springs on Main Street*

"*Hope Springs on Main Street* is a warm, tender story overflowing with emotion. With strong, memorable characters and a delightful small town, this book will surely work its way into your heart. Olivia Miles weaves a beautiful story of healing and second chances."

—RaeAnne Thayne, *New York Times* bestselling author

"Romantic, touching, and deep-sigh satisfying."

—Emma Cane, author

"Appreciation for the setting will gradually grow on you as it does on Henry, which is a subtle and effective draw. With a charming cast of characters, the touching connection of family, and the lovely bloom of romance . . . *Hope Springs on Main Street* is a sweet and worthy addition to your romance collection."

—*USA Today*

"This story is delightfully engaging."

—RT Book Reviews, four stars

"No couple deserved a second chance at love more than this pair."

—*Harlequin Junkie*, four stars

Praise for *Love Blooms on Main Street*

"Lighthearted storytelling laced with humor is the highlight of Miles's latest story."

—RT Book Reviews

"For those who want a deeper small-town read, I'd recommend *Love Blooms on Main Street*."

—*Harlequin Junkie*

Praise for *Christmas Comes to Main Street*

"Readers seeking a peppermint-filled, cozy Christmas contemporary will be satisfied."

—*Publishers Weekly*

Additional Praise for Olivia Miles

"Miles's heartbreaking second-chance-at-romance story features a guilt-ridden hero and bewildered heroine. The author's intuitive dialogue adds authenticity to her small-town setting as she keeps readers guessing until the end."

—RT Book Reviews on *Recipe for Romance*

A
WEDDING
IN
DRIFTWOOD
COVE

OTHER TITLES BY OLIVIA MILES

The Heirloom Inn

Blue Harbor Series

A Place for Us
Second Chance Summer
Because of You
Small Town Christmas
Return to Me
Then Comes Love
Finding Christmas
A New Beginning
Summer of Us
A Chance on Me

Stand-Alone Title

This Christmas

Evening Island Trilogy

Meet Me at Sunset
Summer's End
The Lake House

Oyster Bay Series

Feels Like Home
Along Came You
Maybe This Time

This Thing Called Love
Those Summer Nights
Christmas at the Cottage
Still the One
One Fine Day
Had to Be You

Misty Point Series (Grand Central / Forever)

One Week to the Wedding
The Winter Wedding Plan

Sweeter in the City Series

Sweeter in the Summer
Sweeter Than Sunshine
No Sweeter Love
One Sweet Christmas

Briar Creek Series (Grand Central / Forever)

Mistletoe on Main Street
A Match Made on Main Street
Hope Springs on Main Street
Love Blooms on Main Street
Christmas Comes to Main Street

Harlequin Special Edition

'Twas the Week Before Christmas
Recipe for Romance

A
WEDDING
IN
DRIFTWOOD
COVE

OLIVIA MILES

 Montlake

Published by Montlake, Seattle

www.apub.com

Amazon, the Amazon logo, and Montlake are trademarks of Amazon.com, Inc., or its affiliates.

ISBN-13: 9781662511189 (paperback)
ISBN-13: 9781662512582 (digital)

Cover design by Leah Jacobs-Gordon
Cover images: © IndustryAndTravel / Shutterstock;
© Joao Paulo V Tinoco / Shutterstock; © A.Valentino / Shutterstock;
© Valery Petrushkov / Shutterstock; © Vibrant Image Studio / Shutterstock

Printed in the United States of America

A
WEDDING
IN
DRIFTWOOD
COVE

CHAPTER ONE

Hallie

Hallie Walsh's life wasn't perfect, but it was pretty darn close.

She was the youngest of three daughters and by some people's account the prettiest, having hit the "genetic jackpot," as her eldest sister, Claire, liked to say. She'd inherited her mother's small nose and large eyes and her father's easy demeanor. Her childhood was spent laughing, dressing up, dancing around their Boston home, and collecting shells at the large beach house in Rhode Island fondly known as Beachnest Cottage, where her family spent every summer and holiday break.

Good grades and hard work had gotten her into every college she'd applied to, but of course she'd chosen the one that her childhood sweetheart was attending. They'd spent those four years pursuing the same business degree and summering in Driftwood Cove.

Finding work wasn't an issue, since Josh's parents owned the Harbor Club, a private and exclusive establishment where Josh oversaw the dining room and Hallie the day spa, biding their time as employees until the day came when they eventually took ownership.

Even before Josh slipped his grandmother's engagement ring onto her finger just as the sun was rising over the Atlantic and the entire sky seemed to light up, Hallie had always believed that her future was bright. She had, quite simply, no reason to have ever questioned it.

But the problem with having a so-called perfect life was that it didn't leave much room for things to go wrong. And today, something had gone very wrong indeed.

Hallie fought back tears as she hung up the phone on the wedding-venue coordinator and forced a smile she did not feel as the front door of the spa swung open. As part of her job description at the Harbor Club, she was in charge of making sure that every guest felt special, and that meant knowing each one by name, knowing their spouse's name, their children's names, their grandchildren's names, and yes, even their pets' names. The waterfront club with everything from its own harbor to a sprawling golf course was a highly sought-after destination in Driftwood Cove, and many of Hallie's friends often chided her about the perks of the job, assuming that she had facials and pedicures whenever she liked, or that she could feast at the raw bar or imbibe the club's signature drinks every evening. She was lucky to work there, they all told her, and she was. Full stop. Sure, it had been daunting at first, but now, three years into her employment, she had come to know all the club members, even though some, like Evelyn Steele, she'd probably prefer not to have met at all.

Sure enough, Evelyn was approaching with a sour expression, meaning that whatever she had to complain about today was certainly a bigger problem than Hallie's wedding being canceled.

Hallie blinked quickly. She could not cry. Sure, she was fairly certain that Josh's parents would be hard pressed to ever fire her—they were like family by now. She was the daughter they'd never had, as they always reminded her, and in two months they were supposed to officially become family—only the wedding coordinator had double-booked the venue, and the big, beautiful wedding that Hallie had dreamed of nearly all her life was off.

Her phone buzzed on the desk, and she glanced at the screen to see the venue coordinator's name appear again. A mistake, perhaps? Or just more apologies? Evelyn was quickly approaching, and there was no other staff member around to greet her, but with each buzz of the phone, Hallie's heart beat faster.

The phone silenced itself just as Evelyn approached.

"Hello, Mrs. Steele. I see we have you down for the works today!" Hallie's voice was cheerful, and she could only hope her expression matched.

Evelyn Steele didn't remove her sunglasses, something she rarely did indoors. Years back there had been bets on what color her eyes might be, with most of the staff deciding on icy blue. (In the end they were established to be gray, and spotted only when she started adding facials to her long list of services needed.)

Evelyn leaned into the counter, and even behind the shield of her shades, Hallie detected a narrowing of her eyes.

"It's been a terrible week."

Tell me about it, Hallie wanted to say.

Instead, she nodded in understanding. This was a key part of her job as well—listening to the clients.

Hallie's phone chirped, signaling a voice mail had been left, and her mind went to what it could be—another mistake, perhaps? Maybe the other couple had gracefully bowed out; maybe she and Josh could be married at Cliffside Manor after all, as planned for the past year?

Across the desk, Evelyn cleared her throat.

Right. Hallie stood straighter and forced her attention away from her phone. Maybe the wedding coordinator was just trying to offer another venue—which was not an option. Hallie had already had to give up one tradition, and not by choice. Unlike all the brides that had come before her in her family, her father was no longer here to walk her down the aisle, lift the veil, and kiss her cheek.

Just thinking of it made her chest tighten up, and she blinked away the hurt that still remained eight years after his sudden passing.

It almost hurt to smile, but she did. Trying to remember what Mrs. Steele had mentioned last Wednesday when she'd come in for her weekly manicure, she said, "Oh dear. Did your son not make it to town after all?"

Evelyn Steele's son was two years older than Hallie, a late-in-life baby, and since her husband's early passing, the center of Evelyn's world. Years back, when Hallie was fourteen, he'd made his interest in her known by offering to buy her ice cream from the stand near Stony Beach and then tagged along with her and her sisters for the rest of the afternoon until Amy felt sorry for him and Claire felt annoyed and Hallie felt . . . uninterested.

She'd blamed it on her age, claiming she was too young to date. Not allowed, even, but then Josh had come along and tested that excuse.

Now, every once in a while, poor Max's mother would lament over how much better Max's life would have been if she'd chosen him instead of Josh Goodwin.

"He made it, all right." Mrs. Steele's mouth pinched so tight that her lips all but disappeared into her teeth. "And he brought *her*."

"Ah." Hallie rearranged her expression to one of understanding, even though she was struggling to listen as Evelyn rattled off everything the poor young woman had done wrong since arriving in town. No one was ever good enough for Max, according to Evelyn, and Hallie suspected that she wouldn't have been either. The woman in question was Mrs. Steele's son's girlfriend of two years, a pleasant and lovely young woman that Hallie had met four times, enough to know that she had a labradoodle named Rory, a preference for tea over coffee, and an irreparable relationship with the woman standing here now looking, Hallie realized, like she was going to a funeral.

Despite it being a sunny September day, Evelyn was wearing a formal black dress, a matching shawl, and a look of misery that one typically associated with a great loss—not a day, according to a glance at the appointment book, of pampering followed by high tea in the courtyard garden.

If anyone deserved to don a somber dress or treat themselves to some much-needed pampering, it was Hallie. But instead, she gritted her teeth into a smile, fought back the tears that prickled her eyes, and said, "I see you have a dinner reservation at the club tomorrow. Surely that's something to look forward to?"

"I suppose," Mrs. Steele replied with a sigh. "Josh got us my favorite table, at least."

Josh! What would he say when he learned the wedding news? And she'd have to be the one to give it to him, and soon. His duties here at the club were to oversee the restaurant, located on the other side of the building, with a sprawling view of the harbor. Over the years, he'd worked as a golf caddy, a lifeguard at the pool, and even a busboy. And she'd never once heard him complain or even pine for a day off.

Secretly, Hallie did pine for a day off. Today, especially.

"Well, let's get you set up." She was eager to get the guest on her way before another could waltz through the door. "I'll bring you a glass of the fresh lemonade you like so much."

To Hallie's relief, Mrs. Steele gave a long-suffering nod and slowly made her way through the glass doors that led into a softly lit hallway. Hallie's pace was brisker than usual. She wanted to run, or just point Evelyn in the general direction—she knew her own way. But she forced herself to slow down, to breathe, to brace herself for whatever message was waiting for her when she returned to her desk.

In all her years of living and working here, Hallie had never actually participated in any of the club's services, preferring instead to get her nails done in town, where she wouldn't feel like she was taking advantage of the situation.

Her eyes welled again when she remembered that Josh's mother had blocked out the entire day before the wedding so that all the ladies could be treated to their favorite services. Hallie would have to clear the schedule now. Open it up to the regulars. Probably have to listen to Mrs. Steele complain about her newest affliction the day Hallie was supposed to be wrapped in the plush terry robe instead.

She left Mrs. Steele in the massage room and closed the door behind her, nearly colliding with Coco Goodwin, Josh's mother—or Nicole, as she was properly called. While Mrs. Steele had been too absorbed with her own problems to pick up on anything amiss, Coco's forehead immediately pinched with concern.

"Is everything okay, Hallie?" Her tone implied that she knew better than to think it was something with one of the guests. There could never be a problem with the guests, and if there were, it must be remedied immediately, as if it had never happened at all.

If only Hallie's own problems could be swept away in such a tidy fashion.

Hallie hesitated. It was common knowledge that Josh's parents had hoped that their son would have his wedding reception here at the club, especially when it was such a popular venue for most couples in the area. But they also understood that Cliffside Manor was special to Hallie's family. Not only had her parents been married there, but so had her maternal grandparents. It wasn't just a tradition, as sacred as the family beach house that had been passed along to each new bride and would soon be hers; it was a rite of passage.

And it was also what Hallie had planned since she was just five years old and playing wedding in the attic with her sisters.

And so the club was designated as the venue for the rehearsal dinner, a reasonable resolution, really, given that traditionally the groom's family hosted that part of the celebration anyway.

Still, if Coco found out that Cliffside Manor had double-booked them and then bumped them because the other couple had a larger guest list and thus a bigger budget, then the suggestion of having the wedding here at the club was bound to come up, and Hallie would have little room to argue.

And she didn't want to argue. Not with her future in-laws, who had been so wonderful to her. And not with Josh, who had been just as eager to finally be married as she was.

But she also didn't want to postpone the wedding. And Josh wouldn't, either, not when they'd already been engaged for a year, not when they'd been dating since they were fifteen.

Not when there was, by all reasonable accounts, a perfectly fine and coveted venue right here, beneath her very feet.

"I'm just a little tired," Hallie said with a smile. "I was thinking I might check in with Josh before the lunch crowd hits." It would give her an excuse to duck outside and check her phone.

"You might catch him if you go now," Coco said, looking more relaxed as they walked back toward the front desk. "I can watch your post."

Hallie didn't waste any time speed-walking through the front doors, her phone clutched in her sweaty grip. She hurried to the flagstone path flanked by blooming hydrangeas and toward the waterfront, where she could slip in the side door that led directly to the kitchen and was discreetly hidden by a thick and tall hedge.

But first . . . her thumb hovered over the screen of the device, and closing her eyes, she put the phone to her ear as the message started. More apologies, she realized with a sinking in her stomach. More empty words to try to set things right. She had worked in guest relations long enough to know the drill.

She was just about to disconnect the call when the voice said something else. A cancellation? Short notice. Might not work—or maybe it could!

She started shaking. Head to toe.

They could still have the wedding of their dreams!

Hallie ended the call and slipped the phone into her pocket. She walked into the kitchen on autopilot, her mind somewhere else completely. Two weeks from tomorrow.

Suddenly, it all felt very, very real.

"Hey." Josh came around the counter, where the chefs were prepping for the club's famous lobster rolls, wearing the club-issued navy blazer and khakis. His smile wasn't much different from the first one he'd flashed her that summer before her sophomore year of high school when she and her family dined out on the patio for her birthday and he'd been busing tables. He still had braces back then, and when he gathered with the rest of the staff to sing her happy birthday, the wish she'd made was that one day she'd marry that boy and live happily ever after.

And now, she was going to do just that. In two weeks.

The noise in the kitchen was growing loud, and Josh led her into the dining room, where servers were setting out plates and napkins in the signature club fold. Soon the doors would open, and the morning boaters, the ladies who lunched, or just the regulars looking to socialize with their fellow club members would fill the room. The baskets of warm pretzel rolls would be set on each table, martinis shaken (no judgment passed about the hour), Caesar salads tossed tableside, fresh lobster rolls served with warm butter, followed by the dessert trolley, one of the more charming touches that kept this place popular for generations.

"You look a little tense," Josh said, reaching out for her hand.

"Cliffside Manor called."

"Uh-oh." Josh had left most of the planning to her, knowing that she'd been dreaming of this day since before she'd even met him and that her mother was all too eager to assist.

"Unfortunately, they double-booked us."

That had his attention. "What does that mean? We can still get married?"

"Not on the day we'd planned," she said.

His hazel eyes widened before his face suddenly relaxed into a smile. He squeezed her hand tighter. "We can just have the wedding here!"

They could, and it would be lovely. But this was her one chance to carry on tradition. One chance to be married at Cliffside Manor, just like everyone before her.

Josh picked up on her hesitation. "I know how much your family traditions matter, but I don't want to wait any longer, do you?"

"No," she said firmly. "It was all going so well. I assumed it would . . . all work out perfectly."

Josh hissed in a breath and raked a hand through his light-brown hair. "It's really too bad that Amy wasn't willing to help."

Hallie's middle sister was an event planner in Boston, but her schedule kept her too busy to plan this event, and Hallie hadn't wanted to push, especially when she'd thought this wedding would essentially plan itself. Everything would be just like it had been for all the happy brides before her.

"We can still have the wedding we planned." Or started to plan. Now she realized how much there was to do. Could they even move up the honeymoon? And what about the flowers? The cake? She hadn't made any of these decisions because she'd thought she had time.

Josh was looking at her expectantly, and so she said, "They had a cancellation. Two weeks from tomorrow."

His eyes crinkled when he grinned. "Two weeks? That's more like it!"

She sank into his arms in relief. The wedding would go on. They wouldn't have to wait one more day to start their lives together, officially.

"Oh . . . but there's a lot to do." She chewed her lip, wishing she hadn't said anything until she'd given it more thought. Two weeks. She still had to find the veil. And who knew if the guests would even be able to come! She hadn't even thought about a seating chart.

But maybe . . . Amy could. She couldn't really turn her back on Hallie now, could she? Not in her hour of need, not when their other sister had already let her down.

9

Hallie pushed all thoughts of Claire from her head and smiled up at Josh. He didn't seem to share any of her concerns. "We can pull it together in time," he said. "You already have most of the planning figured out. You have that entire binder full of pictures."

She did. The problem was that she kept adding to it every day.

"I'm sure Amy will be willing to come out a few days early to make sure everything's perfect for you."

If Amy was even available.

And Hallie didn't even want to think about the availability of her other bridesmaid. Her sister Claire hadn't been apologetic about putting work before family functions in the past. And given her thoughts on this wedding, she certainly wouldn't start now.

So many ifs, where once there had been certainty.

"I'll see what I can do about the honeymoon," Josh promised, dropping her hand to wrap his arms around her waist. "Just think, two weeks from tomorrow, we can be getting married. You and me. Starting our lives together at long last. At the manor. Just like you always wanted."

Just like she always wanted.

She managed to nod, but she was feeling a little dizzy, and she was happy that Josh was holding on to her.

A little crease appeared between his eyebrows. "It's what you always wanted, isn't it?"

She swallowed hard and looked up into the eyes of the only boy she'd ever loved. Ever kissed. Ever known.

"It's all I've ever wanted," she said, smiling up at him. Even if she wasn't so sure how it would all come together.

CHAPTER TWO

Amy

Children's birthday parties were not high on the list of Amy's favorite events, but they paid the bills, and so here she was. It wasn't that she didn't like children (although the more meltdowns she witnessed, the less she worried about never having any of her own). It was that she didn't like a mess. Or loud noise. Or two chocolate handprints on the rear of her ivory wool crepe skirt that she really should have saved for tomorrow's silver anniversary party she'd been planning for the past two months.

"Knock, knock" came a voice, which Amy recognized as belonging to Michelle, on the other side of the door.

"Come in." She sighed, turning the lock.

Her assistant swung through the bathroom door and gave a low whistle as her eyes dropped to the stains that Amy probably shouldn't have attempted to clean.

"And here I thought you weren't getting any action these days!" she quipped.

"Very funny." Amy twisted to check her reflection in the mirror and then dropped the paper towel into the bin. "At least there's only half an hour left. If I can keep my back to the hedge until everyone leaves, I should be fine."

"Fine, sure. But still hopelessly single." Michelle raised an eyebrow. "Anyway, I came in to let you know that one of the boys knocked over the goody bag table. Meaning we'll be using those next thirty minutes to reassemble them all."

Since hiding in the bathroom until the party ended wasn't an option, Amy followed Michelle out the door of the pool-house bathroom at the back of the Johnsons' expansive lawn, which had been transformed with a fair bit of effort into a full-blown carnival, complete with a bouncy house, pony rides, games, clowns on stilts, and a cotton candy machine. Even the pool had been reimagined to fit the theme, with a striped awning placed above it like a tent, and filled with floaties in the shapes of various animals to give the impression that they were swimming.

As Amy scooted along the perimeter of the lawn, she eyed the three-tiered red-and-white-striped cake that was already half-destroyed, its chocolate interior on full display.

"Think Gail will notice anything?"

Michelle snorted. "Considering that she left ten minutes ago, I don't think that's possible."

"Left?" Amy kept her eye trained on the seven-year-old birthday boy—the same one who had left the handprints on her skirt—as he made a mad dash for the balloon animals. The balloonist was twisting the last blue tube into the shape of a monkey, and parents were already starting to gather near the garden gate.

In other words, if they didn't want twenty-five rambunctious kids running toward the toppled goody bag display and pocketing whatever loot their hands could grab, they'd better act quick.

"She has the society wedding tonight," Michelle reminded Amy. "You remember. The one she asked you to plan that you turned down?" Her friend gave her a look of familiar disappointment.

"You know that weddings aren't my thing," Amy said.

"Bethany's on that account, isn't she?" Michelle asked as they picked up the clown-faced gift bags and started redistributing the trinkets that Amy had spent a solid two hours hunting down.

"Well, she is her niece," Amy replied.

"Who was only hired because Gail needed help with weddings and I can't do them all."

And Amy wouldn't. She did everything else, from baptisms to corporate events to anything else someone might want to celebrate. But weddings were a deal breaker, and so she was often left reduced to sugar-high kids and their anxious parents.

From across the yard, the sound of a balloon popping made Amy jump, and the wail of tears that followed forecast a headache in the near future. Along with a much-needed glass of wine.

"Drinks after teardown?" Technically, the rental companies would take down the tents and stands and bring the ponies back to the farm where they lived, but there would be no leaving until the yard was exactly as it had been at eight o'clock this morning. Amy's feet were tired, and her back ached, and she could think of nothing better than relaxing in her sweats on the couch with her best friend and—someday—business partner.

"Can't," Michelle said with a little smile as she dropped a rainbow Slinky into a bag and then scooped up some packages of gummy candy that were mixed in with the grass. "I have a date."

"Another one?"

"That's what single women our age do on weekends." Michelle set the last of the goody bags on the table just before a flood of kids came running over.

Remembering her skirt, Amy backed up a step. "Not when they work all weekend."

"Nice excuse," Michelle said, shaking her head.

"Besides, I haven't visited my mother in a while. I might stop by . . ." Both residing in Boston, Amy and her mother usually tried to meet for lunch or dinner once a month, and of course on holidays, especially when Claire couldn't be bothered to visit and Hallie was with her future in-laws. Gone were the days of a loud, full house—they'd died along with Amy's father's laughter, which used to fill the now-empty space.

"Your mother has a busier social life than you do," Michelle countered.

"Well, she's very active with local charities." They each had their own way of handling the loss of Amy's father. Claire worked. Hallie grew even closer to Josh and his family. Bunny—Amy's mother— took the helm at what was once her husband's real estate business and devoted her free time to worthy causes and the occasional bridge game.

And Amy . . . she worked, but not like Claire. More like she kept busy. Anything to keep her heart from dwelling too much on the past and everything—and everyone—she'd lost.

"I'm just pointing out that she owns her own business and still makes time for other things. And she's not in her late twenties, like you." Michelle gave her a pointed look. "Just think, if you found a great guy, you could plan your own wedding and get over this hang-up you have about them."

Amy closed her mouth before she fed into that comment. Michelle didn't know that she'd hit a nerve; only Amy's sisters really understood that part of her heart. They had been there for the dress-up days, the arguments over who got to wear their mother's veil. They knew the dream she'd had for herself. And they knew that the man she loved didn't share it.

At least, not with her.

But Amy's sisters also weren't around to talk much these days, and Michelle was. Somehow, slowly, Michelle had become the person she texted after a long day or laughed with on a Saturday night. She knew the ins and outs of Amy's day, and Claire and Hallie . . . well, they just knew what Amy was willing to share. When they talked at all.

"Weddings are a lot of work and emotions. And I don't have a problem with being single," Amy reminded her friend. She watched as two kids fought over which goody bag they wanted, even though they were all identical for this very reason. It was one of the key things she'd learned about children's parties. No mixing colors for cupcakes. No alternating prints on party favors. No variety when it came to ice pop flavors. It kept everyone happy. Or at least it cut down on the chaos.

"So you say," Michelle said in a tone that showed she didn't believe it in the least. "Come on. Let's start breaking everything down. If we get out of here early enough, I might have time to change my shoes before my date."

Date. That was certainly a foreign concept. And a reminder that she probably should get back out there again. Even if every dinner or coffee she'd sat through, ranging from perfectly pleasant to a complete bust, only seemed to serve to remind her that the connection she'd shared all those years ago had been unique. Special. Maybe irreplaceable.

But it hadn't been enough.

The silver anniversary party was—drumroll, please—silver in theme. Amy couldn't be blamed for the lack of imagination, but Gail tried all the same.

"Silver?" She tsked as she swept a disapproving eye over the room.

"I couldn't exactly go with gold," Amy pointed out. She caught Michelle's eye and gave a little smile.

Gail sighed heavily. "I suppose not. It just seems so . . . expected."

"It's what the client wanted," Amy said, because there was no arguing with that. Sometimes, when Gail had a conflict and the budget was low enough for her to not be too invested, Gail let Amy handle all the client meetings. This had been one of those times.

"Well, the client is always right," Gail said, and not for the first time. It was something that she'd instilled in Amy from her first day on the job. You can advise, you can guide, but you ultimately have to sit back and let the client have the final say. It was their party.

Moving on to make sure that the flower arrangements were all in place, Amy heard her phone ring in her pocket. She crossed her fingers that it wasn't the bakery, which was yet to deliver the four-tiered cake meant to replicate the happy couple's original wedding cake, then felt her shoulders relax when she saw that it was her sister.

Hallie hadn't called in weeks, and Amy realized with a twinge of shame that she hadn't initiated contact in longer than that. The days melted into each other, and the weeks turned into months all too easily. She couldn't let it go to voice mail, even though she probably should.

"Hey, Hallie," she answered, glancing at Gail, who was watching from across the room to make sure there was no emergency. Amy flashed her a smile to show all was well and that she could be on her way now. As the face of the company, Gail would stay until the clients arrived, though, before slipping out the back door, leaving Amy and Michelle to handle the rest. "Can I call you tomorrow? I'm at an event."

"That's sort of what I wanted to talk to you about, actually," Hallie said. "We've had a change of plans with the wedding."

"Change of plans?" This didn't sound like Hallie at all. Hallie always had plans, even if she was much more of a type B personality than say, Claire, who was wound so tight that Amy often had the urge to reach out and tickle her, like she'd done when they were little, just to see her loosen up a bit. Hallie's life fell in stride, neatly ordered in a way that Amy sometimes envied.

"Cliffside Manor double-booked our original date."

Yikes. It was known to happen, but rarely. No wonder she sounded a little off.

"So now we're getting married in two weeks!" Hallie announced.

Amy blinked, wondering if she'd missed some part of the rambling story while she was watching the cake be carefully carried through the ballroom doors.

"Two weeks?" The event planner in her grew suspicious of just how her sister was going to make this happen. The sister in her grew concerned about how she might rearrange her schedule to show up for her bridesmaid duties.

"That's right! And I hate to ask because I know how busy you are, but I don't see how I can pull this off on my own, not now, with so little time and so much to do. And I can't take the time off work, not when Josh is hoping to move up our honeymoon. I know it's a big ask but—"

But many things. Like the fact that Rachel Eisenberg's bat mitzvah was the very same Saturday, an event so large that Gail had her entire team on it. Like the fact that Hallie lived in Driftwood Cove, which was less than a two-hour drive but hardly a place that Amy liked to visit, and that what she was asking for would require days of planning—weeks, really. More than the two she had.

Like the fact that Amy didn't plan weddings. Not her own. Not anyone's.

Not even her kid sister's.

She closed her eyes against the dread that was building inside her. She'd have to say yes. She couldn't say no. But oh, how she wanted to, badly.

Work had been her excuse the first time around, but Hallie hadn't seemed worried then, with a year of planning ahead of her and everything pretty much already set in stone since she was still in pigtails. But this was different.

And Hallie wouldn't press the topic unless she really needed Amy's help.

"I can come out next weekend," Amy said, thinking of the Friday-night retirement party she had to oversee. She alone had handled the account, and there was no way she could let her clients down. Just like she couldn't let her sister down. "But email me all your plans today so that I'm up to speed when I get there. I'll do what I can from here this week."

"Oh, thank you, Amy! I knew I could count on you!" Despite the relief in Hallie's voice, Amy detected another meaning.

One that had to do with their other sister. One that said Hallie could not count on Claire. Amy felt a hint of anxiety when she thought about how things might play out when they were all reunited—that was if Claire even bothered to show up for her bridesmaid duties.

Since the disastrous engagement party last summer, Amy had barely spoken to Claire, and only to beg her to apologize to Hallie, which, to Amy's knowledge, hadn't happened. She'd thought she had a few months to worry about how everyone would behave at the wedding, but with the timeline being moved up, tensions over more than returning to Driftwood Cove surfaced.

"Will . . . everyone be in attendance?"

"If you're referring to Claire, I was going to ask you the same question." Hallie's tone shifted. "I don't even know if she should still be in my wedding party."

Amy couldn't blame her sister. When Claire, a little tipsy and always a little outspoken, had loudly told Amy that she thought Hallie was too young to be rushing into marriage, Amy had tried to laugh it off. But Claire made it clear she wasn't joking. Even Bunny, flustered and wide eyed, couldn't ease the tension, and Amy had been relieved to flee Beachnest Cottage at dawn the next morning, telling herself that things would blow over.

Only a year later, they hadn't.

"Of course she should still be in your wedding party," Amy said now.

There was silence on the other end of the line.

"It will all be okay," Amy told Hallie. Then, because she knew her sister needed to hear it, she added, "It will be perfect. I promise."

After all, at least one of them deserved a perfect wedding.

Stuffing the phone into her pocket, she walked over to inspect the cake, pleased with what she saw.

"Well, someone looks happy," Michelle said, giving her a coy look as she came to stand beside her. "Please tell me you've finally decided to unlock your lingerie drawer and accept a dinner invitation from one of the many men I've given your number to?"

"You did not!" Amy stared at her friend.

Michelle laughed. "No, but I might soon if you don't get yourself out there."

"Forget my personal life. My sister's wedding planner messed up, and she needs me to fill in."

Michelle's expression turned suspicious. "But you don't do weddings."

Amy shrugged. "I do now." She had no choice. "They moved up the wedding. It's in two *weeks*. I told her I'd come out next week to help."

Michelle's face fell. "Have you told Gail?"

Amy flicked a glance over her shoulder. "Not yet."

With confidence she didn't feel, she squared her shoulders and crossed the room to where Gail was alternately looking from her watch to the main doors. The happy couple who had been married for decades would soon walk through the door so they could personally greet the guests, meaning that Amy didn't have much time.

"Do you have a moment, Gail?" she asked, then, seeing Gail's large blue eyes go round, she assured her, "Everything's fine, and I can take it from here. I just wanted to let you know that I need to take a week off the week after next for my sister's wedding."

"You're just telling me this *now*?"

"The date was moved up unexpectedly," Amy explained. "And I'm a bridesmaid." *And the new wedding planner,* she didn't add. "The Eisenberg party is completely planned. Everything is in place, and I confirmed the dessert station on Friday. I'll devote this entire week to anything else that needs to be done, but I'm confident that Michelle and Bethany can handle any assistance you'll need in my absence."

"You mean you'll be gone for an entire week?"

"My family needs me." In all her years of working for this woman, she had never asked for a favor; instead she always did the favoring, handling last-minute orders and overseeing final-hour changes. Giving up her own plans, weekends, nights, and even holidays.

And Michelle wondered why she didn't have time to date.

"Then it looks like you have a choice to make," Gail said coolly.

Amy stared at her, and she thought she heard Michelle gasp from behind her.

"Bethany has been learning the business, and I think she's ready to take on more projects." Gail gave her a long look. "If you'd been willing to move into weddings, all of this could have gone much differently."

And there it was. Her fate had been sealed long before tonight. And she hadn't seen it coming.

Willing herself not to cry, she cleared her throat and said, "I thought you were grooming me for partnership. I've been with the company for five years. You know weddings aren't our only business."

"No, but they're a huge part of it."

It was true, Amy understood, and there was no space for argument. Her boss was right: she did have a choice to make. But was she being given any choice at all?

"I'm sorry you feel that way, Gail," she said evenly. And she was. Gail wasn't perfect, but then other than, say, Hallie and Josh, who was? Amy had liked this job, even loved it at times. She'd thrown herself into it when she moved full time back to Boston, enjoying the creative challenge, the way every project was different from the next. That she was always looking forward to the next event.

That it stopped her from looking back.

"The clients are here!" Michelle trilled, sounding anxious.

Amy stepped forward on shaking legs, but Gail, suddenly composed, cut in front of her and sailed across the marble flooring, hands outstretched, congratulating the happy couple on their special day.

"I can't believe you just quit!" Michelle hissed to Amy.

Amy blinked rapidly, feeling a little disoriented. "More like I was let go."

"Why didn't you just tell her you're *planning* your sister's wedding? That you had a change of heart?"

Amy thought about it but then shook her head.

"Because I didn't have a change of heart," she said.

And that was just the problem.

CHAPTER THREE

Claire

Most people dreaded Monday mornings, but Claire Walsh wasn't one of them. What she dreaded were Saturday afternoons, that long stretch of time when she'd already had her morning run and her second and third cups of coffee and made sure that her apartment was tidy, which didn't take long, given that it was sparse. The thought of lounging around, making an art form of doing nothing, made her so tense that she had to get up and actually do something, and so she couldn't really relax until Sunday, when she knew that the next day would be Monday.

When she'd be back in the office. Her happy place. The place where drama was limited to the clients and swiftly rectified, usually by hers truly. It was a place where she could right the wrongs if not of her own life, then at least of others.

With her usual Monday-morning energy, her usual coffee in one hand and a bakery bag containing a muffin for the building's security guard in the other, Claire pushed through the revolving door of the midtown Manhattan high-rise where she'd worked since graduating from law school, climbing her way up the ranks of the firm with the help of a strong work ethic and plenty of billable hours. She handed the elderly gentleman near the lobby desk his usual and said, "Happy Monday, Bert!"

He gave her a fatherly grin. "Claire, you always know how to brighten my day!"

Try telling that to the soon-to-be ex-husband of the woman she was representing, Claire thought as she stepped into the elevator. She tabulated just how much she was going to take from the lying cheat by the time the doors slid open on the thirty-second floor.

She walked briskly down the hall, eager to get to her office and review her files before her ten o'clock mediation meeting.

On Mondays the office was slower to fill, but she wasn't surprised when no sooner had she settled into her leather executive chair and powered up her computer than there was a knock at her door and Gabe Turner appeared.

"You always know how to brighten my day!" she said, stealing Bert's phrase, which made Gabe's eyes twinkle because he knew it.

"Bert enjoying his Monday muffin?" he asked, stepping inside her office to make himself at home on one of her visitor chairs.

"You know it." She typed her password onto her keyboard.

"Why don't you ever bring me one of those muffins?" Gabe chided. "I'm only your husband."

"Work husband," she corrected, glancing back at him. "And why don't you ever rub my feet? These heels are killing me, and it's barely eight." She lifted a leg up to prove her point, the stiletto poking out from the side of her desk.

"I'll rub your feet," he said with an easy smile.

She dismissed the comment with a wave of her hand, even though she knew he probably would if she asked him—her and half the island of Manhattan whom he dated. She and Gabe had come up the ranks together, having graduated from law school the same year, albeit on opposite sides of the country. They'd met early in her first week, in the break room, when neither of them could figure out how to use the coffee machine. It could have been an awkward encounter, especially considering that they both prided themselves on pretty much always being right, both top of their class, knowing all they could and figuring out what they couldn't. Instead, they'd gone downstairs to the coffee shop next door. It was the start of a beautiful relationship, and one that she enjoyed from Monday through Friday, never on weekends. There was a no-fraternization policy at the firm, and since they were both on partner track, anything beyond friendship wasn't up for consideration. Things with Gabe were black and white, with no gray area. Just the way she liked it.

The phone rang—not an unusual occurrence for a Monday morning—and Gabe stood up.

"Lunch today?" he asked from the doorway.

She glanced at her schedule and nodded while reaching for the phone. "Claire Walsh."

"Claire! I wasn't sure if it was too early to call." It was her mother.

Instinctively, Claire's stomach tightened. The last time her mother had called her this early was when her father had his fatal heart attack. Even though that had been eight years ago, right now every nerve in her body seemed to go on alert, bracing for what was coming.

Claire frowned. "Is everything okay?"

"Oh, fine, fine. Just . . . your sister had to move up her wedding date."

Claire opened her mouth and then closed it. It was common knowledge in the Walsh family that she wasn't quite as enthusiastic about Hallie's plans as everyone else. And because she'd opened her "big mouth," as Amy put it, at the engagement party last summer, it was also common knowledge to the bride as well.

A little over a year had passed since Hallie's engagement party, and she and Hallie hadn't spoken in all that time. Not even at Christmas, when, fortunately, Hallie was on a ski trip with her future in-laws and

Claire was too busy with a custody dispute and a January trial date to spend the holidays with her family.

It hadn't been the first time, so no one questioned things. And it wasn't like she could shelve her responsibilities at the firm just to sip eggnog or decorate a tree that would be hauled out to the curb by the first of January.

But it was more than that. Holidays hadn't been the same for the Walsh family in eight years. Claire dropped in for a night—if she visited at all.

"Let me pull up my calendar." Claire bit back a sigh. How many Fridays did she have open at the moment? It wasn't like she could drive in the morning of the wedding, not when there was a rehearsal dinner the night before that she'd be expected to attend.

Not when she was the sister of the bride. And a bridesmaid.

At least, she assumed she was. Hallie had asked her and Amy together, before Claire decided to be frank. From her perspective, settling down might as well have just been called settling. It started great, and, like most things, ended badly. And, in the case of marital dissolution, expensively.

"Okay, when is it?" She scanned her schedule, wincing at how tight it was.

"A week from Saturday," her mother said.

"A week from Saturday?" Claire sat up straighter and clicked on next week's schedule, even though she knew what it held. Meetings. Casework. No different from this week. "That's really short notice, Mom."

"It's the only time that Cliffside Manor could squeeze them in," her mother explained.

Claire felt the impact of those words. Cliffside Manor was where every bride in the family was married, and Hallie intended to continue the tradition, claiming that it guaranteed a happy ending.

As if there were such a thing.

"There was no way around it unless they wanted to push things off by another year or completely change their plans."

Claire couldn't hold back her opinions, even though she probably should. "Another year might not be a bad idea."

"Claire." Her mother's tone was laced with warning. "Your sister needs your support. She knows you don't approve of her relationship."

"It's not that I don't approve . . ." Except that she didn't. Not completely. It wasn't that she didn't like Josh. He was a perfectly nice guy who seemed to genuinely love her sister. But all they'd ever known was each other. Their entire lives had been set up for them. They were yet to face any hardship. And Claire knew all too well what could happen when they did. "I just think they're very young."

"They're twenty-five. And they'd been dating since they were fifteen."

"In other words, since they were children."

Her mother was quiet for a moment. "If you can't support your sister, then maybe it's better if you don't come at all."

Claire felt her eyes widen. "Of course I'm going to come. How can I miss my own sister's wedding?"

But how could she really go? She scanned her screen again, thinking of which meetings she could reschedule.

"Amy is coming up early to help plan," her mother went on.

Meaning that once again Claire got to look like the jerk for not being able to drop everything last minute to show up to a wedding she didn't even think should be happening.

She didn't have a choice. Her baby sister was getting married, and even though they hadn't spoken since last summer, and even though they had drifted apart in the years since their father's death, Claire would be there for her.

She'd smile and laugh and hug and say all the right things.

And then get out of town before she gave her true opinions away.

Lunch with Gabe was a frequent event, sometimes in their offices, sometimes over a shared case, and sometimes at the sandwich shop in the lobby, like today.

"How was your weekend?" she asked.

Gabe told her about his latest disastrous date as they stood in line, waited for their orders, and then moved to a table just as two businessmen were getting up.

"Didn't even bother with dessert," Gabe said, settling into his chair.

Gabe dated a lot. And none of them went well.

"Did you walk her to the door?" she asked.

"Didn't want to send the wrong message. I waved her off in the cab."

Claire chuckled. "Remind me to never date you. I'm not sure I'd make it beyond the first round of drinks." She sighed as she unwrapped her sandwich from the wax paper.

"You seem stressed," Gabe said, lifting his top slice of pumpernickel to remove the pickle, which he set on her plate without her needing to ask.

"My sister's getting married."

He shrugged. "You already knew that."

"A week from Saturday." She gave him a long look to underscore the magnitude of this turn of events. "They had to move things up, apparently. It just seems so . . . rushed."

"Rushed? Haven't they been together since they were kids?"

"Exactly the problem." Claire pinched her lips. "That was my mother who called, first thing this morning. Of course, she made sure to mention that my other sister will be there for an entire week, meaning that in addition to already being in trouble for not giving my full blessing to this wedding, I'll be judged for only showing up for the weekend."

"So give them one less thing to complain about," he said, biting into his sandwich.

"You mean . . . go up early?" She thought about it for half a second and then shook her head. "I can't leave work for an entire week."

"Do you have any court dates?"

She should have known that a fellow attorney would follow up her excuse with the perfect question. "No."

"Shift whatever meetings you have back a few days," Gabe proposed. "And isn't your family's Rhode Island house huge? You can work while you're there at least part of the week."

She picked at her Reuben. It was possible, but not exactly tempting, if the engagement party was any indication.

"To be honest, I'm not sure they'll even unlock the door for me." She was only half joking.

"You really don't think Hallie has forgiven you yet?" Gabe asked.

Claire didn't need to think about the answer. "No. And Amy has disappeared, too, clearly taking sides. I didn't exactly take back what I said. And I don't think they'd believe me if I did."

She knew her sisters thought she was cynical, that she hadn't ever known true love and couldn't understand. But Hallie was young, even naive, and all Claire wanted was to protect her. She knew more than Hallie did about what could go wrong.

"So make them believe you." Gabe shrugged as if it were that easy.

"And how do you propose I do that?"

He looked at her thoughtfully for a moment. "You've told your sisters that you don't believe in lasting love."

"Because I don't," she said, nodding.

"Well, maybe you should show Hallie that you do."

Claire laughed. "She'd never buy it."

"She can't exactly rebuff your apology if she thinks you're sincere." Gabe raised an eyebrow. "You do plan to apologize, not try to stop the wedding, right?"

Claire paused. "It's not that I want to stop the wedding, I just . . . want her to be sure."

"Who says that she isn't?"

Claire sighed. Hallie *was* sure that she was marrying her soulmate, that they'd live happily ever after in the cottage by the sea, just as their parents had done, but Claire had seen more and understood that life didn't always work out that way. People lied, cheated, and betrayed one another, even in the longest-term marriages. Even in the ones that looked so happy from the outside.

"Even if I wanted to stop the wedding, I couldn't. I'm going there to support her. And . . . to try to repair our relationship." But even she knew that it would be nearly impossible to move past the engagement party. Hallie had looked at her with the hurt in her eyes that Claire had only been trying to avoid.

"Then show her you believe in her marriage. That you believe in love."

"And how do I do that?"

Gabe shrugged, as if the answer were simple. "Bring a date."

Claire considered this. A date would go a long way in selling her story about believing in true love, and she didn't exactly have a better plan of convincing her sister that she supported this wedding—especially when she didn't.

"It's a little late to find a date for the wedding," Claire pointed out.

"Well." Gabe set down his sandwich and wiped his mouth with his napkin. "I could be your date."

"You?" Claire laughed again, but then stopped when she realized he was serious. She shook her head. "I can't ask that of you."

"I'm offering. Your family has a big beach house, and I haven't had a vacation in years. Besides, other people's family problems are sort of my specialty."

"Mine too," Claire countered. Except when it was her own. "I don't know . . ." Ever the practical one, Claire was already thinking of logistics. How could they both take a full week off work? And what kind of rumors around the office would that stir up if they both left at the same time? "I can't ask you to take that time off from work," she said, hoping that would put an end to this crazy proposal, because that's what it was: crazy.

Still, it was also strangely perfect. After all, she and Gabe had maintained ironclad boundaries for as long as they'd known each other. There was never any gray area with them, never any awkwardness that one might typically find in a friendship with the opposite sex.

No, with Gabe, it was easy. They accepted their roles as friends and colleagues. There were no hard feelings. No weird moments. It was all business, really.

And maybe this could be too.

Wait. Was she really considering this?

"Come on. It's just a week. It will be fun!"

Fun was the last description that Claire had for a week at the family's beach house, but maybe a vacation *could* be made out of it. Maybe she could catch up on sleep, clock some longer runs along the shore, and come back to the office rested and ready to go.

And back on speaking terms with her sister.

Or maybe this entire wedding week would be a bigger disaster than she already feared.

CHAPTER FOUR

Hallie

Saturday couldn't come soon enough, but by the time it rolled around, Hallie was exhausted, relieved, and a little terrified.

She woke to the promise of a sunny day, judging from the light slipping through the gap in the linen curtains of her childhood bedroom. When she moved to Driftwood Cove full time after college, she'd fallen into old habits, even though she was the only person living here for most of the year. Her father's study remained unchanged, the door often closed and the bookshelves filled with framed prints that hadn't been replaced with new ones. Her parents' bedroom, which her mother used less and less frequently, was still set aside for her visits, just like the two other bedrooms, which belonged to Hallie's sisters, who came even less often than their mother.

Once, they'd all gathered in the rambling house every chance they had; the car was usually packed the morning of the last day of school, and with the short commute it was common for them to drive down for a long weekend too. But since Hallie's father's death, Bunny preferred to stay in Boston, and Claire made every excuse not to visit the place where he had taken his last breath. Amy hung on for a while, but Logan's engagement was one more heartbreak than she could handle.

Nothing had been the same since Hallie's father died.

Except for the house. And Amy had lost that, too, hadn't she? She'd never said as much, but Hallie sensed it as her relationship with Josh grew stronger and it was clear that they'd eventually get married and Hallie would be the one to inherit the house.

Hallie hadn't dared to change a thing. Not the throw pillows on the sofas in the living room, not even the sun-faded cushions on the chairs in the sunroom. Partially out of respect, partially out of suspicion, she still didn't quite see the house as hers just yet.

But it would be. Per tradition, the house was passed down to the first bride in the family. Another precious, irreplaceable heirloom handed through the generations, soon to fall into her official possession.

Two months earlier than expected.

It's just two months, she reminded herself. Two months from now she could have woken up thinking the same strange thought: that one week from today, she'd be getting ready to be married. To don her mother's wedding dress, which had belonged to her mother's mother before her, and the veil that had been passed down to every bride for so many years that it was a wonder the thing hadn't fallen apart by now.

If it hadn't fallen apart by now. Hallie had idly looked for it over the past few months—a lot at first, after Josh proposed; less so after that disastrous engagement party.

Now, though, she stepped out of bed, stretched her back, and thought about where it could be. Her mother didn't know but had promised to look for it at the house in Boston before she drove in tomorrow. Claire wouldn't be any use, but Amy might have an idea.

Right now she was depending on Amy to solve a lot of her problems.

But her sister wouldn't be able to solve all of them. There was the matter of Claire, of course. Hallie still couldn't believe what her mother had told her. Claire, arriving tomorrow, to spend the entire week in a town she had barely graced in eight years?

There was a part of her that had hoped Claire wouldn't show up at all—the last thing Hallie needed was a naysayer on her wedding day, even if she knew that all the comforting words Amy had told her in the days after the engagement party were true, that Claire was hard and cynical and couldn't understand love when she hadn't experienced it herself.

And then there was the other, smaller part of her that felt not having Claire standing by her side was as equally impossible as not having her at the wedding at all. Sometimes when she walked by Claire's old bedroom, just two doors down from her own, she was reminded of the Christmas Eve nights that they'd all huddle in Claire's big bed, hoping that Santa could find them at their beach home, wondering what joys the next morning would bring. How Claire would read her books until she fell asleep, even when Hallie was old enough to read on her own. How back then, their six-year age gap had felt huge, and Claire took her role as the eldest most seriously. Always holding Hallie's hand across the street, sometimes buying her a treat in town with her babysitting money when she grew older.

Thinking back on those days, Hallie's heart would soften, only to harden again when she thought about how much Claire had changed, distancing herself not just physically but emotionally in the days and weeks and then years after their father died. How it was like her heart had died with him. How she'd gone from being a little bossy to uncomfortably blunt. How she'd gone from being warm to standoffish. How she'd found one excuse after another not to visit for holidays or birthdays, or eventually even to bother with a phone call.

But now Claire would be coming here, tomorrow, to this house, and there was nothing Hallie could do about it, because for the next week at least, it was still her mother's house.

Taking a deep breath, Hallie padded down the stairs, past the front sitting room, which was now the landing spot for all the gifts that she and Josh had registered for back in the winter. More were arriving by the day, each one reminding her that her wedding day was actually almost upon her.

Feeling slightly shaky, she reminded herself that Amy was literally on her way at this very moment, driving toward Driftwood Cove, the miles becoming shorter with each passing second.

Amy had already started tackling Hallie's long list of to-dos. She had the guest list. And more than that, she knew how things should go. She'd pored over their mother's wedding album just as many times as Hallie had as a little girl. She knew every detail by heart. Sure, Hallie had clipped some visuals from magazines, ones that made it possible to recreate tradition in modern times. The bridesmaids' dresses would be blush, not the peach that her mother had chosen. And the bouquets would be a little less leafy. The cake would be tiered and white, like her mother's, but the topper didn't look anything like her and Josh, so that left some room for a bit of imagination.

Taking a deep breath, she reminded herself that it would all be okay. Better than that, as Amy had assured her, it would all be perfect.

Her phone beeped in her pocket, and she pulled it out, hoping it was a text from Amy.

Instead, she saw Josh's name. The countdown begins.

She swallowed hard. Somehow they'd gone from years to months to weeks to . . . days.

She started to push the phone back into her pocket, but it beeped again. Again, her heart lurched. Again, a text from Josh. A week from tomorrow, I'll never have to text you first thing in the morning.

No. Because he'd be right here. Every morning. Of every day. For the rest of her life.

Another one popped up: Have fun with your sister today. I'll check in later.

Of course he would. Because that's what people who were about to get married did. They checked in with each other. They spent time together.

But did they spend so much time together?

To hear Claire say it, no. But then Hallie thought of Josh's parents, who were all too happy working side by side by day and going home together at night. And even her own parents, who had run their real estate business together, had still made time to dance together in the kitchen when a good song came on the radio.

She had reached the back of the house now. She set the phone on the old butcher's rack that greeted everyone who entered the kitchen, next to the framed photos and cookbooks and the mixing bowls from England that her mother collected, even though some were now chipped.

The light streaming in through the kitchen window caught the engagement ring on her finger as she started the coffee. It seemed to blind her, making it impossible to see anything else other than the promise she'd made. And the one she intended to keep.

The one that, a week from today, she'd fully commit to in front of all their friends and family.

Even Claire.

She didn't even realize her hand was shaking until the coffeepot dropped to the ground, shattering at her feet.

When Amy's car crunched to a stop on the gravel driveway, Hallie was waiting for her on the long porch that wrapped nearly completely around the house.

"Tell me you haven't been waiting out there all morning," Amy said with a laugh when she climbed out of the car. Her auburn hair that she alone had inherited from their father was pulled up high in a messy bun, her feet in driving moccasins, her attire a murky cross between loungewear and pajamas.

But Hallie had never seen a more beautiful sight.

"Only for the past hour, since you called from the rest stop." She ran down the porch steps, arms outstretched, and pulled her sister in for a long hug. "It's been too long."

"It has," Amy said, with a twinge of regret in her tone. She didn't make it back to Driftwood Cove often, not when she lived so close to their mother in Boston, and not when this town carried ghosts that they didn't discuss. "But then you were the one who went off to Vail for Christmas this year."

It was true. It was Hallie's year to spend with the Goodwins. Their mother was still working full time and volunteering with her friends in her spare time. Amy claimed to have a hundred Christmas parties to plan anyway, and Claire . . . well.

Hallie helped Amy unload her bags from the trunk and haul them up the stairs to the porch, where they dropped them near the screen door that led to the kitchen.

"Look at that view!" Amy paused to take it in. The house sat close to the water, separated by only a couple of hundred feet of grass. It was a clear day, but the sea was rough, and the water, Hallie knew, would be cold.

Guilt crept in when Hallie watched Amy's face transform. Her sister had always loved this house, perhaps most of all of them, and that was no small feat. Hallie had once dared to think that Amy and Logan would end up together; that, being older, maybe she'd be the first to get married, the one to inherit the house. She knew that Amy thought so too. Or hoped, at least. That she'd hung on for years, waiting for their friendship to turn romantic, until Logan had gone and gotten engaged . . . to someone else.

And if he'd proposed to Amy instead, then this house might have been hers.

Hallie wondered if Amy ever thought of that. All the things that had been lost here, not just their father.

"We could take a walk along the shore?" Hallie suggested. Amy had been in and out in one night last summer, and before the engagement party she hadn't been back to Beachnest Cottage in four years, always claiming work kept her busy, even though Hallie knew that it was more about what happened with Logan Howell.

Amy's smile was tired. "Maybe later. First I want to see the house. As you said, it's been too long."

There was that wistful tone again, the one that made Hallie pause and count her blessings, the one that reminded her of just how lucky she was and how happy she should be.

The screen door creaked when they pushed through. Hallie had opened most of the windows, allowing the breeze to flow through the rooms. It was a comfortable home, large but certainly not fancy, with worn slipcovered sofas and sagging chairs that sat around the stone fireplace, the kitchen in the distance, and a large farmer's table with mismatched chairs that had accumulated over the years completing the dining room. The rooms were large, the walls high and filled with framed photos and watercolors from local artists, but the real view, of course, was the Atlantic Ocean.

Most days, the family bypassed the oversize living room for the screened-in porch with its wicker furniture and weatherworn game boards, the overhead lighting dim but cozy. When they were younger, Hallie's father would read them ghost stories, just enough to thrill them, never enough to scare. Other nights, they were content just listening to the sound of the waves crashing against the shore.

"Your room is all ready for you. I even refreshed the linens." Hallie was eager to show her sister that everything was like it always was. That nothing had changed. That it was still Amy's home too.

"You didn't have to do that!" Amy remarked as they began trudging up the stairs with the luggage.

Oh, but she did. Amy was doing her a favor. A big one. One that surpassed bridesmaid duties. One that she knew couldn't be easy for her sister, not just because it required coming back to Driftwood Cove.

Amy might have used her work as an excuse not to help with the planning originally, but Hallie knew her sister, and she knew her history. She'd been a part of it. She, Josh, Amy, and Logan. They'd been a foursome, a tight group of friends. Until Logan had gone off to marry his college sweetheart—a woman that no one but Logan had ever warmed up to, and the feeling was mutual. Lindsey hadn't liked the Walshes any more than she enjoyed spending time in Driftwood Cove, and over time even Josh had lost touch with Logan.

They'd never talked about that wedding, and none of them had attended it either. And after that, Amy stopped talking about weddings altogether.

Amy's room was beside Hallie's, the walls in a blue-and-white-striped print, the bedding crisp and fresh, the flowers on the dresser straight from the garden.

"We're the ones who are supposed to be pampering you," Amy said with a disapproving glance back at her as soon as they inched into the room, but it was clear that she was pleased.

"There's no way I'll be able to relax this week," Hallie said.

"Let's go over our list," Amy said, getting right to it as she sat on the bed. "Tomorrow is your dress fitting."

"I just need to find the veil," she said.

Amy looked at her a little strangely, no doubt because Hallie hadn't brought it out of storage yet.

"Mom always kept it in her closet," she said, remembering how they'd retrieve it when they played dress-up, how it was always on the highest shelf, wrapped in paper, in a pale-blue box, and each time they removed it, it was like unwrapping a present.

"Well, Mom is arriving tomorrow. I'm sure she'll be able to find it once she's here," Amy assured her.

Hallie dropped onto the bed beside Amy. "And you heard who else is coming tomorrow?"

Amy set down her phone and gave her a look of sympathy. "She must feel terrible if she's coming up a week early."

Hallie considered this, secretly hoping this was the case but knowing that it wasn't. Claire might have grown cold over the years, but she'd never been mean. She'd never say anything just to hurt someone, especially one of her sisters.

No, when Claire spoke, she spoke the truth.

"The only thing Claire feels is that I shouldn't be marrying Josh."

Hallie could still remember Amy defending her, calling Claire out on her harsh words, pleading with her to take them back. And Claire hadn't. She'd apologized, sure, only in the moment, with their mother shooting glances around the crowd, which was oblivious to the family drama unfolding on their very lawn. But she'd apologized for hurting Hallie, not for what she said.

Now, like then, Hallie reminded herself that Claire's opinion didn't matter. That she should consider the source. That she didn't need to give it another thought.

But that didn't mean it didn't still hurt.

"Hey," Amy said, giving her a little smile. "It's going to be fine, okay. Better than fine, it's going to be perfect. This is your wedding week, Hallie. You should be enjoying it. Just leave the worrying to me." When Hallie didn't respond, Amy said, "You're not that upset, are you? About Claire? You know she doesn't understand. The only man she's ever loved was Dad, and after that . . ."

Hallie nodded. "I just wish she could understand that some of us can still be happy." Amy looked down at her hands, and Hallie immediately regretted her words. "Sorry, Amy. I know this isn't easy for you."

Amy shook off her concern, but the look in her eyes told Hallie she had hit a nerve.

"You and Josh are the perfect couple. And, hey, one of us deserves a happy ending, right? And who cares what Claire thinks or says? This isn't about her. It's about you and Josh."

Hallie swallowed hard, unable to fight her anxiety. "I'll just . . . feel better once everything for the wedding is all in place."

Yes, that was it. Of course. Anyone in her position would feel rattled.

"Don't you worry about a thing. If I have to bake a cake myself, you will have the most beautiful cake anyone has ever seen."

Hallie laughed. "I seem to remember you pouring salt into the birthday cake for Dad one year."

"It was one year," Amy corrected. "And he still ate it!"

They both laughed, but the good feelings were all too soon replaced with a familiar tug in Hallie's heart. From the sadness in Amy's eyes, she knew her sister felt it too.

"I miss him," Hallie said.

"Being back in this house reminds me of him," Amy said softly. "Remember how he'd always make pancakes for us our first morning here?"

"He'd make them in the shape of our initials. I always felt like I had the biggest one." Hallie sighed. "But being here does keep him alive." And it was why she couldn't imagine ever changing it.

Hallie flopped onto the bed, feeling better by the second that her sister was here. Her favorite person in the world (well, other than Josh, of course!). The one she could still picture as a little girl, proudly handing their father the cake they'd all made together.

"I wish he could be here," Hallie said sadly.

Amy reached down and squeezed her hand. "He is. In his own way."

Hallie turned to look at her sister, who was staring at the ceiling. "You really believe that?"

After a beat, Amy nodded, and for many reasons Hallie was happy that Claire wasn't here. Claire would have probably said that they were being fantastical. She never liked talking about their father anymore.

And because they all knew it hurt her, no one mentioned him when she was around.

"I have the entire list you sent me," Amy assured her, sitting up. Back to business. It was easier than dwelling on the past. "I plan to work around the clock to make sure that this is the most beautiful wedding that Driftwood Cove has ever seen. It will be perfect."

Perfect. There was that word again.

Only coming from Amy, Hallie almost believed it. How could she not? Amy had been more than a sister; she'd been her friend. Only two years apart in age, they'd lived through everything together. Amy knew the name of her childhood stuffed animal, the one that Hallie still kept in the chest at the end of her bed. She knew that Hallie had a scar on her knee from the six stitches she'd gotten when she'd fallen off her bike because Amy was the one that Hallie was chasing when it happened. She'd been there every Christmas Eve when Hallie would sneak into her room to listen for Santa (Claire had never believed, but at least went along with it), and she'd been there when they'd had to put their dog down, and they'd both been too young to know just how old he was, only that they'd loved him.

These were the parts of her that only Amy shared. Well, and Claire too. Parts of her life that Josh knew about, sure, but hadn't experienced. He didn't get that same sad smile whenever they passed a golden retriever on the road. He didn't laugh every time they saw two little girls on their bikes going a little too fast, knowing all too well what might happen . . .

"I still can't believe you're here," she whispered, reaching for Amy's hand, knowing that Amy had only come because Hallie needed her. And because Amy loved her.

"I still can't believe you're getting married. My little sister." Amy looked at her with such fondness that for a moment Hallie thought she might cry—from relief, sadness, or longing, she wasn't sure.

She looked around the room. It was painted blue, the floral quilt unchanged from when Amy was just a giggling girl full of dreams and ideas. Eventually this room would be transformed, wouldn't it? To a room for her future children. Same with Claire's. Although she'd probably repurpose Claire's first. It would serve her right.

And all those moments and memories they'd made right here in this space would fade into the past. And even though Amy was here, she'd be gone in a week, and they'd never again be those little girls who ran around in their white cotton nightgowns, their hair wet from the shower, smelling like soap, the breeze floating through the windows on their cool skin, while they played dolls, or sneaked a cookie from the stash that their father kept in his desk, or told each other stories, huddled together in bed, dreaming about their future.

Hallie turned her back to her sister, trying to compose herself. "Maybe we can do something special tonight. Just the two of us in this old house."

For the last time, she thought, blinking quickly.

That was the thing she didn't factor into her future plans. That with change came loss. It had sneaked up on her, no different from all the little things that fell into place. She'd grown up. They all had. Each day they were all moving forward.

But worse, they were drifting apart. Maybe it was inevitable.

CHAPTER FIVE

Amy

Morning in Driftwood Cove was so quiet that had it not been for Amy's alarm, she might have slept clear through to noon. She'd always slept well in this house, lulled by the sound of the sea through her open window, usually with the heavy fatigue of a day well spent and the promise of another waiting.

"Hope I didn't keep you up too late last night," Hallie said when Amy padded into the kitchen in search of coffee.

They'd stayed up late, sharing a bottle of wine, sitting out on the covered porch, listening to the waves crashing against the shore until they were both catching each other's yawns and struggling to keep their eyes open.

They'd talked about everything—well, almost everything. Amy wasn't about to share that she'd left her job to come here. How this wedding was costing her something, and more than just a paycheck.

There was no way around it: being in Driftwood Cove was bittersweet. The town, like this house, was full of her happiest memories and her greatest heartbreaks. It was here where her father had taken his last breath. Where they'd spent the last holiday meal together as a family of five, even though they hadn't known it then.

Where she and Logan used to ride bikes into town, sit along the shore until the sun had set, only to meet up again the next day and do the same thing all over again, never tiring of each other's company.

Until it seemed that one day, he did just that.

Shaking away her darkening mood, Amy forced a smile.

"Wow, look at that machine!" Amy admired the shiny cappuccino maker, thinking that it would take her the length of her stay to figure out how to operate it.

Hallie's cheeks flushed. "The other one . . . stopped working. This was one of the wedding gifts. You don't think I jinxed anything by opening it early?"

Amy gave her sister a funny look. Since when was Hallie superstitious? But then, she was a bride, and a bride who had to move up her wedding. It made sense that she was a little jumpy.

"Do we have any dinner plans for tonight?" Amy asked while Hallie worked the machine. Knowing that their older sister was arriving today, Amy shared Hallie's apprehension. Would Claire keep her mouth zipped this time? Bunny assured Amy that she'd made certain of that, but just in case, Amy decided to limit Claire's drinks to two beverages. Especially at important events, like the rehearsal dinner and the wedding itself.

She made the same promise to herself. The last thing she needed was to drown in her stress, especially when her stomach hurt just thinking about the fact that now she truly had nothing to return to in Boston: no love life and no job. And she certainly didn't need her family picking up on anything, when telling them about her job would only dampen Hallie's wedding week.

"I think Mom wants a big family dinner," Hallie said. Her back was to Amy as she prepared her coffee the way she liked it (plenty of cream, and even more sugar), so there was no chance of reading into her expression.

In other words, Mom was hoping for the best. Amy wished she could be as optimistic as her mother was, but then that was how Bunny got through the tough years, trying to hold the family together, smiling through the pain. It was what Amy would have to do tonight, containing her agitation about her career and her future when all she really wanted to do was fall into her mother's arms and have a good cry.

"Will Josh be joining us?" Amy casually asked when Hallie turned to lean against the counter.

Hallie nodded as her gaze drifted into the adjoining dining room, with the long table and mismatched chairs.

"It's funny, but I can't remember the last time we had a family meal."

As much as Amy hated to mention it, she said, "It must have been the night before your engagement party." That was the night that she and Claire had arrived at the house, late, of course, after a long day at work. They'd gathered at the big dining table, which seemed bigger than ever without their father at the head of it, and let Hallie and Josh regale them with details of how Josh proposed. It had been a quiet but calm night, not loud and boisterous like the ones before, when they were younger and their father was still with them.

Or like the night afterward, when Claire had to go and speak her mind.

"No, I meant just us. Just the family," Hallie said.

Amy stared at her now, clutching her mug. Meaning without Josh? Or meaning the way it used to be, when they were kids? Hallie was probably just missing Dad, Amy decided. Or missing the way things used to be when he was still with them. It was easy to do that in this house, even easier when they were together and his absence was felt. How many times had she looked around the lawn at the engagement party last summer, almost willing him into existence, sometimes even looking at the porch and imagining him standing there, talking to one of her uncles in that animated way, moving his hands and arms, putting everyone around him at ease?

It didn't seem possible that they were all gathering here for Hallie's wedding and that he wouldn't be there to see it. Or walk Hallie down the aisle.

Amy pushed aside her own hurt and pity and looked at her sister. They could both say all they wanted, but the sad truth was the wedding wasn't going to be perfect, not like the ones they'd once dreamed of. It couldn't be.

The bridal salon was a new addition to Driftwood Cove, having opened a few years back thanks to the trend of country weddings. Not that Amy would really classify their beach town as country, though it was certainly not big-city glamour.

Amy took in the creamy white walls and carpeting, the glistening chandeliers, and the smell of fresh roses, fighting to push back an ache in her chest that she had managed to keep at bay for most of her adult life.

"Amy?"

Amy startled and turned to see Hallie coming out of the dressing room, a vision in the creamy white taffeta dress that their mother had also worn on her day, the photo proudly on display in the entranceways of both Beachnest Cottage and their Boston home.

"Oh, Hallie. You look beautiful!" It was a cliché, of course, but it was true. Hallie did look beautiful, and not just because of what she was wearing. Her eyes seemed to shine a little brighter, her cheeks were a bit more flushed, and her smile was as wide as it had been on those special summer evenings when they'd run through the yard, catching fireflies.

She walked closer to her sister, thinking that the dress really did suit her. While old, it was a traditional cut, making it a timeless style. The satin skirt was full, the waistline trimmed in crystals that had been repaired and replaced over time, the bodice a sweeping sweetheart neckline with cap sleeves that fell off the shoulder.

"We're missing a veil," Amy said. She walked over to the display, quickly finding several beautiful options. She carried the one she liked best back to Hallie. "Try it on. Just so we get the full picture."

Reluctantly, Hallie did.

"Oh! That is beautiful! Isn't it, Hallie?" Amy couldn't help but touch the soft tulle that was dotted with tiny crystals, adding some much-needed flair to the otherwise simple dress.

"It's a little . . . showy," Hallie said, turning her head in the mirror to look at herself from different angles. "Not like Mom's veil."

Amy had many fond memories of their mother's veil draped over her own head as she walked along the grass toward a make-believe groom, but she also remembered it as slightly discolored with age and very old fashioned. Now, surrounded by so much frothy tulle, she felt a longing in her chest, which she quickly put in check.

This was Hallie's wedding. Her dream was coming true.

Amy stared firmly at her sister. "Of course it's showy! You're the bride! All eyes will be on you!"

"I'm not used to having all eyes on me," Hallie said, looking nervously in the mirror.

"It's your day, Hal. The day you've dreamed of all your life."

Their eyes met in the mirror, and Amy knew that they were both thinking the same thing. That once, Amy had dreamed of a day like this for herself. Trying on the dress, making sure it fit her figure, slipping their grandmother's veil over her hair, and walking down the aisle, all eyes on her, her eyes only on . . .

Well. No sense in thinking about that. Another woman had held the pleasure of picking out a wedding dress, flowers, and a cake, all to plan her special day with the man Amy had loved. While she was kept firmly in the friend bucket.

The two-hour phone calls and shared confidences couldn't top whatever connection Logan felt with Lindsey, the girlfriend he met in college, the one who preferred city life, only visiting Driftwood Cove once—but that had been enough to establish that Amy disliked Lindsey about as much as the other woman disliked her.

"She's jealous of what we have," Logan had told Amy when she voiced her concerns about the girl he'd brought home. Sure, he'd dated over the years, but it had always been casual, and even though it always made Amy's heart sink a little, deep down she thought that none of the girls would last.

But this one did.

"She'll come around," Logan had said. "I told her she has nothing to worry about."

Maybe Amy should have seen then that Lindsey was here to stay. That Logan didn't see Amy as anything more than a friend, his pal, while she saw him as so much more—even though she'd never told him that. She couldn't work up the courage to risk their friendship, afraid to push things too soon and put a strain on a relationship that had always been so easy and enjoyable.

He'd never given her false hope. Never looked at her in a way that suggested his feelings were anything other than platonic. Every moment she spent with him was nearly perfect, but always a little painful, because she was always left wanting more.

Hallie stood in front of the three-way mirror while the shop owner inspected the fit.

"I can't believe that I'm really wearing it," she said. "Three generations. Do any of your clients wear their ancestors' dresses?"

"Oh, I mostly do corporate events and birthday parties," Amy said vaguely. "My old boss handled the weddings."

"Old boss?" Hallie stared at her. "Did you switch companies?"

Shoot. "I mean . . . she's kind of old." Oh, brother. Gail was only fifteen years older than Amy, but then, Hallie hadn't met her.

And now she never would.

Swallowing back the panic that twisted in her stomach and made it difficult to catch her breath, she fluffed Hallie's dress instead.

"You can try on your bridesmaid dress while you're here," Hallie suggested.

Amy shook her head. She'd already scheduled that fitting for the next day, when Claire would be with them.

Just the thought of it made Amy's stomach twist with nerves. She could still remember the hurt in Hallie's eyes last summer when Claire had told her that she was too young to be getting married, too naive to think it would all be sunshine and roses. That she hadn't lived. That she didn't know what she was doing.

But the one who didn't have a clue what she was doing with her life was Amy. Claire had her career. Hallie had true love.

And Amy . . . had nothing.

After another coffee break at the little shop on the corner where they went over more of the details and the week's schedule, Hallie checked her watch and said, "Oh! I promised Josh we'd pick him up and bring him back to the house before everyone arrives."

"Mom is already there," Amy said, looking at her phone. "She just texted."

"You don't mind making a quick stop?" Hallie asked, pushing back her chair.

"No problem." Amy stood up and tossed her paper cup into the recycling bin. She liked Josh. He was a sweet kid who adored her sister, and, having never had a brother, she was excited for the new addition to their family—even if Josh had felt like a member of the family for some time now.

"He's just down the street. He was getting fitted for his tux," Hallie said as they pushed out of the door, the bell above it ringing their departure.

Amy pulled up her notes on her phone and crossed that item off her list, then shoved it back into her bag to enjoy a few minutes with her sister when they weren't consumed with wedding planning.

The town center of Driftwood Cove was, not surprisingly, busy. On weekend afternoons like this, especially on warm, sun-filled days, there were always plenty of tourists in town for the day or weekend, strolling down the cobblestone sidewalks of Main Street with ice cream cones in hand or picking up bags of saltwater taffy to bring back home as a reminder of an afternoon well spent.

Hallie chatted about her thoughts for the wedding favors as they walked toward the corner, where Amy could just barely make out Josh, tall and lanky as he was.

She stopped suddenly, nearly causing a woman with two armfuls of shopping bags from the upscale boutiques to crash into her. Josh wasn't alone. He was talking to another guy. A guy with sandy hair and broad shoulders. A guy who looked a lot like—Amy swallowed hard. It couldn't be.

It wouldn't be. Hallie would have warned her.

"Amy?" Hallie stopped, too, more gracefully, and gave her a questioning look.

"It's Logan," she whispered, because that's all she needed to say. Hallie knew the rest. Heck, even Claire did.

Sometimes Amy wondered if Logan knew too.

Her face burned when she thought that maybe this was why his calls had eventually faded away, and not because Lindsey had a problem with their relationship. Once, Logan had known her nearly as well as her sisters did—maybe better, in some ways. They'd been best friends, starting around the time that Hallie met Josh, when Amy lost her playmate, even though she was seventeen by then. But the afternoons dragged without her younger sister's company, and when she'd taken a job scooping ice cream at the seasonal stand down near the public beach, she and Logan had become inseparable. Everyone said she laughed louder with him, but she soon learned she cried harder too. For five years, Logan had been her person. And for the last five, he'd been missing from her life.

It hadn't taken long for the daily calls and texts to fade to weekly. More and more, if she called, he'd keep it short, because it was obvious he was with Lindsey. Amy told herself that it would run its course, that he'd come to his senses and break up with the girl who didn't seem to have much sense of humor and didn't even like Driftwood Cove. And didn't even want to get to know his best friend.

But she'd been wrong. And for the first time, she dared to wonder if she'd ever known him at all.

By the time the wedding invitation arrived, Logan had permanently moved to New York, and their communication was down to a few texts a month, usually over something silly, like a commercial playing on television that they used to laugh over.

She made up an excuse for why she couldn't attend. But she couldn't watch another woman have the wedding she'd dared to dream about. Marry the man Amy loved more, she was sure of it.

Have the life she'd thought would just continue forever. Amy and Logan. Two peas in a pod. The peanut butter to her jelly.

Her excuse about why she couldn't come to his wedding was her final text to him. And he'd never responded.

Hallie's eyes darted to the end of the street and back to Amy. She looked almost as alarmed as Amy felt.

"I didn't want to mention anything, because I wasn't sure . . ." She swallowed hard as her cheeks turned pink.

"He's coming to the wedding." It was a statement, not a question. One that she had known was a possibility but had thought at least unlikely.

"We all lost touch with Logan when he moved to New York," Hallie started to explain. "But I guess recently Logan reached out to Josh. I didn't ask the details, and I didn't know he was in town . . ." Hallie blinked rapidly. "Maybe it won't be so bad. I mean, you two were so close once."

So close. So, so close.

She leveled her sister with a look until Hallie's smile dropped. But then she reminded herself that this was supposed to be the happiest time of her sister's life, and she shouldn't go ruining it just because of her own romantic disappointments.

"Josh didn't tell him that I'm hopelessly single, did he?" she asked.

"He probably just told him that you're a very successful event planner and that you moved and don't visit much."

Ah, but did he know why? She hoped not. Not that it would go to his head or anything. Logan didn't have an ego. He had a heart. One that he'd given to another woman.

No, if Logan knew that he'd hurt her so much that she'd left behind this town, her family house, and all the happiest memories of her life, he'd feel terrible. Because if there was one thing she knew, it was that Logan had cared about her as much as she'd cared about him.

He just hadn't fallen in love with her.

"I can tell Josh not to invite him if you want," Hallie said with a pleading look in her eyes.

What Amy wanted was to run, get in her car, and hightail it back to Boston. But then she wouldn't be able to see her little sister get married.

She cleared her throat. "It's fine. We're adults." It would be . . . fine. She'd just walk over, say hello, exchange pleasantries, and then go back to the house and bring a bottle of wine into bed with her.

Oh no, they were turning. Josh was lifting his hand. They'd been seen.

Hallie raised an arm, but her face was frozen in terror.

"I'm sorry, Amy. You know Josh has no clue how you felt about Logan because you never wanted anyone to know. He just thought we were all friends who drifted apart. It's not that uncommon as you get older and people get busy with work and—" She stopped short, and Amy was grateful for that.

No, it wasn't uncommon to lose touch with childhood friends, however close they once were. Even her own sisters had drifted away. Josh was none the wiser about her romantic feelings for Logan, and Amy knew there was no malice. Just four good people coming to greet each other. Four people who used to all be tight. One who ended up with a broken heart.

With each step forward, she felt the pull of the past. Logan, seeing her, tipped his head, his expression guarded. Of course, her presence wouldn't be a surprise. She was the bride's sister. Which meant he'd known she'd be here—maybe not today, but this week. That he'd see her again. And how was that supposed to go?

"Amy." His eyes were as kind as always; the only sign of time was the light creases at the corners. "It's been a long time."

She smiled because she always smiled in his presence, but the tug of longing and hurt swelled up in her chest until she felt like it might burst. All that pain and heartache came to the surface, undoing all the years she'd done her best to tamp it down. Box it up. Forget about him. That laugh. But most of all, how she felt when she was with him. Like she was wholly accepted, loved just for who she was. And happy. Oh, so happy.

"It has been." Amy's smile felt stiff as she inched forward at the same time he sort of lifted his arms, and then she lifted hers, all the while feeling Hallie watching her, reminding her of just how awkward this was when once, it had been so natural.

Finally, they hugged. Quick and light, with a pat on the back, when all she really wanted to do was pull him close, feel his warmth, smell his hair. Never let go.

Clearing her throat, she glanced at Josh. "Josh! Congratulations, brother." She reached and hugged him quickly, this time feeling Logan's eyes on her.

She stared at her shoes, laughed at some joke Hallie made that she didn't even really hear, and wondered just what the heck she was supposed to say or do.

"This is a surprise," Hallie was saying to Logan. "When did you get into town?"

"A couple of days ago, but I've been busy with work." Logan kept his eyes on Amy. "I ran into Josh, and he told me about the change in the wedding date. Sounds like there's a lot to be done in a short amount of time. I'm happy to roll up my sleeves and help."

"Great! We need all the help we can get." Josh slapped his old friend on the back.

"Oh!" Hallie looked at Josh for a long time, but he didn't seem to pick up on her stare. "Well, Amy's an event planner, and she's going to be taking over most of the work this week."

Logan caught Amy's eye. "I guess that will give us a chance to catch up."

"I think I have most of it covered," Amy said, tensing.

"We've only got six days," Josh said jovially. "The more hands, the better."

"Six days," Hallie murmured and then shook her head. She flashed a wide-eyed glance at Amy, the fear in her eyes unmistakable.

But where, Amy wondered, was it directed?

"I told Logan I'd drop him off on my way to the house. So I'll meet you over there in an hour?" Josh reached out and took Hallie's hand before giving her a light peck on the cheek.

Amy exhaled a breath, relieved that Josh hadn't asked Logan to join them—until she considered what was stopping Josh from thinking that Logan should join them. His wife, probably. Maybe even children.

She glanced up the street, eager to get away, not wanting to hear any details.

"It was really good seeing you, Amy," Logan said, his gaze seeming to search hers.

"It was good," she agreed. Too good. And that was just the problem.

Neither Hallie nor Amy spoke as they walked back to the car and then started to drive to the house.

"That went . . . okay," Hallie hedged.

Amy kept her eyes on the road. She didn't know how it had gone. Awkward. Surreal. Too many emotions to process.

"Yeah. It's fine. Glad we got that out of the way," she said with a forced smile, but her voice was shaky.

Hallie gave a nod and then turned to look out the window, onto the sea, lost in thought, maybe waiting for Amy to speak, to see if there was more she wanted to say.

But Amy didn't want to think about Logan. No, all she wanted to do was forget him. Forget the part of her heart that still beat only for him.

The part of her that she'd left here, in this town, along with every other dream she'd ever had for herself.

CHAPTER SIX

Hallie

Hallie's mother was already in the front room, stacking up the wedding gifts, when Hallie and Amy came in through the back door a short while later, Amy still looking a little pale.

"There you girls are!" Bunny set down a robin's-egg-blue box that probably housed a beautiful cut glass vase and came across the room to give them each a hug.

Hallie didn't resist. If anything, she clung to her mother, letting her hold her a little longer than usual.

Bunny's eyes were bright when she finally pulled back. "Well, that was a warm greeting!"

Hallie gave a little shrug. "I just missed you."

It was silly, considering she'd just seen her mother last month when Bunny was checking on some of the properties in her real estate portfolio. The trips were frequent, and Hallie knew that her mother's business was just an excuse to stay at the house, not that Hallie ever minded. She liked having an excuse for some girl time, the long evenings spent out on the porch, talking about the old days and sipping tea. The walls of this house might contain her fondest memories, but there was something different about reliving the stories, laughing about how Hallie's father once leaned against the loose porch rail and fell straight down into the bushes, or how he'd brought them fishing one time and only one time because all three girls begged him to throw the first fish they caught back in the water and then insisted on feeding the fish rather than trying to catch them.

It was different, talking with her mother or even Amy, from talking with Josh. Sure, Josh loved this house, and he'd even loved Hallie's father. But he hadn't lived those moments firsthand. He couldn't completely understand.

"You just got in, and you've already gotten straight to work!" Amy remarked, giving her mother a more casual hug. With both of them living in Boston, their visits were more frequent.

"Well, there's no time to waste!" Bunny replied a little breathlessly. It was clear that she hadn't stopped since she'd arrived, but then there was a large group of relatives to prepare for this week. "My, you'll have a lot of fun unwrapping all these gifts after your honeymoon."

"You don't have to worry about these, Mom. I can take care of them later," Hallie assured her.

"Since some of your cousins will be using this room when they arrive on Thursday, I thought I'd get an early start on preparations," Bunny replied.

"Maybe we can have a cup of tea?" Hallie asked her mother. She'd love the chance to slow down for a few minutes, enjoy the presence of her family in this house.

"Oh, there won't be much time for that. Your sister's on her way from New York!" Bunny glanced nervously at Amy, who quickly left the room. As the youngest, Hallie was used to observing these little exchanges, and she'd learned to interpret their meaning.

Amy was upset, but probably not about Claire. Logan Howell was in town. This couldn't be easy for her, and she didn't seem to want to talk about it either.

Hallie, however, didn't want to talk about Claire. Or even think about her. Her mother was right. There was no time to waste, including the rest of today.

"I was wondering if you've seen the veil? I've looked for it, but it's not in any of the usual places."

"The veil?" Her mother's eyes clouded over for a moment. "Have you looked in my closet?"

Hallie nodded. "It wasn't there."

"Well, it must be here somewhere." Her smile looked a little tight when she patted Hallie's arm. "I'll look. It's just been so long since you girls have played with it."

"Well, it's been a long time since we've all been back in this house together," Hallie said. And she for one wasn't going to count last year's engagement party. "It's just that I've dreamed of wearing it since I was a little girl."

"Are you talking about the veil?" Amy asked, poking her head into the room. She was clutching a mug of coffee, meaning that she must have figured out how to use the new machine.

"Why don't I go poke around in some of the closets before Claire gets here?" Amy suggested.

Hallie watched her sister leave the room, waiting until she had slipped up the stairs before turning to her mother and whispering, "Logan's back in town."

"Oh?" Her mother blinked, but she didn't seem completely surprised. "Well, it's nice of him to support you. He and Josh were such good friends once."

"But they lost touch. When he didn't come to the engagement party, I assumed that he wouldn't come to the wedding either." Hallie started to chew a nail, and then, remembering her wedding was now just days away, dropped her hand. "Josh has him helping with the wedding!"

"And Amy's upset about that?"

"Of course! The guy broke her heart, Mom! You remember!"

"It was years ago," Bunny pointed out. So was Dad's death, Hallie thought, not that she'd voice it. There were some things in life people never fully got past.

"Did he . . . say anything more?" Bunny began stacking the boxes in the corner. Come Thursday, this room would house some of the younger cousins who didn't mind sleeping on the floor.

"No, but then we didn't exactly stick around to chat." Hallie pulled in a breath. "I thought Amy was going to make a run for it when she saw him."

"She'd never leave you in a lurch with the planning," her mother assured her.

Hallie frowned at her mother. "You're not worried that Amy's upset?" She knew her sister had gone upstairs to collect herself, not to go searching through closets and under beds for the box containing the veil.

"Maybe it's about time that Amy saw Logan," her mother said; then, seeing Hallie's shocked reaction, she took her hand. "They were so close once."

"And Amy was madly in love with him," Hallie reminded her mother.

Her mother chewed her lip, nodding. "Do you think that she still is?"

Hallie stepped back and leaned against the arm of the couch. Up until now, she might have thought that Amy was more hurt than in love, but now she wasn't so sure. Amy had never dated much. And she seemed to have given up any dream of having a wedding of her own someday.

"I just don't want to see her upset," Hallie said. "She only came back here for me."

"Well, maybe it was time. Your wedding has brought all of us back together again."

Hallie's eyes flicked to the old clock on the wall. "What time did Claire say she would be here?"

"She didn't say . . ." Their mother looked equally nervous. "But I did talk to her, Hallie. She promised me that she didn't have any intention of upsetting you. She's coming to support you. You know how much she loves you."

Hallie nodded quietly. She used to know how much Claire loved her. Depended on it, really. She used to be able to confide in her, talk to her, and share things she'd never tell her mother, like when she'd had her first kiss.

But then their father died, and Claire retreated into herself. In the years immediately following, Hallie sometimes felt like she was mourning the loss of her father *and* the relationship she'd once had with her sister.

"Did Claire happen to mention anything else to you?" Amy asked as she came back into the room. She gave Hallie a look of apology. "No luck with finding the veil."

"Well, there's plenty of time to find it," Bunny said, stacking more of the gifts against another wall. "And what do you mean about Claire, Amy?"

Yes, Amy, do tell. If Claire was planning to drop another bomb when she got here, then she should just stay back at her office in New York, where she likely slept on a pullout couch while she watched marriages unravel and billed by the hour.

Amy looked thoughtful for a moment and then shrugged. "I just think it's unusual for her to come up so early when she was only here for a night last summer."

And any other time she'd visited in the past eight years, Hallie thought.

Amy picked up a box, looked at the label, and set it back down on the pile. "Did she have anything to say to you, Mom?"

"I think she said plenty last time we all saw her," Hallie said in a huff.

"Claire is . . . Claire," her mother said, trailing off.

"But she wasn't always this way," Hallie countered. Sure, with their six-year age gap, Hallie's memories of her eldest sister might be a little rose colored, but not entirely. "She used to love coming here. And she used to laugh more. And . . ." Hallie swallowed hard. "She used to believe in happy endings."

"Claire sees a lot of heartache and disappointment in her profession," her mother countered.

"I just miss the way she used to be," Hallie said quietly. "The old Claire never would have said those things on one of the happiest days of my life."

"I know it doesn't feel this way, but I really think she's just being protective," her mother said. "You know how she always looked out for you. I used to joke that she was your second mother!"

"Yes, but I'm not a little kid anymore. And you were the same age as me when you and Dad got married," Hallie pointed out. "And he was your childhood sweetheart too."

Her mother's hands stilled for a moment before she nodded.

"Oh, Mom." Hallie immediately felt bad. "I'm sorry. I know you miss him."

Her mother's smile turned braver, as it was known to do when their father was mentioned. "I just know how much he would have wanted to be here for you, Hallie. And how much you wish he were here."

"We all do," Amy said. She tipped her head at Hallie. "Is that why you haven't changed anything with the house?"

Hallie hesitated. "It really isn't my house yet, though. I've just been living here."

"Well, that's about to change," Amy said. "As of Saturday, the house goes to you."

Her expression was neutral, but Hallie thought she detected a hint of longing in her voice. She thought back to what her mother had said. There was no doubt in her mind that Amy still had feelings for Logan.

At the least, it was a loss. But it might be more than that. It might be love.

Hallie tried to imagine what it would be like to miss Josh and found she couldn't. How could she, when they were always together? Sure, there had been the early days, when she went back to Boston for the school year and only saw him during breaks, relying on phone calls to bridge the gaps. But they were young then, and those days were so long ago. They shared most classes at college. And then they both started working at the Harbor Club.

She realized that she might very likely spend every day for the rest of her life with Josh, in the most literal way.

"Hallie?" Her mother was looking at her with concern. "Everything okay?"

What had they even been talking about? Hallie blinked rapidly. Oh, right. The house.

"There's plenty of time for change, isn't there? Besides, I happen to like it exactly as it is." Full of memories of her and her sisters, her father coming in through the back door, calling them all out onto the porch to admire the view, her mother wrangling them to do another jigsaw puzzle at Christmas, right here, in this very room, at the table in front of the crackling fire.

Once Josh moved in, he'd bring his stuff. Stuff that would change what was here. That would maybe take its place. Pushing aside all those wonderful memories until they were nothing but the past.

Because Josh was her future. Just as she'd wanted.

"This old house has certainly lasted through the generations," her mother said with a sigh. She looked around, perhaps picturing it the way Hallie did, filled with laughter and music and smells from the kitchen. Dad's weekend-morning pancakes sizzling on the griddle, the girls all gathering plates and silverware, their hair still messy from sleep, while Bunny made freshly squeezed orange juice. "So many memories."

"And now it will have new ones, right?" Amy was smiling at Hallie, but it didn't quite reach her eyes. "You're carrying on all the traditions, Hallie. We're counting on you."

Counting on her. Hallie had never really thought of it that way, but maybe it was true.

She, the youngest of them all, was the first to wear the dress, cut her cake at Cliffside Manor, and fill her album with all the photos that a future daughter might someday pore over, just like they had all once done.

She was the lucky one, she thought, looking at Amy.

CHAPTER SEVEN

Claire

Claire realized five minutes into the trip that she'd never been in a car with Gabe. It was silly, she knew, to feel nervous about being alone with him, trapped in the vehicle, the radio the only other voice to break up the silence. They spent hours together each week, sometimes each day, but this was different. Gone were the boundaries of the workday, the excuse of a difficult case or a need for camaraderie. There was no going back to the desk, no demand of a meeting, no firm timeline. What had she been thinking, agreeing to this ridiculous scheme? And for an entire week?

They'd rented a car, since neither had use for one in New York, and Claire drove because she knew the way. Plus, she took comfort in having a task. Driving gave her something to do. Something to focus on other than the man sitting so close beside her, his presence suddenly all too obvious, or the fact that soon she would be face to face with the sister she'd hurt, badly. And she couldn't even take it all back because she'd meant every damn word.

She could have called Hallie. Or texted Amy. Something to say that she was coming up, to break the ice. But she knew that her mother would have already taken care of that, and the truth was that she wasn't sure what would be worse, a response from Hallie or no response at all.

Or Amy, reminding her of how badly she'd upset their youngest sister, insisting once again that she apologize.

"You do know that your knuckles have been white since you got on the highway." Gabe's voice was laced with amusement, and she wondered just how long he'd been waiting to point that out.

They were thirty minutes into the trip, and she only now realized he was right. Her shoulders were tight—her neck, too—and it took a bit of effort to loosen her grip on the steering wheel.

"I'm not used to driving," she said mildly.

"And here I thought it might have something to do with seeing your family," Gabe replied.

She slanted him a rueful look but quickly returned her eyes to the road. Traffic was bad, and the last thing she needed was a fender bender.

Although . . .

No. No, she would not entertain that thought. Yes, a mild accident would be a perfectly handy excuse for being delayed until, say . . . the morning of the wedding, but she wasn't going to wreck her perfect driving record just to avoid her family.

Because Gabe was right. It wasn't about driving this car. It was about where she was driving it. Back to Beachnest Cottage, where the best but also worst moments of her life had happened. The last two times she'd visited Driftwood Cove had been for her father's funeral and her sister's engagement. Both were events that she'd rather not think about. And bad things tended to come in threes, or so the saying went.

"Remind me again who I'll be meeting," Gabe said.

"Well, the extended family won't descend on us until Thursday." Claire could already picture the chaos of the full house. It was still a family home, meaning everyone was still welcome.

Even her.

"Pam and Ned are the ones we want to avoid," Claire told him. And even though he probably already knew the other main facts, she decided to repeat them, just so things were fresh. Just so there were no red flags. Just so their little ruse was believable. "They're relatives on my father's side." She named the others, thinking of how everyone together would make the otherwise large six-bedroom house feel small.

"And your mom is Bunny, short for Bernice, a nickname that your father gave her on their first date that stuck."

She glanced at Gabe sidelong. "Boy. I've really told you a lot about my family," she remarked.

But she hadn't told him everything.

Still, she was flattered that he remembered until she considered that he, like her, was an overachiever who prided himself on going the extra mile for his clients, putting in the long hours and committing to everything he did.

"You look anxious," he observed.

"Do I?" Claire tried to relax her face, but it was no use. She was anxious, and she wasn't good at hiding it, especially around the person who knew her best. "I'm regretting not texting Hallie to tell her my plans. I'm sure my mother told her, but we haven't spoken since last summer."

"I'm sure once you get past the initial awkwardness of seeing Hallie, it will be like nothing ever happened," Gabe said.

Maybe he was right. Her mother had probably apologized on Claire's behalf. Told Hallie that Claire was coming up a week early to show her support, and to make things right.

Besides, Gabe was levelheaded. Like her, he didn't see the world through rose-colored lenses. He saw the heartache and the grit. He was a realist. And he wasn't afraid to be frank.

"Enough about my family," she said, shifting against the seat back, feeling the tightness in her shoulders. Her fingers were beginning to cramp, and they still had hours more on the road. "Let's talk about the Jones-Smith case."

There. Work she could do. Work kept her mind off her own troubles. And work gave her and Gabe something to talk about. It bonded them. Brought her back to her safe place. One that felt controlled and manageable.

She wouldn't even have to think about what would happen when this car stopped in front of that old house she'd once loved as much as her father himself, and this reunion—and this ruse—became a reality she couldn't avoid.

―――――🙞🙜―――――

All confidence that coming back wasn't a complete disaster, however, seemed to drain away when they crossed the town line and the wooden sign welcoming them to Driftwood Cove.

"If I lived here, I'd never leave!" Gabe said as he swung his head to and from the front and side windows, admiring the small downtown, with its cobblestone streets and charming boutiques, each bay window display more appealing than the last. The harbor came into full view, and a sweeping view of the ocean was interrupted only by the large homes on the bluffs, their crisp white walls in sharp contrast to the brilliantly blue sky.

"Well, I only ever lived here part of the time. Besides, now the house will be passed down to Hallie." And she doubted she'd ever be invited back.

"Does that bother you?" Gabe asked. "Not getting the house?"

Claire almost laughed, but the small part of her that had once loved this cottage stopped her, replacing that bitterness with another emotion—one she tried to avoid. Pain.

"Hallie lives here full time. It makes sense that she would get it. And she's marrying first, so that's just how it's always been, since my great-grandparents' generation." Amy had been the one who loved the house the most, and for a while Claire had even thought she'd be the one to marry first, until Logan broke her heart. Now she visited about as infrequently as Claire, but her excuse was probably understandable, at least for Hallie and Bunny.

Claire couldn't face that house without all the memories that came with it. Early-morning jogs with her dad, their special time when he always raced her to the porch and let her win. Rainy afternoons curled up with a book in his office while he tapped away on the computer keyboard and she was perfectly content with his quiet companionship. The way he'd taught her how to dance in the kitchen, letting her stand on his feet, bumping her into the refrigerator on purpose, just to make her laugh.

A flutter of nerves ran over her stomach as she took the next turn, knowing it would deliver them to Beachnest Cottage in about four minutes, five if she took her foot off the accelerator a bit.

"You really that nervous about seeing your sister?" Gabe didn't miss a thing.

She glanced at him. Were her emotions that obvious?

But it wasn't just the thought of seeing Hallie. Or even Amy. It was facing this house. The past. The feelings it stirred up.

"Please. She's my sister. What's the worst she can do to me?"

But there was plenty that Hallie could do. Kick her out. Tell her she couldn't be in the wedding party anymore. Maybe tell her she wasn't welcome to attend at all.

"Ah, but see, that's why I'm here," Gabe said with a wide grin. "Everyone has to behave in front of the new guy."

She sucked in a breath. She could only hope so.

The house appeared through the trees, some of which had already started to turn now that the days were shortening. It was a house she'd seen hundreds of times in her life, but she still never grew tired of seeing it for the first time after a long time away.

The cedar siding was weathered gray, a contrast to the white trim, which was touched up every four years, if not more, because the salt could be harsh. The last of the hydrangeas were in bloom, their reddening petals lining the length of the wraparound porch.

The ocean was calm today, a blue backdrop in the near distance when she pulled to a stop. A sense of quiet came over the car as they both stared out the window, and for a moment, Claire felt a sense of peace wash over her—until the screen door banged open and her mother appeared, followed quickly by Amy and Hallie.

And before she had a chance to mutter any word to Gabe, he opened the door and stepped out.

"Hello!" he called, holding up a hand with a friendly smile. Claire scrambled to undo her seat belt, then scurried around the car to join him, to stand at his side, not for the sake of appearances but because she needed him close, to ground her. To remind her that she had an entire life away from this house. An honest life, without fanfare or fantasy.

"Claire!" Her mother came down the porch steps first. "I didn't realize you were bringing a friend." Her eyes went wide in confusion as she looked at Gabe. Her expression was almost comically surprised.

Wait for it, Claire thought.

"This is Gabe," Claire said, greeting her mother with a quick hug and a kiss on the cheek. Maybe they could leave it at that. Or just tell the truth. He was her friend. Her coworker. They had a case to work on.

"Her boyfriend," Gabe elaborated, extending a hand.

And there it was. There was no going back now.

Claire couldn't look at her mother. Even the birds seemed to stop chirping in the nearby trees as Gabe looped an arm around Claire's waist and pulled her against him, making her nearly lose her footing in the process.

She clenched her teeth into a grin, resisting the urge to elbow him away. Hard.

"Boyfriend!" Claire's mother looked as overjoyed as if she'd just learned she was about to become a grandmother, which she likely would be soon, but not thanks to Claire.

For a moment Claire felt a twinge of guilt, thinking that they really shouldn't be doing this, but then she looked up at her sisters, standing on the porch, and remembered why she'd agreed to this plan.

Seeing an excuse to free herself from Gabe's grip without sounding any alarm bells, she walked toward the house, where her sisters stood united, looking more than a little shocked.

Good. Already Gabe was a distraction from the tension that lived between them. Hallie was the first one down the steps, her golden hair flying behind her, and Claire froze, trying to process her sister's reaction at the same time she started to open her arms to her. But Hallie dashed right past her to greet Gabe with a big hug, and then, after sliding her a hesitant glance, gave a lighter, stiffer one to Claire.

She had it coming, of course. But it still hurt.

Bunny looked both pleased and a little panicked, her gaze falling on Amy, who would, of course, be responsible for making one extra place at the wedding reception table.

"I hope I didn't inconvenience anyone!" Gabe said gallantly. "I was able to get away from work at the last minute."

Good. Very good. Claire silently nodded and slipped him a smile of approval.

"It's fine. I think there have been a few changes in the attendance list, actually." Amy raised an eyebrow in Hallie's direction and then stepped forward. "Hey, Claire."

"Hey, Amy." Claire hugged her sister, noticing from her middle sister's relaxed smile that Amy didn't seem to retain any of the frostiness that Hallie still held on to. Or maybe she was just relieved that Claire was behaving and that this unexpected guest would likely ensure that.

She'd have to make things right. Clear the air. Maybe even pull Hallie aside if she had a chance tonight.

But give her blessing? That was a tall ask.

"I've started on dinner already," Bunny announced. "You must be hungry from the drive."

Claire was too anxious to eat, especially when the screen door opened and Josh appeared on the porch. He held up his hand in a wave.

No harm done there, it would seem.

"Hey, Josh!" Claire couldn't look at Hallie as she met her future brother-in-law at the base of the steps. God, he still didn't even look old enough to drink!

They exchanged a brief hug before Gabe shook his hand.

Josh, looking pleased with the new addition, said, "I'm not outnumbered anymore!"

Hallie came to stand beside him, taking his hand while giving Claire a pointed look. "Oh, I think you're still outnumbered, but it is nice to have another place at the table."

Like her sisters, Josh seemed confused, surprised, and pleased by Gabe's arrival. Claire realized that Gabe was the first man she'd ever introduced to her family in her entire adult life.

Meaning that they probably thought he was the one. That an announcement might be coming. That things between them were serious.

Oh, how disappointed they'd all be when, the next time they talked to her, they learned that she and Gabe had decided to just be friends.

Or maybe they wouldn't mind. Maybe they wouldn't even like him.

From the way Claire's mother's eyes lit up as she all but clenched Claire's wrist, Claire realized that there was a fat chance of that happening.

Meaning instead of warding off her problems this week, she'd likely just created a new one.

Dinner at Beachnest Cottage was always a loud affair, usually with guests and wine, the food spread out down the center of the table, served family-style so everyone could help themselves. The more formal and busy life they lived in Boston was shed for the laid-back atmosphere that was called for in this big cedar-shingled house, and tonight was no exception.

Claire glanced at Josh as he passed the potatoes with a friendly smile, jokingly helping himself to an extra spoonful first. It would seem that wind of her opinions on his upcoming nuptials hadn't reached him, which made getting through this week and the wedding easier. Her comments had been directed at Hallie, sister to sister, and really, was there anything wrong in suggesting that her sister might want to spread her wings and date other people before she committed to the only boy she'd ever kissed, in the only town she'd ever lived in other than their Boston suburb?

According to her family, there was something very wrong with saying this. In fairness, her timing had been . . . poor. But she didn't blame the extra glass of wine or even the emotions that being back at Beachnest Cottage had stirred up in her. She'd owned what she said.

And that was the problem.

"It's too bad your parents couldn't join us tonight!" Claire's mother said to Josh.

"You know how the club is, especially before the weather turns too cold. Everyone's cramming in last-minute reservations for the patio."

He slid a glance at Hallie, who beamed, probably remembering that it was on that very patio that they'd met.

Claire barely managed not to roll her eyes, instead catching Gabe's, as he was seated across from her. She gave a little smile of camaraderie, feeling like he was the only person in this room who really understood her. And liked her for exactly who she was.

"So, how long have you two been together?" Amy, who had been quiet all throughout dinner, finally asked.

Claire refilled her wineglass, feeling her stomach tighten. "It's sort of a recent thing."

"But we've known each other for years," Gabe added.

"And how'd you two meet?" Claire's mother asked.

It was a normal question and one that Claire had braced herself for. They'd even thrown around a few scenarios on the car ride up here, tossed in some embellishments, and had a few laughs at possible stories, each one more unrealistic than the last (at a cat-breeding seminar; one of them had picked the other up hitchhiking; at a Sex Addicts Anonymous meeting) but in the end, decided to stick with the truth and let people assume what they would. It wasn't fair to expect Gabe to lie on her behalf, and Claire had never been much of an actress. Besides, her family knew her, and they'd sniff out the truth eventually.

Just so long as they didn't pull all of it out of her, she thought.

"We work together," she said. "Gabe's a lawyer too."

No one looked surprised. After all, they knew the hours she put in. They knew she lived at the office, not just worked there. It would make sense that any potential romantic partner might be found where she spent most of her time.

"We actually started at the firm on the same day," Gabe added.

"Oh!" Hallie's eyes went wide as she turned to Claire. "So you two have known each other nearly as long as Josh and I have! And you work together too!"

Claire reached for her wine and took a sip. If Hallie was going to try to compare her relationship with Josh to Claire's (fake) relationship with Gabe, then she was doing a pretty good job of glossing over a few key facts. Like the fact that Claire and Gabe met when they were fully formed adults, nearly the same age as Hallie was now.

It was right there, on her tongue, but she had made a promise. She could feel Amy's eyes on hers, waiting, watching. Her mother looked as if she hadn't blinked in a few seconds and might not until Claire spoke again.

Thankfully, Gabe beat her to it.

"She was my first friend in the office," he said. "Most days, she's the only reason I look forward to going to work."

Claire stared at him. Was this true? But then, she thought, sobering, of course. He was just playing along. Being convincing.

"Do you know, when these girls were little, Claire liked to play office?" Their mother chuckled and ignored Claire's warning glance.

Gabe looked at her and then leaned forward. "Oh, I would have loved to see that."

"She used to put us to work!" Amy added, giving a knowing nod. "She was always the boss, and she made Hallie and me be her assistants."

"I always had to fetch her things," Hallie said ruefully, not meeting Claire's eyes. Still, a ghost of a smile passed over her mouth when she said, "Like cookies. Chocolate from Mom's secret stash."

"Hey! I always wondered why that kept disappearing." Bunny gave Claire a wink across the table, and something deep down in Claire's core went all warm and soft.

She loved her family. She enjoyed spending time with them. But it hurt, too, reminding her of a better, simpler time, when all their dinners were filled with warmth and laughter.

"But of course the game they loved to play the most . . ."

Oh no. No. Claire's eyes flashed to her mother. She wouldn't! But she would. Bunny was looking fondly at Hallie now because, of course, this night was really about her. The entire week was. But Claire was still a part of it, and she'd made a choice to come up early, to sit here at the table. While all the hidden parts of herself were revealed.

Well, not every part.

"Wedding!" Hallie's eyes lit up when she looked at Josh, who leaned into her and squeezed her hand.

Had Claire just pursed her lips? From the look Amy was giving her, she had. Oops.

She relaxed her expression. Took another sip of wine. Careful not to have too much, but then, the night sort of called for it. She was tense and uneasy, and not just because of the unspoken conflict between her and Hallie. Gabe was in her family home. Learning things about her that she'd rather not share.

"Oh, now this I have to hear," he said, flashing her a wicked grin across the table.

"When Hallie was little, she was always the flower girl," Amy chimed in. "She loved picking flowers for the role and then dropping the petals along the aisle we'd make between the dining room chairs."

"And were you always the bride then?" Gabe asked Amy.

"Oh, no. Actually, Claire was often the bride!" Bunny said gaily. "Veil and all."

"Veil?" Gabe repeated.

"My veil," Claire's mother continued. "The one I wore at my wedding, and the one that Hallie will too."

"If we can find it," Hallie said with a sigh.

Claire shot her sister a look. She had almost forgotten about the veil. It was something she'd blocked out, along with all the other silly things she used to do with her sisters under this roof.

But she could tell by the glint in Gabe's eyes that he wasn't going to forget it any time soon.

"Here I would have thought you'd be the officiant!" he said.

"Please. You know how I feel about marriage."

"And how is that?" Hallie asked, her eyes challenging.

Damn it. Claire reached for her wineglass and then, thinking better of it, set it down. She stared at her sister, wanting to be honest without hurting her. Wanting her to understand that getting married at age twenty-five, just like her mother, to the only boy she'd ever dated, just like her mother, did not guarantee a picture-perfect life.

"I just think that not all couples have what it takes to make it for the long term, and even the ones that do aren't always as they appear," she replied carefully.

Hallie's eyes narrowed. Amy reached for her wine. And Josh just helped himself to more potatoes.

"We see more marriages break up than last in our profession," Gabe added quickly.

She gave him a look of gratitude. No more wine for her tonight, even though she'd only had a glass.

"We might see a lot of heartache in our profession, but I think even Claire enjoys a good happy ending now and again," Gabe said.

"Yes, well, all that make-believe was a long time ago," Claire said, hoping these embarrassing stories would come to an end rather than extending into the dessert course.

"Oh, I wasn't referring to your dress-up days with your sisters," Gabe said. Claire held her breath, wondering where the heck he was going with all this. "It's because of Claire that I've become a die-hard Nora Ephron fan. I think I've seen *Sleepless in Seattle* five times. And I might have even teared up the first time."

It was one of the many things they'd talked about, this one early in their friendship. He'd never seen a Nora Ephron movie; meanwhile, she and her sisters had them all but memorized. She'd rattled off the names. He'd promised to check them out. He'd never said if he had.

Probably with one of his many dates over the years, she decided.

Boy, he was really laying it on thick, wasn't he? She'd have to tell him he could back off after tonight. So far, one near crisis had been averted.

She could only hope it was the last one.

"No wonder you've been keeping him all to yourself," Amy whispered the moment they were alone in the kitchen.

Claire just shook her head and kept her focus on making the coffee to go with dessert.

"He's wonderful!" Bunny stage-whispered, joining them with a stack of plates that she set on the counter to deal with later.

Claire glanced back toward the dining room, where a burst of laughter had erupted. She couldn't help but smile at the sound, and not just because Gabe was helping to loosen the tension with Hallie.

A memory of her father sitting at the head of the table resurfaced before she could stop it. She could picture him now, telling a story they'd already heard, putting a fresh spin on it, adding a few details that had grown cloudy over the years, pausing right before the best parts. He was the best storyteller.

Claire blinked at the plates in her hands, forcing herself back to the present.

"Gabe's a great guy," she said firmly, because that couldn't be refuted. He was. Probably the best she knew. Certainly the best friend.

Lowering her voice, she shifted the topic to one she was equally happy to avoid. "I was thinking that I should pull Hallie aside and . . . explain myself."

Their mother looked tense. "Maybe it's better to just let it go for tonight. Josh is here, and everyone's having a nice time, and I stopped in town on my way in and bought a pie for dessert."

In other words, her mother wanted to keep pretending everything was just fine when it wasn't.

Claire hung back with Amy while their mother disappeared into the dining room, announcing that dessert was ready and they should take it out onto the porch to enjoy the breeze.

Amy looked as miserable as Claire felt, and as much as Claire was dreading a tough conversation, she was shuddering at the thought of going upstairs to her bedroom with Gabe even more. He'd be sleeping on the floor, but the room was small, and the bathroom was even smaller, and—why hadn't she thought this through before agreeing to it?

"I didn't mean to upset Mom. Or you," she said.

"It's not that." Amy looked at her sharply. "I saw Logan today."

"He's here?" Claire felt strangely relieved. This, Amy's problem, this she could deal with far better than her own troubles. Logan getting married to another woman had devastated Amy, and even Claire had been on the receiving end of her calls, three years after Claire had stopped visiting Driftwood Cove, stopped making regular appearances with her family in general.

At the time she'd been touched, almost even dared to believe that she and Amy might find a way to be close again. But then Amy had refused to talk about Logan anymore, and Claire could relate to that.

Sometimes it was easier to move on. Or move away.

Amy nodded miserably. "In town. And coming to the wedding."

"How was it? Seeing him again?" she asked gently. She knew better than to ask about his wife, whose name she had forgotten.

Amy shrugged. "About as awkward as you and Hallie hugging on the lawn."

Claire pulled a face, wishing it had been a different reunion. "That bad, huh?"

"That bad." Amy sighed. "Anyway, it doesn't matter, does it? This time next week, Hallie will already be married, off on their honeymoon, and we'll be back to our lives."

Claire nodded, but she knew from experience that nothing was ever that simple.

CHAPTER EIGHT

Hallie

Of course Claire had to go get cynical! She just couldn't hold it in, could she?

Hallie handed a guest a folded fluffy robe with a smile. Told herself to take a few deep breaths and enjoy the soft classical music that was flowing through the discreet speakers that rounded out the true escape that the spa promised.

People paid a premium to come here for a day of relaxation. It was nearly impossible not to find peace in a place as tranquil and soothing as this. But Hallie didn't feel relaxed or peaceful. She felt like she might instead be developing lockjaw.

At least she had the cake tasting to look forward to today.

Feeling slightly better, she walked back to her post at the front desk and, seeing that there wasn't another client due for thirty minutes, pulled out her wedding binder and flipped to the section she'd marked off especially for this. Like so many other sections of the binder, it was overflowing with ideas, each contradicting the other. There was lemon chiffon, vanilla with raspberry, and chocolate with raspberry, just to name a few. And then of course came the actual design of the cake.

Each page she'd cut from the magazines she purchased seemed prettier than the last.

"I was wondering if you do a couples package," a voice said, startling her.

She slammed the binder shut guiltily and then laughed when she saw it was just Josh.

"And here I thought I couldn't surprise you anymore," he said, looking proud.

"More like you sneaked up on me." She reopened the binder. "I can't decide between sugar flowers or real flowers for the cake."

Sometimes she wished that, like the dress and the venue, she could have some guarantee that she was getting this right. But her mother had chosen a red velvet cake for her wedding, to match the red flowers that were fitting for her Valentine's wedding, and her grandmother had gone with all white, for her winter wedding.

She showed him two examples that she'd clipped from a magazine, but, as usual, he said, "Whatever you like best."

"But that's just the problem," she said. "I don't know which one I like best. I like them both."

"No one has it all, babe," he remarked, but something seemed to land square in her gut on the words.

No. No one did have it all, even if it seemed like they did. There were choices that had to be made, even about things as trivial as a cake, and with each person, place, or thing that was chosen, another possibility was left behind. Another path not forged.

"You okay?" Josh asked, his brow pinching. "I'm sure whatever cake you choose will be perfect."

"There's that word again!" Hallie cried.

"What word? *Perfect?*" Josh looked so bewildered that Hallie instantly felt bad for reacting like she had.

She reached out and touched his hand. "Sorry. I'm just . . . stressed. We have so much to do and so little time. Speaking of which, we should probably get some lunch before we head over to the bakery so we can decide with our heads and not our stomachs."

"That's today?" Josh grimaced. "I didn't realize you'd moved it up."

"I had to move it up. I thought that's why you stopped by."

He shook his head. "I can't make it, Hal. The tennis league has their luncheon today."

Right. He'd only talked about that luncheon all last week, and she'd completely forgotten about it in light of bigger issues. It was an annual event, and one that he'd been entrusted with for the first time on his own.

She knew what it meant to him to prove himself to his parents. To show that he had what it took to take control of the operations here eventually.

"It's just a cake," he said.

She swallowed hard. Just a cake. Technically, that's all it was. But it was the only wedding cake she'd ever have. The one she'd dreamed about as a child and fantasized about for the past twelve months. The one that would have to be the prettiest, most delicious cake that she had ever seen or tasted, because she only got one chance to make it right.

Just a cake. But as she looked down at her binder, it felt like so much more than that.

"Did you stop over here for another reason, then?" She was eager to change topics. While it wasn't uncommon for them to visit each other during the workweek, the luncheon was a big deal, meaning he probably wouldn't have left the dining area without a good reason.

"It's about the honeymoon," he said, and he hesitated long enough for her to feel her heart speed up.

Hallie felt the familiar sense of dread. "I thought we had that straightened out. They were able to push it up?"

"They were . . . but when I came into work today, I had an email saying that they weren't able to completely replicate everything we'd planned. It looks like instead of staying in the main resort, we're in one of the outer buildings."

"Oh." Hallie's disappointment was manageable. They couldn't expect everything to be perfect, could they? She nodded. "That's okay."

"It's on the first floor," Josh continued slowly.

Well, that wasn't exactly okay, but maybe they could walk right out onto the sand instead of viewing the ocean from their balcony.

"And there's another thing," Josh said, wincing. "We'll have a view of the golf course instead."

The disappointment returned again when she remembered the view they'd been promised, of the sweeping Pacific, the cliffs in the distance, the palm trees that seemed to reach all the way up to the balcony she imagined sitting on each morning, enjoying her coffee.

"The golf course?" She was aware that she was speaking too loudly. The spa was supposed to be a place of peace, quiet, and calm. A place where you checked your troubles at the door. A place where nothing went wrong.

"You have a view of the ocean every day from both your work and your home," Josh pointed out.

She didn't feel like arguing that this was the rocky northern Atlantic coastline, not a tropical view of the Pacific.

He gave her arm a cajoling little shake. "I know it's not what we'd planned, but we're still going. And we'll be together."

Hallie nodded. "Did they at least give us a discount?"

"Babe, we're lucky they were able to accommodate us at all."

They shared a small smile. So that was that. Nothing to be done. As Josh said, at least they were still able to go. And they'd be together. On their honeymoon. Just not exactly as they'd planned it to be.

"Sorry. I know it will be great. It will be better than great. It will be amazing!" She tried to remind herself just how much she'd looked forward to this trip. She and Josh had talked about it right after they'd gotten engaged. It only made sense, seeing as they'd both dreamed about going to Hawaii since they were kids.

Kids. Claire's voice popped into her head again.

"You sure? Because you don't look like you're that happy."

"Sorry." Hallie reached for his hand and gave it a squeeze. "I'm just a little . . . off. Claire's comments last night at dinner got under my skin."

"I thought dinner was nice," Josh said, looking at her with concern. "You didn't have fun?"

"I did. I mean, it was nice." Hallie pressed her lips together. "It's just Claire. You know how she can be."

Josh shrugged. He did know how Claire could be, but he only saw the side of her that Claire revealed, and he certainly didn't know what her sister thought about Hallie marrying him. He hadn't been in earshot of her comments at the engagement party, and Hallie hadn't wanted to sour the evening any more than it already had been by venting to him. Besides, what good would come from that, other than her husband hating her sister? Holidays were awkward enough when Claire bothered to show up, and this wedding was proving to be more complicated than she'd wanted, in every possible way.

"Did she say something to upset you?" Josh asked.

Hallie stared at him in shock.

"Didn't you hear what she said, about how not every couple has what it takes to stay married?" she asked.

Josh didn't look fazed. "She wasn't talking about us."

Hallie wished she could believe that.

"She's a divorce lawyer," Josh went on. "What do you expect? Besides, that's all talk. I think she was a little embarrassed by that story your mom was telling her new boyfriend. You know that deep down she believes that marriages can last. Your parents were married for decades."

Yes. They were. And happily, too, right up until the sudden end.

"And she's here supporting us, isn't she?" Josh asked.

"Hmm." There was a lot that Hallie could say to that, but to do so would be to give her sister's words merit, not to mention strain Josh's relationship with Claire, which would make family functions forever more tense than they already were, if Claire even deigned to grace them with her presence.

Still, Josh was right. She was here. For the week. Offering her support. And maybe her apology.

But so far she was doing a poor job of showing it.

"Maybe I'm overreacting," she said, only because she wished she'd never mentioned Claire or what she'd said. Josh couldn't understand—why would he? The only way to make him understand would be to tell him what Claire had said.

And that was definitely something she couldn't share with Josh. Not six days before their wedding.

Not ever.

By the time Amy came through the spa doors at their agreed-upon time, Hallie was blinking back tears, but not because of the honeymoon. She could no longer care less about a golf course view instead of the blue stretch of the ocean—well, almost. At least she couldn't care at this moment.

"We have a crisis," she whispered when Amy approached the desk, her brow creased in worry.

"About the wedding?" Amy's alarm was so visible a bystander might have thought she was the one getting married.

"No," Hallie said.

Amy's shoulders sagged when she breathed, "Thank God. You had me worried."

"You were worried? It's my wedding," Hallie said, but instantly realized how insensitive that was of her.

"And I'm the one planning it," Amy reminded her. Doing her a favor. "So, what's going on?"

At that moment, the problem in question burst through the front doors. Mrs. Steele had called not five minutes ago, insisting on a last-minute appointment, even though they were fully booked. Hallie knew without having to consult Coco that declining Evelyn's request wouldn't be acceptable. She was one of their biggest clients—make that their biggest client—and whatever had to be done to accommodate her would just have to happen, even if that meant that Hallie had to roll up her sleeves and give the woman a foot massage herself, which she would be doing instead of going to her cake tasting with her sister as planned.

"Oh, thank goodness you were able to squeeze me in," Evelyn drawled dramatically.

Amy, who was used to dealing with demanding clients of her own, merely raised an eyebrow.

Hallie wished she had her sister's cool edge. Right now her stomach was in knots, and she was starting to pick at her fingernails until she remembered that manicured hands weren't just part of her image here at the spa, they were also sort of a necessity for her upcoming wedding.

"I've had the weekend from hell." Evelyn nailed them both with a look so grave that it didn't matter that her eyes were still shielded by her sunglasses.

"Oh dear," Hallie said sympathetically. "Well, we'll have you feeling better in no time."

"The only thing that could make me feel better would be if my son broke up with that . . . that . . ."

Amy's eyes had widened a notch, and Hallie felt downright panicked. Mrs. Steele was raising her voice, a big no-no in the spa, ignoring the subtle but very real signs asking for quiet.

The last thing she needed was to have her upsetting their other guests today. She knew that Claudia O'Neal was nursing a migraine, and Lily Briggs was enjoying her first time back since recovering from knee surgery after a nasty fall in Killington last spring.

"Now, Mrs. Steele, we have the blue room all set up for you. In fact, I'm personally going to be assisting you today."

Amy looked at her in alarm. "But—"

Hallie took Evelyn's arm and began leading her down the hall. "Anything I can do to make you comfortable."

"Can you find my Max a decent woman?"

Hallie heard Amy bark out a laugh behind her and did her best to keep her composure.

Hallie winced, but the look in Evelyn's eyes, even from behind the shield of her sunglasses, made her nervous.

Sure enough, Evelyn said, "If only you hadn't turned down his advances all those years ago. Just think, you could have been my daughter-in-law instead."

Hallie swallowed hard, wondering if Amy was out of earshot, knowing that she probably wouldn't be able to compose herself if she'd heard that remark.

Just hearing Evelyn hinting at a different future confirmed to Hallie that she was on the right path. Of course she was! She loved Josh and his family. And they loved her. Everything was going to be just fine. She'd grow old with her first love, just as her mother had done, and her mother before her.

It wasn't until she had her best client secure behind the spa door, complete with dim lighting, her favorite classical music, and a calming candle, that she dared to crack a smile.

"What about the cake tasting?"

Hallie looked desperately back at the door. "I can't leave work. I'm already leaving the entire staff in a lurch later this week and next week for the honeymoon."

"But it's your wedding cake!"

Just a cake, she reminded herself.

"I honestly can't decide what I want anyway. If I went, I'd probably be there all day and end up still undecided and unable to fit into my dress to boot."

That was the honest truth. Sometimes having too many options just led to second-guessing and regret.

"I could probably close my eyes, flip through the pages of this binder, and jab my finger at any one of these cakes and be thrilled with it."

She felt better already knowing that was true.

Amy reached out for the binder and began flipping through it. "They are all beautiful," she admitted. "Very traditional," she added.

Hallie just shrugged. She liked traditions, and Amy knew that. Her entire family knew that.

Especially Claire.

"So you want me and Josh to handle it?" Amy asked, closing the binder and holding it to her chest.

"Just you," Hallie said. "Josh is stuck at a luncheon. It's a big deal, and you know him. He'll eat anything."

Once, he'd even eaten a piece of a dog biscuit from the little plate that Trudy left out at the bakery for people to take to their waiting pets outside. He'd thought they were free samples, and Hallie didn't have the heart to tell him the truth.

Still didn't, she thought wryly.

"You know I want you to have a beautiful wedding, Hallie," Amy said with a reassuring pat on her hand. "I'll make sure it's beyond your wildest dreams."

"I trust you, Amy." Hallie smiled, feeling better.

"I'll see you later, though. For the dress fitting?" Amy knew the week's itinerary as well as Hallie did.

"Yes, I will not be missing that," Hallie said, sighing at the thought of missing out on any of the planning, but also thankful that Amy had stepped in to help. "I'll see you later. Then you can tell me all about the meeting at the bakery."

"It'll be just fine," Amy assured her. "Better than fine. It will be perfect."

Her sister would make everything right. Hallie wouldn't have to worry about a thing.

CHAPTER NINE

Amy

The Bittersweet Bakery, like many shops in Driftwood Cove, had been around for as long as Amy could remember, and the storefront was as sweet as the baked goods inside. It was where her mother always picked up pies for their summer picnics, or her father purchased bagels for lazy Sunday mornings.

It was also where Amy and Logan had liked to go on rainy afternoons, tucked into a table near the window, sharing an oversize cookie, talking about nothing and everything all at once.

Pushing aside those memories, Amy focused on the task at hand. It was a big ask, picking out Hallie's wedding cake, but it was also one she knew she could handle. She'd chosen dozens of cakes for clients before, from traditional three-tiered anniversary cakes to brightly hued birthday creations that fit the theme of a children's party.

Hallie was a traditional bride, but she was also a modern bride. Only twenty-five years old, which Amy knew Claire took issue with, thinking that Hallie hadn't lived yet.

Still, when you knew, you knew. Just like Amy had known at that age who she loved.

Leaving Hallie at the Harbor Club, Amy walked toward the bakery, relieved at having time to herself almost as much as having the distraction she'd been craving. Without her family to worry about, her mind wandered, playing back Gail's final words to her, her chest tightening when she counted down the days until the wedding—not because Hallie was getting married but because then Amy would have no purpose. No job. Nothing to return to in Boston other than an empty apartment and a dwindling bank account.

She should be job searching, but that wasn't exactly an option when she had so much to do for Hallie, who, unlike her, had to show up for work today.

Next week, she told herself. Monday. She'd make a pot of coffee and reach out to all her contacts, and every competitor too.

She breathed a little easier as she approached the main street of town, where the road turned to cobblestone and the salty sea breeze filled her lungs.

Until she considered that there was still one problem. Any event planning job she took would likely expect her to plan weddings.

And this was a one-and-done.

Seeing that the crosswalk was flashing, she hurried her pace across the street to where the pink-and-white-striped awning rippled in the wind, not wanting to be late or rushed through the tasting.

She reached for the door at the same time as another hand did, and looked up to see Logan grinning back at her.

Immediately, her hand dropped as her heart began to pound. Again? She'd hoped to dodge him until at least the rehearsal dinner, but that was the problem with a town as small as Driftwood Cove. It was full of shared memories, people, and places.

And Bittersweet Bakery was full of all those.

For a moment, she wondered if she could claim she was just leaving, walk away, and come back at another time. With Hallie—which would be better, of course.

But then she remembered the appointment, how Trudy had barely fit her in, how this was a rush order as it was.

And how she'd promised her sister she'd handle it.

"Logan." She swallowed, struggling to make eye contact. "What are you doing here?"

But that was a silly question, wasn't it? He was probably here to buy some muffins or a pie or any of the other delicious items that the shop was known to offer on a daily basis.

"Same reason you are," he surprised her by saying.

"I'm here for the wedding cake tasting."

"And so am I." Perhaps seeing her confusion, he added, "Since Josh couldn't make it, he asked me to go in his place. I assume Hallie did the same?"

There was no way that Hallie knew about this, or she would have warned her. Still, she'd need to have a talk with her sister after this and ask her to set some boundaries with Josh.

Amy's chin lifted defensively. "I'm the wedding planner. It's my job to help with these sorts of things."

"Consider me a second opinion, then," he said easily, and, before she could stop him, he opened the door.

He was staring at her, the door open, gallantly waiting for her to go first. Her mouth, she was aware, was slackened, her eyes probably popping, and she was at a loss for words to tactfully tell him to please leave, that she had this covered, that she didn't need him here, didn't need him in general. She finally stepped inside, her mind spinning.

The room was filled with tables, mostly occupied by young families with children eating the bakery's famous oversize cookies or cupcakes topped with various pastel shades of buttercream frosting. The long counter ran down one wall, the display case a happy vision of pastries and sweets made with attention and care. She couldn't even look at Logan. Couldn't even believe that he was here, standing beside her, acting as if nothing had ever changed between them, as if all these years could be forgotten and they could pick up right where they'd left off!

As if her heart hadn't been broken in half. As if he hadn't betrayed her in the deepest way, finding another girl who, for whatever reason, was the one he wanted to spend the rest of his life with, even when Amy had been the one he'd devoted all his time to every day for years and years.

"Amy and Logan!" Trudy said as soon as she was finished serving a customer. Like most businesses in town, this was family owned and operated, and Trudy had been working at the bakery since she was old enough to see over the counter. Now, her once-blonde hair was graying, but her blue eyes were still bright and youthful. "What a happy sight this is!"

Amy managed the briefest of smiles. "It's nice to see you, Trudy."

"Here for your usual?" Trudy asked.

Amy felt Logan's eyes on hers as her cheeks heated. Back when they'd been friends, hanging out every spare chance they had, they'd come in here at least once a week. One of many things that they had in common. One of many things that were not enough.

"Actually, a wedding cake," Amy said.

Trudy's eyes popped, and she clasped her hands together. "A wedding! Oh, it's about time! I always thought the day would come for you two."

Amy's cheeks burned, and she was aware that she was gaping at the bakery owner, if only because she didn't dare look at Logan.

"We're here for my *sister's* wedding cake tasting. I made the appointment last week?" Amy tipped her head, then explained. "Hallie and Josh both got stuck at work."

"Oh no!" Trudy looked alarmed. "Do we need to reschedule? Although we're running on a short timeline as it is, with the wedding only days away. If it wasn't the two of them, I honestly don't think I would have made the exception."

Amy understood. Josh's parents were important people in town, and the Walshes weren't far behind. Their history was generations deep, on both sides.

"It's okay," Amy assured her. "I'm an event planner, so I do this sort of thing for my clients all the time." It was true, she did, but never for a wedding, and certainly not one that was so personally important to her.

"And Logan is here to keep you company. Like always." Trudy beamed, and Amy didn't have the heart to correct her. "Why don't you two take a seat in the corner, and I'll bring out some samples. I've got some design ideas here." She handed over a portfolio, which Amy took, even though she had saved plenty of photos on her phone, and Hallie had collected clippings too.

Amy moved to the table, aware of Logan following close behind. She immediately opened the book the moment she sat down, grateful for something to look at. After flipping through the rather uninspiring pages of three-tiered cakes with the usual flowers piped down the sides, she couldn't ignore the pull of his stare any longer.

"So." She closed Trudy's portfolio and forced herself to look up.

"So." He grinned, causing the lines around his warm brown eyes to crinkle. He'd always had a warm smile, kind, contagious really. Still did.

"It seems that you haven't been back to Driftwood Cove in a while," Amy surmised. She'd never been sure, though, and she hadn't been willing to run the risk.

After all, this was her second time back since the big heartbreak, and here he was!

"Work has kept me busy. The pace of New York is . . . well, you understand, being in Boston," he explained.

She wanted to say that she didn't understand anything. Not why he'd gravitated to Lindsey at all, not why he'd committed to her for life. Not why he'd stopped texting and calling.

But then she'd have to explain why she'd stopped too. And that would require telling him how she once felt about him.

Her eyes went to his hands resting casually on the table. No ring, but she wouldn't read into that. Even her own father hadn't always remembered to put on his ring, and of course, Logan had always been busy with his hands. He loved tinkering with old things, from his dad's boat to the old house they lived in on the other side of town. His father was in construction. Logan had talked once about eventually taking over the business.

Maybe he had. But right now she wasn't ready to ask for details. It would lead to more than she wanted to hear, and she had to stay focused.

"You must be eager to get back to the city. Central Park is beautiful this time of year." She busied herself by opening Hallie's binder, even though its contents were far from surprising. Her sister's inspiration was their parents' wedding. Classic. Elegant. A bit too old fashioned. Maybe a bit too safe.

"It's nice to be back, reconnect with old friends." He gave her a sad smile and then cleared his throat. "I haven't spoken to Josh in . . . years. But with old friends, it's like riding a bike."

She raised an eyebrow. Was it? Maybe for the guys, but not for her. She couldn't imagine ever getting back to the way she and Logan used to be.

Even though a part of her longed for nothing more.

"So, you're here for the week?" She turned another page in the binder. She saw where Hallie was going with this, trying her best to imitate their mother's cake, but in a slightly more modern way. Now, if Amy were to pick out her wedding cake, she'd want it to be a showstopper, something as stunning as the venue itself, something worthy of photographs in an album just like the one their mother kept, the one she'd stared at until she'd memorized it. Right down to the sugar flowers.

"Actually, I'm here in Driftwood for the foreseeable future." Logan looked puzzled when she stared at him, the surprise no doubt registering on her face. Didn't his wife hate this little seaside town? Hadn't she insisted on a big New York wedding and an apartment on the Upper East Side that her father was paying for? "I'm surprised you didn't know."

She held his gaze, hating the way it still made her feel close to him even though it reminded her of their distance. She wanted to ask why she would know. Did he think she kept tabs on him? But she knew he wasn't like that. There was no arrogance to him. No ego. No, he was a good, solid, funny, and kind guy, and that was what made all this so damn hard.

"I'm working for Bunny," he said.

Amy blinked at him, happy that their cake samples hadn't arrived yet because she probably would have choked on them.

"You're working for my *mother*?" And she hadn't told her? She'd had a chance, last night! Or earlier. This must have been in the works for weeks, months even! And Bunny hadn't even mentioned his name at dinner.

Of course, that was nothing new. When Amy had stopped talking about Logan, everyone in her family did too. It was like how they tiptoed around Claire with their father.

But this was different. Bunny had hired Logan. She knew he was in town.

And she'd said nothing. Not to Amy. And, it would seem, not even to Hallie.

"It's new. Just worked it out last week, actually. She needed some help with these older properties, and I have the skills and experience." He gave her a funny look. "I've been working for a construction company, on the business side, but I have to say that it's nice to get in there with my hands again and restore some of the beauty in these old homes."

"No one . . . told me."

He didn't seem to read anything into that, but then, he'd never known how much he'd hurt her.

"Your family is probably so busy with this wedding that she didn't have a chance to mention it."

She nodded. "Yes." Probably. But she'd be asking for an explanation the moment she got back to the house.

"So, you're a wedding planner!" Logan smiled at her.

She couldn't bring herself to return the gesture. "I'm an event planner, actually."

"You like your job?"

"Love it!" She realized she was speaking in the present tense, like this was still a job she held, not one she'd been let go from last week. But there was no reason to get into all that, not the least of which was that she didn't need Logan to tell Josh, who would most certainly tell Hallie, upsetting her.

But it was more than that. She was determined to show that her life had turned out fine. Better than fine—great. "I usually have at least one event a week, sometimes two."

"This must be old hat to you, then," he said. He leaned in, giving her a wink. "Don't worry. I'll defer to the expert. Just consider me here for the free food."

Against her will, she smiled. "Josh must have thought I needed another opinion. But then . . ." A horrible image took hold. One of Logan and his bride picking out their cake. "I guess you've done this before."

A strange shadow darkened his eyes. "I have."

She nodded. There it was. The awkwardness still lingered between them.

She couldn't have been more grateful when Trudy appeared with a large plate filled with small slices of layer cake.

"There are nine flavors here, detailed on the little cards. If there's anything you want me to tweak, or mix and match, just ask me. Though, personally, I wouldn't put the chocolate buttercream with the lemon sponge." She winked.

After Trudy excused herself, Amy picked up the fork, trying to focus on the task. "So. Shall we eat? I suggest we start with vanilla and work our way up to the chocolate, but—"

"Amy." Logan stopped her before she could take her first bite.

She looked at him properly, their eyes meeting across the table, his sad, searching; and despite the years that had passed, the connection remained. Her heart squeezed in her chest, filling with love and hurt and a longing she couldn't deny, even though she'd tried, for years, sometimes even successfully.

"I feel bad that we lost touch," he said.

She gave a little nod, swallowing hard. Of course that was all he had to say. What else was there?

He'd made his choice. She'd accepted it. But sitting here across from him, she was achingly aware of it.

She brushed a hand through the air, trying to tamp down any evidence of the pain in her chest. "It happens. Even with you and Josh. You had a lot going on. We both did. We . . . went our own ways."

"And now we're back here. Together."

She felt uneasy, wishing they weren't together at all, because even though they were in the same bakery, sitting at the same table, nothing was the same at all, and each ticking minute just reminded her of that.

"Do you remember when we used to stop in here and get one of those big cookies?" he said, and something in her felt like it was breaking all over again. He remembered.

"No one makes cookies like Trudy" was all she said. She picked up her fork and put a sample in her mouth before she could say any more. "I think we can rule out the chocolate. And the lemon."

"But you love lemon!" he said, looking confused. "You always went for the lemon meringue pie at your family's picnics. And I should know because I was at every one of them."

Until he started attending another family's picnics, she wanted to say.

Instead, she reminded herself of why she was here. She couldn't let herself get distracted.

"Yes, well, it's not my wedding." The words came out with the hurt that lingered in her chest. "We'll go with vanilla. That just leaves the design." She already had ideas for this, ones that she'd envisioned back when she was still hopeful that one day she might be planning her own wedding with the man now sitting across from her.

She pulled up her phone and searched for a visual that would give Trudy an idea of what she had in mind. Three tiers, of course: that much she and Hallie had always agreed on. And there would be flowers, of course, but instead of the sugar flowers that their mother had used, Amy preferred something fresh.

"What do we think?" Trudy asked, coming by their table.

Amy held up her phone and showed Trudy a few of the images that caught her attention. "I was thinking we might use flowers that match the centerpieces and bouquets between the tiers. That would make the cake stand taller and really make each layer pop."

Trudy looked surprised but nodded. "That's certainly unusual but very pretty. I'll coordinate with the florist. I assume you're going with the shop here in town?"

"Of course." Amy couldn't help but feel excited. It would be a beautiful cake. The prettiest she'd ever seen. Everyone would marvel over it. Everyone would remember it.

She knew she certainly would.

She set the phone down on the table, the photo still on display.

Logan leaned in and then looked up at her, a wrinkle appearing between his eyebrows. "Really? You don't think it's a bit . . . showy?"

"This is a large, formal wedding," she pointed out. Hallie had shared the final head count with her this morning, now that everyone had responded to the change of plans. Amy still hadn't brought herself to check if there was a plus-one with Logan. She could only assume that there would be.

"May I?" Logan reached for Hallie's binder and flipped through the pages. "This page is wrinkled the most. Hallie must have kept coming back to it."

Trudy craned her neck for a peek. "Very pretty."

"And very small," Amy said, dismissing it. White buttercream with white flowers that wouldn't even be noticeable from across the room. "I much prefer the look of fondant for this."

Amy looked at Trudy for guidance, but the woman was glancing over at the counter, where a little boy was trying to reach for a muffin in one of the baskets on the counter. She muttered something and scurried over before the entire batch was contaminated by grubby hands.

Logan raised his eyebrows. "If you say so."

Amy bit back a sigh. "I do," she said. They stared at each other for a moment. An opportunity, perhaps, to speak. About the past. Heck, even about the present. Certainly not about the future.

Instead, Amy broke his gaze, her heart beginning to pound.

"Well," she said, tucking her phone back into her bag and taking possession of Hallie's binder. "Looks like we're done here. I have a meeting at the bridal salon, and I can't be late. Thank you for your . . . help."

She stood up and made her way to the counter, hoping that by the time she finished placing the order, he'd be gone.

Only when she turned back and saw that he was, she realized that she hadn't wanted that at all.

What she wanted was to turn back time—to go back to that year before Logan ever met Lindsey. To tell him how she really felt. To know if it could have been them instead, sitting here together, planning for their cake instead of her sister's.

What she wanted . . . was impossible.

CHAPTER TEN

Claire

Claire and Gabe had been sitting opposite each other since the house finally quieted down this morning, their laptops open, files spread around them, fingers tapping in silence. Every once in a while one of them would look up and say, "Coffee break?" and the other would push back their chair, and then they'd head into the kitchen to refill their mugs like they would do if they were back in the office.

It wasn't weird at all, Claire told herself as she sipped her third cup of the day. Even though it was actually very weird. So weird that she was regretting agreeing to this sham.

She didn't know what had been stranger last night—seeing Gabe in her childhood home or closing the door to her childhood bedroom, left alone with him and all the dolls and stuffed animals that hadn't ever been packed away. Fortunately, they were both tired from the drive, and after going through the awkward process of taking turns in the bathroom, brushing their teeth, and changing before eventually turning out the light, him on the floor with a heap of blankets, her in her bed, she'd fallen asleep quickly, thanks to the wine at dinner. She hoped that she hadn't snored. If she had, Gabe would have been sure to tease her about it by now.

Still, she'd woken even earlier than usual and lain in bed, all too aware of his presence in the room, the steadiness of his breath while he slept.

Her mother clearly loved him. Her sisters certainly approved.

Soon, to them, Gabe would be a thing of the past. A friend. A friend who dated other women. While she remained firmly single. Never mind that it would be by her choosing.

"Do you have a red pen?" she asked, forcing Gabe to look up at her with those deep-set eyes.

"Was that the one thing you didn't pack in your suitcase? Excuse me. Suitcases." The corner of his mouth quirked.

"You clearly aren't used to traveling with women," she retorted. "But then, that would probably require taking one on a second date."

"Like you can talk," he teased. "When was the last time you went on a date, much less a second date?"

He was staring at her now, waiting for an answer, and she couldn't think of one that wouldn't give him the advantage in this debate.

"I don't have time to date," she said simply.

"Ah, but you do. If I have time to date, then so do you."

Claire held her breath, knowing he was right, knowing that she wasn't being honest with him or herself right now. It was a convenient excuse and a lot easier than the truth.

She hesitated, wondering if she should unload the painful part of her past at long last, because she'd kept it bottled up for so many years that she'd simply learned to live with it.

Maybe learned to live by it.

But how could she ever give her heart away when she often felt like her father had taken it with him?

"But you don't make time for vacations either," Gabe was saying now. "And you clearly aren't used to traveling at all, unless you count the path you've burned into the pavement between your office and the courthouse. You do know that airlines only allow one carry-on item these days, and that none of your suitcases would be small enough to qualify?"

"Which is why we drove," she said. "Besides, it makes it easier for us to escape if need be."

"I think your family is pretty great, actually," Gabe said, tipping his head, all joking subsided.

"They are." A feeling of guilt crept up, like it always did whenever she thought of her sisters, of her mother, of the holidays and birthdays that she had let pass by, of the calls she didn't make and the visits she didn't take. It hadn't been deliberate. It had just sneaked up on her, the distance, then the excuses, made more frequent each time she did see them and was reminded of how stilted their once-tight bond had grown.

"And Josh seems like a nice kid," Gabe pointed out.

Claire gave him a knowing look. She knew that Gabe also chose his words carefully, a hazard of their shared profession. "He is a nice *kid*. I like him. I just . . ."

He raised his eyebrows. "Careful."

"It's fine. No one else is here." Hallie was working, and Amy was out running wedding errands, and Bunny was also busy getting ready for the last-minute festivities and the dozen or so family members who would soon descend upon the house.

Claire huffed out a breath. "We should get back to work. I need to meet my sisters at the bridal salon soon, and I need to get this contract to my client before I go."

"The bridal salon?" His eyes twinkled. "Why do I suddenly have a vision of you trying on wedding veils in my mind?"

She should have known he'd never let her live that down. "See, that's why I shouldn't have agreed to this ruse," she said. "My family filled your head with all these stories, and now you'll bring it up every chance you get."

"What can I say? They've given me a whole new side of you. And here I thought I knew you so well."

"You do know me. All that other stuff was when I was a child. A kid," she said, choosing her words carefully.

From the way Gabe shook his head, she knew that he understood exactly what she was referring to. Josh and Hallie were young and in love, and everything so far had been easy for them, because both sets of their parents had made sure of that. They'd been given jobs straight out of college instead of having to interview. They'd been provided housing in exchange for some light caretaking, and soon, because of the way the original will and ownership of this house were structured, they'd inherit Beachnest Cottage. There were no struggles. No uncertainties. But it wouldn't always be that way, not even for them. And that was what had Claire worried.

She pushed back her chair and walked down the hallway lined with family photos going back to when the girls were young, some even older, of her mother when she was young, playing on the very sandy shoreline out back with her own sisters. Images of happy times, idyllic really, ones that she now struggled to look at without feeling a knot build inside her stomach.

The door to her father's office was ajar, the light off, and even though Claire's mother had used the space for years, she hadn't so much as moved a book on the wall of shelves. Claire walked behind the desk, her gaze falling to the framed print of her parents, tanned and glowing, their smiles radiant, each holding up a glass of wine.

The golden years, Claire supposed.

She looked away quickly and ran her fingers over the smooth wood, recalling the days of playing office, sitting behind his big antique desk, ordering her sisters to fetch her things, feeling so important.

Hallie had always been the most eager to please. Maybe because she'd been young and still saw it as fun. Claire's heart tugged a little when she thought of the younger Hallie, with her blonde tendrils falling at her shoulders, her chubby cheeks flushed, and her eyes, so dark and bright, so earnest.

She loved Hallie, now as much as then, even if it didn't seem that way.

Eager to get out of this room, she opened a desk drawer, but it was just filled with candy wrappers and an old checkbook. Her hands halted on a notepad that still bore her father's handwriting, and even though his scribblings themselves weren't important, her entire body seemed to tense up at the sight of his smooth, bold strokes.

She slammed the drawer closed, then tried another, thinking that maybe her mother didn't have much point for a red pen. This was just their second home; more and more it was Hallie's house.

About to give up, she opened the bottom drawer, thinking it was a long shot. Her theory was proved correct when all it contained was a large white envelope. She almost closed the drawer and stood up, until she caught sight of the return address. It was from a real estate company; she recognized the name as being local.

Glancing around the room and into the hallway, even though she knew that her mom and sisters weren't home, she lifted the envelope and sat down in her father's old Windsor chair.

The envelope had been opened. More than that. It had been saved. But why?

Probably another investment, she told herself as she fished out the papers inside. Prices were going up everywhere, especially here, in this seaside town. Or maybe Bunny wanted a smaller place, for when Hallie and her future children filled this one? Technically, the house was for the family, and large enough for them all, but the wedding must have stirred up thoughts, scenarios, and preparations.

She skimmed the letter, written on formal letterhead, frowning when she came to the words that were irrefutable. *In response. Per your query.*

Her mother had initiated this correspondence. And it wasn't about another property. It was about Beachnest Cottage.

There was a sum. A potential list price. A list of suggestions for improvements that should be made first.

Claire stared at the letter, reading it through twice more, even though she knew what it said, and worse, what it meant.

She nearly jumped when Gabe appeared in the doorway, his hands in his pockets, his expression open and friendly.

"Everything okay?" he asked, frowning a little.

Claire licked her lips and then shoved the papers back in the envelope and replaced them in the bottom drawer of the desk, where she'd found them.

"Fine. Just fine," she said, closing the drawer and standing up. Even though right now, nothing felt further from the truth.

She wouldn't bring it up. Not today. Not when she had to process it; certainly not when she had to do damage control for last night.

Stepping out of the car in downtown Driftwood Cove, she saw her sisters were already inside the bridal salon, fussing over a rack of white gowns that she knew weren't intended for Hallie. Hallie, being Hallie, was content with wearing that old satin dress Bunny had worn. While some brides agonized over their wedding dresses, trying on dozens, if not more, Hallie was happy with the one that had been sitting in the attic all this time, waiting for her.

Just thinking about that attic made Claire think of the house, which then made her think of the documents she'd found, which made her mind start to spin and her stomach tighten because it didn't make sense. And Claire liked things to make sense.

Did Hallie and Josh not want the house? Maybe they wanted something new. Something to call their own.

She pushed all those theories out of her mind when Amy caught her eye and waved, prompting Hallie to turn as well. Mustering up all the enthusiasm she could for trying on a pink dress she would absolutely never, ever have a reason to wear again, Claire pushed through the door.

Her first realization was that she had never been inside a bridal salon. Her second was that it was actually quite lovely. The lighting was bright, the chandeliers added a touch of glamour, and the furnishings were soft and inviting. Soothing music played from speakers. And everything seemed to sparkle.

Even, she saw, Hallie's eyes.

"Do I get to see you in your dress?" she asked her youngest sister, hoping that they might be able to start the week over, right at this moment.

"Not until the big day," Hallie said, then frowned a little. "And I still have to find the veil to complete the look."

The veil as in the old, antique thing they used to run around the house in as kids? The one depicted in the very story their mother had shared last night?

Claire understood the benefit of tradition, but was anything about this wedding of Hallie's choosing?

"Is Mom here?" Claire asked, looking around.

"She just called me and said she got stuck at the caterers' for Thursday night's big dinner."

Claire supposed she should be grateful for the small group they were right now, but the tension was obvious, and Hallie still wouldn't meet her eye.

"Hallie had her fitting yesterday," Amy explained. "It's you and me today."

Claire refrained from commenting on just how fun that would be for fear that Hallie would assume she was being sarcastic when she only partially was. It had been a long time since she'd gone shopping with her sisters. Longer still since the days of playing dress-up. Besides, when would she ever have a reason to try on fancy frilly dresses in a bridal salon?

Never, unless Amy found love and decided to get married.

"I wasn't sure you'd make it," Hallie said. "We were supposed to meet here twenty minutes ago."

"I got a last-minute call from a client," Claire explained. "Poor woman married her college sweetheart only to find out that he'd cheated on her with her best friend the night before their wedding. And ever since."

Silence fell over the room while Claire flicked through a rack of veils, feeling the weight of her sisters' eyes on her.

"Good thing that my best friend is the man I'm marrying," Hallie said, her tone meant to be light but clearly defensive.

Claire pressed her lips together. "It's sad, though. She thought they were madly in love. She thought she could trust him."

"Claire . . ." Amy's eyes flashed to hers.

The shop owner appeared then, out of a back room, carrying two identical pink dresses in satin.

"Oh. Lovely," Amy murmured, looking longingly at the gowns.

"So the wedding color is pink, then?" Claire tried, hoping to make conversation light and easy.

"Blush," said Amy, Hallie, and the shop owner in unison.

Blush. There was a word for everything, even a particular shade of pink. And because Claire believed words mattered, she went along with it.

"I stand corrected, then." She forced a smile, seeing Hallie's eyes narrow just a notch.

"You would have known the color if you'd bothered to reach out to me since I asked you to be my bridesmaid," Hallie said mildly.

So here it was, then. Claire pushed out a breath, almost relieved for the opportunity to say her piece when no one could accuse her of starting more trouble. "You're right, Hallie, I should have reached out.

And apologized. What I said at your engagement party wasn't intended to upset you. I was just looking out for you."

"By suggesting that I don't marry Josh?"

The salon owner's eyes went wide, and she looked down at the dresses in her hand, to them, and back again before mumbling something about putting them in the dressing rooms and all but running to the back of the shop.

"I never said you shouldn't marry Josh," Claire said, stifling a sigh. "I just mean—"

"I know what you meant. That I don't know what I'm doing."

"I never said that either," Claire said, more firmly this time. "But I see a lot of people who rush into things and only later end up wishing they had taken their time." And each time she sat there, listening to someone's story of heartache and disappointment, she was reminded why it was better to be in her position. Alone. Safe. Untouchable.

"Josh and I have hardly rushed things," Hallie said, but her cheeks turned pink. "Well, except for this week. We've been together for ten years, Claire."

"Yes, but how many of those years were adult years?" Claire heaved a sigh. "You've never even dated anyone else!"

"Neither did Mom! And look at her! She knew she'd found the one, and that was that."

Claire told herself to slow down and take a step back, but this was her sister, her baby sister.

"I just don't want to see you get hurt."

"Why would I get hurt?" Hallie's eyes seemed to be on fire, but a flush was working its way up her cheeks. "Josh loves me."

"I'm sure he does," Claire managed. For now, she thought.

"Claire, you promised Mom that you wouldn't cause trouble," Amy warned.

"I'm not causing trouble. I'm just looking out for you, Hallie. I'm a lot older than you—"

"And you have literally no experience when it comes to relationships," Hallie replied, but then stopped herself. "Well, until now."

Of course. Gabe. Crap. She should have considered her so-called boyfriend might be used against her in this argument.

"You're twenty-five. You have your entire life ahead of you."

"I do. And I plan to spend it with Josh," Hallie huffed. "Besides, I'm the same age as Mom was when she got married, so I think you've lost your argument, counselor."

Claire had to clench her teeth together from snapping back at that, and not just because she didn't like to lose a case.

"I shouldn't have said anything," Claire said because clearly, she shouldn't have. It didn't change the outcome, and it only upset everyone in her family, including her. Frustrated, she stared at her youngest sister until Hallie was forced to look her in the eye. "I'm sorry, Hallie. I am. I know you and Josh love each other, and really, who am I to be giving you marital advice?"

Only a divorce attorney, she finished to herself.

"Mom's on her way," Amy said, looking up from her phone. "Can we move on now? It's your wedding week, Hallie, and you might be the only one of us Mom gets to do this for too. Let's try and make today nice, shall we?"

Claire gave Amy a look of sympathy, knowing that this must be as difficult for Amy as it was for her—but not for the same reasons.

The shop owner, who must have been listening to every word from around the corner, used this time to reappear, looking quite relieved but still a little flushed. "The dressing rooms are ready," she said. "Please come out once you've tried them on so I can pin you for any alterations."

Claire did as she was told, without argument, if only because she was eager to have a moment to herself. She stepped into the small room and shut the door behind her, resting her head against it with closed eyes. It was only Monday, and she and Gabe wouldn't be out of Driftwood Cove until Sunday.

Gabe. He understood her in a way her family never could. He saw the same things she did, day after day, and never bristled at her cynicism.

She changed into the dress quickly, feeling the soft material slide over her skin, hitting right at her knees. The bodice was fitted, the skirt a generous A-line, and the sleeves capped on either side of the swooping neckline. The dress was simple, much like Hallie's wedding gown, and something strange bloomed in Claire's stomach when she looked at her reflection.

The color seemed to bring out a pinkness in her cheeks. A *blush*, she corrected herself. She couldn't remember the last time she'd worn a formal dress. Last year's firm holiday party, she supposed, but she'd been in court that day and had simply shed her blazer, leaving her in a basic black wool crepe shell.

Amy stepped out of the dressing room at the same time as Claire, and even though Amy's hair was darker, like their father's, the color looked just as good on her, if not better.

"Oh." Their mother walked in then and sighed into a smile, tipping her head. "You both look lovely." No sooner did she say it than her eyes welled. "Look at me!" She fanned her face, laughing at herself. "What will I do when I see Hallie in her wedding gown?"

Hallie linked her arm through their mother's and grinned. "Ah, Mom. What will you do when you see me walk down the aisle?"

They all laughed, somehow even Claire, even though when she thought of her sister walking down that aisle, in her mother's dress, without their father at her side, she almost felt like crying. For everything that might have been.

And everything they'd lost.

The shop owner handed out small glasses of champagne. Complimentary, or had she overheard the bits of their conversation? Either way, tension, for the moment, had been forgotten.

But still, Claire couldn't help feeling unsettled while she stood before the full-length mirror beside Amy, letting the shop owner cinch and pull and pin the dress.

"You'll probably be happy to have the house all to yourself by the time the week is over," Claire said lightly, looking in the mirror for any change in Hallie's expression. If the house was going to be sold, surely now would be a good time for someone to speak up.

But Hallie just shrugged and said, "Oh, I suppose. But having everyone there makes it almost feel like old times."

"And you'll have Josh there once we're gone," Amy pointed out. "So you won't have it completely to yourself. Not ever again."

Hallie's smile seemed frozen for a moment, and then she blinked, pulling it wider. "Very true. I guess I . . . never thought of that."

"But you two are so used to being together. At work every day," their mother commented. "Now you'll get to officially come home together each night too."

"Have Josh's parents said what they'll do with the carriage house now that he's moving in with you?" Amy asked.

Claire resisted the chance to point out that Josh, like Hallie, still lived on his parents' property. Instead, she stayed quiet, following the conversation and whatever information she might glean from it.

Hallie, who looked far away, blinked and then shook her head. "I think they had plans to rent it out, but I'm not sure."

"It's a hot market," their mother said, raising her eyebrows. "They'd be smart to do that."

Claire saw her chance, and she wasn't about to let it pass. "Did you ever think about that, Mom? Selling the house, I mean?"

Her mother looked surprised by the question. "Beachnest Cottage? Oh, there's been interest over the years, certainly. It's appreciated in value, too, even though it needs quite a bit of work."

Claire waited to see if her mother would say more, but the shop owner poked at Amy with a pin, causing her to let out a little cry, distracting from the moment. Claire kept her eyes on the mirror, on Hallie behind her, who was frowning now, and not over Amy being jabbed by a sharp object.

No, there was something else worrying Hallie's forehead. Something that had faded in her eyes. Something that left her chewing her lip, staring vaguely into the distance.

Something was going on. And Claire was determined to find out exactly what that was.

CHAPTER ELEVEN

Hallie

Normally Tuesdays faded into the week as a nothing-special day, but this week was different. This Tuesday was the last Tuesday she'd be single. The last Tuesday she would be Hallie Walsh. The last Tuesday she wouldn't have a second ring on her finger, reminding her of the promise she'd made.

The one she'd once been eager to make.

Last night had at least been drama-free. Claire and Gabe had a working dinner at the dining room table, leaving Bunny, Hallie, and Amy to eat something light out on the porch before retiring to bed early. She woke with a number in her head: four. Four days until the wedding. It should feel real by now, especially with her sisters and mother in the house.

But instead, it just reminded her of all those holidays and summers when it was just them gathered in this old seaside home.

Now she wondered if it would ever feel that way again.

Her mother was in the kitchen when Hallie came down the stairs, dressed for the day in a pale-pink shift dress—classic and elegant, just like the spa. The pearl earrings that Josh's parents had given her for her twenty-first birthday were usually the only jewelry she wore.

Well, except for the engagement ring.

"You're going to work again today, Hallie?" Bunny fumbled with the new coffee machine.

Hallie finished tying her hair into a low ponytail and walked toward the coffee maker, happy to help her mother with the new contraption.

"They need both of us there through at least tomorrow," Hallie said, filling them each a mug. Seeing her mother's dismayed reaction, she added, "It was short notice. And they've been good to me."

It was true that Josh's parents had been good to her, and long before they'd offered her a job at the club. From the very start, Coco was always warm and kind, inviting Hallie to family barbecues, special events at the club, later holiday dinners that they split between their two families, and even a couple of ski trips to Vermont. James had stepped in like the father she'd lost, even though they both knew that he could never fill his shoes, and he didn't try to either.

"I just felt so bad that you couldn't even taste your own wedding cake." Her mother clucked her tongue.

"Well," Hallie said briskly. "I would have been too conflicted anyway."

"I just want you to have the wedding you really want," Bunny said gently.

"I already have Claire giving warnings," Hallie reminded her mother.

Her mother set a hand on her arm and looked her straight in the eyes. "I am not warning you away from marrying Josh. I just want to be sure that you aren't rushing things with the wedding."

"Waiting for more than another year didn't make sense," Hallie said firmly. "And having the wedding at Cliffside Manor is not up for negotiation."

Her mother frowned down at the coffee in her hands.

"Mom?" Hallie's tone expressed her concern. "Is everything okay? I didn't cause you too much stress by moving up the wedding, did I?" She knew it was a big ask to expect her sisters to drop all their work plans to come for the week. But her mother had a busy professional and social life; it was possible she'd had to rearrange her schedule too.

"It's just being back here, with all my girls." Her mother gave a shrug, but beneath her brave smile, her eyes looked sad. "Thinking about your wedding makes me remember mine. I'm just feeling nostalgic, I suppose."

Hallie nodded. She understood. More than she was letting on. Somehow this wedding didn't feel like the start of her next chapter. It felt like the end of the one she wasn't ready to turn the page on just yet.

"I thought you'd be happy I'm getting married at the manor," she said.

"Oh, I am! I am! It's your wedding, though, and you know I've never pressured you to follow any traditions."

"I want to!" Hallie exclaimed, knowing this hardly came as a surprise to anyone in her family. "You know how much I've always admired what you and Dad had. And now look at me, getting married at the same age you did."

Her mother stirred her cream into her mug and took a sip. "I always knew you and Josh would end up getting married, you know."

"And if we hadn't?" Hallie blurted. She saw the same surprise register in her mother's face that she felt herself. Where had that come from?

But what would her life have been like if she'd never met Josh that day, on her birthday, all those years ago? Would they have met another day, another summer? What if she'd gone to camp instead, or her parents hadn't brought them here for the season? Where would she be working? Who would she be dating? Would she be like Amy or Claire, a career woman living in a big city?

"What about the house?" she asked, grabbing at the most obvious, thinking of Claire's strange comments at the bridal shop. "If I wasn't getting married, what would happen to it?" Her mother didn't come back often, and her sisters might never even return again, especially Amy, now that Logan was back in town.

"Oh, but you are getting married!" Her mother shrugged off the comment.

But now something was nagging Hallie. "But let's say my life had been different. What then?"

Her mother raised her eyebrows and set her mug down on the countertop. "Well, I don't know. There's always Claire and Amy . . ."

"Speaking of Amy," Hallie said. "Amy told me last night that Logan is working for you! Why didn't you mention it?"

Hallie had been just as shocked as Amy to hear this news, partially because she couldn't believe that Josh hadn't told her first. But lately, it felt like there was a lot they weren't telling each other.

"It just happened," her mother said, not seeming to find it a big deal, even though Hallie was about to argue that it was. Especially to Amy. "These old places need some work, and Logan knows the area, so when he reached out I could hardly turn him down." She winced. "Your sister hasn't said anything to me yet. Is she upset?"

"Um, yes. You know how she felt about Logan! I don't think she ever got over it."

Her mother shook her head sadly. "That's what I've been worried about. She never talks about him, though."

"She's thrown herself into her work," Hallie pointed out. "Like Claire."

"Only Claire has a boyfriend now," her mother said, her eyes glistening. "I like him."

"I do too," Hallie admitted. Maybe Gabe was good for her sister. Maybe he would soften her edges. Remind her of the girl she used to be.

But was he enough to make her rethink marriage?

Getting back to the house, she said, "Realistically, if none of us were ever married, what would happen to the cottage?"

It was a hypothetical, and one Hallie wasn't sure she was so focused on, but now that the question had been broached, she needed to hear the answer.

"I guess I'd sell it," Bunny surprised her by saying.

Hallie felt her eyes go wide. She stared at her mother, wondering if she'd laugh, say it was a joke. But her expression was calm; her tone lacked any emotion.

"Sell Beachnest Cottage?" Hallie barked out a laugh. That was crazy. Preposterous. Impossible!

Or was it?

"Honey, it's a large home that requires a lot of upkeep, and these old homes, especially with the elements being right here along the coast, don't do well empty. They need to be inhabited and taken care of. Amy and Claire never get back here, and most of my time is spent in Boston. So really, that would just leave you."

Just leave her. To follow along the path she'd started. With no room for any doubts.

"Good news," Josh said when she stopped by to see him before her shift started. He gave her a quick kiss and led her outside, onto the patio where their rehearsal would be held, looking toward the water, where right now the boats were heading out for the day.

The water was smooth, the sky clear. The weather forecast said it would stay that way through to Sunday, when the clouds came in. Hallie hoped that it was correct. By then they'd be on their way to Hawaii, and all this planning, all this waiting and dreaming, would already be behind them.

It seemed funny, she thought, that you could look forward to something your entire life only to be so close to already being on the other side of it.

"The hotel called, and they have an ocean view after all?" she asked hopefully.

"Sorry, babe. But I did get our dance lesson rescheduled. They can fit us in tonight. Your sisters can join us if they want too."

Hallie had almost forgotten the dance lesson. Their four-week classes were supposed to start in two weeks.

"Do you think we can learn all we need to in one class?" They were the first in their families to be getting married. The first of their friend group too. They'd never been to a wedding together. Hadn't gone to prom together, either, since she'd been in Boston for the school year.

Sure, they'd goofed around at parties or picnics, but how could she be marrying someone she'd never properly danced with before?

"Oh, I'm sure it will be more than enough." Josh gave her a rueful smile. She knew he was only doing the lesson for her, and she appreciated it. If it were up to him, they'd skip the first dance altogether. He didn't feel comfortable in the spotlight like that. But Hallie didn't see it that way. She saw it as tradition. Their first dance as husband and wife.

"You can dance with me here," she suggested, feeling relieved by the idea. A few steps together and she'd be reminded that all was well, they always fell right into place, and they'd have a beautiful first dance at their wedding. "For practice. I have a few minutes before I have to get to my post."

"Real funny, Hal. People could see us."

"So? We're not on duty yet, and besides, everyone at the club knows that we're getting married." Some of them were even guests. "Come on. Let's be spontaneous."

He gave her a funny look. "What's gotten into you, Hal? All this wedding stuff is making you . . ."

She stared at him, her good mood suddenly gone. "What? Making me what?"

He looked at her for a moment and then shook his head. "Forget it. We have the dance lesson tonight. We can learn then. And it's time for work now. So, I'll see you after?"

She nodded and accepted a quick peck, even though she didn't really lean into it.

"Why didn't you tell me that you asked Logan to go to the cake tasting yesterday?" she asked.

Josh shrugged. "Didn't know you'd have a problem with it."

"It's not that I have a problem with it. It's my sister."

"Amy? But she and Logan go way back. They were best friends."

They were, and that was just the problem.

"You know how Amy is," she said, struggling to meet his eye. "She takes a lot of pride in her work, and she likes things done her way."

"Her way or our way?" Josh countered, forcing Hallie's gaze to dart to his.

"What are you implying?"

"Nothing. But this is our wedding, Hallie. It's great that Amy is helping, but I hope that everything still turns out the way we want it to be."

Hallie refrained from pointing out that already the honeymoon wasn't going as planned, and not being able to go to her own cake tasting had never been something that she'd imagined, but then she remembered that they still had the venue. And that was most important—along with the dress. And the veil.

Which was still missing.

Just thinking of walking down that aisle without her veil made her anxious. It was tradition. It was good luck.

"Amy is an expert at what she does. She works for one of the biggest event planning companies in Boston!" And more than that, she was her sister.

Amy knew what she liked without even asking. Amy knew every part of her heart.

Except for the one part, the part that beat a little too quickly lately. The part that felt panicked and uncertain.

Were they doing the right thing by pushing up this wedding?

"Besides, it's not like we had a choice," Hallie said. "It was this weekend or more than a year from now."

And she couldn't live like this for another year. Putting her life on hold. Waiting, wondering. Besides, there was always the chance that something could go wrong a year from now. Something like the venue burning down or flooding or one of their parents getting sick or one of them getting hurt.

Or one of them changing their minds.

By the time Hallie arrived home that afternoon, she almost wished she had the house to herself. Her feet ached, her head was starting to pound, and she only had a few minutes to change if she was going to be on time with Amy to do a final walk-through of the venue, given how long it had been since she'd last been there.

When she walked up the steps and into the hallway, the house was quiet enough that she thought she was alone for a moment, until her mother called out from somewhere upstairs.

"Hallie? Is that you?"

"It's me, Mom!"

"Come upstairs!" Bunny called, her voice echoing through the rooms, her tone urgent enough to make Hallie toe off her shoes and reach for the banister, stopping herself only when she considered all the things her mother might end up telling her. That Claire had decided she couldn't support this and had left, with Gabe in tow. That they'd had a handful of cancellations, after all, people who couldn't rearrange their plans on such short notice.

That moving the wedding up to this weekend had been a terrible idea.

Hallie briefly closed her eyes with dread, but when she crept up the stairs, bracing herself for whatever news she was about to hear, she saw her mother standing in her bedroom, holding a handful of lace in her outstretched arms, her smile nearly as wide as her arms needed to be to hold it without letting it graze the floorboards.

Hallie heard herself gasp, felt her breath catch and her heart start to speed up. It was the veil. The one they'd worn as little girls, the one that their mother fretted they would trip on or rip. The one that had been misplaced, lost, but never forgotten for all these years.

"You found it? But where? I've searched everywhere!"

"Actually, your sister found it," Bunny said.

"Amy? But she already looked . . ." Hallie turned to see Claire appear in the doorway.

"It was in my closet."

Meaning the one room of the house that Hallie hadn't searched, because going in there hurt too much, reminding her of the sister she'd once had.

Now she saw a glimpse of that old Claire, the one who was happy when she was happy, the one who would always let her have the last ice cream sandwich, even if Claire had been reaching for it first.

Her mother said, "Must have tucked it away one time when you girls were playing with it and forgot all about it over the years."

"Something like that, I suppose," Claire said.

Gabe came to stand beside Claire. "Ah, this must be the famous veil you all talked about so much at dinner. I'm surprised Claire hasn't clipped it onto her head again!"

Claire jabbed him quickly with her elbow. But she was smiling when she rolled her eyes.

Hallie startled for a moment. It had been a long time since she'd seen her sister so carefree. So . . . happy.

So much like her old self.

Maybe that's what love could do to you. Maybe that's all that Claire had needed.

"Are you going to try it on?" Gabe asked, only he was still teasing Claire.

"You wish," her sister said, shaking her head.

Gabe jutted his lip, a gesture that told Hallie he wouldn't have minded at all, but maybe not for the bragging rights that Claire believed to be his reasons.

Hallie and Bunny exchanged a smile. She'd so long ago given up on having a moment like this, with Claire not being so defensive or withdrawn, that Hallie almost hated for it to end for fear that she might never ever find it again.

"Unfortunately, I don't have much time," Hallie said slowly. "We have a meeting at the venue, and then Josh scheduled a last-minute dance lesson with us for this evening."

"How lovely," Bunny said. "I had some paperwork to catch up on anyway tonight, so don't worry about hurrying home."

"Sounds like fun!" Gabe said.

Hallie hesitated for a moment, glancing at her sister, who seemed so genuinely pleased for Hallie to have the veil. "You're . . . welcome to . . . join us," she offered.

Claire's eyebrows shot up in surprise, but before she could respond, Gabe said, "Count us in."

Claire stared at him and then back at Hallie. "Count us in," she said, then backed out into the hallway. "Well, we were just out for a walk, so I guess we should freshen up and leave you to it."

Hallie turned her attention back to the veil in her mother's hands, feeling her mood brighten with each passing second. It was all working out. Even with Claire. She could have made some snippy remark or an excuse not to come tonight, but she hadn't.

Without needing to be told what to do, Hallie walked toward the freestanding brass mirror that stood in the corner of the room, near one of the tall windows that looked out onto the ocean. She watched in the reflection as her mother ever so carefully placed the clips into her hair and then smoothed the veil out around her shoulders and down her back, where it finally came to rest near her knees.

In her pale-pink cotton shift dress, she wasn't quite the complete vision, but it was close enough. Enough to make her feel hopeful that one thing had gone right. That it would all be all right. That she'd made the right choice moving up the wedding date. Made the right choices, from her first date with Josh, to accepting his proposal, to daring to believe that what they had was meant to be, that it could last.

"It's a sign," she breathed, smiling her first easy smile in days. The veil had been found. She'd wear it just like her mother had on the first day of the rest of her happy life. Everything was coming together. Everything would be beautiful.

Everything would be perfect, just like she always knew it would be.

CHAPTER TWELVE

Amy

So the veil had been found. It had been so many years since Amy had seen it that she'd almost forgotten what it even looked like, but the memory had distorted things, as memory was prone to do, putting a glossier coating on reality and making things better than they actually were.

It was a fine enough veil, she told herself, but she still couldn't stop thinking of how much more beautiful the ones at the shop were, how they would bring the otherwise simple dress to the present day, giving it a hint of modernity and the sparkle that would make it feel more complete.

These were the thoughts that went through Amy's head while she and Hallie drove to Cliffside Manor, where they'd be meeting with Josh and the event manager of the property. The old house was stately, the closest thing to a castle that Amy had ever seen, and, as Hallie kept pointing out, family tradition.

"You never wanted to try something different?" Amy mused, her eyes on the road, so she wasn't able to read her sister's expression.

There was a pause before Hallie spoke. "What do you mean?"

"I mean, the venue. The dress. The veil. You didn't want to break from the past and maybe think about what you would have wanted if it wasn't all . . . decided for you?"

"It wasn't decided for me," Hallie replied, a defensive edge creeping into her tone. "It's what I decided. The path was there, and I chose to follow it. Besides, I don't see a reason to make things more complicated than they need to be. The manor is one of the most beautiful buildings in all of New England. And the dress and veil are just as nice as anything I might find in a shop. And given that we've had to rush the date, I think I should just be grateful that I don't have to worry about a dress not being finished in time."

True, all true. But still, Amy wasn't convinced. But then, this was Hallie. Hallie was content, always had been. She didn't yearn for more than she was given and didn't question the path that was placed in front of her.

Once, there was a time when Amy dreamed about her wedding day as much as Hallie, maybe more. She'd been the one most impressed with the wedding albums they'd flip through, the faded photos of this very estate filling the pages. It had all felt like a fairy tale, one with a perfect happy ending guaranteed. Maybe Hallie felt the same way, and that's why she was taking every idea it held so literally. Maybe she was counting on it.

"We haven't talked about the cake yet," Amy said.

"We got a little sidetracked with what else happened at the bakery." Hallie paused. "Do you want to talk about that?"

Amy shook her head. "It shouldn't even matter that he's working for Mom, other than the fact that she didn't tell me."

"I sort of told her you were upset about that," Hallie said.

Amy hadn't brought it up last night over dinner because Hallie and Bunny were too busy talking about all the plans for the week and she didn't want to ruin the moment. Her sister only got one wedding week. And there would be plenty of time for Amy to talk to her mother alone.

"Besides, it doesn't matter what Logan does or where he lives. I have an entire life in Boston."

"A job you love." Hallie was looking at her eagerly.

Amy swallowed hard and kept her eyes on the road, but her grip tightened on the steering wheel. "Right. A job I love."

"So," Hallie said. "The cake?"

"I went with vanilla, of course," Amy assured her. "But I tasted the others since Trudy presented them."

Hallie closed her eyes in relief. "Vanilla is what Mom had at her wedding. It's what I wanted."

"I know," said Amy, but she also knew it was stain resistant and a crowd-pleaser. Besides, it was the cake's appearance that she was most concerned about.

"Of course Claire would say something like that's typical of me. Plain vanilla."

Amy hated this rift between her sisters, especially when she sort of saw both sides but definitely didn't want to get caught in the middle.

"Claire is hardly a risk-taker herself," Amy pointed out, this time drawing a little smile from Hallie.

"And the design? There were so many I loved. It was so hard to choose. Which one did you think would be best, in your expert opinion?"

Here, Amy hesitated. "I had an idea, something that I think you'll absolutely love."

"Wait. Don't show me now. Show me later, back at the house, when Mom is with us."

Amy nodded. They were expected in the lobby for their walk-through in a few minutes anyway.

She turned onto the long drive that led to the massive stone house. Behind it, she knew, were the cliffs that looked out onto the Atlantic.

"I'm going to make this wedding the most beautiful wedding our family has ever seen. Your album will be even more beautiful than Mom's."

And probably the only one of their generation. Amy reached that uneasy thought as she stepped out of the car into the afternoon sun. The temperature had dropped, and a cool, salty breeze was coming in off the ocean.

She had to make this wedding not just beautiful but perfect. And she had one shot to get it right. And very little time too.

But it wasn't her wedding, she reminded herself once again. Because the only man she'd ever really loved, the only one she wanted to spend every day with, forever and ever was—

Standing right there.

"What is he doing here?" she hissed to Hallie, who had also stopped in her tracks.

"Oh!" Hallie put a hand to her mouth. Her brown eyes were wide with worry and shock. "Oh, Amy. Josh must have invited him. I didn't know."

"I know you didn't." Amy fought back her exasperation. "But maybe you can tell Josh that I've got things covered. This is my profession. I know what I'm doing. I don't need . . . help."

And she certainly didn't need Logan popping up everywhere she went.

Hallie nodded furiously. "Yes, yes, I'll tell him." She paused for a moment but not to take in the sweeping view of the weeping willows and the lush green lawn that stretched all the way to the house. "I'm sorry, Amy. If I'd known—"

Seeing the worry in her sister's eyes, Amy pulled in a breath and set a hand on her sister's arm.

"It's fine. Really. Logan and I have a history. A nice one. There's no reason why we shouldn't get along for a few days." Or until his wife showed up and gave Amy the stink eye, like she'd done the one and only time they'd met.

Hallie looked so genuinely relieved, but more than that, so genuinely happy for Amy that Amy felt awful for the dread that was building in her stomach with each step they took toward the guys, who were standing with an older woman, probably the property manager.

When they finally approached, everyone turned to say hello. Somehow Amy got through the motions of shaking the woman's hand, introducing herself, saying a warm hello to Josh, and then looking Logan in the eye.

"We meet again," he said with a friendly smile. But there was something else in his expression too. Something that she'd just seen in Hallie. It was hope, she realized. That the past could be forgotten. Or righted.

But as easy as it would be to fall back into the familiar way of his company, Amy had no hope of things between them ever being what she wanted or needed.

And it was best to remember that.

The estate, at least, was as beautiful as Amy remembered. The ceremony would take place on the lawn, overlooking the ocean, followed by a reception on the large stone terrace off the conservatory. Inside the glass-walled room, guests could relax in the clusters of seating arrangements, and if it happened to rain, which so far the forecast promised it would not, then the entire event would be moved indoors, which wasn't a big concession given the grandeur of the place.

After profusely apologizing for the scheduling error, the event manager walked them through the plan while double-checking the terms of the contract.

"The bar will go here?" Amy confirmed.

"A full bar, yes," the woman replied.

"With the same signature drinks that Mom and Dad had at their wedding!"

Amy blinked at her sister, surprised she would remember such a small detail. But then, Hallie and her mother had probably been talking about this for the past year, and no doubt her mother was reminiscing about her happy day along the way.

She rather liked the idea of that nod to the past, but she also thought the signature drink should be a reflection of the couple getting married, not the bride's parents.

"What about a drink that represents your tastes? The two of you?"

Hallie and Josh turned to each other, each looking a little bewildered at the thought.

"You don't have to decide right now," Amy assured them. She turned back to the facility manager. "Can we get you something by Friday?"

The woman nodded. "Of course."

Josh looked pleased by the idea, but Amy thought Hallie looked more than a little conflicted.

Moving on . . .

"And the people inside . . . ?" Amy imagined that many people might want to enjoy the conservatory before and after the sit-down meal, where the comfortable velvet seating would give them a full view of the grounds and the accompaniment of the grand piano in the corner.

"They can walk out the french doors to the bar," the manager said, a defensive note creeping into her tone.

Hallie looked at Amy in confusion.

"We could set up a secondary, smaller bar in here, perhaps?" Amy suggested. She gave Hallie a reassuring smile. This was what she did: she problem-solved. She'd been around enough formal events to realize in hindsight how they could have been made better.

The manager noted something in the contract.

"And the string quartet," Amy continued. "They'll be on the lawn for the ceremony, but after?"

"Here on the terrace until the toasts," the manager confirmed.

"And the band will be set up—" But Amy stopped when she saw her sister's face.

Hallie looked pale. "We still have to find the band! I completely forgot! How did I forget?" She turned to Josh. "I was going to meet with a few, but that was before the date changed and—"

Sensing the rising hysteria in her sister's voice, Amy set a hand on her shoulder.

"It's fine," Amy said, even though her heart was racing with panic. How on earth could she find a band in four days? Especially when a DJ would not fit Hallie's vision or her own. No, they needed a band with personality, one that played all their favorite songs and got even the wallflowers out of their seats.

"I'll find a band," Amy said firmly. How, she didn't know, but she would. She had to.

Hallie nodded, but the worry hadn't left her eyes.

Amy turned to matters at hand. "If I think of anything else before Saturday, can I contact you directly?"

The manager handed over her card and then left them to explore the grounds at their leisure.

Hallie and Amy walked ahead, and not only because Amy didn't feel like talking to Logan, much less looking at him. Every time she did, her heart seemed to feel like it might burst with a mixture of hurt and longing—the exact emotions she'd tried to keep at bay all these years.

But it wasn't just Logan's presence that made her feel defensive and vulnerable today. She hadn't been back to this old manor since her father was alive, when Hallie had begged their parents to bring them one summer afternoon when no events were being held. They'd gone for the full tour, and Bunny had reminisced about their wedding day in more detail than even the album itself could do.

"Remember when Dad and Mom stood down near the edge of the lawn and recreated their first kiss?" she said wistfully.

There were tears in Hallie's eyes when she looked over at her, but she was smiling too.

"This really is the perfect place to get married," Amy told her.

"The only place," Hallie said, stopping just short of the cliffs so they could look out onto the ocean crashing against the rocks below. After a moment, she sighed. "I could stay here all evening, but Josh and I have our dance lesson tonight."

"You're lucky you were able to squeeze that in," Amy remarked. The first dance was a special moment, and one she shouldn't neglect as the wedding planner.

"Sparklers," she said suddenly, looking at Hallie. Amy had always wanted sparklers at her wedding, lighting up the evening sky, and adding a wonderful glow as she danced in the center. And like so many of her dreams, she'd buried the idea, along with the hopes that it would ever come true. "What if everyone held sparklers during your first dance?"

"I never thought of that . . ." Hallie drifted off, frowning a little. "You don't think it will be too chaotic?"

"Not at all!" Amy quickly made a note on her phone. She was so swept up in the idea that she hadn't even noticed the guys had caught up to them.

Josh put an arm around Hallie's waist and studied her face. "What do you think, Hallie? Do you like that idea?"

"I hadn't considered it . . . ," Hallie said. "But now that you've mentioned it, I can picture it. Are you sure it will be dark enough?"

"We'll make sure it is." Even if they had to extend the cocktail hour by a bit and push back dinner too. "So," Amy said, focusing on Josh and trying her best to not look at Logan. "A dance lesson?"

"You can join us," Josh offered.

Hallie seemed to stiffen for a moment, her eyes on Amy. Amy, for her part, couldn't even look at Logan, who seemed to be taking her lead, waiting for her response.

Was it possible that he was willing to go along with this if she was up for it?

Amy entertained the thought for one glorious second until she remembered that he was a married man. And she wasn't even his friend anymore, not really.

"I should really get back to the house. Focus on everything that still needs to be done. I might try the florist too. If they're still open."

Hallie nodded, not surprised.

"In that case, do you mind giving me a ride?" Logan asked.

She should have known she couldn't have gotten away that easily.

"I tagged along with Josh . . ." He gave her a bashful grin; the dramatic plea in his eyes told her that he wasn't going to take no for an answer.

Amy stared at him, wondering how this was so easy for him, why he suddenly wanted to spend time together when he hadn't reached out in five years. When he had a wife waiting for him in New York, or maybe even here in town.

Oh, God. She might be there when Amy dropped him off. And she'd be about as pleased to see Amy as Amy was at the thought of seeing her.

"We're pressed for time, so it would probably be easier that way," Josh said, checking his watch for good measure.

"Oh, we can probably be a little late," Hallie said, looking a little nervous. "It's no trouble to drop Logan off—"

"I barely got us this dance lesson," Josh told her. "It makes sense to go straight there."

"Where are you staying?" Hallie asked.

"My parents' place," Logan replied. "They're at their main house in Baltimore, so I'm taking care of the house for a while."

Sensing Josh's impatience, and the anxiety in Hallie's expression, Amy saw no choice.

"Sure, I can give you a ride." Amy swallowed hard, but her throat felt dry. "No problem."

Once, riding in a car together had been a regular occurrence, the silence as natural as the conversation. They'd hop radio stations until they found a song they both liked, then sing along, not even self-conscious about their voices. Sometimes it was a running joke about who could sing the worst, whose voice would crack on the high notes, who could go the lowest on the oldies. The back seat would be filled with a cooler, towels, and a couple of books in case they got bored, which never happened, not when they were together. They'd drive out of town, to one of the smaller villages where the beaches weren't so crowded, where they wouldn't be spotted by someone they both knew. Where it was just the two of them.

It was all she needed back then. Just him.

"Well, that was a success," she said, trying to keep the topic of conversation on something neutral, hopefully for the duration of the ride.

"I'm not so sure the property manager would agree," Logan said, chuckling.

She looked at him, then, feeling that pang when her eyes snagged his handsome face, looked away again quickly. "Why do you say that?"

She eased out onto the driveway, trying to remember how long it took them to drive here, and what the speed limit was. If she could push it a bit. Get this little car ride over with a bit early.

"You didn't see her face when you mentioned changing the drinks menu?"

"What did you expect me to do? Stand there and just nod? Hallie asked me to help."

"I think this might have been the one part of the plan that was set in stone. No pun intended." She could hear the grin in his voice.

"I'm just tossing out ideas." She glanced at him sidelong. "That's what any good event planner would do. I'm sure you would know, having been through this yourself."

"I didn't get married," he said.

For a moment it felt like the world stopped along with her breath. She stared at the road, processing what he'd just said, convincing herself that she'd just imagined it, hadn't heard correctly, even though the pounding of her heart told her otherwise.

In all these years she'd never asked, and no one in her family had ever said anything. She'd assumed that his life had marched on like hers had. Except that he'd lived happily ever after. That he didn't look back. That he didn't even think of her.

"What?" Her voice came out in a scratchy whisper.

He gave a little shrug. "I didn't get married. The engagement was called off."

She swallowed hard, wrestling with her conflicting emotions. The first thought was of relief, even—dare she say it—happiness, but the other part of her, the part that loved Logan, wanted the best for him, wanted him to have everything he ever wanted in life, felt sad.

"It was a mutual decision," Logan continued. "We wanted different things in the end. Looking back, we always did, I just didn't see it at the time."

"Like New York?"

"Actually, I like New York. City life suits me, but I'll always be most at home in Driftwood." Logan grew quiet. "I guess when it came down to the thought of spending my entire life with her, the closer the wedding date became, the more I didn't think I could go through with it."

"I'm sorry," she said, and she meant it. Sorry for the way things had ended up. For the fact that they'd drifted apart. That they'd missed out on so many years.

But most of all she was sorry that she hadn't been enough. Or what he'd wanted.

And that try as she might, she couldn't be the friend to him that he'd needed at that time. That she'd put her own hurt first. That she'd let him go.

"It was a long time ago," he said. "I've moved on, moved away. It was . . . a tough time. I could have used a friend." He frowned, for the first time since she'd been back, and everything in her wanted to reach out, pull him close, and bring that light back to his eyes. Because this time it wasn't another girl who had hurt him. It was her.

"Why . . ." She stopped, searching for better wording, one that wouldn't bring up too much hurt from the past. "You could have called me."

From her periphery, she could feel him giving her a long look. "I knew how you felt about Lindsey."

Yes, she'd insinuated her feelings but never voiced her true opinion because she hadn't wanted to completely piss off Logan. Now she almost wished she had been firmer with her thoughts on the woman.

"Well, she wasn't exactly a fan of me," Amy said.

"She was jealous of you," Logan replied.

Amy laughed, out of surprise. But her cheeks flushed with heat. "Of me? Why?"

She swallowed hard, almost afraid to hear his answer but needing to know.

"She knew how close we were," Logan said simply.

"Well, she was certainly possessive of you. And she didn't like coming here."

"I gave up a lot to be with her," Logan said softly. "I guess I just felt like I'd messed everything up here and that I'd brought it all on myself."

"But you could have called," she said again.

She *wished* he'd called. She would have been there, to listen, to offer up a distraction. A vacation maybe. Or a reunion right here, in Driftwood Cove. They would have fallen back on their old routines.

And she would have fallen right back in love with him.

Maybe it was for the best that he had never reached out.

"I wasn't sure I could," Logan replied. "When you said you weren't coming to the wedding, I knew that I'd lost you for good."

Amy pressed her lips together. He'd lost her long before that, when he decided to get down on one knee and propose to another woman. A woman who didn't even like her.

"I'm sorry," she said again, because she was, for many things. But most of all because she had stopped being his friend—when he'd needed one the most.

Because being his friend wasn't enough. Not then. But now?

CHAPTER THIRTEEN

Claire

"I still can't believe you agreed to this," Claire grumbled when they climbed into the car that evening. "We could have used work as an excuse."

It wasn't the time with her sister she minded. It was the activity she had a problem with—especially if it included crossing more boundaries with Gabe.

"Is that always your excuse for getting out of things you don't want to do?" Gabe asked. "Because you and I both know that we weren't working over dinner last night."

They'd eaten leftovers with their laptops open, abandoning the contracts that shone on their screens to talk about the house, the town, even Hallie and Josh.

"We were working. Then we got distracted." It was often the case on the nights they stayed late at the office with the intention to work. Eventually shoptalk turned to personal talk.

"I think you wanted to avoid another sit-down meal with your mother telling me embarrassing stories about you," Gabe remarked.

"I wanted a little space, and using work was the best way to make sure no one tried to pressure me into more." Claire hesitated. "It's certainly easier than telling the truth."

And that was an understatement.

Gabe slid into the seat beside her. "It was a golden opportunity for you to spend quality time with your sister and maybe repair some of the damage."

"True." Claire gave him a rueful look. "Why do I feel like sometimes you know me better than I know myself?"

"Because I probably do." Gabe's grin widened, just bordering on cocky but not quite. "You have a way of making things more difficult than they need to be."

That was true, too, not that she'd be admitting as much. She could only feed that ego of his for so long before he started teasing her around the office.

Not that she'd mind. Gabe had a way of adding levity to things. And he was right that she did take life too seriously at times.

And that she was stubborn.

But dancing? She didn't dance. Never understood it, really. Dancing made her feel vulnerable and out of control, two things that she tried to avoid at all costs.

"You know, it's not too late to skip out and go to a bar instead," Claire suggested. "There's a great pub down near the waterfront."

"Sounds great," Gabe said. Then, just as Claire was finally relaxing, he said, "We can go there after the dance class."

"You've got to be kidding me," she said, glaring at him. "I don't think Hallie even wants me there. She only invited us because you showed interest."

"My read on it was that your sister wanted company tonight," Gabe said.

Claire thought about that as she drove down the road, the ocean to one side, wood-sided homes on the other. Hallie did seem eager to have others joining them tonight. But did she really want Claire there?

Or maybe there was another reason. Maybe she wanted Claire to see how happy she and Josh were. How well they danced together.

Or maybe she was onto the ruse. Wanted to see if Claire and Gabe could handle physical contact for an hour.

At the thought of it, Claire really wished she'd made up an excuse or offered to meet Hallie and Josh on safer territory.

"Well, she did invite you," Gabe pointed out, raising an eyebrow. "Take it as a good sign. I don't think you want to let her down."

"No, I don't," Claire said begrudgingly, but she didn't want to go to a dance class either. She glanced at him, noticing the little smirk that played on his mouth. "You're actually looking forward to this, aren't you?"

He glanced at her. "What can I say? It sounds like fun."

"What part exactly sounds like fun? Getting your toes stepped on or listening to corny music for an hour?"

"Watching you squirm," he said with a laugh.

"Very funny." Still, she was slightly amused.

"Okay, then, how about watching you outside your element? I'm seeing a whole new side of you away from that office."

She swallowed hard, gripping the steering wheel a little tighter. "Dare I ask if that's a good thing or not?"

"Oh, it's a good thing," he said with a chuckle. "A very good thing."

And even though she knew that tonight his enjoyment would be at her expense, she couldn't help but smile.

Hallie and Josh were already in the dance studio, a large, lofty space that occupied the second floor above some storefronts.

"Amy's not coming, then?" Claire couldn't help it: she felt uneasy around her sister and guilty around Josh. It wasn't that she didn't like him; she just didn't trust him not to let her sister down.

But then, did she really trust anyone anymore? Lately, she wasn't even sure she could trust herself.

"I invited her and Logan, but they said they had other plans," Josh said good naturedly.

Claire's gaze swung to Hallie, giving her a look of camaraderie. Few others knew about how Amy felt about Logan or cared about her as much as her sisters did. It was a bond. A special one. And one that made her feel so connected to Hallie at that moment that she hadn't even realized until now just how alone she'd felt.

For just a second she felt her heart soften with so much love for her sister that she wanted to cross the room and pull her in for a long, hard hug, tell her how sorry she was, how happy she was for her, even if that little part of her was still reserved for concern. But Hallie couldn't see that this worry came from wanting to protect her.

"Maybe I should go back to the house and keep her company," Claire said.

"Nice try," Gabe whispered to her, his breath warm on her ear.

Stiffening, Claire stepped to the side.

"Oh, Amy was giving Logan a ride," Hallie said, her eyes widening with meaning.

Claire could only let out a sigh and hope that her sister was being careful. Though Amy hadn't said as much, it was clear that she still held feelings for Logan, who was a married man now—at least as far as they knew. After all, Claire knew too well how many marriages ended in the first few years.

"Is Logan's wife coming to the wedding too?" Now was the time to gather facts and prepare everyone for what was to come.

It was better to see the bad stuff coming. Better than having a nasty surprise when you least expected it.

"Oh, you didn't know? That marriage never happened," Josh said.

"What?" Hallie swung her head to him. "But you never told me that."

Both Claire and Hallie stared at Josh, equally stunned.

Josh gave a good-natured shrug. "Just found out myself when he came back to town last week. You knew as much as I did until then."

Hallie's cheeks were red as she stared at her fiancé. "But . . . but . . . why didn't you tell me?"

"Didn't think it really mattered. None of us ever knew his fiancée, and we had RSVP'd no for his wedding because you planned that trip for us to Vermont."

Hallie caught Claire's eye. It was a story that Claire remembered, Hallie purposely making sure that she and Josh wouldn't be available that weekend.

Josh tipped his head. "Why do you care so much?"

Gabe, who knew all about Amy's heartache, gave Claire a funny look.

So Logan was a single man. But did Amy know this? Claire could only raise her eyebrows at Gabe, silently communicating her confusion.

"I care because I thought we told each other everything," Hallie sputtered to Josh.

"Well, we've had a lot more important things going on in the past few days than worrying about Logan's breakup," Josh pointed out. "Besides, that was years ago. What does it matter?"

Hallie opened her mouth and then closed it, but Claire knew why, of course. It mattered because Amy mattered. Because if she knew that Logan hadn't gotten married, then this would give her hope.

Maybe false hope.

But their sister's welfare now seemed like the last thing on Hallie's mind when she blinked quickly. "I just find it weird that you didn't mention he was back in town. Or this."

Josh widened his eyes and gave a shrug, as if he wasn't sure what he'd done wrong.

"Did you know that he's now working for Mom too?" Hallie asked.

"What?" Claire gasped. "I didn't know this! Who told you?"

Hallie turned to Claire, her cheeks blotchy and pink. "Logan told Amy. I talked to Mom and confirmed it."

"I didn't know that."

"Seems that there is a lot we don't know," Hallie said.

Claire and Gabe exchanged a nervous glance. She wondered if Gabe was finally regretting his offer to come here tonight.

It was too late to bail now. The instructor came through the door wearing a dress with a sweeping skirt and heels. Claire had expected a young woman and for some reason found herself relieved to see an elegant woman, well into her seventies, with a lithe frame. Frowning, she wondered why she cared. Would it have really mattered if Gabe was around an attractive woman who was a better dancer than she was?

She realized that it would have mattered. A lot. And not just because she didn't like being the worst at something—because she liked being held in high esteem by Gabe.

Unlike her sisters, he was never confused by her motives, never hurt by her best intentions. He saw the best in her. And that . . . that was something she should be aware of. Gabe was a friend, sure, but she knew from watching Amy suffer that sometimes even friends could let you down.

She glanced at Hallie, feeling a wash of guilt come over her.

Sometimes sisters could too.

The instructor introduced herself and then, using Josh, demonstrated the waltz. It seemed simple enough, but still, Claire almost wished she could pull out her phone and take notes. She would have, too, if she didn't think that Gabe would tease her.

She watched instead, trying to memorize everything as she'd once done with her vocabulary words for SAT prep, but when the instructor turned on the music, everything seemed to leave her mind.

Gabe opened his palms to her and tipped his head. "Shall we?"

She stared at his arms and then his face, the one that she'd come to know so well, to look forward to seeing every day, that always brightened her day, no matter how bad it might be going.

With more trepidation than she wanted to feel, she stepped toward him, placing one hand in his, stiffening a little when his hand slid around her waist.

"You know it's okay to let me lead," he said, his voice teasing. "If you don't, we'll end up like your sister over there."

Claire glanced at Hallie, who seemed to be struggling with Josh, each moving toward the other at the same time. Each stepping on the other's feet.

She turned back to Gabe and grumbled, "Lead the way."

He wasted no time in pulling her tighter, making her breath catch against her now pounding chest. He moved with ease and confidence, and she had no choice but to follow, a little clumsily but steadily enough.

The last man she'd danced with had been her father, and that had been when she was little, around the kitchen, using his feet for guidance. She swallowed against the memory, tucking it firmly back into place, and forced her mind back to the present.

Gabe must have sensed her taking a step back because he tightened his grip on her waist. "Remember, we can't both lead," he teased.

Claire swallowed hard, nodding. She felt tense, out of her element, and eager to lessen her anxiety. "I didn't realize that you know how to dance."

"Sure do. The salsa, the tango, even," Gabe said, leading her into an awkward twirl. "The waltz."

"But . . . but . . . you never told me!"

He pulled her back in. "There are a lot of things you don't know about me. This just happens to be one of them."

She narrowed her eyes at him, feeling a little unsettled. "Are you telling me that you haven't been completely open with me?"

"I've been plenty open! We share a lot. More than I do with most."

She nodded. "Same here," she muttered. But not everything. She just hadn't thought that he'd been holding back too.

"Ow!" From across the room Hallie cried out, drawing the attention of both Claire and Gabe.

Claire watched as Hallie's cheeks flushed a dark red and she muttered something to Josh, who muttered something in return, eventually leading the dance instructor to walk over to demonstrate once again.

"Yikes," Gabe whispered, his voice husky and warm in her ear.

Yikes was right. Claire used her sister's outburst as an excuse to take a step back from Gabe. She felt her breath steady with relief.

"In order for this to work, one must lead," the instructor was saying. "Not two."

Gabe's eyes met hers, twinkling merrily. Before he even spoke, she knew what he'd say. "You really want to lead, don't you?"

She fought back a smile. "It would seem that in this case, I can't even if I wanted to."

"Then you'll just have to trust me," he said, pulling her closer and expertly sweeping her across the floor to the music.

Trust him. But how much?

"We're going to head down to the pier for a drink. You're welcome to join us," Claire offered when the hour was up. It was an olive branch, and one that she was extending before Gabe could beat her to it or worse—later tell her that she should have asked.

Because it was the right thing to do. And, Claire realized when she said it, it was what she wanted. To laugh with her sister, relax, and enjoy her company. It was something she hadn't done in so long, and she had only herself to blame, not just because of what happened last summer but because she hadn't made time for it, long before that.

Not surprisingly, Hallie shook her head, but the reasons didn't seem to be about the tension that lingered between them. Her cheeks were flushed, her eyes bright, but not in a happy way, judging from the frown she wore, and there was a decided pinch between her eyebrows.

"I should get back home," she said. "It's a busy week, and I still have to work tomorrow."

"How often is your sister in town? It could be fun!" Josh cajoled, giving her a little bump with his elbow.

Hallie shook her head more firmly. "I'm tired. I just . . . want to go home."

Claire knew not to push, but the other part of her wanted to—drinks had sounded like a good idea in lieu of the dance class, but after what she'd just experienced the past hour, she needed some distance from Gabe.

But going back to the house would only confine them further. Sharing a bedroom, a bathroom, pretending that they were romantically involved in front of her mother and Amy. No, drinks it was.

The bar was just across the street and down a bit. It was crowded, but they managed to find a table on the patio, looking over the water. Like at their usual happy hours in their favorite bar around the corner from the office, Gabe ordered a Guinness, and Claire asked for a glass of white wine, extra chilled.

"Cheers," he said when their drinks arrived. "To vacation."

She gave him a look over the tops of their glasses. "You know this is not a vacation. It's a family wedding. And you have now witnessed the tension for yourself."

Something was going on with Hallie, and Claire couldn't chalk it up to prewedding jitters, not when Hallie had never grown out of her wedding obsession, unlike the rest of them.

She'd talk to Amy about it tonight or tomorrow. See if she'd picked up on anything. But then, Amy was probably too focused on Logan to worry about Hallie right now.

"Okay, then, what are we toasting to?" Gabe looked at her questioningly, and for once, Claire felt at a loss for words.

"To getting through the week," she said. "Between this ruse, Logan being back in town and single *and* working for my mother, and Hallie still being upset, it will almost be a relief to finally see her walk down that aisle."

"How about we toast to a happy ending to the week," Gabe proposed.

She raised her glass. "I'll drink to that."

She took a small sip and set her glass back on the table. A pause that wasn't normally so awkward stretched between them. Even during walks to their favorite lunch spots, they could blame lapses in conversation on concentration—their minds were always on work. But here, it felt different. Strange. "So . . . when was your last vacation?"

"I was just thinking that," he mused. "Do long weekends count?"

Like her, Gabe worked many hours. She couldn't recall the last time she was in the office and didn't see him there.

"In our cases, yes."

"I think I went skiing last winter," Gabe mused, eyes narrowing in thought. "Or maybe that was two years ago . . ."

"It was two years ago," she told him, relaxing into their usual banter. When he looked at her sharply, she shrugged. "Remember? You were dating that girl from the gym for like . . . a week . . . and the firm was closed for a holiday on a Monday."

He nodded as the memory came back. "We broke up on the drive back." They both laughed. She'd remembered that, too, but didn't feel like pointing it out.

"Is she the girl who taught you to dance?" Claire asked.

He shook his head and took a long sip of his beer. "No, that was a long time ago. A different lifetime."

"But you joined the firm when I did."

"This was before that. My law school days."

Ah. They rarely talked about those days. And she preferred not to think about them. When her father passed she threw herself into studying more than ever, because thinking of him, of her family and the life they once had, was just too painful.

Eventually, all that energy became routine. A habit.

Maybe a safety net.

"I didn't leave much room for fun in law school."

But it seemed Gabe had at least made time for dancing.

"Let me guess. You joined some ballroom dance class to meet the ladies," she joked, imagining a younger Gabe, even younger than when she'd met him.

"Actually, it was for one lady." He cleared his throat, all hint of a smile now gone. "My fiancée at the time insisted on it."

She stared at him, waiting for him to tell her he was joking, keeping her on the hook, that he'd learned by watching *Dirty Dancing* one too many times—another movie she'd mentioned in passing.

But his eyes were flat, his mouth resigned. He took another sip of his beer while she stared at him.

"Wait. You were *engaged*?" When he just nodded, she remained staring. "But . . ."

"But I never told you?" He didn't seem bothered by this. "It was a long time ago, and I don't see any point in talking about it."

"But . . . but . . . that's sort of a big deal, Gabe." More than a big deal. A huge deal. An enormous part of his life that he had left out, maybe purposely.

But then, she thought, she was guilty of the same, wasn't she? Leaving out major parts of her life because talking about them hurt too much.

And didn't change the outcome.

"Not really." He shrugged. "It was years ago. We didn't get married. I moved to New York. I started at the firm. And you know everything else after that."

She knew things before that. Where he grew up. How he got that scar on his chin. What he always wanted for Christmas and finally got. The dog he'd loved so much that he still kept a framed photo of him on his bedside table, years later. Even though she'd never seen his bedroom. Or the inside of his apartment.

Taking things too far from the office, other than lunch or happy hour, would be taking things from professional to . . . personal.

But Gabe had just gotten personal.

If Gabe could have failed to mention that he was once engaged to be married, what else was he keeping from her?

CHAPTER FOURTEEN

Amy

Amy's phone rang before she had even gotten out of bed the next morning. She'd stayed up late, looking over seating charts, relieved to see that Logan wasn't bringing a guest, even though she knew that didn't really reveal anything about his personal life. Just because he hadn't married his college girlfriend didn't mean he hadn't met someone else in all these years. Just because he wasn't listed with a plus-one for this wedding didn't mean he was single either. He could have someone in his life who couldn't make it this weekend on such short notice. Or maybe he'd just started dating someone, and it was too new to bring it up. She'd gone round and round until she'd finally called Michelle for a distraction, a reminder of her real life, the life that was hundreds of miles from Driftwood Cove.

The life that didn't include Logan. Hadn't for some time.

They'd chatted about the wedding plans, about Hallie's insistence on honoring tradition literally rather than subtly, and about Amy's future employment options. By the end of the call, Amy was reassured that she'd feel better by Monday, when she was back in Boston, meeting Michelle for coffee, and getting her new job search underway.

She just had to get through this week first, and then she could focus on the rest of her life.

But now the phone was ringing. The day had started. Wednesday. Meaning they were down to three days before the wedding. There was still so much to do, and she of all people could not show panic.

She reached for her phone, hidden under the papers she'd scattered on the empty side of her double bed, and felt her heart race when she saw the name.

All this time, she'd wondered if he still had her number. If he'd deleted it.

"Hello?" she asked, her voice hesitant as she sat up in bed, fully awake.

"What are you doing today?" came the smooth voice, as if they talked on the phone like this all the time.

Before she could respond with the litany of items that were on her agenda, he said, "I think I found a band."

"What? Already? But I just dropped you off at your house like—" She pulled the phone away to check the screen.

"Fifteen hours ago," he said.

"I can see you used your time wisely," she said, hearing the smile creep into her voice. A day ago she might have been annoyed. Thought that he was overstepping. But now she felt the comfort of his support. He wanted this wedding to be the same success she did.

"I had a few ideas in mind, so I made some calls when I got back. An old buddy from college isn't too far from here, and he makes the rounds, playing at town events, the occasional hotel lobby."

They were desperate. Not that she'd tell Hallie as much, but it was Wednesday, and most of the better musicians would have been booked out for the weekend for months.

"I know what you're thinking," Logan said. "You're thinking I should have let you handle it. I know you're planning this, but I just wanted to help. If you don't think he's any good, no hard feelings. He still has his day job."

"Which is?"

"He's an accountant," Logan said flatly. She waited to see if he was going to tell her he was joking. "Or maybe an actuary."

Amy sighed internally. "I know Josh asked you to help, so you can't let him down."

"No, but I thought you should check the band out first, seeing as you are the wedding planner. I can pick you up," he offered. "Can you be ready in an hour?"

She caught her reflection in the mirror that hung over her dresser. Pillow creases lined her cheek, and her hair looked like it had been caught in a windstorm. But she couldn't say no. And not just because Hallie was counting on her.

"I'll see you in an hour," she replied and tossed the phone onto the bed before groaning into her pillow.

It was just professional. A problem potentially solved, thanks to Logan.

But there was a bigger problem. The feeling that swelled in her chest.

Reminding her of what she'd once wanted. And maybe still did.

"Well, you're all dressed up this morning!" Claire said pertly when Amy came downstairs forty minutes later, knowing that she'd need a coffee before she began her day, and not just because she was starting it with Logan. She sat beside Gabe at the dining room table, laptops and files covering the surface.

Amy looked down at her jeans and soft ivory sweater. Had she taken extra time with her hair, giving it a little curl at the ends? So what? She was here on business. Meeting with vendors. Planning the best wedding that this town had ever seen. She had to look the part. If she was back in Boston, she'd be wearing a smart wool crepe dress with a matching blazer, not something as casual as . . . cashmere.

"Have you seen Mom around?" Amy asked. She'd hoped to have a nice little chat with her mother last night about how Logan came to be working for the family and how long Bunny planned to keep that arrangement. And why Logan of all people was required for the job, when her mother knew just how heartbroken she'd been over him.

"I saw her this morning before my run," Claire said. "Sounds like she'll be in and out all day getting everything ready for the guests arriving tomorrow. She said she didn't want to disturb us."

"Mom certainly has wedding fever these days," Amy remarked.

"Disturb us from *work*," Claire said, sliding a glance at Gabe and then abruptly pushing back her chair. "I think I need a refill. Are you getting a coffee?"

"Looks like I'm not the only one working on this trip," Amy mused when they were both alone in the kitchen.

Claire shrugged. "Gabe and I weren't able to cancel all of our meetings to come here. But we still made time for fun last night. It's too bad you didn't come to the dance lesson."

Amy said nothing as she reached for a mug and filled it.

"Josh told us about Logan," Claire said, never one to dance around a subject.

"Which part?" Amy asked.

Claire hesitated. "I don't know how much you know . . ."

Amy almost laughed, even though none of it was very funny. "Don't worry. I think I know everything, unless you have even more to share?"

"So you know he never got married," Claire said tentatively.

For once, Amy didn't mind her sister's bluntness. She sighed and said, "I just found out yesterday."

"And how do you feel about that?" Claire asked, looking at her frankly.

Amy felt flustered as she opened the fridge, which had been stocked since her mother's arrival, and found the carton of cream. It was strange, talking to Claire like this. Even though her sister knew the long history of her friendship with Logan, it had been a long time since they'd confided in each other.

Still, if she couldn't talk to her sister, then who?

"I don't think it really changes the outcome, does it?" she asked, knowing that Claire would be honest in her response.

Claire gave her a sad look. "But if you'd known—"

If she'd known. How would her life have been different? Would they have kept on being friends while she waited for him to give any indication that he saw her as something more or watched as he fell in love with someone new?

"There's no sense playing woulda, shoulda." She splashed the cream into her mug and set it back on the counter. "He didn't choose me, Claire."

Just saying the words still hurt, stirring up the pain that had seared so deep and lasted so long.

She'd held out hope for years that one day he'd say the words, echoing her own feelings. And when he made the announcement that he was getting married, when her future felt suddenly so determined, so bleak, it was as if her entire world had stopped. The only other time she'd felt that way was when her father had his heart attack.

When she learned that there were no guarantees in life. That the future wasn't always what you thought it would be.

"He didn't choose me," she said again, forcing herself to face the cold, hard truth. "He only ever saw me as just a friend."

"What do you think about him working for Mom?" Claire asked.

Amy just raised her eyebrows. "Why do you think I wanted to know where she was? A little warning would have been nice."

"I can't believe she didn't tell any of us." Claire looked at her strangely. "What is Logan doing for Mom, exactly?"

Amy shrugged. "Helping out with the properties, I guess."

"And you're okay with that?"

"I would have liked some advance warning, but, yeah, I . . . think I'm okay. I've had five years to get over him." Even if seeing him again was stirring up all kinds of feelings. It was inevitable, she supposed, like being back in this house, surrounded by old memories, reminded of the person she used to be.

"I just want to make sure at least one of my sisters is all right," Claire said.

"What's that supposed to mean? Wait." Amy gave her sister a stern look. "Did you and Hallie fight again last night? Is that why you wished I'd come? To be your buffer?"

"Hardly!" Claire said, stepping back. "You know I've been on my best behavior." Seeing Amy's skeptical expression, she insisted, "I have!"

Amy managed a small laugh. "You're trying, I'll give you that much. And none of us expected you to come for the entire week. Hallie may not have said as much, but I know that means a lot to her." Frowning, she realized that if Claire wasn't worried about her relationship with Hallie, she must be worried about something else. "Is something else going on with Hallie?"

"Well, I was going to ask you that. She seemed . . . stressed last night. At the dance lesson."

"Well, the wedding is just days away, and she had to push up the date," Amy said with a dismissive smile. "Show me a bride who wouldn't be anxious right about now."

"I know." It was clear that Claire had no intention of refilling her coffee and that, as expected, she'd followed Amy in here to have some girl talk.

Amy didn't mind. Once they used to talk like this all the time, but after their father died nothing had really been the same with Claire. She'd taken it hard, having been a daddy's girl all her life, the one who aspired to be successful in business like him, who respected any advice he doled out, who thought he could do no wrong. She hadn't cried at the funeral, or in the days before or after. Instead she'd shut down. Closed herself off.

And maybe, eventually, Amy had, too, in a way, but not until a few years later, after her second heartbreak. Now Amy was just as guilty of throwing herself into work as Claire was.

She understood. It was an easy escape.

Claire's gaze was thoughtful. "It just seemed . . . it seemed like there could be a bigger problem. With her and Josh."

Amy's eyes grew wide. "A problem between Hallie and Josh? That's just what you want, isn't it?"

"That's not fair," Claire shot back. "I never said that."

"You hinted at it, and you didn't mince words." Amy set her coffee mug down before she spilled it. "Claire, you know Hallie and Josh. They're best friends. They're soulmates. They're just like—"

She stopped talking, closing her eyes for a moment.

"Like you and Logan," Claire said softly. "I know."

Amy nodded, then swallowed back her emotions.

"Anyway," she said. "I was just with them yesterday, and everything was fine. Every bride gets nervous before her wedding, and Hallie has a lot more to worry about than most. She realized right before she went to the dance lesson that we don't even have a band lined up."

Claire's brow knitted as she slowly nodded. "That's probably what it was, then," she said slowly, only she didn't sound convinced. "Maybe we should all go out tonight. Girl time. It might be our last chance before Hallie's life changes forever."

Amy stared at her sister. "That is surprisingly optimistic of you, Claire!"

Claire gave her a playful swat. "What do you think?"

"I think," Amy said, "that your boyfriend has had a positive influence on you."

Claire's cheeks reddened. "I mean about taking Hallie out tonight. I didn't see any kind of bachelorette party on the itinerary."

No, that wasn't on Amy's list of wedding-planner duties. And as a sister, it was something she'd overlooked. She'd been so focused on the cake and the flowers. On what she'd do with herself when she returned to Boston.

On Logan.

"Let's do it," she said, giving a firm nod. Amy looked at her watch, her heart skipping a beat when she saw the time. "And speaking of bands, I'm about to go see if we might have found one in the nick of time."

Gabe ducked his head around the entry to the kitchen. "There's someone here named Logan for you, Amy."

The look that passed between him and Claire told Amy that he knew the entire sordid story, and she was too flustered to be embarrassed about that.

Logan hadn't just pulled up front. He had come to the door. He was in her family house.

Like the old days.

Giving her a very pointed look, Claire walked out into the hall crooning, "Logan Howell! I heard you were back in town."

Amy gulped back half the mug of coffee, which had gone colder with their talk. What she really needed was a shot of liquid courage, but seeing as it wasn't even ten, much less five, and she had very important work to do today, that probably wasn't a good idea.

Of course, spending her day with Logan probably wasn't a good idea either.

The accountant slash actuary slash wedding singer was nothing like Amy expected. The meeting location was about a twenty-minute drive outside town, during which she kept conversation neutral, discussing the wedding and the things that still needed to be done.

"I have three other guys with me usually, but it's Wednesday, so—"

"They're at work?" Amy guessed.

"Once we thought music would be our full-time gig, but life has a funny way of changing plans on you," the guy joked.

Amy glanced at Logan. You could say that again.

"I already know your work, but maybe you could play one of your CDs for Amy," Logan suggested.

"Sure." The musician stood up and started riffling through some stacks on his desk. Then he stopped and picked up his guitar.

"You know that there's only one way to see if this music really works," the bandleader said. His mouth crooked into a smile. "The question is, Will people dance to it?"

"Oh." Amy released a nervous laugh. "Well, the first dance song is . . ."

But the guy started playing the first few notes before she could finish. She looked from him to Logan, who was smirking. "You told him the first dance song?"

"It was a wild guess, but I remember you and Hallie always saying that you'd want to dance to the same song as your mother did at her wedding."

Amy flushed, feeling foolish at admitting such a thing so openly, especially when she'd once imagined dancing to it with Logan at their own wedding.

"Well," she managed to say. "You can't go wrong with Sinatra. I'm just surprised you'd remember something silly like that."

"It wasn't silly," he said. "And of course I remember. I remember everything." His gaze was steady on hers, and she felt the heat rise in her face, forcing her to look away.

The tension building between them was as loud as all those years of silence. She motioned to the singer. "This sounds pretty good to me."

"It does, but I think he's right. Should we see if it passes the test?" He waggled his eyebrows as his mouth twitched.

She froze, then stared at him. He couldn't. He wouldn't. But he was. Why?

"You don't mean . . ."

"That we should dance? Since when would you turn down an opportunity to try something new?"

Since you broke my heart, Amy thought. Since you fell in love with someone else. Since I lost my sidekick, my best friend. Since all those adventures, however small, ended.

"You do owe me," he said, giving her one of those wide-eyed looks that she never could resist. The look he used to give on those cold, blustery days when she'd rather be inside than out but he couldn't resist the call of the water, convincing her that it was the best time to go, that they'd have the beach all to themselves. And she'd agree, because the thought of it just being the two of them was all she needed to hear. Anytime. Anywhere.

"For what?" she asked.

"For not dancing with me last night." He gave her a pointed look.

She felt her cheeks color. "I told you. I had to get home."

And home was where she should be now, not here, not feeling tempted by something that didn't hold the same weight for Logan. To him it was just a dance, two good friends enjoying each other's company.

And to her it was so much more. Even though it shouldn't be.

Sensing that this time he wasn't about to take no for an answer, she stepped forward and took his hand, the same warm, steady hand that used to help her onto the old sailing boat his father let him use sometimes, the same sure strength that made her feel like nothing bad could ever happen to her, not when he was around. She moved into his arms and felt her body close to his. It was an embrace not unlike others that they'd had over the years, long, hard hugs when they'd gone for a while without seeing each other.

His hair still tickled her cheek when he pulled her tighter. His body still felt like it was molded to hers, such a perfect fit, her perfect match. And just for this moment, just for now, she let herself dare to fall. To enjoy the warmth of him, the closeness, and that need that had always been there, the emptiness in her heart that was made just for him, momentarily filled.

CHAPTER FIFTEEN

Hallie

By the time Hallie left work that day, she had lost track of the number of guests who had stopped to wish her congratulations, or ask about how the plans were coming or details about her honeymoon. There were reassurances about the weather, comments on her engagement ring, and all the usual general good wishes that came with getting married.

"What did you decide on for your first dance?" one asked kindly.

"'It Had to Be You.'" She barely managed to whisper the name of the song that she had always thought was so romantic, so old-timey, a classic Frank Sinatra tune that stood the test of time. Just like their marriage would. Just like they had, all these years.

Now the song felt like it would haunt her forever, bringing up images of her stepping on Josh's feet, and then he hers, and then their noses bumping, not once, but twice!

"Just think. The next time you come into work, you'll already be a married woman!" Susan Park confided with a wink and a little wrinkle of her nose, the result of so much Botox it made it impossible for her to emote on any other part of her face, so every time she smiled only her nose proved it was genuine.

And the words were genuine. Well intentioned. Heartfelt. But they didn't make Hallie feel anything other than nervous.

Jitters, she told herself as she drove home, even though she couldn't stop thinking that she was leaving the Harbor Club for the last time as a single woman. That from now on, they'd drive to and from work together. Every single day.

That everything would be the same in many ways. But somehow so different.

All the cars were at the house when she arrived, but instead of Hallie being greeted by her mother or the smell of something starting to simmer on the stove, both Amy and Claire came around the corner from the stairs, both wearing pink—even Claire.

"Don't even think about taking off those shoes," Claire said. "We're stealing you for the night."

Hallie stared at her sisters in disbelief. For a moment she wondered if this was an ambush, a last-ditch effort on Claire's part to have it out, convince her to not go through with the wedding, or postpone it. But then she realized Claire was smiling, and Amy too.

They were supporting her, participating not just in the wedding itself but in the events leading up to it. And she couldn't help but feel a little more relaxed by their enthusiasm.

"But I'm in heels!" Not to mention the stuffy shift dress she usually wore to work.

Amy and Claire glanced at each other, and after some silent communication of eye reading and shrugging, both nodded.

"Okay, but you only have five minutes! No trying to get out of it by running off or saying you have plans with Josh," Amy teased. "This is our last night alone as just us girls until you officially become a married lady who has to get home to her husband."

"Don't say that!" Hallie hadn't even realized her tone until she saw both of her sisters' eyes widen. Swallowing hard, she took a breath. "I mean, don't say that I won't make time for you. It's not like you guys ever visit anyway."

Surprisingly, it was Claire who raised her eyebrows and then nodded. "Fair point. I don't visit very often, and I . . . feel bad about that. But we were just joking, Hallie."

Hallie studied her older sister. Claire didn't joke. She was too serious for that.

"Are you sure everything's okay?" Amy asked carefully.

Hallie gave a tired smile. "I'm fine. It was just a busy day at work."

"Which is why we're going to go out tonight and have a few drinks," Amy said firmly.

"What about Mom? Shouldn't we stay back and keep her company?"

Claire shook her head. "When I saw her this morning she told me that she's having dinner with the Goodwins tonight. And Gabe is going out with the guys. When Amy told Logan about our plans for tonight, he and Josh invited Gabe out with them."

"You and Logan, huh?" Hallie asked, arching an eyebrow at Amy.

Amy rolled her eyes. "He found a band for your wedding. I went along to make sure they were okay. You'll love them, by the way," she added.

"I'm sure I'll love anything you decide," she said, realizing that she still hadn't even heard about the cake design yet because everyone had been so busy all week.

"You have no excuse, Hallie," Claire said.

"That's rich coming from the queen of excuses," Hallie replied, but she felt pleased. Warmed by the way Claire was making an effort. By a glimpse of the sister she'd missed so much, not just this past year but long before that.

"And I for one could use a couple of glasses of champagne," Claire added.

Hallie cut a glance at Claire. Somehow she couldn't picture her older sister indulging in one too many glasses of champagne and having fun. But then, up until today she hadn't seen her in a pink shirt since they were kids either.

She nodded, feeling a little more excited about the evening ahead. "I'll be back down in a minute. Should I put on pink too?"

"If I'm wearing it, you're wearing it," Claire said.

For not the first time this week, Hallie's heart softened toward Claire. If even Claire could show up for her, then what reason did Hallie have to worry about something like a first dance?

Amy announced that she'd chosen the place and already secured reservations. A place where they were sure not to run into the guys, she said with a wink, and Hallie exchanged a glance with Claire as they stepped out of the car and looked around the small downtown of Driftwood Cove.

Clearly, Amy wasn't up for another run-in with Logan, and Hallie didn't blame her.

"Oh, the place on the corner?" Claire asked hopefully.

Hallie swung around to see what Claire meant. It was one of the posher places in town, a step up from the many casual seafood joints that served food on paper plates or in plastic baskets, and anchored worn wood picnic tables to their back patios.

Hallie and Josh had tried all of those, making a point of keeping their scoring system to themselves until they'd gone through the list.

In the end, their top picks were the same.

Once, that had been enough reason to think that it meant that they were perfect for each other.

"You okay, Hal?" Amy looked at her with concern.

"Long day at work. Difficult people," she added.

Amy looped her arm through hers. "All the more reason to put the day behind us and start the night off right. The first round is on me!"

She linked her other arm through Claire's. "The rest of the rounds are on Claire."

Hallie felt a genuine laugh slip out at the look on her older sister's face.

"Why? Because I'm a lawyer?"

"And here I was going to say because you're the oldest," Amy said.

Claire could only shake her head. "No problem. It's the least I can do." She slid a glance at Hallie, and for a moment Hallie let her guard down, sensing her regret, if not for her words, then for at least saying them.

Hallie decided to let it go. To stop thinking about the words that had haunted her ever since they were spoken. To stop being mad at her sister. At Josh. Even herself.

"It's been so long since we've done anything like this," she said, hearing the sadness in her voice even though her heart hadn't felt this full in so long, she hadn't even known it was missing something.

"Not since, what . . . the Christmas before last?" Amy looked at each of them for confirmation.

Hallie thought about it properly. It must have been. They'd been in Boston then. Josh had been there, of course, but he'd gotten a headache and gone to bed early, leaving Hallie and her sisters to stay up late that Christmas Eve, much like they used to do as young girls, only this time older, and with eggnog.

For a long time after that, Hallie remembered thinking that had been the best Christmas ever.

It sure beat this past year, when she was alone with Josh and his parents at their ski chalet in Vermont.

She knew that was part of being a couple, trading off holidays, but she longed for the energy and noise that came with more people. As sweet as Josh's family was, they weren't her family.

But soon they would be. Officially.

"I hear good things about this place, so it had better live up to its reputation," Amy said.

It was a new place in town, a wine bar, set up with small tables anchored by flickering candles, a trellis overhead giving the outdoor patio a cozy European vibe, the sound of the waves crashing against the rocky shoreline reminding them that they were in Rhode Island, not France.

Amy ordered the first round, sparkling rosé for the table, and a cheese board in case they were hungry.

Claire held up her glass in a toast. "To sisters. And for this wedding that brought us all back together again like old times."

It was generous, and Amy gave her a nod of approval. But Hallie could only focus on the last words her sister had spoken. Like old times.

Did she mean eight years ago, before their father's sudden death? When the big old cottage on the beach was filled with laughter and music and good food and activity every chance they had? When they could still tell each other anything without fear of judgment? When her sisters were the first people she turned to when she needed to feel better about something?

She clinked her glass against the other two and swallowed back the wine against the lump building in her throat.

"So . . . tell us more about Gabe," Hallie said, eager for the opportunity to finally tease her sister. "We haven't had a chance to interrogate you yet."

"We're far too polite to do that in front of him." Amy nodded dramatically.

"Unlike Mom, who had to share embarrassing stories?" Claire shook her head.

"Those memories were some of my happiest ones of the three of us," Hallie admitted quietly.

Amy gave her hand a little squeeze. "Mine, too, Hallie. Sometimes, it feels like just yesterday that we were three young girls with our entire lives ahead of us. Sometimes I can't imagine feeling that hopeful again."

Hallie couldn't either. Her entire life hadn't felt wide open in a very long time. She'd preferred it that way. Less uncertainty. Less risk of hurt or disappointment. More guarantee of holding on to things just the way she'd liked them.

But people still changed. Look at Claire. Try as Hallie might, she'd slipped away.

"Besides," Amy said, giving Claire a teasing look. "I think Gabe liked hearing those stories. And now you need to share some in return."

"What's there to say?" Claire took a long sip of her drink. "You've met him. And you all probed him that first night, in case you didn't think I noticed."

"He's cute," Amy said.

Claire shook off the compliment, but it was clear from the way she didn't meet their eyes that she was secretly pleased. "He's a great guy."

"Better than that guy you briefly dated in college?" Amy squinted at the memory. "What was his name again?"

Claire's eyes flashed. "Not the one with the ferret?"

Amy whooped in laughter, and Hallie joined in, even though she wasn't sure she'd ever heard this story. Probably because she was too young to have paid attention, or to have been the appropriate audience.

Or maybe because she was off with Josh.

Amy turned to her and said, "Claire met this guy. Said he checked every box. Handsome. Well dressed. Top of his class. He was premed."

"Architecture," Claire corrected. She shook her head and reached for a piece of cheese. "He was perfect on paper."

"Until she went back to his dorm," Amy said, sputtering on a laugh.

"He started kissing me on his bed, and as we leaned back, I thought his sweater was coming around my neck—"

"No!" Hallie laughed, straight from the belly, and oh, it felt good.

"Oh yes." Claire nodded. "It seemed he forgot to mention his little pet."

"He forgot to mention a lot of things," Amy said, nodding.

"Like the girlfriend back in his hometown, who came for a surprise visit the very next weekend?"

"No!" Now none of them were laughing. Amy tsked under her breath. "Was that what turned you off dating?"

Claire looked down at her glass.

"No, definitely not," she said, giving them a shrug. "I guess . . . my priorities just changed."

Change. There was that word again.

"What about you, Amy? You must have a bad dating story or two," Claire chided.

Amy made a show of thinking about it and said, "Okay, there was this one guy. Blind date. Should have known. But I walked into the restaurant where we were meeting, and I was pleasantly surprised. Thought, okay, this has some potential."

"Uh-oh." Hallie's eyes darted to Claire's, wondering if she knew how this ended, too, but she seemed as intrigued as Hallie.

"Next thing I know, he starts crying," Amy said. "At first I thought, Are you serious? Am I that disappointing? But then he started telling me how I looked just like his last girlfriend. The one who had just dumped him three days ago!"

"Did he at least pay for dinner?" Claire asked.

"Oh, there was no dinner. He said he was too upset to eat!" Amy hooted. "I had to order my own wine while I listened to his problems and then finally put him in a cab to go home." She shook her head. "Honestly, I almost didn't mind listening to him talk about his problems. It just took my mind off my own."

Hallie raised her eyebrows. Wasn't that the truth?

The women laughed lightly, but then the conversation turned silent. This was where normally Hallie, as the other person at the table, would share her horror story, but of course she didn't have one, because the only guy she'd ever dated was Josh.

Claire, never one to miss a thing, said, "See, it's a good thing that Hallie found Josh so she was spared these types of moments."

Amy lifted her glass. "Let's play a game."

"A game?" Claire looked doubtful. "Are you going to pull a deck of cards out of your bag?"

They all shared a smile then, remembering how their father often did just that, shuffling the pack and then dealing out the hand while they sat on the patio, waiting for dinner to finish cooking in the oven, or sometimes even at the Harbor Club, their dinner already finished, their parents enjoying a cocktail until the sun set. It was always rummy, and somehow, no matter how often they played it, they always forgot the rules, making up new ones as they went along.

"Do you know that Gabe has a completely different way of playing rummy than we do?" Claire said.

"Gabe . . . ," Amy said suggestively. "We still haven't talked about Gabe very much. All the focus has been on Hallie."

"Please!" Hallie said a little eagerly. "Let's talk about Gabe."

"He's quite a babe," Amy added, laughing.

"Stop. He's just my—" Claire quickly reached for her glass.

"He's just what?" Hallie glanced at Amy, wondering if she knew something that Hallie didn't. After all, she and Claire weren't close and hadn't even spoken for a year until this week. She hadn't even known that Claire was seeing anyone, let alone that it was serious enough to introduce him to the family.

"He's just a good, solid guy," Claire finished, but the way she was staring at the candle flickering on the table instead of looking up at them made Hallie think there was more that Claire had to say about Gabe.

"Well," Amy said. "Onto the game. We'll drag more out of you before the night is through."

"What's the game?" Hallie asked with interest.

"Never Have I Ever." Amy explained the rules. "I'll start. Never have I ever . . . kissed someone from work!"

Hallie, being obviously engaged to the boss's son, whom she saw every single day at work, took a sip of her drink. Both Amy and she stared at Claire, who was staring at them blankly.

"Claire, pay attention. If you've kissed a guy from work, you have to take a sip."

Still, Claire just blinked at them.

Hallie chuckled and looked at Amy, who seemed perplexed.

"Earth to Claire. I don't say this often, but you are the most intelligent of us three. You work with Gabe, don't you? Then drink up!"

"Oh!" Claire's cheeks turned nearly as pink as her shirt. She took a sip from her glass, a rather long one, and plunked it back on the table. "Sorry. Must have spaced out."

Hallie gave Amy a funny look. Since when did Claire "space out"?

"I'll go." Claire tapped her fingers together, then gave a sly grin. "Never have I ever lost or quit a job."

"That's easy. None of us has."

"Actually . . ." Amy looked nervously up at them as her fingers inched toward her glass.

Claire gasped, but Hallie felt horrified. "Since when?"

"Since recently?" Amy took a small sip, then wiped her mouth. "I didn't want to worry you. It actually worked out perfectly so I could devote all my time to making your wedding as beautiful as possible!"

Hallie felt a flush of guilt. Her sister had given up her time when she could've been working for pay to help her plan a wedding that Amy seemed more excited about than Hallie did these days.

"You didn't—" A horrible thought took hold. "You didn't lose your job because my wedding was such short notice, did you? Because I called in a favor?"

"No," Amy assured her, but she'd hesitated before she spoke, and Hallie wasn't entirely convinced. "There was no upward mobility, and it was time to move on. This just gave me the push I needed. Really, I should be thanking you. You did me the favor."

"But—you always loved your job," Hallie said.

"I did. I do." Amy didn't look entirely convinced that losing or quitting her job had been for the best. "But it hasn't been working for a while, and I don't think I realized that until now. My boss brought in her niece recently. I thought I'd eventually move up and become a partner, but now I see that it was never going to happen, no matter how many clients I brought in or how many hours I worked. Her niece doesn't have any of the same qualifications, but . . . she's family, so she gets the job."

Hallie closed her mouth and stared at the center of the table, but she could feel her sisters exchange a glance.

"I didn't mean anything by that," Amy said quickly.

Hallie nodded, but her face was on fire, and she couldn't even look at Claire, knowing what Claire thought about her job at the Harbor Club, how she'd earned it based on who she was—or rather, who she was dating—rather than experience or qualification.

"I mean, you do an excellent job at the club. It's different." Amy took a shaky breath. "I really put my foot in it."

"No, it's fine, really. I mean . . . there's no denying I only got the job because Josh and I were going to get engaged, everyone knew it. It was only a matter of time." Hallie gave a nervous laugh, but she felt the backs of her eyes prickle. She pleaded with herself not to cry. She'd held it together until now. She just had to hold it together for three more days. She'd feel better once the wedding was over. Once she was married.

To a man she couldn't even dance with without stepping all over his feet and he hers.

"Refill?" she asked tightly, and then topped off all their glasses with the remainder of the bottle. She took a long, slow sip until she had steadied herself.

"I suppose the next one is on me, then," Amy said. "Never have I ever kept something from my dear sisters."

Hallie's and Claire's eyes met. "Well, you kept the part about your job from us," Claire pointed out.

"But only because I didn't want to worry Hallie. And I only brought it up now because I've been feeling more . . . optimistic."

Claire narrowed her eyes. "About your job prospects or about something else?"

"Or *someone* else," Hallie added. "Seriously, Amy, Logan's in town. And he never got married. And you two have been spending quite a bit of time together."

"Only because of you," Amy protested. "Anyway, now you know about my job. And you all know about Logan. My life is an open book. Can the same be said for the two of you?"

Hallie glanced at Claire, who wasn't saying anything.

"We haven't had many talks like this in a while," Hallie said. "We haven't had a chance to confide in each other."

"I miss that," Amy said, looking a little emotional.

Hallie and Claire exchanged a small smile.

"Me too," said Claire, surprising her.

Hallie felt her spirits bloom with the exact thing she'd just thought she'd lost long ago. Hope. Not for her wedding day, or the day she'd walk down the aisle in her mother's dress. But for a chance to get back to the way things used to be. For all of them.

"My turn," Hallie said. "Never have I ever . . ."

She swallowed hard, trying to think of what to say, knowing it shouldn't be so difficult. But there were so many things she hadn't done that it felt impossible to nail it down to just one. Never had she ever gone on a girls' trip. All her vacation days and weekends were spent with Josh. Even as far back as when they were in college. Never had she ever had a job interview, because she'd gone straight from graduation to working at the Harbor Club.

Never had she ever had a bad date. The only guy she had ever dated was the man she was marrying in three days.

Suddenly, all she could think about were all the never-would-she-evers. All the things she'd never do or experiences she'd never have because her path was already clear, had been for some time, and she'd chosen to follow it.

"Hallie?" Amy set a hand on her wrist. "Everything okay?"

"Of course! Everything is fine. More than fine. It's . . . perfect."

But it wasn't. And she wasn't so sure how much longer she could pretend that it was.

CHAPTER SIXTEEN

Claire

The house was quiet when Claire came downstairs the next morning, having passed by both of her sisters' closed bedroom doors. She was used to it; she'd always been the early riser in her family, always up with the sun, if not sooner, seeing no point in lying in bed, staring at the ceiling, or closing her eyes against reality, trying to fall back into dreamland.

Besides, it wasn't like she could do that now, not when she had set up camp with Gabe. He'd already been asleep when she'd gotten back last night, a little tipsy, not that it helped her sleep any better. Like her, he was quick to rise—quicker, actually. With the exception of the first morning, he'd been up before her each day since they'd been here, his place on the floor neatly folded up, hiding any evidence of strife or deceit. It was no surprise—most days he beat her to the office, and there was no denying that the promise of seeing him each day made it easy to toss back the covers even on the coldest of winter days.

Today, though, she didn't have to go far.

She stopped in the doorway to the kitchen when she saw Gabe standing over the coffee machine.

"Don't tell me," she said. "You can't figure it out?"

"Guilty as charged," he said, stepping back.

"It's new," she said, giving him an easy excuse, even though Gabe wasn't one of those guys who worried about protecting his ego. "Probably a wedding gift."

"They're arriving by the dozen," Gabe said, referring to the boxes that were stacked high in the front room. All from friends and family who wanted to celebrate and support the happy couple.

Or not-so-happy couple, Claire thought.

"That reminds me," Claire said, groaning. "I haven't bought Hallie a gift yet."

Gabe's eyes widened at her, but she was quick to defend herself. "She's the one who pushed up the wedding! And I still have time." But not much.

Sensing that Gabe still wasn't buying the cause of her delay, she said, "I'm here to support my sister." In any way. If she decided to get married, Claire would do her duty and stand by her side. But . . . if Hallie was having doubts, then Claire was here to listen.

Last night had been fun, like old times in many ways, but Hallie had seemed quiet by the time they'd left the bar and headed home.

Maybe she was just tired, Claire told herself. But she struggled to believe that completely.

"What do you have in mind for the gift?" Gabe asked.

"I'll know it when I see it," Claire replied. Something off the registry felt a little impersonal, given their relationship, but something more personal felt almost hypocritical, given her feelings about the union. "But first. Coffee."

Claire brushed by Gabe as she approached the counter, the usually large space suddenly feeling cramped and tight, even though they were the only ones there. She kept her eyes trained on the machine, on the process that Gabe had already started. Suddenly being alone with him, standing so close, made her feel . . . things she couldn't explain. Or define. Things she just knew she shouldn't feel.

Gabe was her friend. Her closest friend, really, even if he did point out that they never spent real time together outside the office. The office was her entire world, her entire life.

Only now, stepping back from the machine as it started to brew, filling the kitchen with its heavenly scent of fresh coffee, she knew that wasn't true, really.

She had a family. This house. Memories that she'd pushed away.

Even if some were best forgotten.

Gabe pulled two mugs from the cabinet, handed her one, and said, "So today is the day the festivities kick off."

"Yes, all the nosy aunts are descending upon us," she said, shaking her head. "They mean well, but they also forget that I'm not twelve. Last year at Hallie's engagement party they asked about my job as if it were a new hobby I'd just picked up, not something I'm actually trained and qualified to do."

"Oh, it can't be that bad!"

She slid him a look, not matching his amusement. "Trust me. It is."

"Then what do you say we get out of here for the day?"

Claire had planned to work as far into the afternoon as time would allow her, but now she saw that Gabe had a point, that the house would be chaotic today as the door opened, people and luggage filed in, and room after room was filled with new energy.

Nosy aunts asking questions. Gabe having to ramp up his fake-boy-friend act.

"I do need to buy that gift," she said, seeing a good excuse to leave.

"Perfect." Gabe nodded. "You can give me a guided tour of this town."

"The guided tour?" She was skeptical, but one glance out the window at the shining sun and the blue sky made her think otherwise.

The best way to get around town was by bike—too many beaten paths weren't accessible by car. Claire knew that her mother would never get rid of the old collection of cruisers, and she doubted that Hallie had, either, and not just because she was glued to tradition at the expense of forging her own path.

After they'd had their coffees, she led Gabe out to the detached garage, which was mostly used for extra storage.

"You do know how to ride a bike, don't you?" she asked, as she pulled open the large door.

He dipped his chin at her. "Who do you think I am?"

"I'm not so sure," she said, with a shrug. "I'm beginning to wonder if I know you at all."

He gave her a funny look. "How could you say that? You know everything about me!"

Did she, though? She didn't see him on weekends, or evenings, although they both put in such long hours that she imagined all he did was go home and drop into bed just to get up at dawn the next day and back to the office. Sure, she heard all about his weekend activities, which ranged from jogs in Central Park, to dates that ended badly, to the occasional baseball or hockey game with an old buddy from college who was passing through town.

She thought she knew him. Now, she wasn't so sure. Maybe she just saw what he was willing to share.

"And what is it you want to know?" he asked, closing the shed door behind them.

She walked her bike alongside his, over the bumpy lawn and toward the driveway. There was a lot she could ask, she supposed. Silly things, like his favorite color, even though she was sure it was blue. But then, didn't most people prefer blue? Or his favorite food, but again, that was easy: it was sushi, technically a spicy tuna roll, and again, that didn't matter.

What she really wanted to know was more about this woman whom he had once imagined sharing his entire life with. What she was like. What made her so special.

And why it had ended.

"Well, you still haven't answered my question, and I don't know if you can ride a bike," she said, shutting down any chance of discussing his past. It was clear he didn't have more to share on the matter either. At least not with her.

"Oh, I can not only ride a bike, but I'll race you into town," he said.

"I thought I was the tour guide!" She clambered to get onto her bicycle seat and start pedaling faster than he could, but he was swift, and the devilish grin he tossed over his shoulder made her heart speed up from more than the exercise.

She pushed that rush of emotion away quickly, digging into her pedals with more force, until she had passed him by, too far for him to have any hope of taking the lead again.

"You trying to lose me?" he called out, his voice getting lost in the breeze.

She didn't reply, because he wouldn't have heard her even if she did. The wind was in her face, the air filling her lungs, as she charged forward, putting distance behind herself and Gabe and that house—and all the feelings it stirred up.

"One thing you definitely don't know about me! I have a killer sense of direction!"

It was true, she didn't know that about him. But she knew these streets. The town. The best places to go.

And she could pedal faster and outrun anyone if she tried hard enough.

They rode all the way to town, Gabe sailing past her once the storefronts were in sight, and eventually slowing down so she could catch up, riding side by side on the empty roads, single file when a car came along. It didn't take long. Only fifteen minutes, and it was a path Claire knew well, one she had traveled dozens if not hundreds of times over the years.

"My sisters and I used to ride our bikes into town." She was out of breath by the time Main Street approached and they ditched riding for walking. The streets were as congested as the sidewalks, and her legs were tired.

"We'd come in for ice cream," she said, motioning to one of a couple of casual spots on this stretch. She smiled, thinking back on those days she'd taken for granted, assuming somehow that they'd just always be that family, that their traditions and routines would last forever. "Feels like a long time ago now. Like I was a whole other person."

"From what I hear, you were." Gabe raised an eyebrow when they parked their bikes in a nearby rack. There was no sense in locking them up. Tourists had no use for them, and most locals had their own two-wheeled means of transportation.

Claire gave him a rueful look. "I was wondering how long it would take you to bring that up again."

His grin reached his eyes. "I was hoping to save it for the next partner meeting, but I couldn't resist. The image of you in a wedding veil just won't escape me."

"Very funny. I'd have thought it would be nearly impossible for you to picture me as a bride."

"Easier than you might think."

He glanced at her, his eyes locking with hers a second longer than usual. She felt her heart start to hammer as she looked away for a distraction, something to ground her.

She gestured to the bakery up ahead. "We could grab a coffee. Some bagels, maybe?" A memory of going into town with her father to collect a baker's dozen of bagels hit her sharply, straight in the chest, stealing her breath for a moment. Those days were so ordinary, but so special too.

"I'm enjoying just walking for a little bit," Gabe said.

Pushing back her emotions, Claire focused on the man in front of her. The man who wasn't part of that other life, only her current one.

"Happy to be out of the house?" She gave him a knowing look. "Just wait until Aunt Marcia starts asking when we're having babies."

Her cheeks flamed. She couldn't believe she'd just said such a thing!

"Oh, I think I can handle your family," Gabe said easily, clearly not as disturbed by that image as she was. "I had a really nice time with Josh and Logan last night."

Claire had been waiting to ask about this, even if a part of her wasn't sure she wanted to hear Gabe's opinion on the guys.

"Josh and Logan aren't my family," she clarified.

He shrugged. "Josh will be soon enough."

"Please tell me that they didn't interrogate you," she said, feeling nervous. Gabe was having too much fun with this ruse, and there was no telling what he might have said.

He cocked an eyebrow. "Don't you trust me with my responses?"

She didn't, and not just because of their fake relationship. You couldn't trust anyone. Not entirely. Not even the person closest to you.

"What did you think about Logan?" she asked. "Did he say anything more about my sister?"

Gabe shook his head thoughtfully. "No. She didn't really come up. We mostly talked about sports. Life here in Driftwood Cove."

"Did they happen to mention anything about the house?" she asked slowly.

"Beachnest Cottage?" He frowned at her. "No. Why?"

She stared straight ahead. She couldn't talk to her family about this. Not yet. Not when she hadn't figured out if there was anything worth discussing.

But Gabe—she could talk to Gabe about the house. He wasn't emotionally invested in the place.

"I came across some papers in the office," she said. "It was a letter from an appraiser. I get the impression my mom might have considered selling the house. Or maybe she still is." None of it made sense.

"I thought Hallie and Josh were getting the house?"

Claire nodded. "They are. That's tradition. And Hallie hasn't said otherwise." But then, she got the sense that there was a lot about Hallie she might not know.

"And Amy didn't say anything either?"

"No one has." Claire shrugged it off. "Maybe it was nothing. Maybe it had to do with insurance." It was possible, but her instinct told her otherwise.

They'd approached the water's edge now. The Harbor Club wasn't far in the distance, and the boats were out, enjoying a crisp, clear day with a light breeze.

"I'm sure it's nothing," she said, trying to reassure herself. She could go back into her father's office and have another look, but secrets had a way of coming out, didn't they? If Bunny was planning to do something with the house, Claire would learn the truth eventually.

"I'm probably just tired from being out last night," she added.

"It must have been late, because I didn't even hear you come in," Gabe observed.

He'd been asleep when she had, and she'd grabbed a cardigan and gone downstairs to sit on the porch until her eyelids were too heavy to fight anymore.

"It was . . ." She grimaced, moving her hands up and down, unsure if the good outweighed the bad.

"Claire! You promised," he warned.

Her eyes burst open to underline her innocence. "It wasn't me, I swear. I was on my best behavior."

"Scout's honor?" He grinned, but Claire looked at him suspiciously.

"Were you a scout?"

"Of course I was. Didn't you do that type of thing? I thought every kid did."

"Well, I didn't. And for some reason, I can't see you pitching a tent or starting a campfire with two sticks either."

He laughed, taking no insult. "I can do both of those things, actually. And we haven't even talked about my knot-tying skills."

Claire groaned. "Don't let Logan hear you say that. He'll invite you out on his dad's boat, and I'll never see you again."

"Would you miss me?" Gabe bantered, but there was something in his eyes, something that didn't quite match the mischief in his mouth, that made her pause.

She bristled. "Would you miss me if I got lost in these woods?"

"I wouldn't need to miss you," Gabe said simply. "I'd rescue you."

"I don't need a hero," Claire replied. "I'm perfectly capable of taking care of myself."

"So you'd rub two sticks together for a fire rather than let me help you?"

Claire turned to him. "Isn't it better not to have to need someone?"

"Sounds lonely, if you ask me," Gabe said, his gaze steady.

"Anyway, we're not talking about me," Claire said. "We were talking about my sisters."

To her relief, Gabe didn't push the topic. "So really, is everything okay between you and Hallie?"

Claire thought about it and admitted, "I don't know. I get the sense that there's something else going on that she's not telling me."

"You have a good read on people," he pointed out. "And she's your sister. You know her well."

Claire did know her well, and that was what had her worried. The Hallie she knew was sweet and optimistic, easygoing and good natured. But the Hallie she saw this week wasn't any of those things.

"It's probably just all the last-minute plans leading up to the wedding," Claire said.

But she had the distinct impression that Hallie was tense about something. And that, contrary to what Claire would have expected, it had nothing to do with her.

CHAPTER SEVENTEEN

Amy

Never have I ever. The thought lingered with her long into the night and extended far into the next morning.

Never have I ever. The list was long, and single-focused, spiraling rapidly with a laundry list that went back as far as that summer after college when Logan came back and gave her the worst news imaginable.

Never have I ever kissed Logan Howell. Never have I ever been proposed to or worn a diamond ring.

And that begged the question: Would she ever?

To hear Michelle call it, Amy could, if she was willing to put herself out there, and not just half-heartedly. But it was easier to bury herself in work, to find an excuse to stay in on the rare weekend nights that she wasn't covering an event.

Love wasn't supposed to be a struggle. It was supposed to be steady and true. The one thing that could be counted on when nothing else in the world made sense.

Logan had been there for her in her happiest, most carefree moments, and the darkest days following her father's death. He'd gotten her through that unbearable heartache—until he went and broke her heart all over again.

No. At this rate, she never would have a wedding of her own. Which was all the more reason to pour everything into Hallie's.

Amy had spent the morning going over her checklist, making sure that there weren't any last-minute items that needed tending. She called the manor and confirmed a change in chairs—gold would be so much more elegant and dramatic—and then started making some notes about the centerpieces. Hallie was out with Josh, and Claire and Gabe were nowhere to be seen either.

It was just as well. Amy had plenty to do today, and she knew that her mother did, too, preparing for a full house. All the spare rooms had been aired out, the linens changed, and fresh towels stacked in all the bathrooms.

When Amy stopped in the kitchen on her way into town, she saw her mother sliding two pies from Bittersweet Bakery out of their boxes and into ceramic pie dishes.

Bunny looked up guiltily when she saw Amy, but then laughed. "Think anyone will notice?"

"I think the only thing anyone will care about is the taste," Amy said. She braced herself for the conversation they were about to have. The timing wasn't the best, but it had been a busy week for everyone, and it wasn't going to let up until after the wedding.

"And here I thought it was the thought that counted," Bunny replied.

"Not when it comes to hosting a party, I'm afraid," Amy said. She helped her mother transfer the last pie into a ruffle-edged dish, bracing herself for the potentially tense exchange they were about to have. "Besides, this is a lot of work for one person."

"Oh, I don't mind." Bunny gave a tired smile, but she did seem content.

Bunny kept busy—more than busy, really—between running the business and sitting on endless charity committees. Was it any wonder she needed some help with the properties here in Driftwood Cove? And wouldn't she want to hire someone who not only understood the homes here but also knew the family?

Logan had stepped up when Amy's father died. Not just for her but for the family, by offering to run errands, drop off meals from his mother, and even mow the lawn for a while. It was his company that mattered to Amy. It was something she'd never forgotten.

Maybe Bunny hadn't either.

"I know you miss Dad," Amy said gently. "It's strange to think of him not being here for Hallie's wedding."

Her mother looked back at the pies—she was prone to seeking a diversion whenever her husband was mentioned.

"He's been gone eight years," she said with a sigh, as if that was that.

But Amy knew it wasn't. In all these years, Bunny hadn't considered dating, even though plenty of her friends in Boston tried to introduce her to handsome widowers or divorcés at their holiday parties and summer barbecues each year.

"Yes, but your daughter's getting married," Amy said, letting the words sit there. She couldn't believe she hadn't seen it earlier—how difficult this must be for her mother. She supposed that she was too wrapped up in her own feelings about the wedding and the nerves that it hit.

"She's getting married in your dress. And veil." She stifled a sigh. Really, if Hallie could have stuffed her feet into her mother's shoes, literally, she would have. Amy had certainly enjoyed looking through the family wedding album and playing bride, but for Hallie, it was the only inspiration she'd ever needed. "I have to think being back at Cliffside Manor will stir things up."

It had for her, after all.

Her mother pressed her mouth together for a long moment. No doubt thinking of her own wedding day. "I always suspected that Hallie would want to follow in my footsteps. She was so enamored with that album." She smiled, but it didn't quite reach her eyes.

"Well, you and Dad had a picture-perfect love story," Amy replied gently. "It can't be easy on you not having him here."

"At least I have you to keep me company," her mother said brightly, patting her hand. "And really, it's Hallie that I feel bad for. This wedding means so much to her, and she hasn't said it to me, but I know she wishes he were here to walk her down the aisle. I've been so busy between tying up loose ends with work and preparing for a houseful of guests that I think I've failed as the mother of the bride."

"Nonsense!" Amy shook her head. They were all doing the best they could. Even Claire. "I'm the wedding planner. I feel like I failed as a sister of the bride for not agreeing to plan the wedding in the first place. Maybe this mess-up could have been avoided."

Her mother gave her a long look. "Well, you were busy with work, you said . . ."

Amy could tell from Bunny's expression that she knew there was more to her reason.

"But you're here now," Bunny said quickly. "And that's what matters."

"Like Claire being here now?" Amy stared at her mother. Like Logan, this was another topic they hadn't had a chance to cover yet. This was their first time alone all week, and it might be the last opportunity before the extended relatives descended on them. "Gabe is certainly a surprise."

"In every possible way!" Her mother's eyes were bright with approval. "I've always worried about Claire, choosing to be alone like that." She looked at Amy. "I worry about you too."

"Is that why you decided to hire Logan to help out with the estate?" Amy tipped her head, giving her mother a stern look even though she couldn't stay completely mad at her. Not when her mother was already clearly struggling.

"If circumstances were different, I wouldn't have hired him," Bunny replied.

"You mean if he was happily married with two kids?"

"You two were such good friends—"

"Exactly," Amy stressed. "Just friends."

"But that was years ago," Bunny urged. "Circumstances have changed. Maybe hearts have too."

Amy hesitated, thinking for one glorious moment that she had a reason to hope for something more. But then she shook her head. That kind of thinking had led to a broken heart once before. And the fallout had cost her more than his friendship.

She'd shut herself off. From this house. From the people in it. From the possibility of more in her life.

"I'll always care about Logan. And I think he will for me too. But I have a life that I've built without him." Even if she wasn't sure what it looked like now that she no longer had her job to return to.

She fought back her anxiety, seeing the lines of concern in her mother's face.

Bunny nodded. "Just don't lose sight of the one you had before."

She knew what her mother was referring to—this house, which she never visited anymore. This town, which had once been her favorite place in the world. Even the simple pleasure of a beautiful wedding—all things she'd banished along with her hurt.

She hadn't just lost Logan. She'd lost so much else too.

"Well," she said, snapping back to it. There weren't many hours between now and the wedding, and certainly no more time could be spent thinking about her own love life. Or lack thereof. "I have to get to the florist. They're putting together a sample bouquet, and I need to sign off on it. Why don't I bring some arrangements back with me? For tonight?"

Her mother's face lifted. "Oh, Amy, what would we have done without you this week?"

Amy swallowed against the lump in her throat, knowing how easy it would have been to stay away. And how right it was to come back.

Amy had placed the flower order over the phone last week, but she felt better after meeting in person with the owner and seeing the nosegay in real life. The color of the roses perfectly matched the shade of the bridesmaids' dresses, and the berries that Amy decided to add at the last minute nodded to the start of the fall season without taking away any of the elegance.

Still, something was missing.

"Can you show me the vases you'll be using for the centerpieces?" Amy knew that this was one of the most overlooked details, by hosts and planners alike. It was a lesson she had learned the hard way, of course, like most things in life.

"We're going with round," the florist said. She pulled out a simple glass bowl. It was attractive and traditional, and it wouldn't compete with anything else on the table, including the flowers themselves.

But it wasn't a showstopper. It wasn't . . . perfect.

"I think we need something bigger in scale. Something higher on the table." Before the florist could protest, she added, "I know we don't want to block anyone's view, but I want the flowers to be noticeable when people enter the room, not an afterthought."

The florist didn't disagree, instead pulling a few options out of the back room, some more ornate than others.

Amy thought of the venue, the stone mansion high on the cliffs with a sweeping view of the sea, the formality of the quartet, and even the old-school band that would be keeping people dancing long into the evening.

"The gold," she said firmly.

It would be both traditional and unexpected. It would look beautiful with the color scheme. Her excitement started to rise when she envisioned it all coming together.

The florist raised her eyebrows but jotted the change in her order form.

"Oh, and can I get some small arrangements for another event tonight? I think four should be good," Amy said, so caught up in the vision of this wedding reception that she nearly forgot about the promise she'd made to her mother. "Nothing too fancy. We're having an outdoor family gathering at the house tonight. We'd like something to brighten up the yard."

"You can't go wrong with roses," the florist said. "I can do some mixed bouquets?"

"In the round vases?" Amy nodded. "I can pick them up in a couple of hours, if that works. I have some more errands to do in town."

The florist looked relieved to have some time to pull everything together. "Come back in a few hours, and they'll be waiting for you."

Amy tapped out a text to let her mother know the flowers for tonight were taken care of as she pushed out the door, and nearly into Logan's chest.

"Hey!" He looked so pleased to see her that she couldn't help but let her guard down, smiling back. He gave her a funny look. "Is there something you need to tell me?"

Amy felt heat rise up in her cheeks, and her heart began to pound so hard that she was sure he could hear. How did he know? She'd never let on, not back then. Not now.

But then she saw Logan point to the flowers she was clutching. She'd forgotten that she was holding the sample bouquet.

A nervous laugh escaped her. "Yeah. No. I'm afraid my love life has taken a back burner to other people's big plans." She glanced at him, knowing that she'd created an opening to ask about his personal life.

If she even wanted to know.

"I get it," he said before she could work up the nerve to ask. "I've thrown myself into work the past few years."

"It's the best cure for a broken heart," she said, referring to his own circumstances, but he just gave her a funny look.

"I guess we have a lot to catch up on," he said.

Amy nodded, even though she knew that there was very little to share on her end, and certainly not in the romance department.

But when he said, "I was just going to grab a lobster roll over at the Shark Shack if you have time for me?" she hesitated.

"It's a busy day, Logan—"

"But you have to eat," he pointed out. "Come on. We might not get another chance like this again."

She felt the weight of those words sink in along with the realization of the passing of time, and all that they'd already lost. She didn't want to go back to Boston with a broken heart again, or with the sense of leaving things unfinished between them either.

But she also knew that they'd never get back to what they once were. That this time she had to make peace with where they stood, say goodbye on terms she could live with.

"Okay," she agreed. "For old times' sake."

Because that's all they had. A shared past. No future. At least, not together.

The food hut was off the beaten path, known to locals and summer people only, people who didn't need any frills, just good, fresh catch done right. They settled on a picnic table overlooking the harbor, and both of them wasted no time digging in.

"Oh," Amy groaned. "That's good."

"You make it sound like you haven't had it in a long time."

She hadn't. And clearly no one had told him that. Or why.

"Not as much as I wish," she said, realizing now how much this was true. Wondering just how little she'd return now that the house would technically become Hallie's. When her sister and Josh had a family of their own, it wouldn't be like coming back to her second home anymore. It would mean coming to stay with Hallie and Josh.

Rallying herself, she said, "So, I hear the guys went out last night."

Logan shook his head. "I'm sworn to secrecy, if you're looking for details."

"What do you think of Gabe?"

"Like him a lot. Hope he'll join the family!"

This kind of phrase was nothing new, not coming from Logan, but that was just the problem, wasn't it? Logan wasn't a part of the family. He never had been, even though it felt like he was. He'd been there every summer and every break. Every day in between on the phone and by text and email. He'd been there for her father's funeral, sharing her tears. And now he would be here at her sister's wedding.

Josh would be family. Gabe might someday be too.

But Logan would only ever be on the fringes.

"Maybe he will," Amy said, thinking about Gabe. "He and Claire seem to really know each other, but then, they were friends for a long time before they started dating."

Logan was looking at her thoughtfully, his eyes warm and intense, just enough to draw her in and make her never want to look away.

"Do you ever wonder what it might have been like if the two of us had started dating instead of just becoming friends?" he asked.

Amy's hand stilled, and she swallowed against the pounding of her heart, which was so loud that she was sure that Logan could hear it too. But he was just grinning, casually, as if what he had just said didn't cut the deepest part of her.

As if he had no clue that she'd wondered that all the time, for years, even when she'd tried to stop because there was no point.

She wondered now—not for the first time—if things might have been different if she'd just told him how she felt. If he'd known that she saw him as more than a friend, more than a pal. But then she reminded herself that he'd never given her any reason to believe he saw her as anything but that.

"Do you?" she asked, her voice coming out raspy, as if she didn't dare ask the question any more than she could bear to hear the answer.

"Sometimes, sure."

She was aware now that she was staring at him, unable to say anything, not even play along with this hypothetical scenario because there was nothing funny or entertaining about it. This wasn't their normal banter; this was serious. To her, at least.

"There was always one thing that stood out, though," he said, with a shrug.

One thing that stood out? Or that stopped him?

"What's that?" she asked, giving him a look that she hoped passed for teasing, when really, her breath was caught in her lungs, as she hung on to whatever he said next.

"Well, if we dated and it didn't work out, then everything we had would be lost, ruined."

Her mouth felt dry as she nodded.

Logan gave her a wry look. "But then, I guess we lost what we had anyway, didn't we?"

"Logan—" she started, but he shook his head.

"No, please. I need to say this."

She stared at him, her heart pounding so hard that she was sure he could hear it as the rest of the world seemed to fall silent. Maybe this was it. The moment she'd waited for, dreamed of.

"I messed things up with us, Amy," he said. "You were the best friend I ever had, and I didn't know how to balance things." He gave her a look of such regret that she almost didn't notice the heavy disappointment in her chest. But it was there. Reality always crashed her back to the ground again, rooting her in her role.

She swallowed hard and set her sandwich down beside her. "Well, we were young."

"But we knew what we wanted," he said, searching her eyes. "Or at least, you did."

She stared at him, wondering if she should say something, if it even made sense now, after all this time, when he had a new life and she had hers, back in Boston. When they hadn't been close in five long years.

When feelings had changed.

Or maybe hadn't.

She could tell him, she knew. Right now. He'd opened the door, and all she had to do was step through it. *Actually, Logan, I was in love with you from the first time I saw you.* She wondered how he'd react to that. Surprise, she imagined. Maybe even laughter, assuming it was a joke.

Or maybe . . .

She stared into his eyes, thinking how easy it would be, that now was a perfect time, that she had nothing to lose. In three days, she'd be back in the city, the world she'd built for herself, the one without him in it. She'd go back to never seeing his name flash on the screen of her phone. Never hearing his voice. Never talking late into the night about nothing and everything all at once. Or maybe she'd hear from him now and then when he had a major life update.

Like if he met another girl he wanted to marry.

She'd find a new job; her life would once again become routine. She'd plan other people's special events and milestones instead of having any of her own.

Maybe she'd settle for a nice guy. Or maybe she'd hold out for that same connection that she and Logan once shared.

"I shouldn't have asked you that," Logan said, silencing her. "About how things might have been if we'd . . ." He didn't finish the sentence, but his words still cut.

"Romance complicates things," Amy managed to say; then, desperate to get off the subject of herself, to put all those feelings to rest, she added, "Claire's dating her coworker. How's that going to work out when they break up?"

"Who says that they'll break up? Sounds like some of Claire's cynicism is rubbing off on you," he said, the moment lost, his expression not showing the same regret she felt.

Or maybe it was just her own protective layer she'd built up over the years.

"Claire wasn't always so cynical. Life . . . changed her." She frowned, thinking of the smiling, bubbly girl who used to light up every time their father entered the room.

"You haven't changed," he said, stopping her in her tracks. He looked at her steadily, his grin wide, his eyes so warm and intense that it took everything in her not to reach out, pull him close, hold him in her arms and never let him go. She wanted to hold on to that smile forever.

But more than that, she wanted to hold on to how she felt when she saw it.

"Neither have you," she said softly.

CHAPTER EIGHTEEN

Hallie

The festivities were beginning. Officially or unofficially, things were underway.

They had been for some time, she reminded herself after leaving the town hall, marriage license tucked firmly into her handbag.

"Forty-eight hours," Josh said as they reached the car. The plan was to go straight to the house, where most of her aunts and uncles and cousins would already be. Josh's family would join as well, and there would be an informal cookout before the more formal events tomorrow.

Normally Hallie looked forward to these types of gatherings, when the old house was filled with activity. It was impossible to feel alone or sad or even worried when there was always someone around to talk to, cheer her up, or distract her from her problems.

It had been that way when her father died, all those years ago. One by one, the aunts, uncles, and cousins descended upon them, and despite the circumstances, all too soon they were smiling at memories and stories that others shared, learning new things about the man who was gone but somehow had never felt more alive.

She could only hope that the same energy would be felt tonight. That she'd feel supported and celebrated like she had on that sad day all those years ago. That she'd be distracted from all these little worries that were creeping up on her, keeping her awake at night. That she'd be reminded of why she was doing this. That their happiness would spread to her.

That she'd know, like before, that it would all be okay.

"Forty-eight hours. Imagine that." Hallie looked around the town, the very one that had been at least her part-time home all her life. She'd never questioned it before. Never wanted to trade in the harbor or the shoreline for city life, never minded that there was pretty much one of everything—well, with the exception of ice cream parlors and candy shops and other touristy-type places.

She'd liked her world small. But now she wondered if there was a better word for it. If it was actually . . . limited.

"I'm not sure I'm ready to get back to the house and deal with all the well-wishers just yet," she confided. Perhaps, she thought, that was the whole point of a big wedding. You were so busy tending to guests, greeting old relatives, and exchanging pleasantries that by the time it was over, you craved being alone with the one person you had promised to be alone with forever.

Only in her case, she was more worried about what would happen after they'd left. When the aunts and uncles and cousins went back to their lives, taking her mother with them. And her sisters too.

"We could take a walk?" Josh suggested. "I could use a coffee."

Hallie nodded, pleased that she felt as she did right now. That what she craved more than seeing her family or even her sisters was the comfort of her usual routine. The life she loved and the life she'd chosen. The person who was at the center of it all.

They walked down to the Salty Breeze Café, one of a few places in town that sold coffee and baked goods, but this was the local favorite. Like most of the establishments here in Driftwood Cove, it had been around for decades, and Hallie and Josh had been coming here since . . .

She laughed, stopping in her tracks. "You know, I never really thought about it before, but this is where we had our first date."

Josh gave her a funny look. "You never thought about that?"

She shrugged, feeling bad if she'd hurt his feelings. "I mean, only because we've always come here."

"That's the reason we always come here, Hal. Because it's our place. The coffee at the Atlantic Coffeehouse is way better, but this place is special."

She stared at him. "I don't deserve you."

His grin grew, but instead of smiling, Hallie was fighting back tears. She didn't deserve him. Not the quiet way he loved her, not the heartfelt way he cared. These were the things that were on his mind, even if they weren't vocalized. And if he had any idea what she'd been thinking these past few days or maybe even more . . .

It would break his heart. And that was the last thing she wanted to do. She never wanted to hurt him. Not ever. She loved him.

But she just didn't know if she loved him enough.

Enough to never live anywhere but within the confines of this small seaside town. To never work anywhere other than the Harbor Club, which they would eventually take over, becoming the new reigning Mr. and Mrs. Goodwin who were greeted with nods by the staff and shook hands with special guests in the dining room. They'd eat every Sunday night possible in the dining room, just like they had with Josh's parents for as long as she could remember. They'd follow the traditions of his family just as much as she had followed the traditions of hers.

They'd be living on the terms already put in place for them. Following in someone else's footsteps instead of carving a path of their own.

They stepped inside the coffee shop, and Josh ordered their usual, something that Hallie had always liked but now found a little irritating.

"How do you know I don't want a latte or a cappuccino?" she asked lightly when they had collected their paper cups.

"Because you always order an americano," he said simply.

Hallie was quiet while she fixed her drink the way she liked it. The way she always had it. Just as Josh had been quick to point out.

"But what if I wanted to mix things up?" she asked, pushing through the screen door and out into the sunshine. The ocean breeze was strong, blowing her hair back, as if trying to remind her why she loved her life here and why she should stop questioning it when she'd never done so before.

But that was the problem, wasn't it? That was what Claire had been trying to say to her, even if she had really bad timing.

Maybe Claire saw, all along, that eventually, Hallie would question her choices. And she just needed to be sure she did it before it was too late.

Josh didn't look fazed by her question, instead shrugging and taking a sip of his drink. "Then you should have just told me." He stared at her, his brow furrowing as the intensity in his eyes grew. "This isn't really about coffee, is it?"

She sighed. "Of course it's not about coffee. It's about all of it. Our coffee. The house. This town. Our jobs."

"Whoa." Josh looked at her almost sternly. "Our jobs? I thought you loved working at the Harbor Club."

"I do!" she insisted. She was growing so frustrated with herself, she could only imagine how she was making Josh feel. "Forget it. I don't even know why I said that."

"If you don't like your job at the spa, then I'm sure you can transfer to another part of the club, Hallie. And you don't even have to work there if you don't want to."

Up until now, she'd never considered that she had much of a choice. Never cared if she didn't. She'd been grateful for the job. Relieved by the clear, certain path that was their future. She'd looked forward to it.

"I like my job. Really. I mean it. I love it," she stressed. Then, with a little smile, she added, "Well, maybe not when Evelyn Steele comes in, but even then, it's not so bad."

"Then what are you saying? What's really going on here, Hal?"

Hallie sighed. "I don't know. I guess I never questioned our life here before. I've never stopped to think that every day will be more of what it's always been. That it will never be . . . different. That even our house won't really be our own."

"Is this about the house?" Josh was blinking quickly, looking at her with such confusion that she felt like the world's biggest jerk because she couldn't explain this to him any more than she could explain it to herself.

"Maybe. I mean, all this time, we just assumed things, right? Because that's just how it was. But I never even asked you if you wanted to live at Beachnest Cottage." She'd never even properly asked herself.

"It's a great house," Josh said. "And it's your family house. Doesn't it get passed down to the first child to be married as their wedding gift?"

"It does. But my mom said something the other day . . . how if none of us got married she would sell it."

Josh's expression matched her original surprise. "It makes sense, doesn't it? If you didn't want it, that would leave one of your sisters. Claire has way too much going on in New York, and Amy . . . she loves that house, but she never really visits." He stopped, looking at her carefully. "You do want it, don't you?"

"Of course I do. It's my home. I never thought of living anywhere else!"

But maybe that was just the problem.

"Come on," Hallie said, reaching for his hand. It felt warm and familiar and so right that she never wanted to let go of it. "Let's go home." She gave him a smile, a squeeze, a look that she hoped would let him know just how much she loved him and their life.

She just hoped that it could be enough. For both of them. Because what Claire said didn't just apply to her, did it?

If Hallie could be having all these feelings so suddenly now, just days before she walked down the aisle wearing the dress she'd always planned to wear to marry the only man she'd ever loved, then who was to say that one day Josh might not wake up and have the same thoughts?

And that was the part that scared her more than anything else. They were all each other had ever known. Their lives up until now had been easy. Perfect, really.

But if this past week had taught her anything, it was that nothing was perfect.

Hallie's breath felt shaky when she climbed into the car, and she was almost grateful for the distraction of so many people by the time they arrived at the house a few minutes later. Her family wasn't large; her father had two sisters, and her mother had been an only child.

Aunt Marcia was the first to greet her, pulling her into one of the long hugs that she was known for, the ones that made you feel like you couldn't breathe until she finally released you. The ones that almost hurt.

She managed to answer all Marcia's questions, the kind that were to be expected, about the wedding plans, the flowers, the honeymoon, and, of course, Claire's new boyfriend.

"Looks like you may not be the only one tying the knot," Marcia said with a waggle of her eyebrows. She had a glass of sangria in her hand, and Hallie was beginning to suspect that it wasn't her first.

"Do you mean Claire?" That would be a surprise, but then, so was Claire showing up with Gabe at all. Finding out that they'd known each other for years. That they worked together too. That like her and Josh, they spent all day, every day together—something Claire had implied in the past was limiting Hallie's horizon.

"I wouldn't rule her out just yet," Marcia said. "When you find the right one, suddenly your mind is open to experiences and plans that you'd never even considered before. Suddenly the world is just . . . wide open. Love can take you anywhere."

Or nowhere. In Hallie's case, love was keeping her right here, in Driftwood Cove, in her childhood bedroom. Drinking coffee that wasn't the best in town. Working at the very place they'd first met.

Seeing the need to mingle, Hallie squeezed her aunt's hand and then walked across the grass, toward the porch that was filled with faces she knew and loved, people who were here only because they were happy for her. Because they wanted the best for her. Because they wanted to celebrate with her.

"It's the beginning of your new life!" her uncle Ned exclaimed after she'd given him and Aunt Pam a hug.

A new life. But was it? It was really just the same life.

"I just wish that your father had been here to see it," Ned mused, earning him a hard nudge from his wife.

"It's okay," Hallie said, even though it was very far from it. She was the bride, this was her wedding weekend, and the only tears that should be shed were happy ones, right? "I feel that way too. But I'd like to think he is here, in some form. At least in spirit."

She wanted to think that, at least. But she knew that if her father was watching down on her, somehow, he'd send her a sign. Help clear this fog that she couldn't seem to make her way out of.

"Of course he is," Aunt Pam said so firmly that Hallie could only love her more for saying it. "And, of course, he just loved Josh."

It was true. Her father *had* loved Josh. And it gave her comfort to know that her father had known the man she was going to marry.

Something that Claire would never be able to say.

Only for the moment, that didn't bring her any satisfaction. The anger that she'd carried for her sister all year was fading, and in its place was a sense of nostalgia, a longing for the way their relationship used to be. Maybe could be again, even if it would never quite be the same.

They hadn't just grown apart. They'd also grown up. And that part, she supposed, was just inevitable.

"A new addition is just what the family needs," Pam said. "And, of course, what's better than a wedding to bring everyone together?"

"I can think of a few things," Hallie's cousin Jenny said, patting her baby bump. Hallie had it on good authority that it was a girl, and due in January. But she could still remember Jenny shoving her dolls into the old umbrella stroller when they'd come to visit, taking them for walks, then changing their clothes and settling them in for naps under the shade of the old willow tree.

They'd never been especially close—Hallie had her sisters for that. But now Hallie was hit with a feeling of the passing of time. It seemed crazy to think that Jenny was actually having a baby now. Even though she'd been married for years, it felt like she was playing house.

Much like Hallie felt at times.

"What better way to start your year." She greeted her cousin with a careful hug.

"You've got a full house," Jenny remarked.

It was full. By now, everyone would have settled into their rooms, the younger cousins in the front living room and on the pullout couch in the office Bunny still used. Hallie had offered to room with her mother, but Bunny insisted she keep her room, being the bride and the guest of honor. With only two spare bedrooms in the house, accommodations would be tight.

"Having fun yet?" Jenny asked as she sipped her juice.

"Oh, it's . . . exciting, that's for sure."

Jenny leaned in and whispered, "Now you know why I eloped."

"I heard that, young lady!" Aunt Pam said, rolling her eyes. "At least Hallie is giving us all a good wedding to enjoy!"

Hallie gave a nervous laugh, but she suddenly felt a little sick.

"Of course, our side of the family doesn't have a beach house to host everyone," Pam said. Then, giving a wistful sigh, she said, "Your father sure did love this place."

Hallie gulped, afraid for a moment that she might tear up. She could picture her father now, sitting on the deck, watching the waves, unloading the trunk on their first drive up for the season, giving one last glance in the rearview mirror every time they left for the school year.

"At least your mother knows she has you to pass it down to," Ned told her. "Isn't that how things work in her family? The house is given as a wedding gift to the first child of the generation to be married?"

"You're a lucky girl, Hallie!" Pam marveled, opening her eyes wide.

"And I know that your mother can't wait to start shopping for baby clothes."

Baby clothes? Sure, she and Josh had vaguely talked about kids someday—more like assumed that they'd eventually have them. But baby clothes? She was only twenty-five!

Only twenty-five. Claire's voice echoed in her head.

"Mine too," Josh said, coming up to stand beside her. He slipped a hand around her waist, but this time, maybe for the first time, she stiffened.

"Oh, that's a long way away." Hallie gave a nervous laugh. Josh, however, was frowning. She swallowed hard. "But it would be nice to have one down the road. Or two."

"One or two?" There was an edge to his tone, one that implied he was only still smiling because they were not alone.

They'd vaguely talked about kids, but it was always someday. A distant thing. When they were settled. When they were older. There were other things to talk about: the house, their jobs, their honeymoon, the wedding.

She'd assumed it would, like everything else, just work out in due time. Fall into place. But now, she wasn't so sure.

"Two. Maybe a dog. Or two." She laughed loudly, shrilly even. It didn't sound like her, and she saw the funny look pass through Josh's eyes.

"Three can be a crowd," she told him, shutting that down right now. He knew that as much as she loved her sisters, they hadn't been close in years, and that sometimes when she was younger and still at home and her sisters were in college or law school, she felt like they shared a bond that she didn't.

"Oh, I wasn't thinking three," he said, and for a moment, she sighed, thinking that she'd really overreacted, that really, her doubts and worry were getting to her. That she should just relax and enjoy the night. Really!

But then Josh said, "I was thinking . . . five."

Her eyes must have surely popped enough for everyone looking to notice. "Five?" Gone was the smile. In its place, she was sure, was a gape, one that matched the blaze in her eyes, because this was far from funny, far from banter, and far from appropriate conversation to be having in front of—

Oh. But her aunt and uncle had scurried off.

She looked back at Josh. *"Five?"*

He shrugged. "Why not five?"

Hallie knew that if she spoke, it might come out as a scream. Why not five? Why not six? Or ten?

"Kids are a lot of work."

"And a lot of fun. And we have this big old house with all these rooms to fill. And we've always talked about having kids."

"Kids, yes. But five kids? We never discussed that."

Her heart was pounding so hard that for a moment she felt like she might pass out. The house was large. But the rooms were already filled with Claire's bed and books and Amy's dolls, and the walls were lined with family photos that she never wanted to take down.

Or replace.

"We have a long time to decide," she said, not wanting to continue this conversation right now, on the lawn, when anyone might overhear them. She forced a smile when she caught Josh's mother's eye and gave a little wave.

Josh, however, hadn't said anything more.

Didn't he agree with her? They'd never not agreed! Not on where they would live or where they would work or even where they would take their honeymoon.

But that had all been predetermined, hadn't it?

Whereas this . . . this was the one thing that was all their own. A family of their own. A future that they decided . . . when and how.

And for the first time since she'd met him, long before they'd ever even gotten engaged, she wondered if she and Josh had the same vision for the future at all.

CHAPTER NINETEEN

Claire

The house had slowly filled with aunts, uncles, and cousins all day. The bedrooms were filled to capacity, and the front two rooms of the house were laden with luggage and bedding. The backyard was lit with torches to ward off bugs, and the strings of lights that draped from the porch had been flicked on even though the sun still shone low in the sky. A long buffet table had been set up and filled, and everywhere Claire looked, she saw someone she knew.

"Who are we hiding from?" Gabe whispered in her ear when they finally stepped outside a solid thirty minutes after the party had started, and only after the noise through the bedroom window made it almost worse to stay inside.

Claire skimmed her eyes over the guests and kept her voice low. "Those two teenage boys over there are my cousins. My mom's cousin is their father, and he's a great guy, too, so long as you don't mention baseball. You'll never get away from him." She looked over her shoulder at his amused expression. "No, I really mean it. He'll tell you the history of the Red Sox until everyone's gone to bed, and even then, he'll suggest you take the conversation inside."

"Something tells me that by living in New York, I'm an easy target."

She raised an eyebrow. "You're an easy target because you're here with me."

Gabe laughed and walked over to the drinks table to get a beer. Claire, feeling more anxious than she had that first day in court all those years ago, stuck close by, pouring a glass of wine with a heavy hand, then taking a large gulp, both for liquid courage and because of the realization that someone was bound to comment on the size of the pour if she didn't.

"That's my aunt Pam down by the picnic table," she continued. "And . . . oh dear." Claire started to back up, straight into a wicker coffee table, and nearly lost her footing before Gabe grabbed her by the arm and pulled her upright. Her eyes darted to the left and then the right, but it was no use.

"Claire!" Uncle Jeffrey had reached the top of the porch stairs and pulled Claire in for a bone-crushing hug before she had time to duck or run.

"Uncle Jeffrey," she managed to grunt. Over his shoulder, she could see the whites of Gabe's eyes.

Finally released, she took a moment to collect her breath before giving a light hug to her aunt Marcia and turning to Gabe. "This is Gabe. Gabe, my aunt Marcia and uncle Jeffrey."

Aunt Marcia's eyes went wide. "So this is the famous Gabe? Everyone was wondering when we'd meet the man who finally stole Claire's heart." She gave a look of approval. "We were disappointed you weren't at the house when we arrived. But imagine our surprise when we learned that you had met this strapping man!"

Beside her, Gabe coughed on his drink, and Claire swallowed a sigh.

"It's been a busy week for our family, as you can imagine. Gabe and I were running errands in town all day."

"Oh, it all makes sense now. I'm sure the two of you were eager for some alone time." She waggled her eyebrows, and her husband just gave a loud guffaw.

Gabe, however, used the opportunity to slide a hand around her waist and pull her a little closer. "You couldn't be more right," he said, then grinned down at Claire. "Isn't that so, Claire Bear?"

Claire Bear? Claire felt her eyes blaze, but Gabe's smile just widened before he nuzzled her hair. She stiffened at his touch, but he didn't release the hold on her waist, and her heart rate was struggling to come down at the contact. She knew she should probably snuggle closer and play the part, but she felt frozen in place instead.

Aunt Marcia clasped her hands at her chest and all but swooned. "Claire Bear! Isn't that the sweetest? And do you have a special nickname for Gabe?" She blinked at Claire expectantly.

Gabe the Babe was what came to mind, not that Claire would be saying that. "Oh, plenty."

He took the moment to lean in—and for one heart-stopping moment she thought he might actually kiss her. Right here on the lawn in front of everyone. Her chest seized with panic, and her breath caught in her lungs. He was close, so close. His breath was on her face, his skin almost touching hers, until it was: nose to nose.

He rubbed against the tip of her nose, his eyes gleaming against her glare.

"Oh, I can't. I just can't with these two!" Marcia was crooning. "You know, Gabe," her aunt confided, setting a serious hand on his elbow. "We were beginning to think it would never happen for Claire."

"Is that so?" Gabe glanced at her.

Claire was eager to take back control of the conversation. "So, Aunt Marcia—"

But her aunt kept her eyes trained on Gabe and said, "I'm sure you know that you have tough competition when it comes to our Claire."

"Oh?" Gabe looked at her with interest, but she just gave him a shrug to convey her own confusion.

"For a long time, we weren't sure if she was chained to that office!" Uncle Jeffrey hooted.

"Actually, Gabe and I work together. He's an attorney too."

"Oh! Is that so? Bunny must have forgotten to mention that part," her aunt said, looking miffed.

They were saved from further interrogation by her uncle Ned, calling from the grill, needing an extra set of hands.

"Duty beckons," Marcia said, grabbing her husband by the shirtsleeves. "It can't be easy for your mother, handling all this on her own."

Claire managed a frozen smile, reminding herself that her aunt was just being kind, even if it stirred up memories and feelings that were best left in the past. "Not at all! My mother loves nothing more than a full house."

"Only it won't be her house much longer," Marcia pointed out.

For a moment Claire wondered if she knew something that Claire didn't. News about the house. Details on the strange envelope that Claire had found tucked away in the desk drawer.

But then she realized her aunt was referring to Hallie. Of course!

"It will always be her home," Claire corrected her. "Hallie would always want her here. She's a lot like my mother."

In many ways. But not, Claire hoped, in all.

She didn't even realize she was holding her breath until her relatives finally crossed the porch, out of earshot.

She stepped back from Gabe's hold on her and took a long sip of her wine.

"I think we need a code word," she said, realizing that she might need to leave if things got too weird.

"A code word? What are we, twelve?"

She gave him a pointed look. "You know what I mean. And trust me, you'll thank me for it. So, what should it be? What's our excuse to leave?"

The glimmer in his eyes told her that she should have known better. "Hanky-panky? Pillow talk? Or how about a good old-fashioned—"

"Stop." She gave him a hard look to show how far from funny this was for her. "Our code word will be *big day*."

"That's two words," Gabe said, clearly enjoying this.

"Big day," she repeated. "And trust me, you'll be using it."

"Oh, I doubt that." Gabe looked relaxed as he stood, looking down from the porch. "You're not having a tiny bit of fun?"

She scoffed. "No, I don't call this fun. I call this stressful. I'd rather be at work, pulling an all-nighter, with that crappy takeout from the diner around the corner."

They'd spent many a night like that. Too many, to hear her relatives' opinions on her commitment to her career.

"I would too," he admitted, but his gaze lingered on her for a fraction longer than usual, making her heart speed up.

She opened her mouth, trying to think of what to say, when she saw her aunt Pam turn and wave eagerly in her direction.

"Code word," Claire blurted. "I mean—damn. What is it again?"

But it was too late. Aunt Pam had hitched her long, flowing skirt and was making her way up the steps, calling out to Claire while her gaze remained firmly on Gabe.

"And here is the happy couple!" she cooed, leaning in to give not Claire but Gabe a big, long, lingering hug.

Claire raised her eyebrows at him, waiting to see if he'd be ready to bail, but he just played along.

"I hope you had an easy drive from New Hampshire," Claire told her aunt. "It must have been a *big day*."

She shot a look at Gabe, but he seemed determined to ignore it.

"Oh, not as big as tomorrow will be. Or Saturday!" Aunt Pam saddled up closer, wedging herself between Claire and Gabe. "Now, Hallie and Josh aren't the ones I'm interested in. I'd much rather hear all about the two of you. Will wedding bells be ringing again soon?"

Ten minutes later, Claire had endured one more round of questions that put the worst trials she'd been in to shame.

"I used the code word," she whispered to Gabe from the corner of the porch she'd managed to escape to, after another long and chatty conversation with Aunt Marcia, whose eyes had never been wider and whose head seemed to steadily bob rather than nod. Marcia had hung on Gabe's every word, even though it was unclear whether she was actually listening or just taking in his dark hair and deep-set eyes and wondering just how long it would be until he dropped to one knee and slid a ring on Claire's finger.

Last summer, Marcia's head had consistently slid side to side instead of up and down while she tsked and clucked, as if everything about Claire's life was just sad and not meeting with her approval.

"It seemed a little too soon into the night," Gabe replied.

True, the sun had started to set, and there was a glow over the yard, enough to almost make Claire relax, tell herself it would all be fine.

"Oh no," Claire said, stealing a glance around the corner of the house.

"Another ambush?" Gabe's voice was low and warm in Claire's ear, sending a ripple of activity down her spine. She hadn't realized he'd come to stand so close behind her, and now she couldn't even turn around without being nose to nose with him. Again.

She swallowed hard, freezing in place.

"It's Amy. Marcia's got her cornered now." Focusing on her sister she could do. But this shift in her dynamic with Gabe she couldn't. Not here. Not now.

Not ever.

Behind her, she heard the soft rumble of Gabe's laugh against her neck, and she shivered.

"Cold?" Gabe asked, stepping back.

Claire turned around, looking straight at him. For some reason, she struggled with the simplest of words. It was still Gabe, with the same dark eyes and hair and teasing grin, but somehow it felt different. She felt different.

Attraction, she realized. Sure, the guy was good looking, but that was a fact; even her sisters had commented on it. It wasn't something she hadn't realized until now.

It was more that it hadn't gotten under her skin before now. Because he'd never touched her this way before. And she'd never let him.

And he might be getting carried away right now, but she certainly wouldn't.

"No." She managed to shake her head. Then, suddenly eager to get back to the crowd and all their speculation, she raised her empty glass. "Time to reload."

Or maybe it would be better to keep a cool head.

"Claire!"

She turned to see Josh's parents waving from down on the lawn. "Groom's parents," she said to Gabe as they descended the steps to the grass.

"Mrs. Goodwin." Claire leaned in to give the petite woman a hug. "Congratulations to you both!"

"Oh, the congratulations are really best directed at the happy couple," Mr. Goodwin said, looking around for Hallie and Josh.

Claire did the same, but the lawn was small and filled with people.

"I'm sure they slipped away for some alone time," Gabe said gallantly. He extended his hand to Josh's parents. "Gabe Turner. Claire's guest."

Mrs. Goodwin's eyebrows lifted just enough for Claire to notice. It would seem that Josh hadn't mentioned this to them. But then, Josh probably didn't give much thought to Claire or her love life.

And, sadly, she couldn't say the same in return.

"And how are you two . . . acquainted?"

Clearly, the woman was discreet. Probably from years of ownership at the biggest social club in the area.

"We work together," Claire said, hoping to leave it at that. But just then, she felt a hand slide around her waist, causing her eyes to pop as her back stiffened.

"What Claire means to say is that we met at work." Gabe was grinning wildly, refusing to meet her eye.

Coco Goodwin looked nearly as thrilled for Claire as she did for the bride and groom, who were now visible on the steps.

Hoping to steer the attention from herself for a few minutes until she had an excuse to slip away, Claire waved to Hallie.

"There's the happy couple now."

Only they didn't look very happy, at least not from this distance. And not, after a brief hesitation, when they came down the steps and approached the small group. Josh looked a little shell shocked, and Hallie looked as if she'd been crying. Her smile was strained when she greeted Josh's parents.

Claire almost forgot about Gabe's hand all over her waist as she studied Hallie's behavior. She'd pull her aside if she could—and soon.

If only so she had an excuse to break away from Gabe.

"I think they like me," Gabe said when they were finally in the shelter of their own room. Make that her room.

For good measure, she took the extra pillow off the bed and handed it to him, then recovered the folded bedding from the chest.

"Of course they like you," she said. "But you didn't need to ham it up so much."

His eyes glinted in the dim lighting. "Ah. So you noticed."

"It was a little hard not to notice when you were groping my ass." She raised an eyebrow, showing her lack of amusement.

"I wasn't groping you. I was playing the part of the attentive boyfriend. And my hand was nowhere near your . . ." He looked down at her rear, and she picked up her own pillow to swat him.

"Oh, you definitely skimmed the tailbone a few times," she said, shaking her head. She set the blankets down on the floor and started to spread them out for Gabe. He picked up an end and started to help. "You know you don't need to take it that far."

"Out of curiosity, are you this . . . standoffish with all of your boyfriends?" he asked casually.

Claire forgot about the bedding situation for a moment while she stared at him. "First off, I'm not standoffish, and secondly, you're not my boyfriend."

"Yes, but everyone is supposed to think that I am." He shrugged. "I just think it could help you if you let yourself loosen up."

She blinked at him. "Help me in what regard? Getting through this wedding or in general?"

He shrugged again. "Both."

She was gaping at him, and when she spoke, it came out too loud. "I'll have you know"—she stopped herself, remembering where she was and who might hear—"that I am not stiff or uptight or any of the other descriptions that you are implying."

"When was your last boyfriend?" he asked, sounding more curious than usual. When she didn't respond right away, not because of shock but because she couldn't think of an answer that wouldn't prove him right, he said, "Come on. Fair's fair. You know all about my romantic past now."

"Not all of it," she said. She still didn't know how the engagement had ended or why.

For some reason, she didn't want to know. Maybe because she was afraid of what she might hear. If she'd see him in a different light.

If she'd feel let down somehow.

She stepped away, busying herself with the stack of pillows. "You know that I date here and there." That was a stretch. The dates were few and far between and had been increasingly less frequent in recent years. "It just never works out."

"Maybe you don't want it to work out," Gabe said.

She caught his eye. All joking was set aside. He had seen through to something deep down, something that her lame excuses of work couldn't hide.

Love didn't always work out: that was the cold hard truth. Sometimes it was love that cut the deepest and hurt the most. She would know. She saw examples of it every day. Some closer than others.

She balled a fist at her side, fighting against the emotions that were building inside her. She'd had to listen to her relatives voice their uninformed opinions on her love life for long enough. She certainly didn't need to hear it from Gabe too.

Not when he was just a coworker. Just a friend.

"Maybe that's true," she said with a shrug.

"You admit that I'm right?" Gabe looked surprised. It was no secret that Claire liked to win an argument—especially in the courtroom.

"I'm saying that maybe I don't have a desire to get close to anyone."

His brow furrowed as if he wasn't pleased with her answer. "But is there a reason for that? Other than work?"

She hesitated before shaking her head. Needing to lighten her mood before she said something she regretted, she added, "I can assure you that it is absolutely not because I'm . . . stiff."

He looked at her frankly. "We're both divorce attorneys. Plenty of the people in our firm are happily married."

"Maybe they are," Claire said simply. "Or maybe that's just how it appears."

He raised his eyebrows but said nothing. They were both very aware of how possible this was.

She perhaps more than others.

A knock on the door made them lock eyes, their expressions frozen in such mutual horror that she'd have laughed if she didn't think it would draw more attention.

"Yes?" she called out, hoping to sound casual.

"It's just me." *Me* being Aunt Marcia. "I wanted to give you a little something I brought from home. But I don't want to interrupt if you two are . . . busy."

Her tone was laced with suggestion, and now, as Claire's cheeks burned, she saw Gabe fighting off a laugh. She shot him a warning glance: *Don't you dare.*

"I can come back if you aren't decent." A giggle then, from her sixty-year-old aunt.

Claire grabbed the pillow from the floor and tossed it onto the bed. Gabe looked at her in alarm but caught on quickly.

"We're *decent.*" She rolled her eyes skyward at the word. "I just, um . . . one second. I, um . . ."

For once, she was at a loss for words. She started grabbing the blankets frantically while Gabe pantomimed something to her. The phone. Yes, the phone.

"Sorry, I'm just on hold with a client."

"At this hour?" A loud tsk then. As always, Claire's life choices were met with disapproval.

Her shoulders dropped in defeat as she walked slowly to the door, taking one last glance behind her to make sure all evidence was put away.

With a steadying breath, she turned to open the door, just in time to hear some rustling behind her.

Aunt Marcia's expression went from curious to downright gleeful when she finally looked up at Claire.

"Oh, I see you two are just settling in for the night."

Claire frowned; then, as Marcia pushed into the room, she saw Gabe under the covers, his arms folded behind his head against the pillow, drawing attention to the T-shirt that pulled against his broad chest.

Claire quickly looked back at her aunt.

"I have this lovely scented candle that I brought with me for nights when I can't sleep, and I thought that with how *wound tight* you tend to be, Claire, it might help you get some rest before the big day!"

Big day. Claire heard Gabe's muffled laughter behind her.

"But now I see that you probably won't be getting any sleep at all . . ."

Claire felt her cheeks burn, and she was happy that her back was to Gabe, who would no doubt never, ever let her forget this night.

"Yes, well, it's been a long day, and we have a *bigger day* ahead of us," Claire added, shooting Gabe a stony look over her shoulder that he didn't catch or chose to ignore.

Finally, with a suggestive wink, Marcia slowly closed the door behind her.

Claire wasted no time in turning the lock. But when she turned back to the bed, Gabe was still there, showing no signs of moving.

"Okay, the coast is clear." Claire went to pull a pillow from the bed to toss on the floor, but Gabe yanked it from her instead, his strength almost pulling her completely onto the bed.

They were nose to nose, and she could see the laugh lines around his eyes, feel the heat of his body, smell the musk of his skin.

"You're enjoying this," she accused, still annoyed at her aunt's comments. If she was so "wound tight," did anyone ever stop to consider that maybe she had reason to be? Or that maybe they should be a little less cavalier with their feelings?

"It's a wedding week," Gabe told her mildly as he climbed out of the bed. "There's nothing wrong with having a good time."

Only there was a problem with letting your guard down, Claire thought as she settled into the empty bed and turned out the light, eager to put an end to this conversation, this day, and the fresh hurt that squeezed her chest, so tight that it almost felt like it could break all over again.

If she let it.

CHAPTER TWENTY

Amy

The next morning, the house was strangely quiet, considering that it was filled to the rafters with guests. The party had lasted long into the evening, a festive and loud occasion that made Amy remember just how much she loved being back in Driftwood Cove.

And how much she had missed it.

Now, trying to keep the creeping nostalgia and regret at bay, Amy did what she did best. She worked. With tomorrow being the wedding day, she had no excuse not to.

She sat at the dining room table, a spread of tulle, favor boxes, and name tags covering the long plank of wood. Hallie had already ordered most of the items for her favors, but Amy had a few ideas of her own to make them better.

Hallie, however, paused when she came into the room.

"What are these?" she asked, holding up a small white box tied with a gold ribbon.

"I thought they'd round out the favors," Amy explained. Then, hoping to show how much better they looked, she held up a finished product. "See how the gold really makes it pop?"

"But those aren't our colors." Hallie gave her a questioning look.

"Yes, but you already have the colors in the flowers," Amy said. "And a blush-colored ribbon on a white box won't even be noticeable. Speaking of which, I asked the florist to use gold vases. They're larger in scale, and they'll create a better sense of height and drama. I really think they'll anchor the tables and give the sense of mood that we're looking for."

Hallie just stared at her, neither smiling nor saying anything.

Amy knew that it was a lot to take in, but she also knew that Hallie would love the end product.

"You have to trust my vision," she assured Hallie. "I've planned hundreds of events."

"But the crystal vases are classic. Timeless."

"But you've dreamed of your wedding all your life," Amy pointed out. "Don't you remember how our imaginations would run wild when we looked through Mom's album?"

"Of course I remember," Hallie said. "And that's all I ever wanted. A wedding just like hers."

"Yes, but she already had her wedding. This one has to stand apart a little." Amy searched for the best word to convince her sister. "It has to be . . . special."

Hallie's jaw slacked. "It is special. And I thought you understood how special traditions are to me."

Amy pushed away the favors. "Of course I know, Hallie. Everyone knows. You can still honor tradition, and you are. But things have changed a bit since the last generation." She tipped her head, hoping that Hallie could recognize this.

Eventually, Hallie nodded. "I just don't want the vases to take attention away from the flowers."

"Quite the opposite!" Amy was all too happy to agree. "The flowers you chose are classic, but they risk being . . . an afterthought. Now they'll stand higher on the table and be more noticeable. The gold will make the blush roses pop against the candlelight. And it will go better with the gold Chiavari chairs."

Hallie's eyes widened, and Amy realized that in the chaos of having all their relatives descend upon them yesterday and the party going so late, she hadn't had a chance to tell Hallie about this last-minute change.

"I chose the white slipcovered chairs."

"Against the white tablecloths?" Amy wrinkled her nose. "That's a beautiful look, don't get me wrong, but sort of . . ."

Hallie, however, finished her sentence for her. "Boring? Is that what you were going to say?"

"I was going to say safe. Expected, because that's what Mom had, I know, and you loved what she chose. But this is your chance to add some new personality."

"My personality or yours?" Hallie asked.

Amy blinked in surprise. "I'm only trying to help."

"You think my wedding ideas were boring. You're no different than Claire, you know!" Hallie's voice rose.

"What's that supposed to mean?" Amy asked, forgetting all about the favors, the vases, and even the chairs for a moment.

"I mean that you don't agree with my life. My choices. Not even for the wedding!"

"Whoa." Amy held up her hands, her mind spinning at these accusations. "I'm here, aren't I? I gave up my job to be here. A job I loved."

She hadn't let herself go there until now, to blame her sister for the choice that she alone had made. But there it was. Out. And she couldn't take the words back.

Hallie looked shocked. Maybe even a little stung. And hurting her sister the day before her wedding was the last thing that Amy wanted to do. It defeated the entire purpose of coming here at all.

"I never asked you to choose between my wedding and your job," Hallie said firmly.

"You didn't, but did you really think I was in a position to turn you down? And what were you going to do if I hadn't come?" Amy motioned to the table. "Sure, you had a map to follow, but you hadn't gotten very far along with the process!"

"Well, I'm sure I would have found a way," Hallie said, but there was doubt in her voice. "Mom might have helped more if I didn't have anyone else."

Maybe their mother would have, but Amy had the impression that this wedding was stirring up a lot of emotions for Bunny that she hadn't expected. Tending to her guests was an easier task to focus her energy on, a way to stay helpful but distracted.

Amy sighed, taking a moment to calm herself. "I'm supporting this wedding now, and I supported it last year at the engagement party too. I defended you to Claire, so please don't compare me to her."

Hallie said nothing.

"I'm just trying to help," Amy said carefully. "Hallie, you know that I support you and Josh. You're following in Mom's footsteps, just like you always wanted."

Hallie's gaze swept toward the hallway, where their parents' wedding photo was visible. "They had a wonderful marriage. And it started with a wonderful wedding. I just . . . want to make sure that I start things off the same way."

Amy studied her sister. Hallie was easygoing, sometimes to a fault. But superstitious? Never.

"What's this really about?" she asked.

"Nothing." Hallie shook her head. "Just . . . jitters. Everyone gets them, right?"

"I'm sure that's it," she assured her sister, because how could it be anything else? Hallie was marrying the love of her life. She got the guy, the wedding, and the house. A life that many, including Amy, could only dream of having. "Pushing up your wedding didn't leave much time to plan everything. You know I'm doing the best I can. I'm just trying to show how we can do that but also make things fresh."

Hallie nodded, but her expression showed that she wasn't convinced. "I'm going out for a bit."

"Hallie," Amy pleaded with her. "Don't leave like this."

"I have stuff I need to take care of," Hallie said, already backing out of the room. "I'll be back later."

"We have to go to the bridal salon later," Amy reminded her. It was on her calendar, and an alarm was set to leave fifteen minutes early. She made a mental note to remind Claire, too, wherever she was. She hadn't seen her yet today, come to think of it. The last time she'd seen her was at the party, and only briefly, before Amy had slipped away to the comfort of her bedroom, where she could focus on the wedding and not on all the emotions that being here stirred up. "I guess we'll meet there?"

But Hallie was already walking out of the room. A second later, Amy heard the door close.

"Hallie!" Amy pushed away her chair to chase after her sister, but from somewhere beneath the mountain of tulle and ribbon, her phone started to ring. Cursing under her breath, Amy rummaged for it, worried it could be one of the vendors calling with a sudden crisis—it was known to happen the day before a big event.

But the name that flashed on the screen wasn't local.

"Gail?" Amy answered, frowning with confusion.

"Thank God you answered" came her former boss's husky voice. "We're having a problem with the corporate party tonight."

Amy was aware that at this point her eyes were probably comically large. "And you're asking me to help?"

She blinked rapidly. Had Gail forgotten that she no longer worked for her? Or did she just not care?

Then another thought occurred to her. "Wait, I'm not on that account. Bethany took that one over herself."

"I'm aware of that." Gail grew quiet. "And I'm aware that she wasn't ready for that type of responsibility."

Amy sat down and sank her head into her hand. She didn't know much about the event Gail was describing or see what she could do from Rhode Island, and certainly not the day before Hallie's wedding, but she could also hear the desperation in the woman's voice.

"I'm sure Michelle—" Amy started.

"Michelle's already scrambling to find a hotel with a large enough meeting space," Gail replied.

Oh, this must be bad.

"Okay, Gail. I'll try to help. Just tell me what it is you're asking. What do you need?"

There was a beat of silence before Gail replied, "You. I need you back, Amy. I was rash, and I see that now. You've only been gone a week, and already things are falling apart."

Amy sat up straighter. "You want me back?"

All that worry, all that uncertainty about her future was gone. Instead, she could relax, knowing that come Monday she could slide into her desk, go home to her apartment, and fall right back into her steady routine.

Even make that partnership at some point.

Maybe even plan a wedding. It wasn't so bad, really. Actually it was more fun than she would dare to admit to Gail. For a little while, at least.

"Check my files for the Stewart-Hanson corporate account," she told Gail. "That should give you a road map for tonight's event."

"Thank you," Gail breathed. "And the other thing? You'll come back, won't you? Give things a second chance?"

A second chance. Amy almost couldn't believe that one was being presented to her, but she wasn't about to let Gail off the hook so easily, not after the hell she'd put her through this past week.

"I'll call you Monday morning, after my sister's wedding," she said and then, after disconnecting the call, fist-pumped the air and raised her hands to the ceiling, overjoyed with relief.

"Looks like I just walked in on something," a voice said from the doorway.

Reddening, Amy dropped her hands to the table and looked up to see Logan. "I just received some good news."

"Anything you care to share?" he asked.

She hesitated. Once, she would have grabbed Logan's arm and told him they were going out to celebrate, but she'd learned a long time ago that it was better to keep some things to herself.

She shook her head. "Did you see Hallie on your way in?"

"I passed by her on the way to the house. She looked a bit distracted," Logan said, pulling out a chair.

Distracted was one word for it, but Amy couldn't open up to Logan about her concerns. Maybe once she might have, but things were different now.

"We were working on the favors and had a disagreement," she replied.

"Well, I have a meeting with your mom about some business things, but I'm happy to be put to work while I wait. I'm a bit early."

Amy looked at the table, thought about today's tight schedule, and pushed some ribbon toward him. "Thanks. I need all the help I can get."

Spending the morning with Logan hadn't been on her agenda, but for once, she was happy to stray from her carefully detailed schedule.

Her heart sped up when she handed him the supplies and explained her system.

"And we have to make how many of these?" he asked, looking a little afraid.

"About one hundred and . . . nineteen," she said, doing a quick count of the ones she'd already completed.

"Yikes. Well, if I'd known that, I wouldn't have offered my assistance." But he showed no signs of moving. "What do I have to do?" he asked, scooting his chair a little closer to hers.

She felt her heart swoop and soar at the proximity. Logan. Her Logan. Right here. So close.

She kept her gaze trained on a favor box, demonstrating how it had to be unfolded and assembled, filled with the personalized candle, and then secured with the ribbon.

"There's no way I can tie a bow like that," he said with a low rumble of laughter.

"It's not as bad as it sounds. Although I'm not sure that my sister would agree." Amy started folding a box.

"Didn't she pick out these candles?"

"She did." And they'd had to pay rush delivery to get them here in time. "But she doesn't seem as thrilled by the ribbon color or some of the other changes I've made."

He gave her a sharp look. "Changes?"

"Improvements, not changes." Amy was certain that Hallie would love everything once she finally saw it come together.

"Isn't the client always right?"

"Of course, but an event planner usually has ways of taking their clients' ideas and making them even better." Amy dropped another finished favor into the storage box. "I can see the big picture. I can see how this wedding can be spectacular."

Logan shrugged. "Seems to me that Hallie was always content with keeping life simpler."

"Yes, she is, but this is a wedding," Amy stressed. She didn't add that it was the wedding they had both dreamed of for half their childhoods.

"And it's her wedding," he said slowly. He slid a box to her, and she tied the ribbon.

"Exactly," Amy replied. "I'm just trying to show her that she can change things up, make it her own, create some of her own traditions, even." Another one went in the storage box. At this rate, she might be finished before lunch. Even if she was no longer enjoying the task.

They'd always been honest with each other—well, except for her deepest, truest feelings. But now she wondered if that aspect of their relationship was lost along with the five years they could never get back.

She stopped to look at him. "What are you saying, Logan?"

He hesitated for a moment. "I just think that you need to set aside your preferences and do what she wants."

"Then she should have just hired a personal assistant to place all the orders and run all around town for her." She set her hands flat on the table, forcing a few calming breaths. "I gave up a lot to be here."

"But it's not about you, Amy," Logan said, firmly but gently. "It's not your wedding."

No. It wasn't. And she didn't appreciate the reminder, especially coming from him.

Tears prickled her eyes, and she stood up before he could see them. Turning her back to the table, she pretended to be carefully arranging some finished favors in a large storage box.

"Isn't my mother looking for you?" she asked, unable to look at him.

Finally she heard his chair push back against the wood.

"Let me know if you need more help," he said before leaving the room.

Amy waited until the sound of his footsteps finally disappeared in the far distance of the house before turning back to the room, only to wipe her eyes.

Forty-three favors and a muttered self–pep talk later, Amy looked up to see Claire standing in the doorway.

"Amy? Everything okay?" Her blonde hair was pulled back in a sleek ponytail, and her cashmere sweater and jeans complemented the simple ballet flats that graced her feet.

"Sure! Just . . . busy." Amy's hands shook as she stuffed another favor into its box, and she wondered if Claire noticed.

"I just saw Logan—"

"Oh." Amy shook her head, looking up. "It's fine. He stopped by to see Mom."

Claire walked into the room and surveyed the table. "I thought that Hallie's colors were white and pink." She stopped herself and said dramatically, "I mean . . . blush."

"They are!" Amy set down a favor box, hearing the exasperation in her voice. "Sorry. It's just been a bad morning. Hallie's not as excited about my ideas as I'd hoped, and Logan just told me that I'm pretty much being selfish."

"Whoa." Claire sat down and reached for some supplies. She assembled a favor box without asking for instruction. But then, Claire had always been like that. Independent, self-sufficient. But once, she'd depended on her sisters. Leaned on them too.

And once, Amy had done the same.

"It's not easy," Amy admitted.

"Having Logan around?" Claire's gaze was soft with understanding.

"All of it. Being back here. In this house." She swallowed hard. "I feel bad that I haven't come here more. But . . . it's hard. Everything changed after Dad, and then Logan, and now it will be Hallie's house."

Claire nodded, looking thoughtful. "I wonder what Mom would have done with the house if Hallie hadn't gotten married."

Amy's eyes popped. "Claire!" she warned.

"I'm not insinuating anything about Hallie." Claire clucked her tongue. "I'm just speculating about the house."

Amy hadn't considered this. She didn't have to, not when Hallie and Josh had never shown any hint of trouble and then went on to get engaged, cementing any last hope she had that someday the house might be hers.

Now she felt like she was losing it instead, even though she knew Hallie would always welcome her. It wouldn't be the same. But then, nothing had been in a while.

"I never asked Mom what she would have done with the house. Did you?"

Claire shook her head. "No," she said quietly. "But . . . I might."

Amy shrugged that off because really, there was nothing to read into. Claire was no doubt still hanging on to some hope that Hallie wouldn't marry Josh. At least not yet.

A sudden thought took hold.

"Is this why you want Hallie to push back the wedding? So you and Gabe can get the house?"

Claire looked at her with such surprise that Amy knew she had it all wrong. "Me? You know I don't like coming back here. I mean, I love this house. But . . ."

Amy shook her head. She was rattled and emotional. She wasn't thinking straight. "Sorry. It's been a rough morning, and it's going to be a long day, with the wedding tomorrow." She gave her sister a look of apology. "I know it's the hardest for you to be here, where Dad died."

Claire fell silent for a moment. "I'm only worried that Hallie hasn't sown her oats yet. She's making a big commitment."

"Seems to me that you're protesting a bit too much," Amy teased. "You really don't think that you might change your mind about marriage now that you're with Gabe?"

"Why does everyone have to talk about marriage all the time?" Claire replied, looking annoyed as she focused on the task at hand.

"Maybe because there's a wedding tomorrow," Amy replied, but she felt it, too, and it stung.

Claire, however, didn't seem to share her emotions. No, Claire looked troubled, as if she were wrestling with something. She looked up and around the room a few times, even though the house was quiet and there was no one within earshot.

"If I tell you something, do you promise to keep it between us?" Claire looked so serious that Amy felt she had no choice but to nod. It had been a long time since her older sister had confided anything in her, and she could only hope that it had nothing to do with thwarting her efforts to make this a perfect wedding for Hallie.

Immediately, she felt bad for thinking such a thing. Her sister was turning to her, confiding in her, for the first time since their father had died.

"You can tell me anything, Claire," Amy said quietly. "You know that, don't you?"

Claire hesitated. Maybe she didn't know it, and maybe that was partly Amy's fault. It wasn't like Amy had exactly reached out this past year.

Or maybe Claire had changed her mind. Decided that bottling up her feelings was still best.

Amy reached for another favor box, feeling the sting of disappointment, when Claire suddenly blurted, "Gabe isn't really my boyfriend."

Amy felt her eyes widen. "What?"

Claire swallowed hard. "It's true. I mean, everything I said about him is true. Just not the boyfriend part."

Amy wasn't really sure how much more this day could bring her. She stared at her sister, trying to understand what currently felt more surreal: that Claire had actually brought a fake date to Hallie's wedding or that she was admitting it to her.

She would have felt touched if she weren't so damn mad.

"You're lying to Mom? And Hallie? On her wedding day, Claire?"

Claire's shoulders slumped. "I did it for Hallie, don't you see? She was never going to believe that I suddenly supported her decision unless she saw that I believed in love."

Amy searched her sister's face, feeling sadness on her behalf. "You really don't?"

Claire lowered her eyes. "No, I really don't. And I haven't done a good job of hiding that, much as I've tried. You know how I come across. The things I say."

Amy stared at her flatly. "You've made your opinions very clear, yes."

Claire sighed. "We thought that if she saw that I was in love and that I believed in love, she could believe that I could support her . . . being in love."

Amy blinked, trying to follow this strange logic. "It almost makes sense when you put it that way," she said with great reluctance. "But when were you planning on telling her the truth?"

Claire chewed her lip. "Never, I guess. Some things . . . don't need to be shared."

"So, what, you were just going to pretend he dumped you?"

"Or I dumped him!" Claire looked aghast. "Look, Amy, Gabe is a great friend. It isn't all an act, just some of it. He's like . . . he's . . . my work husband."

This was getting interesting. "Your work husband." When Claire nodded, Amy could only laugh and shake her head. She reached for another favor box and started the task. "You would have one of those."

"What's that supposed to mean?" Claire asked, growing defensive, as she usually did when her job was mentioned.

"I just mean that you're always at work. So of course the person you're closest to would also work there."

Claire looked surprised by the response. "We're very close. And everything we said was true."

"But why?" Amy asked. "Why is he only your work husband?"

Claire narrowed her eyes. "Because sometimes it's better to keep things as friends, Amy."

Well, that silenced her. Leave it to Claire to always home in on the truth, no matter how hard hitting it was.

Claire immediately set a hand on Amy's arm, trying to apologize, but Amy just waved her concern away.

"No. It's true. I mean . . . that's all some people are meant to be, right?"

She picked up the favor box again, but fresh tears blurred her vision. She blinked them away quickly, not wanting to admit that she still cared to Claire, or to herself.

Besides, she could have her old job back now. Come Monday morning, she could be back in Boston with Michelle, back on her old accounts, looking forward to the events she'd already started, planning new ones well into the future.

And Logan would just once again fade into a part of her past.

"So there's really nothing at all going on between the two of you? Nothing ever happened?" Amy couldn't help but feel disappointed. She wanted her sister to be happy and carefree and believe in all the fairy-tale magic like she had as a little girl.

She missed that side of Claire. And she'd thought Gabe had found a way to bring it out of her.

"Just what you see," Claire said. Then, setting down the favor box, she said, "Though he did ham it up a bit for the cookout last night."

Amy nodded, detecting a hint of a smile passing over her sister's lips.

"Too bad," she said with a sigh. Stealing a glance back at Claire, she added, "I thought you two were good together."

Claire didn't say anything as she finished tying a bow with care.

"Do you ever . . . regret being married to your career?" Amy asked.

Claire bristled. "I wouldn't say that I'm married to my career. It's important to me, and it takes up a lot of time and . . ."

"And it comes before anything and anyone else?" Amy gave her a knowing look.

"If you mean that it's kept me from visiting, I feel bad about that. Sometimes you just don't realize how much you miss something until it's too late to go back."

Or someone, Amy thought.

Claire just reached for another favor box without saying anything. "Why do you ask?"

Amy hesitated. "I guess being here has me thinking about the past. And Hallie getting married, well, it changes everything, doesn't it? We can't go back. And . . . I wish I could. I wish that I'd visited sooner. More often."

Maybe that she'd never left.

"We're adults now. We have our lives. You can't stay in your childhood home forever." She paused. "Well, unless you're Hallie."

"Claire," Amy warned. But she knew what her sister said was true. You couldn't stay a child forever. And she hadn't known what she knew now when she'd left all those years ago.

But if she went back to Boston again, this time she knew exactly what she'd be leaving behind.

CHAPTER
TWENTY-ONE

Hallie

Hallie stood inside the bridal salon in her wedding dress, the family veil on her head, staring at herself in the mirror and trying to force a feeling that she didn't feel.

She should be basking in this moment—should have a tingle of nerves in her stomach, sure—but in the place where excitement should be sat something cold and hard. Something like dread.

Claire had been right. Hallie didn't know what she was doing. It didn't matter that she and Josh had been dating since they were fifteen years old, that they never argued, that their life was charmed.

That, perhaps, was just the problem. She'd been lulled into a false sense of security. A path had been presented to her, and she'd taken it.

Five children. Josh said he wanted *five* children. Where had he even come up with such a specific number? And when had this even come about? He'd never mentioned such a thing, never alluded to anything close. At best, he'd complained here and there about being an only child . . . but *five* children?

And did he just think that she'd go along with it the way she did everything else, without questioning, without arguing, without wanting something else for herself?

She realized that he likely did. That she'd given him no reason to assume otherwise. Because that was the way it had always been.

She'd thought, naively, that was how it would always be.

The door to one of the dressing rooms opened, and Amy stepped out in the dress that had been hemmed to fit her shorter figure.

"That looks nice." Hallie managed to collect herself. The bridesmaids' dresses did look nice. Better than nice. They looked perfect. Just as she'd hoped they would look. It should make her feel at ease—happy, even—but right now, all she could think about was *five children*.

"We didn't discuss jewelry yet," Amy said, looking a little alarmed at the possible oversight.

Hallie, however, had this covered. It was something she'd planned last summer, even before she'd officially asked her sisters to be her bridesmaids. Before the engagement party. Before Claire had to go and make her question everything. Before it was too late to change her mind about including Claire in her wedding party.

She'd seen a delicate seashell necklace in a shop one day that she knew would perfectly complement those colors. They had three in stock; it had felt like fate. Like a sign, even.

"Oh, we have some lovely pieces over here." The bridal-shop owner was quick to jump at the opportunity of a sale, and before Hallie could object, Amy was already standing at the counter, oohing and aahing over some necklaces and earrings that held no sentimental value whatsoever.

"Gold would be best" she heard Amy say to the shopkeeper, meaning that Amy was sticking with the gold vases and chairs.

Hallie was about to protest, but a moment later, Claire emerged, looking less annoyed by the color than she had when she'd first tried it on.

She smoothed the dress at the hips and came to stand beside Amy, who had stopped just short of the pedestal where Hallie stood in the center of the shop. Like a doll on display. Like a princess.

She figured that's how she was supposed to feel. Special. Beautiful. The center of attention.

"Oh, Hallie." Amy walked closer to the mirror. "That veil. It really does finish the look."

"I thought you preferred one of these others," Hallie said, motioning to the pile of tulle in the corner of the room. "You certainly liked the one you had me try on."

"I never said I preferred the others. Just that they were new. Fresh. That you might want to bring a touch of your own personality to things, that's all."

Her smile was kind, but her words cut nearly as deep as Claire's had, just a few days earlier, in this very shop.

Hallie reached up and pulled the hair comb from the crown of her head, handing the veil to Amy.

"Maybe you're right," she said briskly. "Something about that veil doesn't feel right anymore."

Really, none of this felt right anymore. Not the veil. Not the dress. Not the carefully selected bridesmaid necklaces that had made her think of so many seaside summers with her sisters.

Maybe not even the groom.

Amy and Claire shared an alarmed glance, and Amy inched toward Hallie, extending the veil with a pleading look in her eyes. "I didn't mean to upset you, Hallie."

"You didn't upset me," Hallie replied simply. She was plenty upset, all right, but for once, it had nothing to do with her sisters. Or maybe it did. Maybe having them here, making them a part of her wedding, had been a giant mistake.

Claire didn't even think she should be getting married, and Amy just cared about the wedding looking nice for the guests, nothing else.

Hallie had thought this week would be special, that she'd look back on it as a time she'd cherished with her sisters, even that she and Claire might move past things, especially after Claire had apologized.

But Claire had said what she needed to. What would get her through the week. And much as Hallie used to chalk up those words to Claire not understanding, never having been in love, she couldn't use that excuse any longer, could she?

Claire had found a great guy. Claire was happy.

And Hallie didn't know what she was anymore. She just knew that right now, she needed to get out of this dress. The dress she'd once longed to wear.

"The veil was a plaything. Something we used to run around in, dressing up, like it was all pretend," she said, walking over to the display of veils that came in different fabrics and lengths. All new and unmarred by memories of three little girls laughing and dancing and dreaming.

They hadn't been those girls in a long time. Maybe they never would again. Girls who encouraged each other, who shared the same optimism, who dared to think that they could all have everything they ever wanted. That it wasn't even a question.

Her sisters hadn't just moved away and stopped visiting. They'd moved on.

While she clung to those memories, those dreams, that feeling as tightly as she'd clung to the veil itself all these years.

"Don't you think it's a little late at this point to change anything?" Amy pressed gently.

"You've been changing things all week!" Hallie pointed out. She pulled a lace veil from the rack, held it up, and then set it back.

Amy looked momentarily shocked but quickly recovered. "I have not! I've just pushed forward with plans. On very short notice, I'll have you know."

Hallie relaxed her shoulders. She was being hard on Amy, maybe. Her sister was just trying to help. Except she was only making matters worse.

"This is a tight timeline," Amy said, more gently. "I've just taken your plan and run with it. I've tried to give you the wedding of your dreams. I've tried to make it beautiful. Perfect! But the wedding is tomorrow, Hallie."

"It's not too late, is it?" Hallie bypassed her middle sister to look straight at Claire. "There's still time to change my mind . . . about anything."

Claire's eyes widened, and she flitted a nervous glance at Amy. Her oldest sister knew when to keep quiet, that was for sure. But for once, Hallie longed to hear what she really thought. What advice she might give.

She'd chalked her sister's advice up to nonsense coming from someone who hadn't found true love and had barely even made it past a few dates. But she'd underestimated Claire. She was in a wonderful, mature, adult relationship with a great guy.

And much as Hallie might hate to admit it, she knew what she was talking about.

She always did, as far back as when Hallie was six and Claire was twelve and old enough to earn her own money from babysitting and old enough to go into town on her own to spend it. She'd always bring Hallie along, always carefully guiding her along the busier roads, always giving up a portion of her earnings, sharing what she had. Not just her wisdom. But her heart.

And as much as Claire might have changed, Hallie knew that she still cared. And that her words were still worth listening to.

"What do you mean by that?" Amy asked, looking a little worried.

"I mean . . ." There were so many things she could say, she couldn't choose just one. And was she really thinking of changing her mind about this wedding? And where would that leave her and Josh? Was she really thinking of ending it completely, going out on her own, starting her life completely over, fresh, with no clear path or path at all? No more job at the Harbor Club? No more lazy evenings or weekends walking through town, going into the familiar shops and restaurants that she never tired of, even now? No more ski trips with the Goodwins or holiday meals with Josh beside her at the table, always there, even when her sisters weren't?

And would she even remain in Beachnest Cottage? If she didn't get married, then the house would be sold. Her mother had been clear about that.

Hallie felt a wave of nausea, and she pressed a hand to her stomach, telling herself that she couldn't be sick, not when she was wearing her mother's wedding dress—her wedding dress.

Aware that her sisters were waiting for her to explain herself, she settled on the easiest excuse, the most obvious at least, her eyes resting on the necklace in Amy's hand. "I don't like that necklace."

The shopkeeper pressed her lips together and accepted Amy's muttered apologies as she set the necklace back in the case.

Through the reflection, she saw Claire and Amy exchange nervous glances. The shop owner disappeared into a back room, not that anyone could blame her, and the only thing that Hallie could be thankful for right now was that her mother wasn't there.

Before she could stop herself, the tears began to flow, fast and warm, steadily down her cheeks.

Amy rushed to pluck a tissue from the box on the counter—probably typically reserved for tears of joy—and handed it to her with a worried frown. "I'm sorry, Hallie. I didn't mean to upset you."

"Me neither," Claire said, stepping forward, her face creased with worry. "If this is about what I said last summer, honestly, Hallie, I'm sorry. I'm here to support you. Tomorrow is the day you've been dreaming about for your entire life!"

"I know." Hallie sniffed and carefully dabbed at her face. Was there any worse scene than a woman sobbing in a wedding gown? She turned her back to the mirror, facing her sisters, sensing the confusion in their expressions, and she knew that she could just say exactly what she feared, but she wasn't ready to see the knowledge in Claire's eyes, the confirmation that she was right.

"If this is about the veil, then of course, wear the family veil, Hallie," Amy pleaded. "And if this is about the necklace, of course we'll wear whatever you picked out!"

Claire nodded her agreement eagerly.

"No," Hallie said, stepping off the podium. "It doesn't matter about the veil. Or the chairs. Or the vases. I don't even care anymore. About any of it!"

"You don't mean that," Amy said gently.

"But I do," Hallie said, wishing she could stop herself but knowing that she couldn't. "I . . . can't walk down the aisle feeling like this." Her heart was beating so hard against her chest that she could feel the blood rushing in her ears. For a moment she wanted to take it all back, but that would just be taking back words. The feelings would still linger.

"Honey, you're nervous. It's a lot of pressure. And the rush—" Amy looked as alarmed as Hallie felt, and even Claire didn't seem happy at Hallie's declaration.

"It's not that," Hallie said, shaking away Amy's reach for her arm. "I thought I knew what I wanted. Not just for the wedding, but . . . for life. And as you can see, I don't really know what I want!"

"Hallie!" Amy's voice carried through the store as Hallie closed the dressing room door behind her.

She couldn't look in the mirror. Couldn't see herself in this dress again, the dress she'd dreamed of wearing, just like her mother had, and her grandmother before her. She'd always thought it was the happiest of dresses because the women in her family had looked so happy wearing it.

And now she couldn't help but feel like she was letting them down. Her mother. Her grandmother, even if she wasn't here to know it.

But worse than anything, she felt like she was letting herself down. And maybe Josh too.

CHAPTER TWENTY-TWO

Claire

"What just happened?" Amy pulled Claire aside the moment they were outside, after a hasty goodbye to the shop owner and a pleasant promise to stop by in the morning to pick up the dresses.

Amy's eyes were as wide as Claire's felt, and they stood on the street corner in silence, staring at each other, no doubt each willing the other to know what to do. When she was younger, Claire always stepped in when there was a problem, however trivial, like a loose chain on a bike. Claire prided herself on taking care of her sisters.

But she was out of her element here.

"I don't know what's going on with Hallie," Claire said, looking down the empty sidewalk where Hallie had last been seen, leaving Amy to make up some excuses to the shop owner about a last-minute appointment, given the rush of the entire week.

"You didn't—" Amy started. But one sharp look from Claire made her stop in midsentence. She sighed and shook her head. "She seemed off this morning when I was working on the favors. I didn't read too much into it, but now . . ." She stared at Claire, as if hoping Claire could shed some light.

"She's seemed a little off to me this week too," Claire admitted.

Amy shook her head as they wandered slowly in the direction of her car. "I kept telling myself it was the stress of the wedding, but I can't help but feel like there's more to it."

"And she hasn't told you anything?" Claire asked. She knew that if Hallie had a problem, she would turn to Amy, not her. And she realized with a heavy heart that she had only herself to blame for that.

"You know Hallie. She, more than either of us, has always longed for a wedding just like the one in Mom and Dad's album. Remember how she would look through it so often that Mom finally let her keep it in her room?" Amy gave a small smile, but it was clear the memory hit her just as hard as it did Claire.

But not for the same reason. Claire had thought she'd pushed the images from her mind, the ones of her parents dancing and gazing into each other's eyes, laughing while they cut their cake. They'd looked so happy, and maybe they were. But were they as happy as they'd led everyone to believe?

"She's looked forward to this all her life. It's probably just a lot of emotions at once now that it's finally happening." But even as Claire said it, she wasn't so sure.

Amy nodded. "You're probably right." She sounded about as convinced as Claire.

"I feel bad," Claire confessed. "That she's upset. I know I've had my reservations about the wedding, but that doesn't mean I'd take pleasure in her having doubts or calling it off."

Amy looked startled. "Do you think that's what she's going to do?"

Claire didn't know. And she hated not knowing. It made her feel uneasy and vulnerable, when all she craved for herself and her sisters was stability. A sure thing.

"I'll try calling her," Amy said, already putting her phone to her ear. A moment later she shook her head and stuffed the device back into her pocket. "She turned her phone off."

That wasn't good.

"We'll go back to the house and wait for her. Maybe we'll spot her on our way back," Claire said.

"Maybe she went to Josh's," Amy speculated, but her tone was a question, uncertain.

"Maybe," Claire said, though she wasn't sure if that was a good or bad thing at the moment. "Maybe she just needs some space. To clear her head."

"But she always told us everything," Amy said, sounding on the verge of tears.

Claire nodded thoughtfully. It was true that Hallie had always been open with them, but they'd moved away, grown apart.

Or maybe it was more than that. Maybe this was too big for Hallie to share.

Maybe Claire wasn't the only one in the family keeping some secrets to herself.

"How was she last night at the cookout? I didn't see her much," Claire confessed.

"Neither did I," Amy said. "I just stopped in for a quick bite but otherwise stayed in the house, working out some last-minute wedding details."

They'd arrived at the car, and Claire paused before opening the door, tossing her sister a rueful look over the hood. "Nice excuse."

"What?" Amy feigned innocence, but there was little use in trying. "I did have to count out all the favors for the guests, and make sure all the place cards were accounted for, and—"

"And hide from Aunt Marcia?"

They slid into the car, and Amy quickly merged onto the road. "I admit that if I had a reason to avoid Aunt Marcia pestering me about my life, I was going to take it."

"If I'd known it could be so easy, I might not have brought Gabe along this week," Claire said.

"I'm glad you brought Gabe," Amy said, silencing Claire.

Claire sat with that thought for a moment as she looked out the window, onto the clusters of shops selling everything from saltwater taffy to fresh catch, the water glistening in the distance. No sign of Hallie.

"Yeah, I guess I am too," Claire said. There was no telling how much worse the week might have gone if he hadn't been here, forcing everyone to at least stay polite while he was within earshot.

"You guess? He's a great guy, Claire. Handsome too." Amy hesitated for a moment. "You really never thought about turning your friendship into something more?"

"No," Claire said quickly and honestly. She hadn't. In all the time she'd known Gabe, she saw him as a friend, a good friend, and maybe even her favorite person, at least around the office, which meant that he was really her favorite person in general, because she didn't exactly go anywhere else.

"I wonder if he has," Amy mused, and this time Claire couldn't respond.

Because it was becoming hard to ignore the fact that Gabe really might have feelings for her that extended beyond friendship.

And she didn't know what to do about that.

There was no sign of Hallie back at the house, and after trying her phone once more, Claire and Amy decided the best thing to do was keep acting like the wedding was still happening unless they heard otherwise.

"Question for you," Gabe said when Claire walked into their bedroom, having all but tiptoed through the rest of the house, hoping to avoid a run-in with one of her extended relatives who would probably next be asking when she planned to start a family. Only now the bedroom she'd made her own had evolved, and not because Hallie had changed anything. Gabe's stuff was everywhere, his toothbrush in the holder next to hers in the en suite bathroom, his clothes hung in the closet beside hers. The room even smelled of him. She knew that smell, recognized it from so many long talks, lunches, and drinks after work. It was one of many small parts of him that had sneaked up on her, made her get comfortable and even put her guard down.

"So long as you're not going to ask me to proofread one of your contracts, then I'm all ears," she said, sliding off her shoes.

He reached for two ties and alternated holding them up. "Light blue or navy blue tonight?"

"Navy," she said without having to think about it. It was much more formal, and tonight's event would certainly be formal if it was being held at the Harbor Club. "But you might not have to worry about that," Claire said, dropping onto the bed. She looked up at Gabe. "Hallie just stormed out of the bridal salon. She said, and I quote, 'I don't really know what I want.' She also said that she didn't care about any of this anymore."

Gabe's expression morphed into one of understanding. "Claire . . ."

"I swear, I didn't say anything!" But Claire couldn't fight the guilt that mixed with panic at the possibility that she might have had something to do with this sudden doubt that Hallie seemed to be facing. If she'd never opened her mouth last summer, would Hallie still be acting this way?

But if she hadn't said anything, then she'd always worry that Hallie wasn't being fair to herself, that she might end up disappointed. Or worse.

"I've been on my best behavior all week," Claire insisted, as much to Gabe as to herself. "Come on. You've been here. You've seen me. I couldn't have been a more supportive sister."

And it was true, wasn't it? She was here. She wasn't complaining, even about the color of the bridesmaids' dresses or the pink shirts they'd worn out for drinks. The last thing she wanted was for Hallie to be unhappy.

Gabe seemed to sense her shift in mood and dropped onto the desk chair. "What happened exactly?"

"I don't know." Claire blinked in confusion, trying to process their time at the shop as she recounted the events. Amy had looked as stunned as Claire felt when Hallie disappeared into the dressing room, and no amount of coaxing could get her to talk.

"Jitters?" Gabe ventured. "The wedding is tomorrow, and they have rushed things."

She gave him a look that said she wasn't buying his theory. "They've been dating forever. This is hardly a shotgun wedding."

She picked up her phone again, checking for any messages from either of her sisters, but as usual, her inbox was filled with work memos, which for once didn't serve as a distraction.

"Engagements do end." She looked at Gabe pointedly.

"You don't really think she's actually calling off the wedding, do you?"

Claire replayed her sister's words today, yesterday, and every day this week. She even replayed the hurt in her eyes last summer when Claire had spoken up.

"She loves Josh," Claire said. Of this, she was certain.

But she also knew all too well that love wasn't always enough. And that sometimes, it caused the most damage.

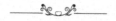

Hallie came back twenty minutes before it was time to leave. Claire had been waiting in Amy's room by then, and when they heard the bedroom door across the hall open, they rushed to greet her, but Hallie had already closed it again, calling out that she was getting into the shower.

"Good sign?" Amy asked, searching Claire's face.

"Maybe you should stay back and ride with her to the Harbor Club," Claire said, and Amy nodded eagerly. They both knew that what she really meant was that Amy could make sure she got in the car.

"Oh, Amy, Claire," their mother said as she stepped out of her bedroom at the back of the house. She was outfitted in a light-blue shift dress with a string of pearls at her neck that Claire remembered her receiving on her tenth anniversary. Claire was probably the only one of her sisters old enough to remember that. It came with being the eldest, she supposed. She was privy to more than they were.

The good, and the bad.

"I thought you and I could ride over with Hallie, Mom," Amy said, almost desperately.

Their mother nodded. "I wouldn't have it any other way!" She turned to Claire. "Did you want to ride over with us or Gabe?"

Claire felt the heat of Amy's eyes on hers, and she refused to look her way. "I'll go over with Gabe, since I know the way."

Gabe stepped out of the room then, looking very much as she was used to seeing him in the office in his suit and tie. For the first time all day, she felt her shoulders relax.

"Ready?" he asked.

"Oh, are you two heading off?" Marcia cried out, hurrying down the hall as best she could in heels.

Claire shot a warning glance at Gabe. There was no way they would be trapped with another inquisition for the car ride, no matter how brief. The night would be long as it was, with even more people to mingle with than last night.

"I'm afraid we don't have any extra room in our car," Claire said apologetically. "Hallie's gift is in the back seat, and since it's not yet wrapped, I don't dare sneak it into the house."

She didn't dare do anything to add further possible disaster to this wedding.

Still unable to shake her unease, Claire saw a reason to quickly make an exit. She was eager to get away from this house, at least for a little bit, to be alone in the car with Gabe, where she didn't have to pretend to be anything other than herself. Claire waved to her family and hurried down the stairs and outside, exhaling only once she was settled in the car. Things were going to be okay. Hallie was getting ready, and at worst she'd be a little late to her own party. The week was almost over, and Claire had gotten through it, keeping her mouth shut just like she'd promised everyone she would.

Just like she'd promised herself.

Gabe drove, following her directions, and Claire glanced behind herself at the large gift that even Hallie would probably deem too much. A full copper cookware set, about eight pieces more than she'd registered for too.

It was Claire's way of showing her support even when she had more doubts than ever before. She'd thought it had been difficult when Hallie was all wide eyes and smiles, but now that Hallie was so far from the starry-eyed girl she'd been at her engagement party, Claire felt a bigger urge to protect her.

She just didn't know how. It wasn't as simple as fixing a bike chain or making sure that Hallie had enough sunblock on her nose. She had to tread lightly. To say the right thing.

To not say too much.

"Parking lot is full," Gabe commented when they arrived at the Harbor Club.

Claire nodded, seeing that as a good sign as well. "Remember, no one but Amy knows about what happened today."

Gabe turned off the ignition and stared at her. "Claire. You don't really think that I'd say anything?"

"Who knows, maybe by tonight it will all blow over and Hallie will be back to her usual self." Claire realized that the thing that shook her up the most wasn't that Hallie might be having doubts about her wedding but that Hallie wasn't behaving like she always did—the way that Claire had come to count on her being.

The way that Claire valued more than she'd known.

"Everything okay?" Gabe asked, never missing anything.

"I guess I just wonder what would happen if Hallie didn't get married to Josh tomorrow. Her entire life is wrapped up in him, in his family, in their life here together." And what would happen to the house? Claire hadn't been back much in years. It was easier to stay away from the memories. But that didn't mean that she wanted the house to be sold or, worse, torn down for something newer and shinier.

A replacement model, she thought angrily, then banished the thought.

"Wasn't that the very life you questioned?" Gabe pointed out.

"I guess I can't imagine Hallie any other way," she said. But could Hallie?

"Well, I don't think you have anything to worry about," Gabe said, interrupting her thoughts. "I just saw Josh walk in looking very happy and relaxed."

Meaning that whatever had troubled Hallie, she hadn't shared it with Josh.

By the time they walked into the elegant building a few moments later, Claire was once again feeling anxious about Hallie's whereabouts, especially when she saw Josh looking around the room, presumably for her, and then checking his phone. Claire did the same, and, seeing nothing, fired off a quick but vague text to Amy: Almost here?

She swiped a glass of champagne from a passing waiter, waiting for the phone to vibrate in her hand, knowing that she wouldn't fully relax until it did. Hallie might have come home, might have gone straight into the shower, but that didn't mean whatever was troubling her was forgotten.

"Swanky place," Gabe observed.

Claire forced herself to look around. The lobby was dimly lit, the warm wood tones and shades of blue, gray, and beige perfectly complementing the seascape that was visible from most of the floor-to-ceiling windows. The dining room was decorated with overflowing centerpieces, the french doors open to the deck and the view of the harbor and the sailboats docked there, their masts down. The ocean breeze flowed through the room as gently as the piano music from the corner, and to ward off the chill, a fire crackled in the oversize stone hearth.

Gabe nudged her with his elbow. "There's your mom and sisters."

Claire swung around to follow his gaze and held up a hand to wave at her family. Bunny smiled brightly, Amy looked a little tenser, and Hallie didn't acknowledge her at all.

Just what she was afraid of. Now wasn't the time to confront her sister, not when Josh was making long strides toward Hallie. Claire observed their interaction from across the room, but her attention was pulled away by Gabe leaning in to whisper in her ear. "Your aunt Marcia just noticed us. She's headed this way. And three . . . two . . ."

"Marcia!" Claire realized her voice was tight as her aunt descended on them.

Claire darted her eyes back to where Hallie and Josh were, but they were no longer visible, surrounded by well-wishers and a thickening crowd of people.

Frustrated, she turned back to her aunt, but the anxiety was building in her chest, and she felt suffocated. Like she needed to get out of this room. Outside. Or anywhere where she could clear her head.

"I was hoping I'd be seated at your table," Marcia was saying, "but it seems that there is no formal arrangement today. Tell me, where are you two going to be?"

One problem was quickly replaced with another. Claire used the excuse to scan the room again, looking for just two open spots and nothing more. Her mother was now chatting with the Goodwins, and Amy was alone at the bar, nursing a glass of white wine and glancing at the lobby every few minutes, no doubt waiting for Logan to appear.

"Oh, um . . ." Claire craned her neck, looking for a glimpse of Hallie. She just needed to see her face. Her eyes. Her smile. One look would confirm her fear. Or put her mind at ease.

But then she heard Gabe say, "I just realized I haven't had a tour of the place, and dinner will start soon. You don't mind if we slip away, do you, Marcia? I'm sure we'll have plenty of time to connect later. Tomorrow is such a *big day.*"

That managed to pull a smile from Claire, and as Marcia started to protest and talk about seating, Claire muttered her goodbyes, and they dashed out one of the open doors.

"You saved us from an hour of tricky conversation," she told him once they were alone on the patio. She pulled in several deep breaths, allowing the ocean breeze to fill her lungs, to calm her. "Actually, I'm surprised you did that. I thought chatting with my relatives was a new hobby of yours."

He gave a little shrug. "I like our alone time better."

Before she could react, she realized that he'd been looking at her, closely, for longer than usual, that his arm was still around her waist, holding her close, even as she now turned to face him. And that the deck had cleared out. There was no one around. They were alone. And they could stop pretending.

Only she wasn't so sure that they were pretending at all.

Her heart began to pound as she stared into his eyes, all too aware suddenly of his grip on her waist, the warmth of his body next to hers, and the curve of his lips as he leaned in and—

"Oh! There you are!"

Claire jerked back to see her mother standing in the doorway. "The toasts are starting. I know that Hallie wouldn't want you to miss them."

Bunny slipped back into the dining room, leaving Claire and Gabe alone once more.

"Maybe she saved us from a tricky conversation," she joked, lightening the mood. Maybe giving the moment a pass.

"Oh, there's plenty of time left in the evening. The trip, though, it's coming to an end." Gabe hesitated for a moment. "I meant it when I said I was having fun. This week . . . it's been really nice."

She nodded, pulling away slightly, and his arm dropped. "It has."

"Looks like the bride and groom are okay after all," he said, jutting his chin to the open doorway where the couple was standing up, Josh saying something to the guests.

Claire tried to see Hallie's face, to catch her eye, but she didn't have a good angle.

"You don't think they're okay?" Gabe asked.

Claire studied her sister from this vantage, trying to shake the doubts she was feeling. She focused on the facts. They were here. Together. Holding hands. Josh beaming into the microphone. Hallie standing at his side.

"They must be fine," she whispered, because anything else would imply that she was doubting them and their marriage. And she'd promised not to do that, hadn't she?

"Well, we should get back in. Shall we?" He held out his hand.

Claire smoothed her dress, feeling the burn in her cheeks when she slipped her hand in his, telling herself it was okay this once, that she was just playing a part. His palm was warm and smooth, and it felt foreign, a part of him that she didn't yet know.

She couldn't even look at Gabe as they made their way into the dining room, but when they sat down at the two open seats, fortunately nowhere near Marcia, she stole a glance, and the smile that still rested on his face only filled her with more confusion than was already there.

The party showed no signs of slowing after the dinner, and neither did the crowd. Claire tried to make eye contact with Hallie several times, but unless she wanted to barge in and pull Hallie away from Josh, a conversation would have to be saved for after the party.

"How was the ride over?" Claire asked Amy once she could be sure they wouldn't be overheard. She was picking at her dessert, and Amy, beside her, had barely eaten her meal—whether out of worry about Hallie or feelings for Logan, who was seated on the other side of the room, Claire couldn't be sure.

"She seemed okay," Amy said slowly. "Quiet. Mom did most of the talking. And it was a short drive. Maybe she got it out of her system."

Maybe, but Amy looked as unconvinced as Claire felt.

"You want to come back to the house with us?" Claire asked. She was tired, and tomorrow was going to be a big day.

Big day. She couldn't even find humor in that right now.

Amy's gaze flicked across the room to where Logan was still sitting before she shook her head. "You go on. I'll stay and keep an eye on Hallie."

Claire nodded, and gestured to Gabe that they should head back.

"We could sit on the porch and listen to the ocean," she offered when he pulled the car to a stop outside Beachnest Cottage a few minutes later. They were the first ones back, and she longed for one more chance to sit outside this great house, knowing it could be the last. Or at least the last time for a while.

Plus, she wasn't exactly eager to get upstairs to the bedroom just yet.

"You seem a little sad," he observed after they'd settled into two wicker chairs.

She shrugged. "Just remembering all the other times I've sat outside here. When I'm in New York I don't think of this place much at all. Being here just brings everything back."

"You're thinking about your father?"

She knew what he was implying. That her father was gone, gone for eight years now, but it was more than that. So much more.

"We used to sit outside here in the evenings, until nightfall. Sometimes, because I was an early riser like him, we'd enjoy the sunrise. Just the two of us. We'd take long runs along the shore and then race back to this porch. He'd always let me win, even though the older I got, the more I tried to slow down to let him catch up."

"He sounds like a really special man," Gabe said.

Claire swallowed the lump in her throat. "I thought he was."

She cleared her throat, straightening up in the chair. Being back here always stirred up emotions she could better contain in the city. She calmed herself by counting the hours until she was back at work, behind her desk, handling the problems of people from arm's length, not within her own life.

"Less than sixty hours before we're back in the office," she said. "When should I break the news to my family that we broke up?"

Gabe rubbed his chin, sliding his gaze from the ocean back to her. "Oh, I don't know. Maybe you don't need to tell them just yet."

"They'll be heartbroken," Claire admitted.

"They won't be the only ones," Gabe said, his eyes locking on hers.

Claire quickly looked away, out onto the water, which was visible only by the light of the moon.

"Yes, well, all relationships must come to an end at some point, and lots should end and don't."

And lots that you thought would last forever never really stood a chance, she thought bitterly.

"Claire." His voice was husky, insistent, forcing her gaze to return to his. "You really don't believe that anyone is truly happy being married?"

Once she had, but not now. She wasn't the little girl playing wedding anymore. She'd never again take her turn with the family veil, imagining a bright future with a guaranteed happy ending.

They simply didn't exist.

"You asked me something the other day. You asked me how I can still believe in love after my engagement ended."

She nodded. "You didn't tell me why."

"Because I wasn't ready then. Because I didn't know what you'd say. Because I didn't want to risk ruining what we have. But I don't want to risk missing out on all that we can be either." He looked her in the eye. "The reason I still believe is because of you, Claire."

Her heart sped up with alarm. "Me?"

He reached out and took her hand, holding it tightly, firmly. "You. Of all people, you, the girl who claims not to believe in any of this. We made a connection right from the start. I never thought that I'd find that after my engagement ended, but with you it was easy. It was better. It felt right. And it confirmed I'd made the right choice." He grabbed her by the shoulders and gave a little shake of the head. "You mean something to me, Claire. Not just as a friend. Or a work wife. But as something more. Something special. You made me believe in love again, even if you don't believe in it for yourself."

She stared at him, all too aware that he was probably waiting for her to say something, to return his feelings or admit that she didn't. Couldn't. But she couldn't do any of that. Nothing would ever be the same between them after this. She knew it. He knew it, too, even if he wasn't saying that.

All she'd wanted was to hold on to what they had.

And now he'd gone and ruined it. She set her jaw, angry and upset. With him—for destroying what had been a good thing up until now. A safe thing. And with herself—for not being able to do what came so easily to others. To give in. To trust. To risk her heart.

With a little shake of his head, he dropped her hand and stood.

"Gabe," she pleaded, not wanting him to go, not like this. "I . . . I don't want to complicate things between us."

"Too late," he said, leaving her alone on the porch.

CHAPTER
TWENTY-THREE

Amy

"Well, I have to hand it to the event planner," Amy told her mother while they sipped after-dinner drinks near the bar. Whoever it was had done an exquisite job with the already beautiful venue, turning the cozy and nautical-themed dining room and waterfront patio into an elegant enough space to have been the wedding reception itself.

"Oh, I think this was Coco's doing," Bunny said, setting her glass of champagne on the bar top.

Amy was surprised to hear this. "Really? But then, Josh is her only child. I suppose she wanted to personally take on the task."

Bunny winced. "I feel like I haven't done enough for Hallie. But I had so much going on with the business, and then with the date being pushed up." Her mother shook her head. "Thank goodness you were able to step in and help out."

"If you could call it helping," Amy grumbled, nearly drowning out the words as she took a long sip from her glass.

"What do you mean? You've devoted yourself to this wedding all week! The flowers. The appointments. Even the cake!"

Amy nodded. There was no denying she'd been busy. But busy making whose dream come true?

She looked at her mother, sensing the apprehension in Bunny's eyes. This was her daughter's wedding weekend, and Amy would be damned if she upset her mother as well as Hallie.

Just thinking about her little sister made her suck in a nervous breath. She flitted her eyes around the room, but it was thick with people, gathered in groups, mingling merrily.

"Did you talk to Hallie tonight?" Amy ventured, hoping her tone remained light.

But Bunny shook her head. "Not since we walked in. With so many of the Goodwins' relatives wanting to have a chance to say hello, it's been a little hectic." She suddenly lifted her chin. "But there she is now!"

Sure enough, there, near the Goodwins, was Hallie. Josh said something to the group, and Hallie tossed her head back, her golden hair falling at her shoulders, her laughter its usual contagious peal.

Amy hadn't even realized she'd been holding her breath until it released in a long sigh.

"I should thank them for such a wonderful night before I leave," Bunny said.

"Go on," Amy said to her mother, who was clearly torn between keeping Amy company and chatting with the hosts. "I'll be fine on my own."

And she was, she reminded herself, casting one last glance in Logan's direction. For the past five years, she'd been just fine. A little bruised. A little lonely. But fine, really.

Amy watched her mother cross the room, another single woman with her head held high, not afraid to brave this weekend on her own, and then took in the choice of centerpieces and candles, as well as the layout of the room. The dinner had been delicious, not that she'd eaten much, but of course the standards were high here at the Harbor Club.

The bar was full, for those seeking something else, and the music was soft and jazzy, setting a perfect evening mood. The large french doors that spanned an entire wall of the dining room had been opened so the outside extended in, and people could come and go as they pleased. The sea breeze filtering in was warm and calming, reminding them of where they were, even as the mood seemed to sweep them away.

But Amy wasn't getting sucked into all that, not tonight. No, tonight her eyes were on the room, on the guests—or rather, the guests of honor. She needed to be sure that she hadn't upset Hallie, hadn't ruined something so special that she could never get back.

She knew she couldn't take it personally that Hallie was occupied all night by other guests. But if she could just have a private conversation with her sister, assurance that she hadn't made a mess of planning Hallie's wedding, Amy would sleep a lot better tonight.

She moved toward the bar, watching through the open doors as Hallie and Josh now chatted with some of Josh's relatives, most of whom had flown in this morning for the weekend. Hallie wore a simple pink silk dress, her feet in strappy sandals, and an ivory wrap hung low at her back for when the chill picked up, which it would. Josh was laughing at something one of his cousins was saying, and Hallie did too. By all appearances, they were the vision of a happy couple on the eve of their wedding, but Amy knew better.

And she knew her sister. And Hallie's smile was strained. There was something bothering her, more than a veil or a piece of jewelry from a shop in town.

It was a look of loss, Amy realized, wishing she could unsee it. Hallie's eyes were flat, resigned, just like they were at their father's funeral.

It was a look of awareness. Maybe even resignation. That she was losing someone she loved more than anyone. Maybe that person was Josh.

Amy was so busy worrying about Hallie and whether this wedding was going to happen—and what it meant if it didn't—that she didn't even notice Logan come up beside her.

"Just a friendly reminder that this is a party. You're supposed to be having fun." He grinned, but she struggled to match it.

"Sorry. Just . . . a lot on my mind."

"Is it me?" he asked.

Amy's heart sped up. "Why would you say that?"

"About this morning," he clarified.

Oh. Of course. She shook her head. Her argument with Logan felt like days ago, with how much had transpired since then.

"You made a fair point," she said. Even if it hurt to hear it. "Besides, I could never stay mad at you for long."

He opened his eyes in surprise. "You could have fooled me. I spent the past five years wondering what I'd done to make you so upset you wouldn't even want to come to my wedding."

"Well, the bride didn't exactly like me," she pointed out, hearing the defensive tone of her voice. "And the ball was pretty much in your court, Logan. I wasn't about to become a third wheel. And I never knew that you didn't end up getting married."

"I regretted not reaching out after that," Logan said. "It was . . . one of my biggest regrets when it comes to you and me."

"One of them?" She stared at him, her heart pounding, wondering what the other ones were.

"Well, for starters, I'm sorry. For what I said this morning. For how I've been this week. You've put a lot of thought and effort into making this wedding beautiful for your sister."

So that was all it was, then. Regret for pointing out the obvious. That she'd overstepped. Upset her sister. Who seemed to have recovered for the toasts but who maybe was just putting on a good show.

"I have, though I'm not sure if tonight was all that Hallie hoped it would be." And that just about broke her heart. The moment Hallie had dreamed of, ever since she was a little girl, with big shining eyes, was here. And none of it was going as she'd planned.

And maybe that was all Amy's fault.

"Do you get the sense that anything is . . . wrong?"

"Wrong?" Logan looked surprised and darted a glance around the room as if he should be looking for something obvious. "You mean, like with the food?"

Amy laughed. If only it were that simple.

"Have you had a chance to talk to Josh tonight?" she tried again, taking a sip of her chilled white wine to calm her nerves.

Logan shook his head. "Only to say hello. Everyone wants a few minutes with the bride and groom before tomorrow. A lot of out-of-towners haven't seen him in a while." He tipped his head. "What's going on?"

Amy almost wished she hadn't said anything. She shrugged it off, hoping to dismiss his concern as well as her own, but there was a panic building in her chest, one that wouldn't go away until she was alone with her sister.

If Hallie would even hear her out. Or open up.

"Nothing. Just . . . well, too much, really." She forced a smile she didn't quite feel, but one glance at Logan's face had the same effect on her it always did, and her mood started to shift.

She took another sip of her wine, telling herself that she was overreacting. Hallie was stressed; it was understandable. But she was here. And actions spoke more than words oftentimes.

"Let me guess. Marcia's been asking you when you'll be settling down now that Hallie's spoken for." His eyes glimmered, and Amy wondered if he had any idea what the mere mention of a wedding did to her.

She laughed, but it didn't come easily. "I think, for the time being, I'll continue living vicariously through my clients."

Or her sister, she realized with shame. She'd thought she was giving Hallie the perfect wedding, but instead, she was giving Hallie the wedding of her own dreams.

"Wish I had the same excuse. Marcia has already had some words with me."

Amy closed her eyes. She could only imagine how that had gone over. Like Josh, Amy's extended family had known Logan for years and treated him like one of the fold, which meant they felt free to speak candidly in his presence.

Or at least, they did. But then, that had been years ago.

"Only to tell me that she's missed me," he added.

The silence was a strain between them, reminding them of years spent apart.

"And to tell me that she's happy I didn't end up getting married."

"She didn't!" Amy stared at Logan in horror, all worries about her sister and the wedding momentarily forgotten.

"Said she'd always wanted to keep me in the family, and now she had hope," he said.

Amy felt her cheeks flush. There were a dozen excuses she could make for her aunt's comment, but none of them would be true. Marcia had just said what she felt. What probably they all felt.

"But to say that about your wedding." Amy grimaced. "Sorry. She's not the most . . . sensitive."

"And that's what I always liked about her," Logan said, no hurt feelings. "She tells it like it is. Life would be a lot easier if everyone did, don't you think?"

He was staring at her now, his gaze deep and challenging, and for a moment, the room grew hot, until a breeze made Amy shiver.

"Why? Something on your mind?" she managed to finally say.

He raised an eyebrow, his mouth lifting at one corner. And for once she couldn't read him. Couldn't figure out what he was thinking or what he might have to say but felt he couldn't.

All she could think was that the only thing sadder than the time they had lost was the ground they were now making up for.

"Are you . . . happy?" she asked. Then, feeling the need to clarify her question, she said, "That you didn't get married?"

Logan frowned slightly, like he was considering the question for the first time.

"I am," he said.

Her heart seemed to swoop, pulling the blood from her face before filling it again. Her cheeks burned.

"Oh, it's getting warm in here now that the room's filling up," she observed.

He gave her a funny look. "But you just shivered a moment ago."

"Did I?" She moved toward the door. "Well, when the breeze hits . . ."

But he wasn't buying it. He knew her too well.

"They did a lovely job with this," Amy commented. "I can only hope that it doesn't overshadow tomorrow." She laughed, but there was a nervous edge to it. It would be so easy to be that girl again—the girl who lived at Beachnest Cottage and saw Logan all the time, the girl who used to laugh at all his jokes because they were genuinely funny. The girl who woke up every day with him on her mind. The girl who held out hope that eventually, one day, he'd tell her that he loved her. As more than just a friend.

"So long as the bride and groom are happy, that's all that matters," Logan said mildly.

"How I wish it were that simple." Amy sighed. "I just hope I didn't upset her . . . with my suggestions."

"You didn't mean any harm," he said gently.

No, she hadn't. But some may have been done anyway.

"I know you, Amy," he said again.

Did he, though? Now? Or even then, years ago, when she thought they were so close?

Amy slurped from her wineglass. "I guess you can't understand. You got to plan your wedding—"

"My wedding was called off," Logan said, his voice dropping to a whisper.

"Yeah, well, that was your choice, wasn't it? It was all your choice."

"What's that supposed to mean?"

She shook her head. "Nothing. It doesn't mean anything. It's . . . moot." A legal term her sister loved to use, but it worked here. "I shouldn't have to explain. There was a time when neither of us ever had to explain. But that doesn't mean you knew me. Not as well as you thought."

"Amy? What are you talking about?"

She knew she could leave it alone. Blame it on stress, the wine, or the long week. She could go back to Boston on Sunday, call Gail, and be at her old desk by Monday, and life would just continue along as it had for the past five years.

But she didn't like being misunderstood. Not by her sister. Not by the man standing in front of her, wondering just why she'd skipped out on his wedding that never happened.

She owed him the truth. And she owed it to herself, too—if only to remind herself that she wasn't the same girl she was the last time they'd stood together in this room. She'd pieced together her broken heart, made a whole new life for herself, one that was waiting for her, the day after tomorrow.

"I'm talking about you and me, Logan. I'm talking about how all this, this could have been us. We were just as close as Hallie and Josh. Closer even. But it wasn't enough for you, was it? I wasn't enough for you."

He stared at her, his expression giving nothing away.

"You wonder why I didn't want to come to your wedding? Why I didn't reach out all this time?" Her heart was racing, and her hands were shaking, but she knew that if she didn't say it now, she never would.

She might not even see him again after the wedding. If there even was a wedding. "You broke my heart, Logan."

There. It was out. She didn't know what kind of reaction she'd expected, but his expression was frozen, unreadable even to her.

"I loved you, and you loved someone else more." The reminder of that hurt felt fresh and raw. "And there was no way that I was still going to be the girl you texted and called and laughed with and confided in all the time when you were choosing to share your life with another woman."

He blinked in confusion. "Amy. I had no idea you felt that way."

"No. You didn't. It didn't even cross your mind." And didn't that confirm all her deepest heartache? "So excuse me if I got a little carried away making this the wedding of my sister's dreams. It's the first wedding I've had a chance to plan, if you can believe it, and the way it's going, it could easily be my last. And maybe you're right. Maybe I did make it too much about me. What I would have wanted. Because it was the closest I got to having my dream come true."

She was fighting back tears now, trembling, and she realized that she'd spoken loudly. She looked around, but the crowd was thick, happy, and completely absorbed in their conversations. Couples grouped with couples. Music playing over the tinkling of glasses. An ocean breeze dulling all the sounds to a silent hush.

No one would even notice if she left, she realized. They'd all found their people. Their groups. Their path.

And she'd only ever hit a dead-end road with Logan.

"Amy," he said, but stopped there. His forehead was lined with confusion—she wouldn't read anything more into it. Not anymore.

She paused only to look around the room for Hallie, who was now standing beside their mother, surrounded by a group of people that Amy didn't even know.

"I should go," she said. Back to the house. Back to Boston. Back to the life that she'd made without him. She started to walk away, because she'd given Logan enough chances to speak up, to tell her the words she'd longed to hear and never would. Still, a tiny part of her that held out for hope, that clung to that fairy-tale dream that was at least coming true for one of them, listened for his voice, slowed her pace for his arm, waiting for something that didn't come.

CHAPTER
TWENTY-FOUR

Hallie

Hallie didn't know how she was getting through the night, not when her eyes kept cutting to the old nautical clock near the bar, not when she now knew that in less than twenty-four hours, the wedding ceremony would have passed and guests would be gathered at the manor, eating the appetizers she'd selected—unless Amy had gone and changed them without mentioning it.

She hadn't seen Josh all day between his tux fittings and her dress appointment, and hadn't had a chance to really speak to him all night. For the second night in a row, they were engaged in small talk instead, thanking guests for coming, talking about their honeymoon, their jobs, the house, and this club.

When Marcia and Pam excused themselves to say hello to Coco, whom they hadn't seen since last summer, she saw her chance.

"We need to talk." There. It was out.

"Now?" Josh looked startled.

She nodded. "Now." Because if not now, then when? It was bad luck for a groom to see the bride on their wedding day, and she didn't need to tempt fate any more than she already had.

"No one will even notice if we slip outside for a minute." She took his hand and led him onto the patio, where the fresh air filled her lungs but the salty breeze did little to calm her.

The moon reflected off the water, where boats bobbed on the soft waves, docked and dark for the night. The music faded behind them as they cut across the grass, distancing themselves from the party.

"Did you mean what you said last night?" she blurted. When he didn't react, she clarified. "About having *five* kids?"

For a moment, Josh looked surprised, and then he started to laugh. "Is that what this is about? Jeez, Hallie, you were scaring me for a minute there."

She felt a nervous laugh escape her. Maybe she had overreacted, let her emotions get the best of her, after all. "Yeah, well, you scared me for a minute too. I mean, five kids."

Now, Josh's laughter did stop. "You know I always hated being an only child, Hallie."

Hallie swallowed against the pounding of her heart. "Yeah, but you aren't a kid anymore. You're an adult. And you're not alone. You have me."

"That's different," he said.

"You're right. It is. Having a bunch of kids doesn't change your childhood, Josh. And who has five kids these days?"

"Since when do we do what others do?" He shrugged, giving her a little grin that made her realize he wasn't going to back down. He wanted this. But did he honestly think she did too?

She stared at him pointedly. "You can't be serious. That's all we do. We do what others did before us; we follow the path they've carved for us. We didn't even get jobs on our own! Or a house!"

Or plan their own wedding, she thought, thinking of how resistant she was to any change, to anything that would make it her own.

"Is that what this is about?" A frown pinched his eyebrows. "The wedding? The house? I told you that if you don't want to work here, my parents would understand. No one made us do any of this. It was there, and we took it, and I thought that's because we both wanted it."

"It's not about the house. Or where we work." It wasn't even about the wedding. She'd hoped it was, even if deep down she knew it was so much more. "It's like we never talked about our future, not really. We just fell into it, because it was there and it was obvious. But we never talked about kids, Josh. Not seriously. And certainly not five."

He stood back a little, seeming thrown. "You have two sisters. Beachnest Cottage is a huge house. You always talk about how you miss the days when it was filled with laughter and noise and activity. I just assumed that you'd want a big family."

"Well, I don't. Or I don't know if I do." She paused, sensing his frustration that matched her own. He was right. She'd always loved a full house, that big summer home full of energy and noise, but she'd also come to love the quiet and the peace. But she'd liked it as it was, and she just couldn't picture it like he was imagining. "I guess I never really thought about it," she finally said.

Josh nodded, his face so serious that she felt guilty for making him as unhappy as she was right now. This was the eve of their wedding. Something they'd been moving toward for ten years.

"We don't have to make any decisions now," Josh said.

It would be easy to agree, to go back to the party, to shove this discussion away for another, distant time. But she'd never doubted a future with Josh before. And she couldn't wake up on her wedding day feeling as confused as she did now. "We're supposed to be getting married tomorrow, and we haven't even agreed on one of the most important parts of our lives together!"

She shook her head, wondering how she could have missed this, how she could have overlooked something so huge.

But then it hit her. She'd done exactly what she accused him of doing. She'd assumed that he'd want what she did. Because they'd always gone along with things. Until now.

He reached for her hands, giving her a little smile, but his eyes were pleading. "Do we really have to decide now? Like you said, we're getting married. Tomorrow!"

She shook her head. "Josh, what do you really want? I need to know. Would you be happy with one kid, or two? None? Because nothing is guaranteed."

"Can't we just see?" Josh asked, growing exasperated and dropping her hand. "Can't we just let one thing be uncertain? Everything else is planned out."

"And that's worked for us," Hallie said. "That's what's kept us together. We've followed a plan until now, but life doesn't always go according to plan. And this is the first time we want something . . . different."

And would it be the last? Probably not if this could happen.

"Tell me what you really want," she said to him softly. "In an ideal world. If everything just continues along, falling into place."

He hesitated, as if he knew what he was about to say would be a problem, and she already felt the tightening of her stomach before the words came.

"I always wanted a big family, Hallie. It was something I dreamed of my entire life. Just like you dreamed of this wedding. I dreamed of something else."

Something else.

She swallowed hard, blinking back tears. She couldn't fault him or blame him for wanting something she didn't.

"Well, I guess it's good that we're finally getting this out now before it's too late," she said, fighting not to cry.

"Too late? What are you saying?" He pulled back, blinking at her.

"I just think that maybe we never stopped to ask ourselves what we wanted." She hesitated, hating that she even thought what she was about to say next. "And now I'm not so sure that we want the same things after all."

"Hallie!" He stepped toward her, but she was already backing up.

"The dinner's already over," she said, her mind spinning, thinking of where to go, what to say. Everyone was here at the club. The house would be empty now. "No one will notice I'm gone. And I need to go. Home. Alone."

Even though there was no chance of her being alone at the house tonight, and he knew it.

The anguished look on his face told him that he also knew what she meant. That she wasn't talking about getting away from her sisters or mother or aunts and cousins.

She was talking about him.

"Hallie, we need to talk." His voice was firm as he quickened his stride toward her.

"We already have," Hallie said, her voice pleading as she fought back tears. "It was something we should have done a lot sooner."

How much else was there that they hadn't considered, hadn't thought about? Everything had been laid out for them: their jobs, their house. But what went on inside that house, when it was just the two of them, was all up to them. And right now they couldn't even agree on how many children they wanted.

Or what other things they might have wanted and found some-where else. With someone else.

"Hallie, it doesn't have to be this way."

She wavered for a moment, thinking that maybe he was right, that they could just put this conversation to rest for the night and forget it ever happened, but how long would it be until it came up again?

They could go back to the party, hand in hand, and she could wake up tomorrow, knowing she was going to cement her future with the man she loved.

The only thing she was certain of right now was that she loved him. But for the first time since she'd first set eyes on him, she wasn't sure that would be enough.

Hallie sat on the porch in her pajamas and a soft wool wrap pulled tightly around her shoulders, replaying the conversation with Josh over and over again, fighting the urge to pick up her phone and call him, or respond to the numerous texts he'd sent asking her to do just that. She felt sick to her stomach every time she remembered the look on his face before she'd left, and a huge urge to reach out and make things right, to take back what she'd said and go back to that place of comfort and certainty. Only right now, marrying Josh made her future feel as uncertain as not marrying him. She knew that if she went to bed, she might wake up feeling better, with a clearer mind, but she didn't see how she could sleep after this, not when tomorrow she would wake up to what was supposed to be her wedding day.

Claire poked her head around the doorframe still wearing her navy lace dress.

"I thought you were asleep," Hallie said, confused. "I heard snoring when I passed your bedroom door."

"That must have been Gabe," Claire said, frowning. Something must have been troubling her, because she didn't even bother to argue the point that she never snored when, in fact, she did. "I was taking a walk, but the mosquitos are bad, so I turned back."

"Without Gabe?" Hallie asked.

"Uh-oh," said Amy, coming up behind her.

Hallie was equally surprised to see her home when the party was still going on at the Harbor Club—without the bride. "I didn't know you were already home."

"We didn't know you were home either," Amy replied.

"I caught a ride with Mom," Hallie replied. "I think some of the Goodwins' relatives intend to stay up half the night."

"Weddings are certainly an excuse for a family reunion." Amy was already dressed in her pajamas. "I guess we all decided to call it an early night, then." She gave Hallie a nervous glance. "I suppose you'll need some beauty rest for tomorrow?"

Hallie just shrugged and looked out toward the ocean, the waves visible in the moonlight. If she started to talk about tomorrow right now, she might start to cry, and right now she could barely even process what had happened tonight.

"I might, uh . . . need to sleep in your room tonight, Amy," Claire said. "If you don't mind."

Amy frowned at her but then nodded. "Of course. I have some clothes in there too. If you'd like to change."

"I think I might." Claire sighed deeply and disappeared into the house.

Hallie shifted on the wicker sofa, giving Amy room to sit beside her. It was becoming clear that she wasn't the only one in her family who was troubled tonight, and she was grateful to think about someone else's problems other than her own—for a few minutes, at least.

"Think she'll tell us what's bothering her?" Hallie asked. She doubted it, considering that Claire hadn't even let anyone know that she had a boyfriend up until this point. She was hardly likely to tell anyone what was going on between the two of them.

"Are you going to tell me what's bothering you?" Amy asked. Then, more gently, "What happened this morning, Hallie? You had me worried that you were going to call off the wedding or something."

Hallie swallowed hard. Was that what she'd done? She was dizzy with how many times she'd replayed her conversation with Josh, and each time she saw the pain in his eyes, she had to close her own against the image.

But Hallie knew that she couldn't keep it in any longer; the emotions were building by the second as the clock ticked down to her wedding day. Her wedding day!

"Josh wants five kids, Amy," she said. There. It was out. And the look of horror on her sister's face was strangely satisfying.

Yep. She'd done the right thing. Called a halt to things before she made a huge mistake she couldn't take back.

"And I take it you don't want five kids?" Amy hedged.

"Of course not!" Hallie huffed. At least, she didn't think she did. She didn't plan on it, at least.

Claire appeared in the doorway. "What have I missed?"

A lot, Hallie wanted to say. *Eight years of my life.* But instead, she tossed her hands in the air, thinking that if there was ever going to be a time she would confide in Claire again, it may as well be now.

"Josh wants to have five kids!" Hallie all but shouted. Surely Claire would have a "told ya so" moment now. "There. Happy?"

Claire looked so injured that immediately Hallie regretted her words.

"Why would I be happy?" Claire asked quietly, dropping into one of the wicker chairs. In Amy's pink flannel pajama pants and white T-shirt, she seemed softer than usual, less harsh. "Hallie, I just want you to be happy."

"And Josh has always made you happy," Amy insisted.

Hallie nodded, blinking back hot tears. He had. He always had. But. There was now that *but* hanging over things.

"But that's because I never questioned things before. I didn't have to. It was always easy. We just always wanted the same things. Now . . . now I don't know what I want."

"Is this really just about how many kids you may or may not want or even actually have?" Amy pressed.

"This is the first time we've disagreed about something in our future. It just makes me worried that we don't have what it takes." Hallie leaned into Claire, resisting the urge to point at her. "You said so yourself, that first night at dinner. Not every couple has what it takes to make it long term."

"They don't," Claire said, huffing out a sigh. "But I wasn't talking about you and Josh."

"That's the problem, though, right?" Hallie countered. "You're seeing the ones who come to you. Needing a divorce. The ones you don't see . . . well, those are the ones who probably did have things planned, or at least, agreed upon."

Claire opened her mouth and then closed it again, as if rethinking what she wanted to say. "I don't know about that, Hallie. No one has everything planned. And no matter how people might present themselves, you never know what's really going on."

"But there are some couples that are just perfect. Meant to be. Soulmates. People who die within minutes of each other because they can't live apart. People who still hold hands, even when they're eighty years old."

"We can all aspire to that," Amy said. "But not many people are lucky enough to find it."

"Mom and Dad did," Hallie said firmly. "They had the perfect marriage!"

Amy nodded, but Claire was quiet, quieter than usual, especially when she wasn't exactly known for holding back her opinions.

"Claire? Why are you frowning like that?" Hallie stared at her sister. Surely even Claire couldn't dispute the fact that their parents were an example of wedded bliss.

Claire swallowed hard, hesitating.

"I just . . . don't think you should base your relationship on Mom's or even Grandma's," she said. "This is your wedding. Your relationship. And ultimately, your marriage. Measuring it against someone else isn't fair to either one of you."

Hallie saw her point, and she knew it wasn't much different from what Amy had been saying all week. But somehow she couldn't help it.

"Don't you see? You were right, Claire. Mom and Dad had what it took. Grandma and Grandpa too. But Josh and I . . . I thought we were so close, so right for each other, and now I really don't know what he wants out of life. Or what I want."

"So you're willing to call off your entire wedding and end things with Josh, the only guy you have ever loved, because you don't think you and Josh have what Mom and Dad did?" Amy stared at her, and it was clear that she didn't agree.

Hallie gritted her teeth. On the spot. A yes-or-no answer.

"You win, Claire. You were right. You're always right," she said, the bitterness seeping into her voice even when she knew that maybe she wasn't being fair. "You warned me last summer. You knew that Josh and I didn't have what it took."

"That's not what I said," Claire ground out. "I was just trying to get you to readjust your expectations."

"Of what? A happy life? With the man I love?"

"Of everything always being easy," Claire said firmly. The color was rising in her cheeks. "Of everything always being . . . perfect."

"What's wrong with perfect?" Hallie cried. "Mom and Dad had a perfect life!"

"No, they didn't," Claire shot back.

"How can you say that?" Hallie recoiled.

Claire's shoulders rose and fell with her breath.

"Because," she started and then stopped. "No one does."

"Oh, there you go with that cynicism again! Mom and Dad weren't your clients, Claire! They weren't one of these sad stories you hear every day! They weren't what hardened your heart!"

Claire's eyes blazed, but for once she didn't say anything.

"Maybe it wasn't perfect, but it was close enough," Hallie said. "You saw how they always laughed, always held hands, danced cheek to cheek at every family party, even if it was just here in the house."

"Dad cheated on Mom," Claire blurted. She closed her eyes, and when she opened them again, she looked like she might burst into tears.

And Claire didn't burst into tears. She didn't cry. Not even at their father's funeral.

The silence was so long and so pure that it was almost audible. Hallie stared at her sister, only the sound of the ocean louder than the rushing of blood in her ears. Her heart was pounding against her rib cage as she tried to come down from this argument, from the level of their voices, from the words that they'd spoken. From what Claire had just said.

"I'm sorry!" Claire cried, reaching for Hallie's hand, but Hallie snatched it back. "I'm sorry. I never wanted to say anything. I didn't plan to tell you. But—"

Amy turned to Claire, her voice incredulous. "What are you saying, Claire? That's crazy."

"It's true," Claire said softly, her voice grave, her eyes filled with regret. "I heard them arguing one night. It was about a month before he . . . died. I was home from law school for the weekend and up late studying. I came down to get some water, and there they were. Right there in that kitchen." She swung her arm toward the door, to the kitchen beyond it. The one where they'd all gathered so many times, the one where their father used to flip pancakes and call out orders like he was running a diner.

Hallie loved that kitchen because she loved the way they'd filled it. But now . . .

"He'd been seeing another woman," Claire said angrily.

"I don't believe you," Hallie snapped, even as doubt settled deep into her stomach, making it ache. "That kitchen was full of happy moments. Dad adored Mom. They did everything together. They ran a successful business together. They raised us. We were a happy family before Dad died."

"We were," Claire said quietly.

"So see? You must have misunderstood." Hallie folded her arms, only to find that they were shaking. She looked at Amy, who seemed lost in something far away, but not arguing, not lashing out, but maybe, worse, letting it sink in. Believing it. And then Hallie looked at Claire, who looked like she wanted to take back what she'd said.

And oh, how Hallie wished she would.

"You must have misheard them," Hallie said again, pleading, almost begging for it to be true.

Claire gave her a look of such remorse and genuine sympathy that she didn't need to say another word. Hallie knew it was true. "I wish I had. More than you know."

"Did you ever think that maybe you did mishear?" Amy demanded, shooting a look at Hallie. Their roles had reversed, and it was now Amy who couldn't accept it, while Hallie felt her shoulders sink, and she turned toward the house, wondering if it would ever feel the same again.

"Come on, Claire. He was a hands-on father. He was always here, always around. And he was happy with us." A single tear rolled down Amy's cheek as her voice broke on the last word.

"Maybe he was," Claire said sadly. "But it wasn't a onetime thing. I can't say for sure how long it had been going on or why or how. I just knew that everything I'd once believed to be true wasn't true at all."

"And Mom knew!" Hallie cried, the idea just occurring to her. Her mind was spinning, playing back every conversation she'd had with her mother about her father, how there'd never been a hint of this. Not a suggestion. "And she never told us!"

"I don't know if she confronted him or he decided to confess. I walked in midconversation. They were speaking quietly. When I'd heard enough, I ran back upstairs." Claire sighed heavily. "Mom doesn't know that I know. I never wanted to tell you."

"So you held on to this, all these years?" Amy's tone was full of wonder, but there was something else there. Sadness.

And understanding.

"That's why you changed," Hallie said aloud. She stared at her sister, almost accusatory. "That's why you went into divorce law. That's why you stopped believing in love and romance."

Claire didn't argue. "Like I said. Things happen that change people."

"I just can't believe it," Amy said, shaking her head.

Hallie stared miserably up at the house. All her life she'd seen the happy snapshots and thought of her parents in their wedding album like a princess and her prince in a fairy tale.

And maybe that's all it was. A fairy tale. Fiction.

She turned to Claire, the one person she could be sure always had her best interest at heart, even when Hallie didn't want to hear the truth. "If Mom and Dad didn't even have a perfect marriage, then what hope is there for any of us?"

And for once, Claire didn't have an answer.

"I need to go to bed," Hallie said, standing up on shaking legs.

Both her sisters rose to their feet. "Hallie, please—" Claire started, but Hallie shook her head, stopping her.

"I can't talk about this anymore tonight. Or think about it. I need to be alone." She gave them a pleading look. "Please."

They didn't follow her as she walked back into the house, up the stairs, and into the quiet respite of her childhood bedroom. And when she closed the door behind herself, she finally felt the tears she'd been holding back spill down her cheeks, hot with anger and loss and need.

For the second time in one night, she'd walked away from someone she loved.

But now she realized that someone she'd loved had turned his back on her once too.

CHAPTER
TWENTY-FIVE

Claire

Claire woke up with a pounding headache that she wasn't entirely sure a strong cup of coffee could fix. Last night was a blur, but as her eyes adjusted to the light streaming through Amy's windows, it came back to her, one awful piece at a time.

Hallie. And Amy. The looks on their faces.

She'd told them the one thing she'd held on to all these years, keeping it tucked away, telling herself it was better if they never knew.

It would have been so much better if she never knew.

But now it was out. The damage was done. And she'd gone and done exactly what she'd promised her mother and Amy and even Gabe that she wouldn't do, which was ruin this wedding.

And worse, hurt her sisters. The one thing she'd vowed never to do.

Beside her, the bed was empty, meaning Amy had already gotten a start to the day.

Or that she didn't want to be alone with Claire when she woke up. They'd said nothing more last night after Hallie had gone to her room.

Maybe there was nothing more to say. Or maybe Amy, like Hallie, simply longed to be alone.

She put on a robe—Amy's, but they were roughly the same size—and carefully opened the door, straining her ear for sounds from the far corners of the house and hearing nothing.

Across the hallway, the door to her bedroom was closed, and she hesitated for a moment, wondering if Gabe was inside, if she should knock, if there was anything that she could say.

But then another door opened, and Hallie appeared, looking disheveled and tired. And nothing like a bride should look on the morning of her wedding day.

Claire considered how different this morning might have been if she'd held her tongue last night or said something different—what her sister needed to hear, not what Claire had been withholding from her for so long. She could have paused, taken a few breaths, and found another way to get through to her sister and get her to stop comparing herself to their parents all the time. To stop using their marriage as some unreachable standard.

"Coffee?" Hallie asked softly.

Claire felt her eyes well with hot tears. It was a simple question, but the implication meant so much more.

Careful not to wake the rest of the house, they padded down the stairs like they once did, long before Claire's perception of her family had changed, back when she still had an open heart, one that she shared with her sisters.

Before she shut them out. The world out.

"I wasn't sure you'd speak to me again after last night," she told Hallie once they were tucked away in the kitchen.

Hallie gave her a long look of sympathy. And maybe understanding.

"I'm so sorry, Hallie," Claire pressed. "I never meant to hurt you. I just wanted . . . to be there for you."

"I feel like I'm the one who should be apologizing," Hallie said, stepping toward her. "It was easy for me to assume you'd just hardened yourself since Dad died. That you let your job turn you cynical. That you stopped being a part of the family. Stopped caring."

"I did care!" Claire protested. Then, lowering her voice, she whispered, "You have no idea how much I care."

"Oh, I think I have an idea." Hallie tipped her head. "I always expected you to take care of me when I was a kid. It never occurred to me that you still were."

"Of course I was," Claire said gently. "I always will. You're my baby sister."

"And I'm no longer a baby, Claire." Hallie reached out and took her hand. "And you could have come to me with this. You could have made me understand why you stayed away and shut yourself off. Then you wouldn't have had to."

"I didn't want you to hurt as much as I did," Claire ground out. Even now, standing in this kitchen, she could feel the panic squeezing her chest tight, the blood rushing in her ears when she allowed herself to understand what she was overhearing that night.

"But by telling us the truth you made it possible for us to be close again. Didn't you want that?"

"So much," Claire admitted on a breath. The tears spilled down her cheeks now, all the pent-up pain finally finding a release. "I've missed you so much."

"Oh, Claire." Hallie reached out and pulled her close, and this time, for maybe the first time, it was Claire who rested her head on Hallie's shoulder instead of the other way around.

"You never have to miss me again," Hallie said when she pulled back.

Claire brushed at her tears. That was one good thing to come of all this, she supposed. But the only thing. She had her sisters back. She no longer felt the need to keep them at arm's length. To keep this house and this town far from her life. But the cost was steep.

And Hallie was paying the price.

"Hallie, please don't let what I said last night impact your choices for yourself," she pleaded. "But you've spent so much time comparing yourself to Mom, and I just . . . I had to tell you the truth. This is your life, Hallie. Your relationship. You can wear the dress and the veil, but it's still your life. And . . ."

"And you just didn't want to see me make the same mistake Mom did." Hallie looked miserable as she started the coffee and then took two mugs from the cabinet. "I get it now."

"I didn't want any of us to make that mistake. Me most of all." Claire sighed heavily. She'd deal with her own mess later. Today was about Hallie. "But I also didn't want you to think that Mom and Dad had this perfect fairy-tale life."

"You used to think that, too, once," Hallie said. "You used to wear the dress and the veil." She stopped, frowning at Claire. "But you found the veil. You gave it to me, Claire."

"Because I knew how much it meant to you." Claire sighed. She'd known where that veil was all along because she was the one who had buried it, deep in the back of the closet where she would never have to see it or be reminded of it ever again. Of the fantasy they'd all fed into. Of the imaginary life they'd all envisioned. "That night, after I came back to my room, I saw the veil hanging on a hook in the closet, left over from years before, probably the last time we'd all played with it together. I . . . I wanted to rip it, I was so upset."

"What made you stop?"

Claire shook her head. She could still remember holding the soft fabric in her hands, her eyes blurred with tears, her hands clenched into fists. The veil was so light, so old, and the material was so thin that she knew how easily she could rip it. They'd been warned countless times by their mother. And that was what had made her stop. Shove it far back in her closet, under a heap of old stuffed animals she'd also outgrown.

"It wasn't mine to ruin," she said quietly. She looked at her sister for a long moment. "And neither was your wedding."

"You didn't ruin my wedding," Hallie said sadly. She finished making her coffee, and Claire did the same, but with far less enthusiasm than she usually did with her first cup of the day. "Let's walk down to the water. I'm not ready to see anyone yet and deal with all the well-wishers."

Claire nodded and untied her robe. She draped it over the back of a kitchen chair.

"Still not sure about today, then?" Claire felt her heart sink. "I'm so sorry, Hallie. I feel like I've let you down in the worst way. I scared you off of your own wedding. Away from the person you love most. And all I really wanted to do was protect you."

"Is that why you never told us about Dad?" Hallie's eyes were filled with tears as they pushed out the back door and started toward the beach path. It was a warm day for September. The sky was a bright, cloudless blue.

Claire realized that it was the perfect wedding day. Or that it might have been if she had kept things to herself.

But she'd kept them to herself for so long. And the damage that had come with keeping them inside was almost worse than the fallout of sharing what she knew.

She'd lost belief in love a long time ago. But somewhere along the way, she'd almost lost her sisters too.

"All I ever wanted to do was see you have everything you wanted," Claire said. "This day. The way you wanted it. The life you dreamed of. But I also knew that everything you admired and looked up to wasn't real. I wanted you to stop measuring yourself against what Mom had. Start living your own life. Make sure it was the best one for you."

Hallie nodded. "You were right. I haven't thought about what I really wanted from my life. I never had to question it before."

Claire looked at her with growing concern. "I apologized for that comment at your engagement party, and I meant it, Hallie."

"But you also meant what you said," Hallie said, stopping Claire before she could protest. "You did. I know you did."

Claire let out a sigh. She couldn't lie to her sister. But she didn't want to hurt her either.

"I . . . don't think I can go through with this wedding," Hallie said.

"What?" Amy's shriek cut across the grass, halting the conversation. Both Claire and Hallie turned to see Amy, already dressed in jeans and a soft pink sweater, taking long strides toward them, blinking back tears that were quick to form.

"Oh, Hallie, please don't say that." Amy reached out to take Hallie's hand. "I was wrong to push my ideas onto you. I was trying to help, trying to make it extra beautiful, but I wasn't listening to what you wanted. I was doing what I wanted. What I . . . dreamed of. For myself. And . . . I plan to spend the morning undoing it all. It's going to be the wedding of *your* dreams, Hallie. It's going to be just the way you always wanted it to be."

Now Hallie was the one whose eyes had filled with tears. "Oh, Amy. That's just the problem. I don't think I ever stopped to really think about what I wanted."

"You know that you love Josh," Amy said.

Claire nodded. "You two have been together for ten years, and not a lot of people can say that. Trust me, I know."

"Yes, but we were kids when we met," Hallie pointed out, using Claire's own words against her.

"But you knew what you wanted," Amy said. "And who you didn't. You could have fallen for Max Steele's charms, after all, and you didn't."

Hallie visibly shuddered. "I can't imagine if I had! Can you imagine Evelyn as a mother-in-law?"

Claire managed a smile when Hallie laughed. Maybe they were getting somewhere. Maybe there was hope for them yet.

"See?" Amy begged. "You knew you didn't want Max. For good reason. You had a good sense about this. Even back then."

"Even when I was just a kid?" Hallie shook her head, not convinced.

Amy gave a shrug, but her sigh was long, wistful. "I was a kid when I met Logan, and if he asked me to marry him today, I'd say yes in a heartbeat. When you know, you know. Some people have to wait years to find the right person. Some people never do. You're one of the lucky ones, Hallie. Don't fight what you have."

Hallie brushed a tear from her cheek. "What happens if I wake up one morning and start wondering how things might have turned out if I'd tried something my way? If I'd taken a risk instead of the safe path?"

"I never said that marrying Josh was the safe path," Claire said firmly. She tried to remember her exact words but couldn't.

"The truth is that no path is safe," Amy said sadly.

"So what you're saying is that it's a risk? Getting married?" Hallie stared at Amy.

"Telling someone you love them is a risk," Amy said quietly.

Claire nodded, thinking of Gabe, of what he'd said. Of how she felt.

Of what would happen if they tried for more than what they had. And what would happen if it didn't work out.

"Maybe," Claire said quietly, "it's more of a leap of faith." And one that she hadn't ever dared to take. "And besides, why are you suddenly listening to what I have to say?"

"Because I'm not sure if Josh and I want the same things. Or if we always will. And then what?" Hallie's eyes filled with tears.

"Then you work it out," Amy said. "You're not Mom. Or Grandma. For the good or the bad, you're your own person, Hallie. This is your life. Your relationship. Your wedding day. Besides, Claire's right. Why take her advice?"

She gave Claire a wink, and Claire couldn't take any offense, not in this case.

"Because look at her!" Hallie said, tossing a hand in her direction. "You have a huge career that you love."

"I help people going through a divorce," Claire said gently. "I'm biased. And a little cynical. And . . . careful. Maybe to a fault."

She thought of Gabe, the hurt in his eyes last night. Maybe definitely to a fault.

"Careful enough to find a great guy!" Hallie said, and now Claire froze. Hallie sniffed. "All this time I thought you just didn't believe in love, marriage, commitment—none of it. Now I see that you were just waiting for the right guy instead of rushing into things with the wrong one."

Claire looked at Amy, whose eyes were as wide as Claire's, no doubt.

"You're hardly rushing into things with Josh," Amy pointed out.

"How could I?" Hallie countered. "I met him when I was fifteen years old!"

"But you love him," Amy insisted.

Hallie stopped crying, but the tears continued to slip down her cheeks as she blinked, her eyes going wide and earnest. "I do. I really do. I can't imagine my life without him. I just . . . don't know if that's enough for a lifetime."

Enough was enough. Claire led her sisters over to the old picnic table on the shoreline. It was weathered and gray and smoothed from years of rain and wind, but somehow it was still standing, after all the knocks it had taken. It might not be shiny and new like it was when they were all little girls, their feet dangling, enjoying a summer dinner of potato salad and fresh corn, their laughter lost in the ocean breeze, but it was somehow more beautiful nicked and imperfect.

Claire looked at her younger sister until she finally met her eyes. "Gabe is not my boyfriend, Hallie. I brought him here as . . . a buffer, a date, whatever you want to call it. Everything we said was true about how we met and how well we know each other. But we're not romantically involved, and I am the absolute last person you should be taking relationship advice from, okay?"

Hallie stared at her with watery eyes. From the set in her jaw, it was clear that her own problems were at least momentarily forgotten. "Are you serious?"

Claire sighed. "I'm not proud. About any of it. Amy knows. I told her yesterday."

"But . . . why lie? Why bring him at all? To show me you knew something about everlasting love?"

Quite the opposite, Claire thought miserably, even as she nodded. She waited for Hallie to yell at her, but instead, Hallie said, "You're good together, you know. You're different with him. Happier. More like you used to be back when you believed in happy endings."

Claire nodded quietly. She knew it was true. She'd just never thought of it that way. Gabe did make her believe that two people could be a match. But enough to last?

"I'm a coward," she muttered. "I've hidden from the one thing I can't control or guarantee. I've been so focused on the worst possible outcome that I stopped believing in the possibility of something wonderful."

"I'm just as guilty," Amy said. "I never told Logan how I felt about him and watched him propose to another woman instead. I lost my best friend for five years. And maybe I just lost him all over again." Amy looked at them both. "Last night I told Logan how I feel."

Hallie gasped, and even Claire was surprised. "But . . . why?"

"You mean why now?" Amy shook her head. "I guess I felt like I had nothing more to lose. Our friendship ended five years ago, and I have an entire life in Boston waiting for me on Monday. And . . . he pushed me. To understand why our friendship ended. Why I wouldn't come to his wedding. Why I never reached out again."

"So he knows." Claire felt almost dizzy at the thought. Of openly telling someone how you felt about them, that you loved them, without being sure that they would return the feelings, that they wouldn't hurt you or let you down.

"He knows how I felt then, but as for how I feel now . . ." Amy blinked back tears. "I'm still in love with him. Time didn't change that. Neither did distance. When your heart knows, it just knows, even when you don't want to listen to it."

Claire fell quiet for a moment. When was the last time that she had stopped to listen to her heart? To ask herself what she really wanted, more than anything else?

"My heart knows," Hallie said quietly. "I love Josh. I always have. I always will. I never thought about another life because I didn't need to. Or want to. I had everything I ever wanted, right here. In this town. At the club. With Josh. I don't think I've been taking the easy path. I think I made a choice to follow it. And I'm making the choice again. I don't want to live my life without Josh."

Claire reached out and squeezed her hand. "Then don't."

It was so simple. But was it? She glanced back at the house, thinking of the man who was still inside, hoping that she wasn't too late.

Hallie stood up. "I just hope I can make things right. I all but called off the wedding to Josh last night." She started to tear up again.

Claire stood and put her arm around her baby sister, pulling her tight. But that was just it. Hallie wasn't a baby anymore. She was a grown woman, the first of them to reach this milestone. To take a chance on love.

"Why do you think Mom never told us about Dad?" Amy wondered aloud as they walked back to the house. "She's never even hinted at having anything but good feelings toward him."

"I've thought about that too," Claire mused. "Do you think it was because she didn't want to tarnish our memory of him? He died not long after that conversation I overheard. What was the point by then?"

"Maybe it just doubled her sense of loss," Amy said sadly.

But Hallie just smiled at both of them and shook her head. "No. No, I don't think that was it. I think she's only ever said so many good things about him since he died because what they had was real. They were in love. It wasn't perfect, but maybe it was close enough. And maybe it was worth it."

Claire pulled in a breath.

Maybe it was true.

———— ✦ ————

Gabe was in the bedroom, packing his suitcase, when Claire burst through the door and closed it shut behind her.

"Wait."

Gabe dropped the bag and turned, ever so slowly, to look at her. He didn't speak, didn't even look particularly curious. He was relaxed, at peace with himself and what he'd said.

He had no regrets.

But she would. If she didn't put those warning voices in her head away and listen to her heart for once.

"I accused you of not telling me about parts of your life," she said. "And the truth is that I've been keeping a part of my past from you too."

He tipped his head, looking curious.

"You know that I had my reservations about my sister getting married, but it's not because I'm cynical or jaded or that I don't believe in love." She stopped herself. "Or maybe it's because I don't. Or I didn't. But I once did, and I want to believe again."

He nodded slowly, as if he wasn't sure if he believed her, and why should he? He'd only known the hard part of her, the woman with the wall up, protecting herself from pain and disappointment, the woman who stiffened under someone's touch, who announced to the world that she didn't believe in marriage. For anyone.

"I don't talk about my father much," she said, sitting down on the bed.

Gabe looked a little confused by this shift in topic but gave an understanding look as he joined her. "Some things hurt too much to talk about. I get it."

She nodded. "You're right. But not for the reasons you think." She took a breath and looked up at him, into the kind, warm, familiar eyes that greeted her every morning, making her world feel as bright as the sun, even on the rainiest weeks of April or the grayest days of January. "I was always closest to my father, maybe because I was the oldest, or maybe because our personalities just clicked. My sisters used to tease me about it, but they didn't mind. He was a big guy. His hugs were like big bear hugs. His laughter rumbled through the walls of this house. He used to dance with our mother in the kitchen. He was the perfect father. The perfect husband."

"And then he died," Gabe said quietly.

"Then he cheated on my mother," Claire said flatly.

Gabe's eyes widened.

Claire felt her eyes well with tears, and she brushed one away before it could fall. "I overheard them, a few weeks before he died. I don't know how long it had been going on. I know that he didn't intend to leave my mother. And then he died. My mother never knew I found out. My sisters never knew."

Until now. Until they needed to know.

"I guess my world changed that day," she said with a shrug. "The life that I knew felt thrown into question. Every memory, every happy moment, I didn't know what was real anymore."

She thought of her father, his hair graying at the temples, standing out on the porch overlooking the water, telling them all to come outside and enjoy the moment with him. To not take any of it for granted.

She always went. She always joined him.

They all did. He'd bound them together in many ways.

And he'd torn them apart.

Or maybe Claire had done that instead. Her own mother had chosen not to let his affair define their marriage. But Claire had chosen to leave, to distance herself, to put the past in the past, locked up and forgotten.

"After that, it just became difficult to spend time with my family. It didn't feel honest. So I threw myself into work. I used it as an excuse to stop visiting, to keep holidays short. I couldn't talk about my father because I didn't want to confront the truth."

"And you stopped being the girl who played wedding day with her sisters," Gabe said quietly.

Claire nodded. "I used work as my excuse for everything because it was easier that way." She swallowed hard, knowing that now was the time to come out with the rest of it. All the truth. On the table. All her fears, sadness, and worry, out there.

"Everyone says that I'm married to my work . . ." She stopped, staring at him, into his kind eyes, the same ones that crinkled at the corners when he laughed and never strayed from hers when she told a story. She swallowed hard, fighting against the hesitation, against the little voice in her head that had kept her safe all these years. But alone. "Everyone says that I'm married to my work, but I think the truth is that . . . I'm married to you. It's not my files or my clients I'm getting in early to work on each day; it's seeing you. You're the reason I get in early and stay late. Why I love where I work even if I don't always love what I do. Because . . . I love you too."

She sat there, her heart beating hard against her chest, all too aware that until this past week, she hadn't used those three words in years. Not since her father's funeral. Not even with her own family.

She'd hardened herself to all the good things in life. Put up walls. Kept people out. And oh, it had felt so good to take them down and let her sisters back in.

But this was different. Gabe wasn't family. And even family could still break your heart.

But the reward, she knew now, was worth it.

"I don't recall saying the words *I love you* last night." His brow pinched a little, making her heart speed up, but then the corner of his mouth quirked, and he reached out and took her hand. "But I'll say it now. I love you, Claire Walsh. I have loved you from the moment you first walked into that kitchen and found me unable to work that damn coffee machine. And I would have kept on loving you even if you never loved me back. You can't change this." He tapped his chest. "You can't fight it."

She smiled through her tears. "And I don't want to anymore."

His grin widened. "So you gonna let me kiss you for real now, or only if your aunt Marcia comes bursting into the bedroom again?"

Claire gasped, but she was laughing. "She didn't!"

"First thing this morning. Good thing I took the bed last night." He raised an eyebrow.

"I don't care if Marcia walks in. But I hope she doesn't. I love my family, but I love my life in New York. With you."

"I do, too, Claire Bear," Gabe said, pulling her close and kissing her slowly. "I do too."

CHAPTER
TWENTY-SIX

Hallie

The house was still quiet, but Hallie knew it wouldn't be for long. It was her wedding day. Or it was supposed to be. The happiest day of her life. The one she had dreamed of since she was just a little girl, holding a photo album on her lap.

"You're sure you don't want me to try to change the vases back to the originals?" Amy asked Hallie again as she rummaged through her handbag for her keys. "She had them ordered, and I could run over there, offer to help transfer the arrangements—"

They'd been talking about the wedding plans since they got back to the house. And right now, Hallie had never been surer of anything, most of all that she wanted to marry Josh. Today.

Hallie shook her head, not only because she knew that what Amy was offering was impossible but also because she didn't care what the flowers looked like; they'd be beautiful either way. All that really mattered was that she and Josh were happy. With each other. Not with a vase.

"I actually really like your idea. At first I was just alarmed, because it wasn't the way it's always been, but . . . now it's grown on me. This is my wedding. If there is even going to be a wedding." This time the doubt wasn't coming from her. Now she wondered if Josh would still want to go through with it.

Amy gave her a smile of encouragement. "There will be a wedding."

Hallie wanted to believe her sister. And her tone was so convincing that she almost could. She knew that her sister would never mislead her or give her false hope. Neither of her sisters would.

"How can you be so sure?" Hallie asked, her voice in a near whisper.

"Because I have never seen two people more suited for each other," Amy said. "There are some things in life that just go together, that you never have to question. Like peanut butter and jelly. Like you and Josh."

"Like you and Logan?"

Amy's hands stilled on her handbag, but she cleared her throat and swung it over her shoulder. "Maybe all we were meant to be was friends."

"Will that be enough?" Hallie asked gently.

"I learned a lot these past five years," Amy said. "I learned that I can live without people I care about, even if I don't want to."

"Like Claire?" Hallie nodded because she understood.

"I think that all of us are tougher than we give ourselves credit for. Me. Mom. Claire. You."

Hallie raised an eyebrow, because as much as she wanted to believe that, she still wasn't sure. And maybe she wouldn't be until she'd had her talk with Josh.

Just thinking of it made her stomach turn over.

"Time has a way of making things clearer," Amy said. "Look how much we've overcome this past week."

There was a lot that Hallie wished she could change about this week, and maybe Amy did, too, but she wouldn't trade the experience. Not when it had brought her sisters back into her life.

Not when she had finally stopped and asked herself what she really wanted in life. And knew the answer.

"It's weird," Hallie said. "I've tried so hard to hold on to the past, but now, I don't think I ever want things to go back to the way they were."

"Me either," Amy said. "And that's why I'm not going to be returning to Boston."

Hallie gasped. "You're not?"

"My old boss offered me my job back, and I thought that all my problems were solved." Amy smiled. "But that would be the easy path, wouldn't it? Not the one I want for myself."

"So what is it that you want?"

"I want to put down my walls. Let the people I love back into my life. Maybe even open my heart to new love." Amy shrugged, but there was a light in her eyes that hadn't been there all week. Maybe not in years. "I'm tired of running away from the things that might cause me pain. Especially when that meant turning my back on the things that brought me the most joy."

"What are you planning to do?" Hallie asked, because it was clear from the confidence in Amy's tone that she'd made a decision already.

"I was thinking about asking Coco Goodwin if she was in need of an event planner at the Harbor Club."

Hallie raised an eyebrow. "I happen to know that there is not an in-house event planner."

"Well, that's a conversation for another day." Amy was quick to shut the topic down, but it was clear that she was trying to temper her own enthusiasm for the idea. "Right now, I am on the clock. And you need to go talk to Josh."

Hallie smiled against her building nerves. Only this time, she realized that funny feeling in her stomach was different from what she'd been experiencing these past few days.

It wasn't nerves. It was excitement.

"I will," she promised. But there was someone else she needed to talk to first.

Her mother was in her bedroom, up and ready for the day, when Hallie knocked on the door, quietly, so she wouldn't rouse the rest of the house.

"Hallie?" Bunny looked surprised to see her. "Aren't we supposed to be leaving for the salon soon?"

"Not for another hour," Hallie told her. She walked across the room to join her mother where she sat on the ledge of the big bay window overlooking the ocean. The sea was calm today, and the sky was clear. It was a picture-perfect day. One to enjoy.

"I always loved this view." Her mother sighed. Then she looked at her a little sadly. "But you and Josh should have this room now, Hallie. I've had my turn. Now it's yours."

"I don't want this room," Hallie told her firmly.

Her mother frowned. "But surely you don't want to stay in your little room at the front of the house?"

Hallie swallowed hard. "That's what I came in to talk to you about. I . . . I don't want the house, Mom."

Bunny's eyes widened. "You don't want the house? But you love this house!"

"I do," Hallie said, nodding to show how much she did. "I love this house. But . . . I love it for how it is. And how it was. I don't want to change it. I want some things to stay as they are."

"Oh, Hallie." Her mother clasped Hallie's hands in hers. "Nothing stays the same forever. That's not how life works. That's not what makes it . . . wonderful."

"Josh and I never really had a reason to stop and think about what we might want. I think that's important for us, don't you? To have something of our own, even if we argue, and even if it's a struggle, to come together and start something fresh, just for us?"

Bunny's eyes misted. "When did my little girl grow up?"

Hallie squeezed her mother's hands back. "But I don't want you to sell this house, Mom. I want to still be able to come back here, with you, Claire, and Amy. And my children someday."

Bunny nodded sadly. "This house holds a lot of memories. Not just from you girls, but from my childhood too."

"Then why would you think to sell it, Mom?" Hallie needed to know.

Her mother hesitated, and for a moment Hallie wondered if she was going to tell her the truth, what Claire had shared about the affair.

Instead, she just said, "I'm selling all of the properties here in Driftwood Cove, Hallie. That's why I brought Logan on, and I've told him not to tell anyone. It's time for me to start the next chapter of my life."

"But . . . why now?" Hallie asked. Sure, her mother wasn't exactly getting younger, but she supposed that none of them were.

"Knowing that you were getting married made me think about the passing of time, I suppose. I assumed that the house would be passed on to you and that it was my turn to step aside."

"Oh, Mom." Hallie's heart hurt that her mother would ever think such a thing. "This will always be your house."

"I haven't spent much time here over the years," Bunny said. "I told myself it was because I was transitioning the house to you, but the truth is that there have been times when I felt like even though coming here brought back happy memories, it also brought back painful ones."

She swallowed hard. A day ago, Hallie might have thought her mother was referring to their father's death. Now she wondered if there was more.

Either way, she was referring to loss. The loss of love. However it had happened.

"The happiest moments of my life were spent in this house," her mother surprised her by saying. "With you girls and your father. And my parents." She brushed a tear from her cheek. "But then everything changed. Claire stopped visiting. Eventually, Amy did too. And it felt like it wasn't the same anymore. It made it easier to hand it over to you. To give it life again."

"I'll keep it then, Mom," Hallie insisted. "But . . . I'm not going to have Josh move in."

"Hallie!" Bunny's hand flew to her chest.

"That's not what I mean," Hallie reassured her. "This is Amy's house as much as mine. And your house. And Claire's," she added, knowing that one day Claire would be able to see this place for all the happy memories it held, not just the sad ones.

"What are you suggesting?" Bunny asked. "Are you saying you don't want to honor the tradition of receiving this house as a wedding gift? Starting the next generation under its roof?"

"I'm suggesting we start a new tradition." A week ago it might not have been an option, but now she couldn't imagine it any other way. "The house should go to all of us." Already she could see holiday dinners at the big dining room table, even another generation of girls scurrying around in their pajamas, playing dress-up with the old lace veil.

Time would pass, they'd all move on, but this house would always bring them back together.

"But who would live here if you don't want to?" Bunny said. "These big old homes fall by the wayside if they sit vacant for too long."

"I was thinking maybe Amy could stay here, at least until she settles into town."

Bunny's eyes went wide. "You mean she and Logan?"

Hallie shook her head. "I don't know about that, not yet, at least. But this is Amy's home too. She loves it as much as I do, maybe even more. And . . . it's her turn now."

"She always loved this house. And Logan."

"I'm just not sure she can have both, but can she at least have one?" Hallie asked.

"Who says she can't have both?" Bunny replied, looking knowingly out to the ocean.

Hallie had to laugh. Her mother was full of secrets. Some were probably best kept that way.

"You knew he was single when you hired him, didn't you? You were matchmaking! Otherwise, you could have waited and had him start working for you after the wedding," Hallie pointed out.

Bunny's smile grew. "What can I say? Sometimes two people just need a little nudge. A setback is just a setback. True love weathers any storm."

Hallie looked down at her mother, knowing that she would never reveal what she knew. Her mother had chosen to stay with her father for reasons Amy didn't know, and which were none of her business either. But she did know that they loved each other. That it was all true.

Even if it wasn't perfect.

Hallie was a woman who honored traditions, and one of the most obvious was that the groom was never supposed to see the bride on their wedding day before the ceremony. It was bad luck. But Hallie was willing to risk that—and break tradition too.

She drove to the Goodwins' cedar-shingle home and around the back to the matching carriage house. She knocked on the door, knowing he'd be inside because his car was down below, beside hers. The same make and model. Bought the same year. Gifts from Josh's parents when they'd graduated from college and started at the club together.

Life had come easily to them so far. Maybe they'd even taken it for granted. But she also knew that things wouldn't always be so neat and simple. Today was proof of that.

"Josh?" she called out, beginning to worry that maybe he wasn't home at all. Maybe he'd hitched a ride with someone. Maybe he'd even left town.

He'd tried calling last night, and left texts asking her to call back. She hadn't. Instead she'd come here. But now she wondered if she might be too late.

"Josh?" She knocked again, but she could tell through the windows that the apartment was dark and quiet and that he wasn't inside.

Holding back tears when she considered where he could be and how she could fix this, she pulled out her phone and dialed his number. It rang three times, almost enough for her to think he'd given up, that he wasn't going to answer, when his familiar voice finally came on the line.

"Hello?"

It was amazing how one simple word could have so much power.

"Josh! You answered. I got your calls; I'm sorry I didn't call back. I had some things to think about, and I came to your place, I tried to find you but—"

She had reached the base of the stairs now, and there, coming around the side of the garden gate, was Josh, with the phone pressed against his ear, a grin growing on his face.

"But . . . I'm going to hang up now," Hallie said, matching his smile. Quickly she shoved the phone into her back pocket, hurrying toward him. To his lanky body, to the tousled hair and big eyes, so sincere and, she realized, a little hurt.

"Josh! I'm sorry—"

But he said it at the same time as her.

"For what?" she asked.

"For assuming that you'd want what I wanted," he said.

"But I'm just as guilty," she replied, her voice rising. "It's always come so easily for us, maybe it was bound to happen that there would be something we wouldn't agree on. But . . . it doesn't mean I don't love you, Josh."

"I don't need five kids." Josh squeezed her hand. "And I don't need to take over the Harbor Club."

"And I don't need to take over my family house," she said, realizing that she'd never even asked him, had she? She'd just assumed. "In fact, I told my mother I don't want it."

"What?" Josh stared at her. "But you always wanted that house. It was always part of the plan."

"To hell with the plan. When did we ever stop and ask ourselves what we wanted?"

His expression softened. "All I wanted was you, Hallie."

She felt her shoulders relax. "Me too," she said in a rush, reaching out for his hands. "Me, too, Josh."

"I do like it here, though," he told her.

"And I do like working at the Harbor Club," she agreed.

"Even if it was just you and me, that would be enough for me, Hallie. It has been so far. And all those things you talk about, all those places, I never longed for any of it, because I've just been content here with you. I don't need all those things. I just needed you."

Hallie brushed aside a tear and swallowed the lump in her throat. "I don't either. I never even thought about them. I just . . . I think I let this past week get into my head. But not into my heart, Josh. That's all you. Always was. Always will be."

"Hallie Walsh," Josh said, dropping to one knee, his hand still holding hers. "Will you marry me? Today? It might not be the wedding we planned, but it will be perfect all the same. And tomorrow may not be all that we hoped, but it will be better together. That I can promise."

Hallie dropped down to her knee and took his other hand in hers. "I can't think of anything I want more than to marry you. Today."

"You don't think it's bad luck that we saw each other before the ceremony?" He gave her a knowing look as they stood.

"Who cares about all that?" Hallie said, pulling him closer to her. "We can make our own rules. Starting today. And I think I'd like a kiss before our wedding."

CHAPTER TWENTY-SEVEN

Amy

If Amy thought the last week was a scramble, it was nothing compared to today.

They were due at the salon for hair and makeup by one o'clock. By three thirty, back at the house, which would hopefully be cleared of guests by then, all eager to arrive at the venue early in hope of a good seat. The car would be arriving at four thirty to take the wedding party to the manor for the five o'clock ceremony, but Amy wouldn't be joining—she'd be one step ahead, at the manor, making sure that everything was in order.

"Oh, Amy," Bunny said, as Amy hurried down the stairs. "I'm glad I caught you. I just saw Hallie. We had the most interesting conversation."

Amy froze, wondering if Hallie had actually confronted their mother about what Claire had told them, but then she read Bunny's face, which seemed more relaxed than she'd seen it in . . . years, she realized.

"We were talking about the house," Bunny went on.

Amy felt her shoulders sag in relief. The last thing she needed was one more thing to interfere with the plans she'd made for the wedding.

"Hallie has decided that she doesn't want it," Bunny said.

"She said that?" Amy's heart was pounding. Had Hallie decided to call off the wedding after all? To not go see Josh?

"What exactly did you say to her in your conversation?" she asked her mother slowly.

"Nothing!" Bunny's brow furrowed in confusion. "What would there be to say?"

Amy scanned the room, even though she knew Hallie wasn't in the house—she'd watched her car drive off while she was on the porch. But she'd also watched Hallie rush toward it as if she were running for her life.

To her life.

Turning back to her mother, she looked into her soft eyes, now worried by Amy's reaction, and she knew that what Claire had told them last night remained between the three of them. It wasn't Claire's burden anymore. It wasn't something that would keep them apart. Now, it strangely tied them all together.

"Nothing," she told her mother. "I just . . . Well, Hallie loves this house. And she loves tradition."

"She does," Bunny agreed. "And this house is full of traditions that she doesn't ever want to part with. And now she doesn't have to."

Now it was Amy's turn to frown. "I don't understand."

"She wants this house to remain as it is. For all of us." Bunny gave a little smile. "It will always be your home too. And Claire's. And mine. And the next generation's . . ."

Amy felt the breath escape her. So Hallie was going through with the wedding.

"She and Josh need to figure some things out on their own, build their own future," Bunny said. "And in case you're going to be staying in Driftwood Cove, you know you can always stay here . . ."

"Me?" The word barely came out, but Bunny nodded firmly. Her.

She'd given up on this house, on the dreams made here under its roof, but if today had proved anything, it was that anything was possible if you opened your heart to it.

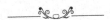

Amy's mother hurried upstairs to move everyone along, and Amy, armed with her list, decided to head into town to have one last check on the flowers and the cake.

She pushed back through the door to the porch but halted once she got there.

There, coming up the pathway, was Logan.

Her heart lifted and swooped like it always did when she first saw his face, but this time she put it back in check.

Today had been a good day. A wonderful day. A day where dreams came true, not just for Hallie but for her. Maybe even for Claire.

She wouldn't let anything ruin it for her.

"You here to check on the bride and groom?" she asked.

Logan raised an eyebrow. Clearly he had heard about the fight last night.

"Did Josh send you to check on Hallie?" she clarified. Then, thinking about all the changes she'd made to the plans, she said, "Or me?"

"He just wanted to get a pulse on how things were coming along for the day. If any last-minute help was needed."

More good news. Josh had no intention of not getting married today. She smiled, thinking of how happy this would make Hallie. How nothing could stop today from being perfect. At least in Hallie's eyes.

"I think I have it all covered," she said, her tone clipped, the hurt feelings creeping in despite her effort.

Logan held up his hands. "I didn't mean to upset you. I know that you're doing all of this because of Hallie. I know you only have the best of intentions, Amy."

"Actually, Hallie asked me to make sure that they did use some of the ideas I had after all," Amy said. Then she added, "But . . . not all."

Logan climbed the porch steps, stopping when he was only a few feet away from her. "You have a good eye for this. I wouldn't be surprised if your boss gave you a raise after this."

"Oh, I don't think so," Amy said, shaking her head, but she was smiling now, straight from the heart.

"Why would you say that? You have a happy bride, and you love what you do. And it shows."

"I do love what I do," Amy agreed. "But I don't want to run away from the place I love most. Or the people," she added, looking him in the eye.

His brow pulled tight. "What do you mean?"

"I mean . . . that I'm going to be staying here, in Driftwood Cove."

"That's fantastic!" Logan's eyes lit up, and he took a step toward her. Then, perhaps seeing her tense at his approach, he said, "But are you sure it's what you want?"

She nodded. Certain of her decision. So very sure of it. "It wasn't what I planned, but it's definitely what I want."

Maybe it was what she'd always wanted. Or maybe it was just meant to be. In time.

"I guess we'll both be staying on in town, then," he said, giving her a slow grin. "I don't know if you've heard that I'm taking over your mother's portfolio. Fixing up the places, but buying them off her too."

Amy looked at him in surprise. Another thing her mother had kept from her—or was waiting to share. She let it sink in. Her mother was passing down the house this weekend, not to Hallie but to all three of her daughters. And she was selling off the properties in town to Logan.

She was saying goodbye to the past, to the life she'd shared with her husband. Maybe she was letting go. Or maybe she'd just been waiting for the next generation to come along and take care of everything she loved the most.

"I didn't know. But . . . that's a good thing." Neither she nor her sisters had ever taken an interest in the business. They'd all forged their own career paths instead. Even Hallie, she thought, with a private smile.

But those properties, that business, felt like an extension of their family. And so did Logan. He always would, in a way.

"It's a very good thing," he said, looking excited at the prospect. "This is where I'm meant to put down roots. It was always where I was meant to be."

"Me too," Amy said. She gestured to the beams of the porch ceiling, to the grass that met the shore, to the beautiful property that housed so many wonderful memories . . . and so many more to come.

"Hallie and Josh aren't going to be moving in here, after all," she told him. Maybe they'd end up in one of the houses that Logan was now renovating. "My mother's giving it to all of us girls to share, so that it always stays in the family, just as it is."

"But who will take care of it?"

"Me, for now, at least."

"I guess that means we'll be seeing each other around a lot more again, then." Logan looked at her questioningly, and, after a pause, she nodded. "Maybe we can even start over right where we left off."

Amy hesitated. There was so much hurt. So much history. So much time lost. "I don't know, Logan. A lot has happened."

"It just about broke my heart to lose you," Logan admitted, his eyes locking with hers.

"Same here," she said quietly.

"And now it doesn't have to happen again. Now we've been given a second chance," Logan said.

A second chance at being reunited with her best friend. Her favorite person. The peanut butter to her jelly. Both in Driftwood Cove again. Their old stomping grounds.

"I think . . ." She paused, looking into the eyes that she'd memorized over the years, the ones that she still saw when she closed her eyes.

"I think our friendship definitely deserves a second chance," she said.

"Oh, I wasn't talking about friendship." Logan stepped toward her. "I meant as something more."

Her heart skipped a beat when he stopped right before her, so close she could feel the heat of his body, so close that she might bump his nose if she even moved. Or maybe . . . brush his mouth. "Something more?"

"Come on, Amy," he said, looking at her softly. "You asked why I called off the wedding. Because of you. Because I missed you so damn much I couldn't think about anything or anyone but you."

She stared at him, barely believing she'd just heard him correctly. Once there had been a time when she'd dreamed of this moment, him finally speaking the very feelings that she held in her heart. And now that it was happening, she almost couldn't even believe it could be true.

"But why didn't you just tell me?"

"Because by the time I realized how I felt, it was too damn late," he said. "I'd already lost you."

"And what if I'd never said anything last night?"

"When I saw you again, Amy, I knew that everything might have changed between us but that my feelings hadn't. It confirmed that I was right to call off the wedding. But it also confirmed something else."

"What's that?" she whispered, almost not daring to speak.

"That I can't lose you twice." He took a step toward her. "I thought I'd tell you after the wedding and before you left town, because I had nothing else to lose. I'm just sorry it took me so long to say it."

"I am too," Amy said, thinking of how much easier things might have been if one of them had dared to speak up. To risk their heart.

To risk everything they loved the most for the hope of more.

But then she thought of everything she'd gained these past five years. A job she loved. A friend she cherished. The awareness that even when it felt like everything was lost, it wasn't.

"We have a lot of lost time to make up for," she said. "I'm not the same person I was five years ago. I've . . . changed."

"Only for the better," he said.

Amy didn't even realize that he'd wrapped his arms around her waist and pulled her close against his chest until his mouth was on hers, a groan escaping from her lips. She'd hoped for this kiss for so many years, dreamed of this moment, and finally given up on it.

But her heart never had. And she knew, as they held each other on the porch of this house that had held so many happy memories, that someday they'd look back and remember that this was right where they'd had their first kiss in the house she could always call home.

CHAPTER
TWENTY-EIGHT

Bunny

Bunny Walsh could never forget her wedding day—and not only because her daughters hadn't let her. It had been far from perfect, even though the photos told another story. She'd forgotten something blue, and the baker had made the wrong flavor of cake. The veil that her mother insisted she wear kept whipping her in the face in the wind and got a lipstick stain that had taken several careful scrubbings to remove afterward, because even though she'd considered donating it, there was something special about having worn her mother's veil, and there was always the possibility that she might have a daughter who'd want to wear it too.

One thing had been perfect, though. Or at least indisputable. Her feet might have cramped the entire walk up the aisle because she'd forgotten to break in her new shoes before the big day, but the smile on her face had never been more genuine. She'd held on to her father's arm until she swapped it for her true love—the man with the big bear laugh, the man who could light up any room, the man who had stolen her heart the very moment she first met him, down at the public beach, right here in Driftwood Cove.

Now, as Bunny walked down the aisle, smiling and nodding at all the friends and family who were gathered at Cliffside Manor on this picture-perfect day, she thought that it was just that: picture perfect. The sky was a brilliant blue, completely cloudless, and over the cliff she could see the waves rolling in the sea. The breeze was light, just enough to remind them that autumn was coming, and with that, change.

She took her place in the front aisle, beside Gabe and Logan, and turned as the procession started, fighting off the tears in her eyes, wishing that her husband could be here to see it, but knowing somehow that he was.

Once, the idea of a daughter had just been a dream, along with so many other parts of her life with her husband that were so uncertain, their stories yet to be told. There was Claire, coming down the aisle now. Her firstborn. The apple of her husband's eye. Of all her children, Claire adored him the most, and that was how Bunny always hoped it would be. But in Claire's eyes her father was superhuman; he could do no wrong. And Bunny knew that like a wedding day, like a marriage, no person was without flaws.

As Claire passed by her chair, they exchanged a glance, one that tugged straight at Bunny's heart, one that told her that everything was going to be okay now. That they'd weathered their storm and now clearer skies were coming. That the future was bright.

She turned back to see Amy, moving up the aisle a little slower, as if she were taking in every step, much like a bride might do. Or maybe, Bunny thought, she was just practicing. Because Amy might have given up on love, but it was just a matter of time before she found it again. It had always been there, after all. Sometimes two people just had to go their separate ways to remind them what brought them together in the first place.

She tried to catch Amy's eye as her middle daughter reached the end of the petal-strewed aisle, but there was someone else who had her attention today. The man sitting to Bunny's left. The man Bunny always knew she could trust the most with the business she and her husband had built together—it had to go to someone who didn't just understand the work, but someone who knew what it meant to her. She wasn't just selling him properties. She was giving him a piece of her history, and in that, a piece of her heart.

And now the music swelled, everyone stood, and there, standing on the stone steps of Cliffside Manor, was Hallie. Her baby. And by far the most beautiful bride that Bunny had ever seen.

Bunny watched, barely daring to breathe, as Hallie began her walk down the aisle, clutching the bouquet in both hands at her waist. The veil reached her midback, blowing slightly behind her, tissue thin and catching the slightest breeze, and all Bunny could picture was the little chubby-cheeked girl with the bright brown eyes running down the stairs in her white nightgown, the veil, down to her feet back then, flying high behind her.

"Don't rip it!" Bunny would cry out, even though she didn't expect any of her daughters to want to wear the old thing when their day came. That veil had come to mean more to her than it ever had on her wedding day—for something so fragile it was strangely resilient, much like life itself.

And somehow, almost miraculously, it never did rip but instead trailed the bride as she made her way toward her future.

The people sighed as she walked by them, taken by the smile she wore—more beautiful than the dress itself. Bunny was sure that later, everyone would be commenting on Hallie's expression when she finally took Josh's hand, but for Bunny there was another moment that stood out, one that others might not have caught.

It was the look that passed between Hallie and her sisters. A look that could only come with time and understanding and even hardship.

It was a promise. The promise that distance and time and circumstances might change a person and lead them astray, but they might also, eventually, lead them home.

And it was hope. Disagreements and hurt feelings could damage even the closest of bonds but never fully sever them. Sometimes they just made them tighter.

It wasn't perfect, or even easy. But it was better than that.

It was love.

ACKNOWLEDGMENTS

Each book is a journey from the blank page to the finished project, and it wouldn't be possible without the help and input of so many along the way. I'm forever grateful to Lauren Plude for believing in my work and taking on this story. Many thanks to Tiffany Yates Martin for challenging me to bring the Walsh family to life on each and every page. Thank you, as always, to my longtime agent Paige Wheeler for her ongoing support. I'd also like to thank the entire team at Montlake for doing their part to make this book shine.

And as always, thank you to my dear readers for spending a few hours with this book. I hope it makes you smile.

ABOUT THE AUTHOR

Olivia Miles is a *USA Today* bestselling author of heartwarming women's fiction and small-town contemporary romance. RT Book Reviews hailed her as "an expert at creating a sweet romantic plot." She has frequently been ranked as an Amazon Top 100 author, and her books have appeared on several bestseller lists, including Amazon, Barnes & Noble, BookScan, and *USA Today*. Olivia lives on the shore of Lake Michigan with her family and an adorable pair of dogs.